AN EASTER K

Paul Toolan is the author of the crime r
January Killing, and *An Easter Killing*. ... apple-
orchard landscape of the West of England, they feature Inspector Zig Batten and the cider-friendly Sergeant Ball. The books can be read standalone or in sequence.

Other writing includes the "beautifully poignant and funny" stories in *A View from Memory Hill*.

Paul was born in urban Yorkshire but now cheerfully admits to being a Southern softie living in rural Somerset. After a successful career in Colleges and Universities, he wrote book/lyrics for musicals before 'turning to crime'. He writes plays, too.

Like Inspector Batten, he enjoys walking, fishing, gardens and the occasional whisky. Unlike him, he appreciates sport and the taste of mushrooms, and loves travelling to sunnier climes, Greece in particular.

AN EASTER KILLING

D.I. Zig Batten 3

Paul Toolan

Published by Paul Toolan

Copyright © 2019 Paul Toolan

All rights reserved.

This is a work of fiction. Names, characters, places, and incidents are products of the author's imagination or are used fictitiously and should not be construed as real. Any resemblance to actual events, locales, organisations or persons, living or dead, is entirely coincidental.

No part of this book may be used or reproduced in any manner whatsoever without written permission, except in the case of brief quotations embodied in critical articles and reviews. For more information e-mail all enquiries to: paul.toolan1@gmail.com

To Charlie, who gave me the idea...

AN EASTER KILLING

Good Friday	Page 1
Easter Saturday	Page 105
Easter Sunday	Page 173
Easter Monday	Page 219
Easter Tuesday	Page 283
Wednesday and After	Page 309

Good Friday

One

On Crown of Thorns Hill, the last remaining thorn-tree clawed its jagged branches at the mist like a witch's hand. Nearby, a clump of ancient oaks stared up at their wind-scarred cousin, but whether with concern or indifference, only the trees could say.

Two strong men grunted in the near-darkness, slicing their spades into the hilltop and throwing aside turfs and dry soil to form a deep, square slot. Deeper they dug, lining the sides with old planks to make a solid housing.

The clean-shaven man pulled a face when his bearded companion spat on the ground.

'What?' said the beard.

'Nothing,' said the other, shaking his head and reaching down to the heavy wooden cross, lying unceremoniously at their feet. Together, they hefted it aloft, firming it upright in the newly-pierced earth. The last glint of evening tinged the varnished wood, sharply silhouetted above them now.

'We dug the hole too deep,' said the clean-shaven man. 'Reverend Kerry wanted ten feet of cross sticking up.'

His bearded colleague grunted a reply. 'Kerry can stick it up himself. Ten, nine, eight, I should care.'

Hurriedly, the men wrapped the crossbeams in plastic sheeting, tied in place with baler-twine, to disguise the shape till tomorrow. They were a day early, but needs must. The apologetic blue mask would be removed at sunrise on Good Friday, in preparation for the Easter rites.

The clean-shaven man peered at the hill's old and new inhabitants. 'Not so lonely now, that thorn tree?'

'I'm off,' said the other, with a glare at the deepening mist. 'Creepy as hell, this place.'

Spade in hand, he grunted down the slope of Crown of Thorns Hill.

His colleague followed - watched only, he thought, by a single ancient thorn-tree, and its new twin-branched companion.

Two

From a hilltop near Caerwent, Sergeant Ball gazed at the distant beauty of the Severn Bridge, a giant cheese-wire slicing the Bristol Channel in two. Bank Holiday cars stuttered at each end. By mid-morning, they'd struggle to move at all.

Gus, the black Labrador, dropped an over-chewed stick on his master's foot, but Ball was tired of throwing wet sticks for a carefree dog. He gazed again at the Bridge, its towers and cables laddering their way from an overcast Wales towards Bristol. Fifty miles beyond lay the CID centre at Parminster, and Ball's home village of Stockton Marsh, surrounded by Somerset orchards and familiarity.

He liked Wales. Liked the Bridge.

But he was the wrong side of it.

'Lost the use of your arms, Chris?'

'Ungh?'

Ignoring her husband's grunt, Di Ball reached down and threw the stick for Gus. The dog lolloped downhill, tail a propeller.

'I thought you liked Wales?'

'I do.'

'Not showing on your face.'

Ball's face turned towards England. He and Di were staying with relatives, near Caerwent. *Her* relatives. He had none left alive.

'Oh, well, you know.'

She did. Good Friday not eight hours awake and Chris Ball's Easter was on the down-slope. Policing tugged at his sleeve, drawing his mind - and eyes - back over the Bridge towards the workaday world.

'Despite everything?'

Broad shoulders shrugged. Di was touching scar tissue. Tensions with his boss had eased, but not departed. Chris Ball and Inspector Zig Batten still quaffed cider together, but less often, and without the easy freedom of before.

'I know we don't have sunshine, Chris. But the view from up here - just look. And there's birdsong. And a fresh scent of morning dew. Can't you smell it?'

Ball pretended he could. But it was crime he could smell, fifty miles to the South. His gaze crept towards the cars heading for the far side of the Bridge.

'You're two peas in a pod, pair of you.'

'*Peas?*'

'Peas! You and Zig, tuh, got to have your fingers on the pulse. At work, I mean. They could blast you into space and you'd still wonder if the CID cat's been fed.'

'*Cat*? No room to swing one of those in our office. You've seen it.'

'I can see it now, behind your eyes. It drove to Wales, with *us*. It'll still be there when a fresh pint lands in front of you.'

Ball perked up at the thought of cider. Too early though, even for him.

'Parminster's closed for Easter,' he said. 'Well, skeleton staffed. The crooks have gone on holiday.'

'What, like you?'

Chris Ball managed half a smile, till Gus plonked a stick dripping with dog-drool on his foot.

Di folded her arms. 'Your turn,' she said.

Finding a dry handhold, Ball waved the stick for Gus to jump at, and with an ex-rugby player's arm sent it spinning down the grey hillside. It whistled through the early morning air like a grenade - towards the Bridge, and the cars edging their way back into England.

As an over-chewed stick bounced down a Welsh hill, fifty miles away in Somerset a muscled hand flicked aside the bedroom curtains.

Mike Brean's gaze fell on the upslope of a different hill, steep and close. Crown of Thorns Hill rose like a green wall above the tidy village of East Thorne. The hill had acquired its name centuries ago, long before age and canker killed off most its trees. Now, only a single thorn-tree graced its crown. A clump of stubborn old oaks and a dozen newly-planted saplings did their best on the wind-disturbed slopes below.

Light winds today, but enough to disturb the grey mist clothing the hill last night. A reluctant sunrise cast a thin light over the village. Beyond empty streets, Mike saw rooftops of thatch and tile, magnolia blossom in a dozen gardens and flashes of yellow forsythia. In the lower distance, faint specks of blossom dotted the gnarled trees in the old apple-orchard at Turks Lane. His gaze swept across the greening of copses and the faint, pale-gold gleams of early sunlight on stone.

'Two reasons to live here,' he said to himself. 'The peace, and the view.'

His gaze drifted higher, to the crest of the hill.

'Strange.'

Shielding his eyes, he peered up through the final threads of mist.

'Nina.'

'Whuh?'

Nina Magnus was on leave for the entire Easter weekend, and glad to be.

'*Nina*. Come and look at this. I can't make it out.'

'It's *Easter*,' she groaned. 'I'm on *holiday*.' She pulled the duvet over a holiday head.

Mike Brean stumped downstairs, to fetch his binoculars.

Three

'Ah-chh.'

'Aaah-chhhh.'

'Aaaah-chaaaa-hoooo! Bugger!'

A pomegranate now, Zig Batten's nose. A scarlet blob, exploding twice a minute. He blew again, wiping mucous from his moustache for the umpteenth time, and flinging the soiled tissue at the bin.
Missed!
Through a chink in the curtains, a weak sunrise tried to distract him, squeezing through cloud and turning the distant stone scar of Ham Hill blood-red and gold. When he threw open the window, birdsong fluttered in.
Do songbirds catch flu, Zig? Flu should be against the law. You're a policeman - suggest it, next time you bump into a judge.
Dragging on a dressing gown, he made his solitary way downstairs. No green-eyed Erin today. Easter weekend, him on leave, and she's abroad, working. At Christmas, it was the other way around. Together, but apart.
He wondered if Good Friday would be any good for either of them.
Between sneezes, he switched on the coffee and the radio. And if the news is earthquakes and explosions, he thought, I don't give a monkey's tit. My holiday's been downgraded to sick-leave, my woman's *overseas*, and there's a bonfire where my nose used to be.
I'm taking my coffee back to bed - and bloody well staying there till Easter Monday!

While Detective Inspector Zig Batten blew on the red-hot coffee he could neither smell nor taste, Mike Brean rummaged in the coat cupboard for his field-glasses.
Yesterday, Mike climbed the rear slope of Crown of Thorns Hill, spade and boards in hand, to dig out a footing for the cross traditionally carried in procession, from church to hilltop, every Good Friday.

For the umpteenth time, East Thorne's Reverend Kerry had explained how 'witness walk' religious rituals went back centuries. Like other English villages and towns, East Thorne still clung to such Easter rites, though with a tighter grip these days. Kerry told villagers and strangers alike 'how Easter *used* to be celebrated' and would treat them to a long stare of admonishment - as if they were put on God's earth to share the blame for a weakening of church traditions.

That same priestly stare pierced Mike each time he walked into The Rising Sun, because Reverend Kerry was usually buttressing the apple-wood bar.

'When first I came to East Thorne,' Kerry too often said, 'a hundred parishioners followed the cross in procession from the church, all the way up the slope to the crest of Crown of Thorns Hill. And every voice would *sing*, Mike, to the glory of God. Imagine, will you? A hundred voices, all praising the Almighty, rain or shine?'

Mike's polite nod was wasted. Kerry needed no encouragement.

'Many a Good Friday I've stood atop the hill and watched a pair of strong lads slot the cross into place and raise it up to Heaven. Oh, and felt the pain and joy of remembrance, sure enough, and preached my sermon sometimes with the rain dripping from my spectacles. But the Lord's rain washed our sins away, my son. Washed us clean.'

Reverend Kerry washed his insides, too, Mike recalled, at this point in his tale. He liked a whisky, and two was better.

'Oh, these so-called *modern* days, Mike. Not the word *I* would use. God-forsaken, that's what they are. You live in the village, boy. You have eyes. If thirty souls manage the hill this year, Good Friday will be a good day, and that's a fact.'

Mike could only nod again. He was God-forsaken too, despite Reverend Kerry's sly attempt to convert him.

'But you're a carpenter, Mike! As was Joseph. Can you not see the young Jesus, in his earthly father's workshop? An apprentice, splicing two planks of wood together?'

The two planks reminded Mike only of school, where he'd nagged Miss Batty to explain Joseph's sudden disappearance from the Jesus household.

'Were him and Mary divorced?' he'd asked. And got Miss Batty's ruler across the knuckles for his pains.

Kerry's subtler methods were no more effective.

'I cannot persuade you, Mike? You're certain now?'

'Certain, Reverend. A bit too hypocritical, for me.'

Kerry wanted Mike to carry the full-sized cross in procession, up Crown of Thorns Hill on Good Friday afternoon, 'in memory of God's own son, who died for the salvation of all mankind - including you, Mike.'

'A true believer should carry the cross, Reverend. I keep a Christian household, but that's as far as it goes.'

'Ah well, bless you for your honesty, my son. Bless you for it.'

Though a Detective Inspector by trade, Zig Batten couldn't detect the bottle of aspirin he'd put on the bedside table last night.

Searching under the bed sharpened his headache. He scoured the kitchen, the bathroom, the study. He knew it wasn't in the airing cupboard, but he looked anyway. No sign in the wardrobe, nor the laundry basket.

Miserable, bone-ached, swollen-nosed and cursing, he thrust his hands into his dressing-gown pockets.

Bottle of aspirin, *duh*.

He shook out white pills, humphed back to bed.

Mike Brean trudged upstairs, muscled fingers pulling at the stuck catch on his binocular case.

'Fiddly damn thing!'

Emerging from the duvet, Nina Magnus admired the strength of his naked buttocks and back. She waited for him to turn round, all six foot of him, consistently proportioned. His skin was everything hers was not, the white muscles a perfect foil to her black sheen.

'Nice bum,' she said, drawing a smile from Mike. 'Is your nice bum coming back to bed, or have you and your window still got naked meditation to do? And by the way, early morning village folk are getting an eyeful.'

'There aren't any,' he said, pulling on his dressing gown. '*Too* early.'

He never wore pyjamas; hated them. But he also hated village gossip, and East Thorne did what villages do. Having a black girlfriend in the white wastes of South Somerset was still considered racy in East Thorne's stuffier households.

'I was trying to look at the hill.'

'What, never seen it before?'

'*No*. There's something funny about it today.'

'Yes, there's a hole in it, and a pair of crossed planks sticking out the hole. You dug and delved, remember, yesterday? Because you couldn't say *No* to that whisky-priest pal of yours.'

Reverend Kerry was used to snaring sinners, and Mike hadn't escaped without a penance - 'a Joseph you may not be, Mike, but a carpenter you are. And since I cannot persuade you to carry the cross in procession...'

Mike had agreed to ferry the cross up the hill and secure it, a day in advance, ready for the service on Good Friday. Reverend Kerry's skills of persuasion - and his intimate knowledge of frequenters of The Rising Sun - also roped in Chas Janner, reluctant orchardman but keen cider-slugger. If Mike was big, Chas was a bearded giant.

'Now, with four strong arms between you, and the Lord on our side, a ten-minute task, lads. And all's ready for the morrow.' He winked at them. 'Of course, I'll see you right with a drink or two.'

Kerry waved a half-quaffed whisky at the bar - before his smile disappeared.

He lowered his glass, his voice and his features.

'But do it discreet now, boys,' he whispered, 'and do it late in the day, in the dimpsy light. And use the track on the far side of the hill, where no busybody will see. Because tradition should not be done this way. And that's a painful fact.'

Even Chas Janner nodded in sympathy. The painful fact was etched into Reverend Kerry's face. Of the dwindling number of 'believers' in the village, none were young enough any more - or strong enough - to drag the heavy wooden cross up the steep side of Crown of Thorns Hill. Tradition had lost out to the ageing process.

'To be sure, they're all as old as Methuselah - or as old as me. And I draw the line at asking the God Tourists. Some decorum has to be preserved.'

'God Tourists' was Kerry's name for outsiders who turned up once a blue moon to church events, for 'entertainment'.

'A religious rite, Mike, central to our doctrine. But to them, humph, a day at the races!'

Mike smiled. Kerry still made sure the God Tourists swelled the collection plate, because 'even Mary and Joseph had the gas bill to pay'.

Chas Janner's only contribution - after Kerry had swallowed his tot and tottered home - was to bet Mike a pint they'd never see a pint for their pains.

Reverend Kerry had all the arts of the forgetful, when it suited him.

'Hey, Mr Deaf-Bum!'

Nina was talking.

'I said how come a green pointy thing is funny, all of a sudden? What's it doing, your hill? Stand-up comedy?'

Mike Brean wasn't sure *what* it was doing. He pointed the binoculars at the crest and twiddled the focusing ring.

Yesterday, he and Chas hauled the cross to the peak of Crown of Thorns Hill, in the half-dark. Chas could have managed it himself, his cider-worker arms as big as legs. He'd refused.

'Feels weird enough doing it with you, Mike. But on my tod? In this mist? Too bloody creepy for words.'

After planting the cross, they'd wrapped the cross-beams in blue plastic to mask the shape. Yards and yards of baler twine, wound tight and knotted, ensured the wind couldn't carry it away. At sunrise on Good Friday, Mike would climb the hill, check the footings and remove its disguise in readiness for the service on Good Friday afternoon.

He sensed how powerful an image the cross would be, silhouetted at the hill's peak, towering above every villager – cynic, sceptic and believer alike. In his mind's eye, Mike saw a dark wooden crossroads on a landscape of blue.

But Chas Janner struggled with the gawkiness of it all.

'I'll not do this next year, Mike. Old Kerry can *inject* me with cider and I'll still tell him to bugger off. I mean, where's the…decency? Sneaking two crossed planks up a hill, the back way, in the dark? Shoving 'em in a hole in the ground, and wrapping 'em up in blue plastic? And what are we tying it on with? *Bright orange* baler twine? Well you can untie it yourself tomorrow. I'm done. The whole thing's bloody Mickey Mouse!'

'You could pretend to be Jesus, Chas, if you like? On Good Friday afternoon? Shall I put in a word with Kerry?'

'Huh, he asks me as often as he asks you. No bloody chance. I told him straight, I'm a fully-registered heathen. Passed the exam. All this...claptrap - they should do a proper job or kill it off altogether. Doing it like this is a bloody insult.'

'Whatever we think, Chas, they're still doing it. Give them a bit of credit, eh?'

Chas drained his cider without a word, and scooted off to his house in Turks Lane.

He had bigger fish to fry.

Nina Magnus yawned unashamedly as Mike peered at the hill through strong binoculars. Throwing back the covers, she arranged herself in a comic parody of a Playboy centrefold.

'I betcha the view sure is better over here,' she said, in a Hollywood bimbo voice, while watching his back and shoulders tighten as he re-focused the lens.

'Why dontcha turn around, stranger, and point them there binoculars at *me*?'

She ran her eyes up to his face as he turned. Kind eyes, Mike.

Not today.

Stark-white, his face. One quivering fist held out the binoculars, the other shaking at the window.

Mike Brean pointed upwards, at Crown of Thorns Hill.

'Get up, Nina,' he said, his voice flat. 'Up! *GET UP!*'

Straight-backed, she did - a naked Detective Constable Nina Magnus, on-leave-no-longer.

'I can't look,' he said.

She prised the heavy glasses from his clamped hand.

'Your job, this.' He slumped onto a bedroom chair too small for his big body. 'Y-your job, Nina,' he stuttered.

Magnus pointed the binoculars at the peak of Crown of Thorns Hill.

Foolishly, she turned the focusing ring. Across distance, the sight still repulsing Mike Brean punctured her eyes too, filling them with the same foulness scarring Mike's handsome face, and turning his features to chalk.

The glasses grew heavy. The dead weight of the image they bore encumbered her arms, dragging them down, dragging at her wrists, at her hands and, one by one, at every joint and knucklebone and fingernail.

With a thud neither of them heard, the binoculars tumbled, corpse-like, to the bedroom floor.

Four

Father Dominic Kerry rose late from his bed - late by his standards. Normally he was up and about by 6am, but no morning service awaited him today. The Good Friday ceremony, this afternoon, was 'the main draw'. He tutted at the phrase.

'The main draw, indeed!'

Leonard Tull, the churchwarden, insisted on calling it that.

'*Pharisee* Tull,' Reverend Kerry muttered, under his breath. 'Godless creature. His mind, if he has one, is on Mammon. Humph, heart too.'

Kerry had no need to lower his voice. Even had Tull been in the room, he was deaf as any post - and proved it, whenever he joined in the hymns.

But if Leonard Tull was short on hearing, Reverend Kerry was short on sight. He scrabbled on the bedside table for his spectacles, the lenses thicker, heavier, these days.

'Where's our Saviour when he's needed, to heal the deaf and blind?' he asked himself. His glasses revealed a bedroom door, which he stepped through, into a kitchen/diner. The old oak table held an impromptu still-life: whisky bottle with empty glass, and next to it a coffee-jar.

'Now isn't life full of daily dilemmas?' he mumbled to himself.

Pulling back the kitchen curtains, he squinted at the day and raised his eyes to Crown of Thorns hill.

'Heavens,' he said. 'Mike must be an early-riser.'

As far as he could tell, the crucifix had been unclothed. He squinted again. Yes, the unmistakeable shape of a cross pointed to heaven from the peak, framed like a halo by the cloudy gold of morning.

'Fitting,' he chuckled to himself. 'God the Son, light of the world, ushering in the daylight.'

As he stared, a sudden ragged movement caught his eye.

'What in heaven's name have they done with the damn plastic sheeting?'

Even through pebble lenses he could make it out, one corner trapped in the branches of the last defiant thorn tree, the rest flapping at the sky like a massive blue 'V'. Kerry rapped the window-frame in frustration. *A giant two-fingered expletive*, he thought, *sent to mock the seriousness of the day.*

'IDIOTS!'

When Mike and Chas agreed to wrap the cross in tarpaulin, he assumed it would be well-secured. Or had Mike gone up there, removed it, and lazily cast it aside?

'The hill's a garbage tip!' Kerry hissed.

Ugly blue plastic waggled on the wind like an insult. Barely sunrise, and Good Friday was an embarrassment. He shook a sad head at Mike and Chas.

'Trust the job to heathens, and what do you expect? Two strapping lads and they bugger up a task so simple an un-raised Lazarus could manage it!'

He tutted, at his own blasphemy, his language, his lack of grace. And at these modern times.

Kerry's hand wavered by the whisky. Sighing, he picked up the coffee jar.

No time to wash.

Nina Magnus struggled into yesterday's clothes and grabbed her phone.

Dead!

Last night, in holiday mode, she'd forgotten to plug it in. Flinging it onto the chaotic bed she rummaged in Mike's jacket for his. Mike was still slumped in the tiny chair by the window, the leather strap of the binocular-case wrapped round his giant hand, a reminder-knot he had no need for.

'I'm borrowing your phone.'

Mike stared at empty space.

Right now, you could borrow his eyes, Nina, and he wouldn't notice. His phone was switched off. Cursing, she booted it up. It had the nerve to ask for a password.

At a time like this! Bloody robots!

'Mike? *MIKE!*'

He peered at her, a robot himself now.

'Your password? For the phone? *Quick!*'

She waved the phone under his nose till he shook himself. Dulled fingers fumbled at the touch-screen and after a year it sang 'Pennies from Heaven'. The screen's wavy lines took another decade to stop waving.

They both stared at the phone now, she wanting to throttle it, Mike's eyes seeing only the hilltop - where the last grain of his innocence lay dead.

Wait till you get up close, Mike, Nina Magnus wanted to say. *Wait till you get a proper eyeful. It'll gut you. Except you won't get up close, will you? Because that's not your job. It's mine.*

She hugged him, knowing the hug was for them both. His broad shoulders were tiny today.

When the screen finally opened, she rapped fast fingers at the 'phone' symbol, and punched in the too-familiar CID number with a workaday fury.

A sniffling, on-leave Zig Batten plonked his coffee mug on the bedside table and squirmed his man-flu body under the warm duvet. Propped up on two pillows, he was about to blow on his red-hot liquid breakfast when the phone rang.

It better not be you, Erin, ringing to say *happy holiday!* I've just crawled back to bed with a box of tissues, a pepper-pot nose and a handful of aspirin - in lieu of your warm female flesh.

He grabbed the phone.

It wasn't Erin.

It was Parminster CID.

'Ask Sergeant Ball,' he almost said, but Ball was fifty miles away, in Wales. After five seconds, Batten jerked bolt upright, and flung aspirin at the bedroom window. The pills clattered against the pane before bouncing onto the carpet, where they lay like dead white islands in a seagrass sea.

The coffee was still too scalding-hot to drink.

He was out the door before it - and him - had time to cool.

Reverend Kerry was dunking yesterday's croissant into instant coffee when he heard the sirens.

Moving to the window, he watched two police cars and a white van swing past the church and skid round the s-bend on their noisy way to somewhere.

'Have a smidgeon of deference, please,' he hissed at them, 'on the day Christ was crucified! *For heaven's sake!*'

Returning to his stale breakfast, he failed to see the Ford Focus of Detective Inspector Zig Batten as it, too, swung and skidded past the church. Nor did he see the driver's left foot jiggle the clutch, one hand spinning the wheel, the other plonking a used tissue on a nose redder than nappy-rash.

Earlier, Reverend Kerry was singing hymns in the shower when DC Nina Magnus skidded past, a grim expression on her face and a white-faced Mike Brean in her passenger seat. At first, he'd refused to come. Now, he sat like a stone statue in the little Toyota.

'I don't want you to come either, Mike. But we'll be first there. Or I hope to god we will. I need you to block the track, at the foot of the hill. And to keep the early morning dog-walkers away, so I can secure the cr-.'

She stopped. It wasn't officially a crime scene yet, and Batten was a stickler for detail, when it suited. But if not a crime scene, Nina, tell me what the bloody hell it *is*! She shuddered and switched off the thought.

'I need to secure the *scene,* Mike. Your job is stopping busybodies clomping up to join me.' She chose not to add, 'and chucking up their breakfast.'

Reluctantly, Mike Brean agreed.

'If there was anyone else I could trust, I wouldn't be asking.'

Because she did trust Mike. First man in a while she *had* trusted, too. Or the first one she'd trusted without the trust being thrown back in her face. She smiled at him.

He could not return the smile. He was in shock but didn't know it.

Nina knew. But crime comes first. When the car jerked to a halt behind the church, at the foot of Crown of Thorns Hill, and Nina flew out the door, Mike struggled to emerge, and not because the car was smaller than him. Big as he was, and brave, there's always something you can never be prepared for.

They'd arrived at his.

Five

Andy Connor's job title - Scientific Services Manager - went to the wall during the recent 're-organisation'.

'Huh. *Cuts,* they mean,' he'd told Batten over a pint. Now, he was 'Principal Officer (Science)'. Colleagues, scientific and otherwise, instantly abbreviated him - to Pee Off or Prof. He encouraged the latter. 'Someone has to be the brains,' he told them.

Today, he was wired, and in no mood for jokes.

'Promise me something, Zig. If you're ever in a position, kindly make sure my passing comes with a bit more dignity, eh?'

He swiped a latex hand at the crucifix, framed by cloud on the peak of Crown of Thorns Hill.

Batten nodded. *Do the same for me, Prof. Please.*

'Who would plan this, Zig? What kind of 'person' puts their mind to...to *this!*'

His other hand gave the hilltop a second swipe. As if in response, the blue tarpaulin trapped in the hill's one remaining thorn tree swirled and crackled.

'At least you didn't get here first, Prof,' said Batten, thanking his lucky stars he didn't either, and pleased to have an excuse for blowing his nose. The thorn-tree looked as half-dead as he felt, its gnarled branches a handful of dry bones. Batten liked trees. But not this one. His brief experience of Somerset included happy walks through woodland - and less happy visits to open-air crime scenes punctuated by one kind of tree or another.

'That's the trouble with Somerset,' he told Connor. 'If we find a body outdoors, it's either down in a swamp or up on a hill. Next to a creepy bloody thorn tree like *that*.'

'Crataegus monogyna, I think, Zig. Not much life left in this one.'

Batten's eyebrow brought a nod of apology from Connor.

'Life, Zig. Why do we spend so much of our time delving into the opposite?'

'We were bad boys, in our youth, and the payback is turning up to *this*.'

'Surprised to see you here at all, Zig. Thought you were on leave.'

'Supposed to be. But Ballie's in Wales. And bloody Wallingford, the Area Super's...'

'Don't tell me. France? Un petit peu de Provence?'

'Further. South Africa. Wine trail and a bloody safari.'

'Hope a lion gets him.'

'Wallingford? He'd poison it.'

Neither man liked the new Area Superintendent, nor his habit of taking the credit while avoiding the work.

The person who had arrived first, DC Nina Magnus, sat on the stump of an old fencepost, her clothes stale and crumpled. At a scene, she knew her first duty was to preserve life. Well, fat chance. She stared - glared - at anything but the cross, her face somehow blacker today.

Batten sometimes had candid chats with Magnus. It was hard to tell when she was upset, he'd told her, because of her facial colour.

'Yes, sir. My face only turns white on the inside. After many hours of contamination.'

She'd added a smile. Batten too.

'You're an experienced detective, sir,' she'd said. 'I have every confidence in your ability to examine other signs and draw conclusions.'

If he couldn't before, a fresh opportunity faced him now. Her eyes were the size of golf balls. When she tried to close them, the lids were too small. Magnus was not much shorter than her Inspector's six foot, and admitted to having a 'robust' frame. Today, she looked frail. Except for her hands, clenched, two iron claws in search of a culprit's throat. Sensing Batten's eyes on her, she jumped up and stomped over.

'Sir?' She gestured at the hill. 'We need to... *cover* this. It's just not right.'

'Wait for the tent, Nina. Holiday traffic, that's all.'

'*That's all?*' She hissed out more breath. 'I'm not a prude, sir.'

He knew. She'd once hitched up her skirt in the office at Parminster, to show the team what a thug's cosh had done to her thigh.

'Come on, Nina. You know the score, and backwards.'

'We should do *something*, sir! I'm not religious, but for heaven's sake it's Good Friday!'

My Good Friday too, Batten almost said.

'We could blank off the scene with that sheeting. For now, at least!'

She flung an arm at the blue plastic, trapped in the old thorn-tree's tangles, jagging and crackling at the sky in an uncaring breeze. A forensics team painstakingly combed the ground beneath it, for wind-shaken trace. Soon, they would attend to the tarpaulin itself. Magnus knew it was a ridiculous suggestion. But to do *nothing*?

Even with the flu, Batten wasn't crass enough to remind her of their duty - preserve the scene; secure the evidence. His mood was much the same as hers. But being in charge means you're not encouraged to show it.

'You know we can't, Nina.'

Magnus let out a breath strong enough to spin a turbine.

'Prof Connor was ear-wigging, and loped over. He took Magnus by the arm and drew her away. He and Batten had things in common: an occasional night in the pub, and a touch more human sympathy than some of their male colleagues. Connor walked Magnus down the slope to his van, parked as far up the hill as it could go. The need to preserve a wide perimeter was the reason.

'Prone to asthma,' he said, pointing at the engine. He pulled open the rear doors. 'Here, give me a hand.'

Together, they drew out thick rolls of dark plastic sheet and two dozen long metal rods.

'Not what they're for, but they'll do as a stop-gap. You take this end, right?'

The photographic team, recovering from their grisly work, watched Connor and Magnus push the tall rods into the ground and hook sheeting over them. Once dressed in its improvised skirt, Crown of Thorns Hill was a giant cup-cake, topped by a poisoned cherry.

'It'll block the view from directly below,' he said. 'Slow the ghouls down a bit.'

He knew it wouldn't stop determined oglers with a better angle of sight. Nothing would. On his way up, Connor had passed a window and clocked a pair of binoculars trained on the crucifix. Professional to his boots, he'd recorded the house number. He trudged back up the hill, while Magnus tutted at their handiwork.

The plastic sheeting would be next to useless.

But anything was better than...*that*.

Connor and Batten tapped impatient feet. Their crime-scene bootees made a rustling sound as they hit the turf. Waiting, waiting, for the tent, for the Doc.

'I always feel like a professional mourner, Zig, at this point. You know, paid to turn up at a funeral.'

Batten nodded, eyes drawn unwillingly from his wristwatch to the wooden cross, its grisly silhouette sharpened by random flashes of sunlight.

A bloody neon sign, Zig, flashing on and off. What we need is dense cloud. Or fog.

He failed to lever his eyes back to his watch. They remained clamped on the crucifix, its naked body screaming in silence.

For the corpse, swaying in the breeze, time was irrelevant. For all who'd viewed it, the image was imprinted now in the dark sump of memory - as was the bright orange absurdity holding the body in place.

Lengths of vivid orange baler twine, secured to each cross-beam, were looped crudely around the victim's arms and shoulders. The stark body dangled and swayed, like the puppet it had become. Though small and fine-boned, the weight of the corpse pulled at the twine which was cutting through dead skin into bloodless flesh.

Connor knew the depth of the wound was a useful indicator of time. And felt ashamed for knowing it.

The head, unsupported, lolled lazily, pointing at the soil it was destined to lie beneath. Both eyes were wide open, staring at nothing. Simple gravity, Batten thought. Or had a human hand - a killer's perhaps - callously neglected to close them?

More lengths of orange twine crudely secured the legs in place. Twine snaked down the shins and coiled around naked feet, pinning them to the base of the cross. Above them, a white shirt was wrapped around the groin, its long sleeves encircling slim hips. The arms of the shirt-cum-loin-cloth were tied together with a granny knot.

It was the body's only dignity.

Nina Magnus, the first 'professional' to clamber up the hill, had fought against her human instinct to cut the body down for decency's sake. A body it clearly was, beyond all human help. Instead, Magnus did what she was trained to do, while averting her eyes from both cross and corpse.

'Prof' Connor, staring at it now, struggled to prevent disgust seeping through the neutral frame of his science.

Batten saw a waste of life.

'You'll grow no older,' he silently told the body.

He wasn't sure if it was pity he stared at.

Or shame.

Six

Being allergic to police cars, Chas Janner knew something was wrong when he drove into East Thorne, early on Good Friday morning. Police cars were everywhere, their wheels angled up on kerbs or plonked askew on grass verges, ruining the turf.

'Bet *they* don't get a ticket,' he muttered to himself. It was far too early for him, but he'd overdone the cider last night - and all that followed - and had to sleep it off on the dirty mattress he kept in his lock-up.

Right now, he needed to get back to Turks Lane, soak himself under a shower and change his smelly clothes, before scooting back to check his supplies. The holiday weekend would be busy, and profitable. He had the 'needs' of his regulars to see to - and some bonus holiday extras to sort.

In the street, villagers he recognised were pointing up at Crown of Thorns Hill and whispering together. Peering up through the car window, all he could see was a vague blur of activity. It's not just police cars, his stay-out-of-trouble antennae told him. Too many people in the streets, too early in the morning. Too many people craning their necks at that bloody hill.

Pulling his little blue Renault into the lay-by near All Saints Church, he grabbed a pair of folding binoculars from the glove compartment. The first thing he spotted - to his surprise - was Mike Brean's black girlfriend, Nina. He couldn't remember her surname and didn't want to. That she was a cop was enough for Chas. He watched as she and a shorter man shoved long poles into the hillside and draped sheeting over them. Scanning the hill, he saw figures in paper suits and masks, like in the cop programmes on TV.

Before the sheeting obscured it, his binoculars found the crucifix he and Mike Brean had dragged up that bloody hill last night.

A tremor rocked his stomach, before an earthquake turned it over entirely.

He'd missed breakfast, but it wasn't hunger.

His fingers shook on the focusing ring as the naked body hanging there came into view. And the face, clear as day.

Crystal clear enough.

Dead enough.

'Jesus Christ!' he whispered, with not the faintest grain of irony. 'Jesus Christ! Isn't that the lippy sod from last night?'

He looked again, to be certain.

'But who parked the bloody lippy sod up *there*?'

'Chas,' he told himself, 'forget your shower. Get away, now. Trouble's coming. Clean out your lock-up. Cover your tracks, man. Fast.'

He rammed the binoculars back in the glove compartment and started the engine.

Driving away, he had to wind down the window to remove the smell of sweat - his own.

'You, boy, are in the shit,' he told the empty car.

'And you're in it deep.'

PC Jess Foreman was less than pleased to be called in on his holiday weekend, but got on with it, as usual. A distracted Chas Janner failed to spot his vast bulk emerge from an unmarked car that seemed relieved when he vacated it. Nor did Janner spot Foreman's notebook and pen, nor Foreman's beady eye.

Into the notebook went Chas's car registration, with a brief description of a giant bearded man with binoculars, acting suspiciously at the foot of Crown of Thorns Hill.

Further up the slope, squeezed into Nina's tiny white Toyota, Mike Brean was wintry cold. Warm air had no effect on his frozen legs, jammed up against the noisy heater, nor on the steamed-up windows. But he chose not to wipe them. Why look out? Hadn't he seen enough?

He dreaded what Reverend Kerry would make of the sight, should he have the misfortune to confront it. An attack on his church? A crude mockery of the central icon of his faith?

Mike Brean pushed cold hands into padded pockets as the car's throbbing heater became a drone. Shivering in the too-small passenger seat, he struggled to blot out the bloodless face dangling from the cross.

Despite his frozen bones, the shock of recognition burned into him.

The hair was different, yes, shorter now. And the body thinner. But the dead face hanging there was all too memorable.

Strong binoculars had confirmed what he feared.

The unique tattoo was there, still, etched into the skin below the navel. A delicate tattooed bird, its wings in the air.

Mike's fingers - all those years ago - they'd caressed it.

'Thanks, Nina. An improvement,' Batten said, as Magnus approached. He flicked a hand at Connor's improvised screen.

'Not for the corpse. Sir.'

Batten didn't need the nudge. None of his team were stones. If procedure allowed, they'd remove the body in a blink. But all they could do was wait. Wait for the Doc, for more of the on-leave team to arrive from warm beds and barbecue-ready patios, or from jammed-up cars on the A303. Bank holidays are a productive time for murder.

Unless you work for the police.

He corrected himself. Is it murder, or something else? He turned to ask Sergeant Ball. But Ball was in Wales. He fell back on training and experience. Not sure? Then assume the worst, while waiting for evidence. His personal mantra said much the same, in a Northern sort of way: *if it's not ruled out, it's still ruled in*. Both reminders had served him well enough, over the years.

But if not murder, *what*?

He ran through some possibilities.

Manslaughter?

Prevention of burial?

Blasphemy? No. Nigh on impossible to prove in a courtroom.

And desecration's no longer in the Statute Book - *though it ought to be*.

Does a naked corpse, on a cross, on a rural hilltop, constitute 'stirring up religious hatred?' He doubted the CPS would think so, Good Friday or not.

Straightforward intimidation, then? But intimidating who?

Against his better judgement, he looked back at the scene. The cross itself was corrupted, yes, but intact. They wouldn't even be able to do the culprit for damage to property.

Magnus was tapping her foot so hard he could feel the vibrations through the turf.

'I know, Nina, I know.'

'With respect, sir, you don't. You don't, at all.'

She flung a sisterly arm at the cross. The groin was covered but the torso was bare. The victim's breasts, as dead as the rest of the body, had the gall to sway left and right when the wind shifted.

'It's worse than a strip-club,' she snapped.

Batten found himself turning away, but not from Magnus. Her golf-ball eyes held him there.

'At the very least we should -'

Batten raised a palm in surrender.

'The team's onto it, Nina. Not their fault the A303's a car-park today.'

D.C. Hick, more SOCOs and a protective crime-scene tent were struggling through bank holiday traffic jams.

'We'll not screw up our chance to solve...*this*...by tramping through the evidence, as well you know. Be just the same if it was a naked man.'

'I doubt that very much, sir -'

Batten raised both palms now, and lowered his voice. 'I share your feelings, Nina.'

She was about to tell him how impossible it was, but he pointed downhill to a line of grumpy forensic staff, dragged out of holiday beds and shoved into reluctant work clothes. The anger of frustrated Easter-weekend partners lay thick as dust on their stooped shoulders.

Surrounded by SOCOs, a collapsed police tent appeared to walk itself up the slope like a giant white cicada. Behind it twitched a figure who any detective would swear had just emerged naked from a ditch and, chancing upon a beggar's discarded rags, had struggled into them. But this was DC Eddie Hick, unlucky enough to be duty CID this Easter weekend.

Batten watched Hick twitch uphill, the lobster pink of his shirt-tail growing longer and louder as it wriggled from unbelted moleskin trousers. Today, the trousers hovered somewhere between burnt umber and mud.

Would Hick be better off naked, Zig?

The body's naked resonance pushed the thought aside.

'Even Hickie's got feelings, Nina.' Batten pointed down at the scruffy DC, to ease the tension. 'Despite being unable to dress himself. As an experienced detective, I have every confidence in your ability to examine other signs and draw conclusions. Once he's viewed the corpse, that is.'

DC Magnus would ordinarily have smiled at Batten's echo, if only because it proved he listened. Today, her face was stone.

Batten watched Hick wrench his goggle-eyes from the body on the cross, and pretend to supervise the staff positioning the police tent with trained care over body, cross and scene.

Another significant body was still missing from Crown of Thorns Hill.

'*Hickie!*'

Hick twitched towards Batten, glad of the excuse to put distance between himself and the corpse.

'Where the bloody hell's Doc Danvers? Forgot to adjust his sun-dial?'

Hick stuttered an answer. 'Er, Scotland. Sir.'

'No wonder he's late. Is he on leave? Or was it forced repatriation?'

A white-faced Hick was unsure if Batten's bluster was real, or a defence.

'British history tour, sir. Bonnie Prince Somebody. So they said.'

Busman's holiday, Zig. History's all bodies too.

'Replacement?'

'On his way, sir.' Hick peered at his notebook. 'Sorry. *Her* way.'

Batten lifted an eyebrow. He'd never worked with a female pathologist before. Let her not be a graduate of the Doc Danvers School of Riddle and Evasion, he thought.

And let her be quick.

'This'll be her, sir.' Hick pointed at a suited figure, tackling the hill, lugging a medical bag. DC Hick knew his duty. 'I'll give her a hand.'

Batten watched as Hick hopped down the slope like a three-legged rabbit. The ensuing exchange went straight into the DC Hick archive.

'I'll take your bag, Miss.'

'Why?'

'Er. Heavy?'

'Yes. It is.'

'Right.'

Hick's strong right mitt leaned across to take the handle. Doctor Sonia Welcome failed to live up to her surname, flicking the bag away from Hick's grasp and flashing a pair of eyebrows Batten would have been proud of.

'But, Miss, you said it's heavy.'

'I did. What a miracle a mere woman has managed to carry it this far. Constable.'

Hick's face dropped. The least she could have done was assume he was a Sergeant.

'If our paths cross at my gym,' she added, 'perhaps we can lift weights together?' And without another word she strode past the pink and mud-orange ball of twitches to present herself to Batten.

A breathless Hick caught up and did the introductions. Batten was careful not to remind Dr Welcome to stay on the tape-marked track, or warn her about the state of the body. He stopped himself imagining what she'd do to it at the morgue, sharp scalpel gripped in the cool, firm hand he'd just shaken.

As if sensing his thoughts, she pulled on latex gloves and wafted past him up the slope, to view and delve. She smells as much of formaldehyde as Chanel, Batten thought, but he couldn't help admiring her bottom, shapely even within her crime-scene suit. She was about the same age as Erin Kemp.

'Woman, sir.'

'Cuh. Sherlock-Hickie-Holmes, you.'

'No, sir, I mean, you know.'

Batten waited his usual five seconds.

'I mean, always a bloke. Used to it being a bloke.'

Batten gave Hick a blokey tap on the arm, to ease him upright, but decided against tucking in his shirt.

'All part of your learning process, Eddie. I'm sure Nina Magnus will happily extend it, if you'd like to share your thoughts with her?'

Even Hick could read the grim expression on Magnus's face, and had the sense to stay away.

Batten left him to it, trudging along the taped track towards 'Prof' Connor. The two men traded looks, sighed, and tapped their crime-scene bootees, eyes focused on the walls of the white tent. When they could no longer stomach the *click-click* of camera shutters from within - and what the sound signified - they shuffled a pace or two away.

'Is it a cross, Andy?' Batten asked. 'Or a crucifix? I'm never sure which?'

'Both, Zig. Crucifix when there's a body - a *corpus*, to us posh folk.

They'll have taken the body down by now. Plain old cross again, I suppose.'

'Less intimidating, without the body.'

'Indeed. A naked female corpse on a cross, on Good Friday. Not going to log it as accidental, are you?'

Batten shrugged. If deliberate, why? Who *for*?

They shuffled further away.

'A better view down than up, Zig,' mumbled Connor, turning his back on the tent and surveying the pretty village of East Thorne below. If the hill they stood on was prominent, so was the Church of All Saints. Its hamstone tower dwarfed the village's two-storey houses, robust though some of them were.

All Saints commanded all it surveyed. Roads moved aside for it. Rival services, in the form of shops, school, village hall and The Rising Sun, were banished to the village's lower fringe. Further along, smaller houses merged into the unmistakeable geometry of an old apple orchard. Some trees seemed gnarled and dead. From others, defiant flecks of white blossom were beginning to emerge.

Batten's gaze returned to the church. He wondered how many parishioners bent their knees there on Sundays, in these less godly times.

'Perpendicular Gothic, Zig, Somerset version. Fourteenth century, at a guess. Square tower, no spire. Big tracery windows. External stair turret. Stop me if you're bored.'

Batten gave Connor an encouraging eyebrow.

'Mostly hamstone, from Ham Hill. But at the corners, see, the frilly bits, a different stone?'

Another admiring eyebrow.

'Probably Doulting stone, from Shepton Mallet. Rewarding to carve, apparently.'

'You're a mine of surprising information, Prof.'

'Evening class, Zig. Architecture. We did Somerset churches, last month.'

'Evening class, Prof? Didn't think you were...you know.'

'Need to clear my head, just like you lesser folk. Your distraction's hoofing along country tracks, or squatting by a lake with a fishing rod, right? Buildings, me. Old, new, big, small or in-between. I like them.

They're important. They're where people go, aren't they? Where we live. You still live in one, don't you?'

'Yes, Prof. When I'm there.'

Batten wished he was there right now. With aspirin, a duvet, and Erin. Or Dr Sonia Welcome. He killed the thought.

'My very point, Zig. We're never there, to clear our heads, either of us. Your village. My village. God knows, *this* village.'

Connor flung an arm at the rooftops of East Thorne.

'Fine buildings down there, and we're stuck on a hilltop. With *that*.'

He cocked a thumb at the temporary white building, and what it hid.

Seven

Below, in East Thorne village, rumour was busy.

Eyes trained on Crown of Thorns Hill tracked the comings and goings of the police. Whispered voices shared theories and inventions.

'Terrorists,' said one.

'The work of Satan,' said another.

'On Good Friday,' said a third, 'please have some respect for the dead!'

The more ghoulish gossipers whined in disappointment when their view was diminished by a screen of plastic sheeting. But it didn't move them on.

At one particular window, a pair of strong binoculars continued to watch a dark crucifix point its strange cargo at the sky - before a police tent sprang up and resurrected the image as a tall clean shroud of white.

Scouring the hilltop, twin lenses picked out the tent's white door as it swished aside, and focused on a woman in a white crime-scene suit, her delicate finger beckoning at two loitering men.

Dr Sonia Welcome closed the tent door behind D.I. Batten and 'Prof' Connor, who waited with mixed feelings.

'I'm still amazed, gentlemen, how the process of evolution has failed to provide humankind with tougher skulls.'

She flicked five fingers at the anonymous body, thankfully removed from the wooden cross, which still pointed at the heavens, though empty of its burden now. The police-tent, just tall enough to contain it, was a tiny, claustrophobic cathedral to Batten, and he a poor sinner staring heavenwards in childish awe.

'Mm, I thought it might be a skull job.'

Even from distance, Batten had spotted a faint trickle of blood, a mere dark line on the victim's neck. Face down and much closer, as the body now was, he saw more than he cared to - the awkward angle of the head, and was it bruising, or shadow? The dead still managed to surprise him.

'Skull job, yes, Inspector, and very likely the cause of death. Alas, I cannot yet say what weapon, if any, was employed.'

Sonia Welcome waved her hands again.

'Coffin position, please,' she said, and her helpers carefully turned the slight body face-up.

As they did, Batten looked for signs of rigor, making a rough calculation the far better qualified would check.

'Dead for some hours?'

'Indeed. Ten to twelve - my initial estimate. A cool night, which must be taken into account.' She peeled off her used gloves and stared at the victim. 'Such a pity, for life to end like this, and for such an attractive woman. She might almost have fallen asleep in prayer.'

Just as you did, Zig, when the school dragged you and your classmates to mid-week church, to grudgingly worship a crucifix. You were ten years old though. This woman here...

'I'm guessing somewhere around mid-thirties? Thereabouts?'

Dr Welcome gave a careful nod. 'A reasonable estimate.' She peered once more at the body. 'If only we could ask her, poor love.'

Batten appraised this 'new' doctor. In contrast to the protective irony of Benjamin Danvers, Sonia Welcome seemed to favour an approach bordering on the humane. Welcome indeed. He silently thanked her for it.

'What else can you tell me, Doctor? At this stage.'

'You can observe most of it yourself, Inspector. At this stage.'

She pointed to various body parts with a precise finger.

'Slim waist. Fine bones. Petite. After she was taken down -' Welcome wagged an indicative finger at the empty cross - 'it was clear her biceps and thighs were well-formed, despite the damage caused by the thick string holding her in place. Muscle tone suggests an active lifestyle, or time in the gym. Though fails to prove either, of course.'

Batten hoped Ms Welcome hadn't done a refresher course at the Doc Danvers School of Riddle and Evasion.

'Small but full breasts - almost certainly her own. No scars, no obvious cosmetic work. Apart from said damage, no significant natural blemishes anywhere on the skin. No moles, no birthmarks.'

Doc Danvers would have added, 'no bar-code, how thoughtless.'

'As to the non-natural blemish - well, clear enough.' She pointed at a prominent tattoo, an inch or so below the navel. 'A bluebird, Inspector. So I am informed by my colleague.'

Again, she waved a hand, this time at a smiling helper.

'Clive here is an amateur ornithologist. When time allows.'

Clive the ornithologist looked pleased with himself.

'It will be double-checked,' she added, and Clive's smile disappeared.

'Her fingernails are interesting. Professionally painted, expensive. Yet clipped, crudely. And clipped recently. And short. Done elsewhere, too, since no clippings have come to light. Which may suggest whatever it suggests, Inspector.'

Sonia Welcome's 'so be careful' glance had a hint of kindness behind it.

'A faint speck of what may be blood is just visible beneath what remains of the right thumbnail. If the remainder hold any useful information, Mr Connor and I will doubtless inform you, soon enough.'

Connor nodded at Batten, both with the same thought: whose DNA did the missing nails scratch? And who crudely snipped them off?

Batten saw two delicate hands, dead, their protective bags like gift-wrap.

'Moved, was she? Or died in situ?'

'Moved, without doubt. Early lividity suggests she lay for a time on her side. Like so.'

Dr Welcome mimed a half-turned body.

Batten added an invisible killer, saw a boot nudge the body onto its back. To check it was dead.

'No obvious signs of recent sexual activity. And, skull apart, no sign of invasive trauma. Later, we shall see.'

'The shirt?'

The white shirt that had brought a tiny amount of dignity to the corpse lay like a folded shroud in an evidence box.

'A tiny bloodstain on the left collar. But three more specks of blood on the upper left sleeve.'

Experience cajoled Batten into seeing a strong right-handed killer, probably male, and wielding whatever was to hand. A broken branch from an apple tree? A chunk of hamstone? A church candlestick? He moved well away from the body, to sneeze.

Serves you right, Zig, for getting ahead of yourself.

Sonia Welcome glanced at the bright red beacon of Batten's nose. Concern? Or simple medical curiosity?

'I shan't attempt to do your job for you, Inspector, but logic may suggest the bloodstains belong to the victim, rather than a second or third party. Mr Connor and I will doubtless know more, once we...' She waved a desultory hand at due process.

Batten recognised the gesture. He used it himself, to avoid explanation. Short cuts to preserve your voice.

And your sanity.

'The shirt is hers?'

'I can tell you it's her *size* - size 8. Petite. Oh, the heady days when I could struggle into anything so small.'

If she was fishing for compliments, she had no need. Batten gave a non-committal nod as he glanced at the size 12 outfit she pleasingly filled. She caught his eye.

'But was she wearing the shirt, Inspector, when she was struck? Or fell?'

'And the answer?'

'Somewhere between possible and likely. Wearing it on her torso, I mean, rather than as an impromptu loincloth. And rather an expensive loincloth. Not polyester, but pure silk, if I'm not mistaken.'

'I was wondering about the shirt. You know, how the victim lived might tell you how she died - etcetera.'

'And polyester and silk tell different stories, yes.'

'Whatever the cloth, did she drape it over her own private parts?' Batten asked, half to himself, half to Sonia Welcome. 'Some kind of sex game? Some kind of fetish?'

'Fifty Shades of Loincloth? What a strange world we inhabit, Inspector.'

'Or did someone else wrap the white shirt round the body? And before or after death? *And why*?'

'If something other than sexual activity, Inspector, you may have your work cut out.'

Batten was thinking the same. He blew his nose.

'Loincloths,' he said, loudly. It came out like a sneeze.

Sonia Welcome gave him a puzzled look.

'Loincloths. They take me back to childhood. Enforced visits to church. A not-quite-naked figure of Christ on the cross, modesty intact.'

'But at some cost to historical likelihood?'

Batten nodded. 'If someone - not the victim - added the loincloth, could it be a deliberate religious reference?'

'A sort of parody, you mean, of Christ-on-the-cross? It being Good Friday?'

He realised he was casting Sonia Welcome in the role of his Sergeant, Batten/Balling ideas backwards and forwards. Despite hating cricket, he batted on. 'Why would someone choose to do that?'

'Crown of Thorns Hill is suggestively named, I would have thought?'

Batten thought of the tower and graveyard of All Saints Church. And prayed it was coincidence.

'Could be simple propriety, I suppose.'

'Death with decorum, Inspector?'

'What a change that'd make.'

'At least the cross is well-cared for.' Sonia Welcome waved her fingers at the fresh coat of varnish on the smooth wood.

Batten had noticed the varnish, and sent DC Magnus down to All Saints Church to discover where the cross was stored, who maintained it, and how recently. What she discovered at the church might or might not prove useful.

His covert motive was to give her golf-ball eyes a brief respite from the crime scene.

Eight

Nina Magnus stumbled down from hill to church in a daze. She should have been able to tell Batten the history of All Saints' crucifix, but she was in holiday mode last night when Mike was telling *her*.

Didn't last long, Nina, did it? she mumbled to herself as she pressed the Vestry bell.

Its *buzz* was distinctly non-rural. *Baaa* wouldn't have surprised her. Nothing would, today.

Reverend Kerry did, his dog-collar more yellow than white but the top of his skull bright red. He's recently shaved it, she guessed. This would be the first time she'd actually spoken to him. In The Rising Sun he was always at the far end of the bar, clustered among what Debra, the barmaid, referred to as 'the men'.

A hint of recognition passed from Kerry to her, quickly squashed by professional circumstance. She wasn't altogether sure if he knew she was Mike Brean's girlfriend, and wasn't about to tell him.

'The cross?' he said. 'The *cross*?'

He wanted to say *how dare you ask! Isn't Good Friday in tatters enough?*

'What of it?' he asked. '*It*, at least, is where it's supposed to be. I imagine you've come to tell me I won't be allowed to join it?'

Not my decision, Magnus told herself. She ignored Kerry's questions, and his mood, by explaining her presence.

'Andrew Holt,' he told her. 'The village knows him as 'Handy Andy'. Because he is a handyman. He maintains the church grounds, and indeed the church itself, in extremis. Andrew very kindly sanded down the cross, and re-varnished it. Without charge. Of all my parishioners, he is perhaps the poorest. Yet he gave his services for free. Lo, the wonder of God's way.'

'He did that here, at the church, Reverend? Or...wherever he lives?'

Kerry caught up. 'Andrew loaded the cross onto his pickup - it just about runs - and drove it to the workshop at his home. He calls it a workshop. It's a large shed. The Churchwarden helped him load and unload. Somewhat reluctantly.'

'And his home is where, please?'

'Andrew lives in Turks Lane. Number 3. With Biddy.'

'His wife?'

'His daughter. There *is* no Mrs Holt. Well, you will struggle to find her on *earth*, at least.'

Magnus wished she was back on Crown of Thorns Hill, rather than chasing a wild goose round a testy vicar.

'And it was returned here, was it? Before it was taken to...' She pointed vaguely upwards.

'It was not. Two strapping fellows kindly collected it from Turks Lane and ferried it to the peak.

On foot. Yesterday evening.'

Mike and Chas, Magnus could have said.

'But now,' moaned Kerry, '*now*, I wish they had not. If only our Father in Heaven would grace me with the skill to turn back time.'

'These strapping fellows, Reverend. Which route would they have taken, with the, er, cross?'

Kerry hesitated, raised a bony finger and jabbed it away from the Vestry. His arm and finger became a snake, curling along the side and rear of Crown of Thorns Hill.

'The back way,' he said, with a touch of embarrassment. 'For the purposes of discretion. I saw no need to advertise the unusual circumstances. In these *modern* times.'

'The cross wasn't stored in the church and taken directly up the hill, on this track behind?' She pointed directly above her, at the path she had driven to, this morning, a frozen-faced Mike Brean jammed in the passenger seat of her little car.

'Correct,' he said.

'So your two strapping fellows didn't use this track at all? Only the other one - at the rear of the hill?'

'I'm certain I said precisely that, Constable?'

Between thoughts, Magnus nodded a thank you. Mike probably told her all this on Thursday night, when she wasn't listening. Her CID ears were listening now.

And they'd heard something useful - the cross was to be moved from Turks Lane on Thursday night, rather than Good Friday afternoon. And the 'back-way' route was not common knowledge. Whose eyes, then, watched it being planted on a dark hilltop covered in mist?

How significant this was, she didn't know. But if it narrowed down the parameters...

'I'm sorry if I've have wasted your time, Reverend,' she mumbled.

Stepping through the Vestry's heavy door, she wondered if she'd wasted hers.

Dr Sonia Welcome replaced the lid on the evidence box containing a carefully folded white silk shirt, size eight.

'The sleeves, Inspector, were tied in their unaccustomed place with nothing more complex than a now much-photographed granny-knot, I'm afraid.'

Batten would get to the crime scene photos and video soon enough. His eyes turned from the evidence box to the victim's skin, scanning it from groin to torso, and back.

'Real? Or sun-lamp and spray? The tan?'

The victim's breasts were as evenly tanned as the rest of the body. Only a thin line of white groin-flesh was visible.

'My guess - note the word, Inspector - is we have the real thing. Sunlight, in quantity, I'd suggest. No signs of a cosmetic tan, and it lacks the tell-tale sun-bed orange hue, so...'

Batten was wondering how the victim managed to maintain a natural tan, given the long grey winter the UK had suffered. Or *where* she managed it. Sonia Welcome was of the same mind.

'And only faint tan-lines on her feet, Inspector. Which may suggest a barefoot lifestyle - in a place with copious sunshine? By the way, no tan-gaps on her fingers, so perhaps not a wedding-ring-wearer. Do we have an unmarried nudist here?'

'Not quite.' He pointed at the groin, where golden brown met a thin frontier of white.

'Ah yes. Perhaps a semi-nudist, who retained the limited decorum of a thong? Or is it a *naturist*, these days? I'm unsure.'

As a rookie, Batten would have been embarrassed to view dead female nakedness in the company of a clothed female pathologist, who was very much alive. And very much attractive. But in these modern times...

'Was she wearing one, or not? A thong? Beneath the loin-cloth, I mean.'

'No thong, Inspector. No underwear - indeed not a stitch of clothing - of any kind. Other than the size 8 blouse with a label I've never heard of.'

Batten raised an eyebrow and a pen.

"Disaya', Inspector.'

He puzzled up an embarrassed eyebrow.

'*Desire?*'

And received an eyebrow back, with the slightest of smiles.

'Not that kind of 'Desire'.' She spelled it out for him. 'D.I.S.A.Y.A. I've never heard of it, but then I'm Pathology, not Fashion. Doubtless you'll *detect* it, soon enough.'

He jotted down the unusual combination of letters.

Sonia Welcome closed her medical bag. 'Anything further?' she asked.

Coffee? A glass of wine? Dinner for two? The words flashed into his head. And stayed there.

'Er, if we can rewind a bit? You said, "was struck, or fell." Any sense which? Could it have been a collision? An accidental fall?'

With an upward turn of her palms, Sonia Welcome became Doc Danvers.

'Well, possible.'

'Probable? Improbable?'

'At present, unknown. What I *do* know is this poor soul here, whether killed by accident or design, did not afterwards disport herself upon a handy wooden cross.'

Batten nodded. His team were tracking the various routes the victim could have travelled to the peak of Crown of Thorns Hill. Dead on arrival seemed likely.

'It may be Easter, Inspector, but she did not resurrect, nor tie herself in place with plastic string. There may be epithelial and other traces on the string.' She pointed to a cluster of evidence bags, each filled with carefully removed orange twine. 'Plenty to keep Mr Connor busy, I imagine?'

Andy Connor was already busy. Batten watched his eyes tracking between the baler-twine, the tall wooden cross and the faint footprints at its base.

'Can I borrow the Inspector, just for a mo', Doc, please?' he said.

Outside the tent, Connor pointed to the backs of two SOCOs, crouched above indentations in the ground.

'More footprints out here, too, Zig. Traces, anyhow. Same size or thereabouts as those near the cross. Best guess, tens, at least. My *suggestion* is they belong to whoever dug the footings. Two big-footed bods, anyway. I know you spotted the pile of turfs lower down the hill, because I could hear the cogs in your brain ticking over.'

They were ticking over still, picturing Sonia Welcome's feet. A five, or smaller? A simple equation: gender and shoe size?

'Not female, then, Andy? Not two Amazons?'

'Likely male, yes. But careful now, because Bigfoot A and Bigfoot B are not all we're finding. Thought I'd better show you.' He pointed again at the SOCOs. 'Taking casts. Traces of smaller feet.'

'Smaller? How small?'

'Size eight at a guess. Or seven. Or nine.'

Connor was treated to a low groan. 'Another male?' asked Batten.

'Given the absence of after-shave and lager, Zig, I can only speculate – partly from the strength required to hoist the body. Though, having said that, there's not much to hoist, is there? The footprints might turn out to be circumstantial.'

Batten shrugged. Forensic evidence was always circumstantial, blast it.

'Could it be a woman's shoe? Pointed toes? Shaped heel?'

Connor rolled his eyes. 'Zig, you'll be cross-dressing next. There's a faint suggestion of shape and size, no sole-pattern to speak of and, would you credit it, no maker's logo.'

'You were doing so well, Prof.'

'Best I can tell you, Zig, is the toes - probably - have gone a tad deeper into the turf than you'd expect from normal walking.'

'Someone reaching up, carrying the weight of a body? Winding baler twine round the victim's arms? Hoisting, even?'

'Plausible, Zig. But it wouldn't take much of a hoist, would it, to reach the cross-beams? All you need do is raise your arms. Whoever dug the hole for that cross, they must have been aiming for hell, not heaven. We'll have fun getting it out. But your maybe size eights is definitely some*one*. A single pair of shoes, no more.'

'So could it be two Bigfoots *and* a size eight?'

'Plausible again, Zig. Except the smaller footprints - such as they are - they're *on top of* the two Bigfoots. They came after.'

'Soon after? Long after?'

'Connor shook his head. 'Beyond guessing, Zig. And neither could I swear to Your Honour in a courtroom that two big-footed males didn't just stand around watching a smaller-footed person hoist a body onto a handy cross, without offering to help.'

'Before the three of them nipped off for drinkies after, to celebrate, yes. But as to likelihood?'

Connor raised both hands in surrender.

Batten blew out a breath. He trusted Connor's judgement, even when unhelpful, but concocting scenarios to explain how the body found its way onto the cross was proving tough. Two male perpetrators? Three? One?

Sonia Welcome stepped from the tent and stood in the doorway, arms folded. Batten and Connor had cut her out of the discussion. We wouldn't have done the same to Doc Danvers, Batten realised. Or any male pathologist. He sneezed, to cover his tracks.

'I take it, Inspector, you have no further pressing questions about the plastic string? Mr Connor?'

Both men flashed sheepish grins of apology.

'The bindings and the knots were thoroughly photographed before being removed,' she said. 'We had to cut them, at several points, but preserved the knotting. Reef-knots. Every one.'

'But the loin-cloth is a granny knot?'

'It is. Why, I cannot say. Nor why every reef-knot is neatly tied, and almost identical. Military precision?'

'Funny things, knots,' Connor mumbled, and slipped away to check.

Batten decided not to remind Sonia Welcome the correct term for the 'plastic string' was baler twine, altogether tougher and more durable. Does her ignorance of baler twine suggest she's urban, he wondered? And not local?

Like you, Zig.

And is the *victim* local?

'No purse, bag, wallet, keys? No phone?'

'None, Inspector. And, alas, no convenient name-tag on her sole item of clothing.'

'Identification's going to be fun. A naked corpse wearing nothing but a loincloth.'

'And carrying not a single personal object. We do so take for granted the daily luggage of life, don't we? The clutter we carry around in our pockets and bags - till death intervenes?'

Batten nodded, wondering if the victim left her clutter at home.

But where is home?

Another sneeze bit him, and he wagged his tissue by way of apology. Sonia Welcome awarded him a smile.

Better looking than Benjamin Danvers, Zig, by a distance. And slimmer.

He remembered Doc Danvers once referring to an obese body as 'a proper slab-filler.' By contrast, this victim was slight.

'At least she won't take up much room in your path-lab,' Batten sniffed.

'Tragically, we always find room for the dead. Seven days a week.'

They stepped away from the tent.

'Not spoiled your Good Friday, I hope,' he said.

She shook out her blonde hair. 'I was dealing with the backlog of paperwork, until...'

Welcome again waved a desultory hand. Her helpers prepared to move the body, with what dignity remained.

'At least I'm not suffering from a cold.' She flicked a sympathetic finger at Batten's pomegranate nose.

It's *man-flu,* he wanted to say.

'Whisky, honey, lemon and hot water, Inspector. Flimsy medical evidence to underpin the recommendation, but rather pleasant.'

He shrugged out a half-smile, which she returned.

'Assuming you like to drink whisky?'

Zig, was that an invitation?

He could manage a tot right now, sandwiched as he was between two bright attractive eyes and a pair of dead ones. In the awkward pause, he caught her eye, she his.

The white tent broke the moment, flapping in a chance gust of wind.

'Whoever she is, poor love, she can speak no more. The likes of you and I, Inspector, will need to be her voice.'

Batten nodded, and sneezed. He almost said, *you see, men can multitask*. But a growing list of tasks killed the thought.

And no Sergeant Ball to manage them.

His Sonia Welcome fantasy blew away on the breeze as the long list hit him, like a bare-knuckle punch to the gut.

Nine

The Reverend Kerry's Good Friday was in shreds, and, his blood up, he was determined to visit the cause. His eyesight was not the best, he owned no binoculars, and the black detective he'd recognised from visits to The Rising Sun had made sure he answered *her* questions without answering any of his.

Stepping onto the track behind the church, he began to tackle the slope of Crown of Thorns Hill, looming above him in a natural coat of Spring grass, below an unnatural swathe of plastic sheeting, topped by a white police tent.

Inside, he knew, his beloved cross was imprisoned.

As the gradient increased he slowed and slowed again, gasping for breath by the time he reached the large frame of the uniformed constable whose job it was to bar his progress. PC Jess Foreman, an old hand, recognised Kerry straight away. Foreman's mental address-book contained anyone and everyone within a ten-mile radius who'd ever stepped across the threshold of a pub. Because Jess Foreman had stepped across all of them too. And when off-duty, he rarely stepped out again till the early hours.

'Now, now, Reverend. You don't want to be going up there. Not today.'

'Today? *Today*? Today is *Good Friday*, unless you too are a heathen who cares nothing for its significance! I have a service 'up there', this afternoon. Crown of Thorns Hill is *my* hill. The Good Friday service has taken place there since...the Flood!'

Kerry ignored the momentary lapse in religious chronology, and pushed his body at the space beyond PC Foreman, who didn't budge. As colleagues pointed out, Jess was six-foot-two in all directions. Thwarted, Reverend Kerry changed tack.

'Village rumour tells me someone is hurt, up there. I am a priest. My duty is to the sick, to the disturbed, and you shall let me pass.'

'Well, sir, if someone *is* sick up there, I doubt they'll want to be disturbed as well. So I'll be asking for your patience.'

Jess Foreman's big feet were firmly planted. Kerry recharged himself with a long breath but before he could apply it, Mike Brean was tapping him gently on the shoulder. He'd witnessed the confrontation from the cramped passenger seat of Nina's Toyota and welcomed an excuse to clamber out.

'The Constable's right, Reverend. You don't want to go up there.'

'I beg to disagree, Mike. I -'

Kerry's gaze fell on the chalk-white features of a strangely sunken Mike Brean. Priestly eyes flicked at the hill, at the roadblock of Jess Foreman, and again at Mike's pallor. Kerry knew the sick and the disturbed when he saw them, and knew his duty.

'Mike. My boy. Whatever has happened to you?'

All Mike could do was point a pallid finger upwards, at the hilltop. 'You don't want to go up there. Believe me.'

Mike closed his eyes, but two magnified circles of death were etched into the eyeballs. He sensed their imprints would be slow to fade. If they ever did.

'What has happened, Mike? Tell me. Please! It is *my* hill!'

'Someone beyond your help, Father. Beyond yours and everyone else's.'

'Who is it, Mike? *Who*? Not someone from my flock?'

Mike said nothing.

Reverend Kerry was the first person to ask him who the body was.

Nina hadn't.

Nor the police, yet. Nor the forensics team.

Too busy.

'Who can it be, Mike, up there?'

Mike closed his eyes.

But the bluebird tattoo remained.

From the hilltop, Batten heard the commotion below, and watched as wise old monolith Jess Foreman took it in his stride. His eyes fell on Mike Brean, hunched, despite his escape from the cramped car. Even without his walking coat, he'd be close to Foreman's size. Both had shoulders like wardrobes. Batten pulled out his mobile and rang Magnus.

'Sir?'

'Nina. This Mike...Brean, is it?'

'Correct, sir.'

'He's the one you roped in? The one in your car?'

'Yes, sir.'

'Does he live local?'

'He does. Sir.'

Batten looked down towards the white Toyota, and up at the white police tent encasing the wooden cross and its grim body - a body someone strong had hoisted up to the crossbeams and tied firmly into place. He glanced downhill at the clumpy feet of Mike Brean - unlikely to fit into a size eight shoe. All the same, if it's not ruled out...

'Got an alibi, has he, for last night?'

Magnus sucked in air, her golf-ball eyes glowering at the phone. For a retaliatory moment, she imagined 'forgetting' to tell Batten what Kerry had revealed about the cross's half-hidden journey from Turks Lane. Then she remembered she'd 'forgotten' to tell Batten about Mike and Chas Janner, the two heavyweights who dragged the cross up the hill in the first place. Her mind was a jumble, struggling to be two different minds in the one body.

Steady down, Nina, she told herself. No reason why Batten should remember the name of your significant other. And the wrong time and, Lord knows, the wrong place to remind him.

Not even time for breakfast, today.

All the same, she'd had a belly-full.

'Yes, sir, he has got an alibi. He's got *me*.'

Ten

The mobile incident room had engine trouble so the temporary command post, Batten discovered, was set up in the skittle-alley of The Rising Sun. If only Sergeant Ball was here, he thought, for skittles, cider, and a murder board.

DC Hick twitched an uncoordinated arm at Batten who - daily - was amazed how Hick, who still hadn't tucked in his shirt, could coordinate *anything*? Batten knew the reasons: training, and hard yards. Despite the limitations of the long, thin space, the command post was ticking over, equipment plugged in, tables and chairs occupied, screens blinking and fingers tapping keyboards - recording little, so far.

'Well done, Hickie.' He gave Hick the avuncular pat on the elbow each had come to expect, while raising his eyes and voice to the room in general. 'Top work, everyone. Appreciated.'

Any response was internal, the correct place for pride in one's job when the job in question is murder. *If* it was.

Batten turned back to a twitching Hick.

'What is it, Hickie? Spit it out.'

'Nothing, sir.'

Batten gave Hick both eyebrows, one encouraging, one the bum's rush.

'It's just...they're saying we have to have a Sergeant, sir, at least. For this. Instead of us lot.' Hick jagged an arm at himself and the Incident Room, his face glum, his body a live snake on steroids.

Batten was too full of flu to sit explain why urgency also needed the balance of 'slow time', the cool, steady time for careful thought - the kind stemming from experience Hick had yet to acquire. If Sergeant Ball was here, no reminder would be needed. But he took Hick's point.

'I expect 'they' are also saying we need an Area Superintendent, Hickie. Instead of *me*. But until 'they' make up their minds, or the staffing budget wins the lottery, we'll just get on, eh? Now, any progress to report?'

'There is, sir.'

'Well?'

'No ID yet. Still delving. If anyone's recognised her, you know, through binocs, they've kept their gobs shut. Photos are coming. Can't troop a load of tom, dick and village folk up there, can we?' He jerked a crooked arm at the hill. 'For a gander, I mean. At a naked corpse. Or to the morgue.'

'Assuming she's actually *from* the village, you mean?'

Hick shrugged. *If it's not ruled out, it's still ruled in.* His boss said it twice an hour.

'Whatever, sir, we're waiting on a cleaned up mug-shot. One safe for these village folk to take a gander at, without chucking up their breakfast. So. No ID yet.'

'And that's progress, is it?'

'No, sir. And nothing from Missing Persons, neither... All the usual's under way - vehicle registrations, door-to-door. Trying to establish a vicinity, but...'

'Best stop calling it progress, then?'

'Yes, sir. I mean, no. There is some, see. Access routes. To up there.' Hick jerked a possibly intentional finger towards Crown of Thorns Hill. 'There's two tracks. One from behind the church, this way.' A left hand finger shot upwards. 'And one round the back of the hill, near that old orchard, over there.' This time Hick's right hand jerked across, in a vaguely different direction. 'Place called Turks Lane.'

'Turks Lane?'

'Four old cottages, sir. Thatched. Opposite that orchard thing.'

'Why's it called Turks Lane?'

Hick stared at his Inspector as if he'd been asked to explain nuclear fission. He shook his head, face, hair. Most of his body followed. '*I* dunno.'

Sergeant Ball would know, mused Batten as he turned away. A Hick finger jabbed him in the back.

'But I've got the list, sir. What you asked for.'

Batten took a printed sheet from Hick's febrile fingers. In Ball's absence, Hick and the rest had done a professional job. The list sported two columns of 'general suspects'. At this early stage, they could be potential witnesses or mere passers-by.

Batten hated lists. Clutching the single sheet of paper, he fought off an irrational desire to blow his nose on it.

The first column showed the names of anyone with the slightest connection to the wooden cross currently shrouded in a crime-scene tent. Batten cursed when he totted them up.

Six!

He ran his finger down the names, and the scribbles beside them. Hick's handwriting looked as if a chimpanzee had stolen a pencil and entered for The Turner Prize.

Reverend Dominic Kerry, All Saints Church.
Leonard Tull, Churchwarden of ditto.
Mike Brean, Carpenter. Helped erect the cross, Thursday evening.

Batten assumed Hick hadn't scribbled down the connection between Mike Brean and Nina Magnus, because he didn't know there was one. Yet. Batten still carried the embarrassment of having to be mirthlessly reminded of it by Magnus, her phone voice an icicle.

It was a relief to return to the list.

Charles Janner, helped erect the cross, Thursday evening. Cider worker?

Hick had added the question mark, and scrawled, 'to be chucked.' Discreetly, Batten changed the u to an e, while guessing the Bigfoot traces found on Crown of Thorns Hill probably belonged to Brean and Janner.

Andrew Holt, handyman. 3 Turks Lane. Sanded and varnished the cross.
Harry Finn.

A blank space followed.

'Harry Finn, Hickie?'

'Oh, sorry, sir.' Hick abruptly grabbed the list from Batten, and scribbled on it.

Batten thought it now said, 'landlord of The Rising Sun,' but it could have been 'warlord of Afghanistan.'

'Harry, sir. Harry Finn. Runs this place. Him'n his wife, Cat. They own it. A free house, not a brewery rental-'

'I know what a free house is, Hickie, thanks.'

'Sir.'

'What's he on the list for?'

'Ah, sorry.' Again Hick grabbed the list, scrawled 'loaned plastic sheet and baler-twine to Brean and Janner,' and thrust it back.

None of the names screamed 'vicious killer'. Batten shrugged. When it came to murder, surprise was what you got.

The second column had but two names - corresponding to the house and car where 'Prof' Connor and PC Foreman spotted binoculars trained on Crown of Thorns Hill. Batten didn't need to cross-reference. Hick had done it for him, with two jagged arrows from a red marker pen. Each name also appeared on the first list.

Leonard Tull, Churchwarden.

Charles Janner, cider-worker-question-mark.

Both had pointed binoculars at Crown of Thorns Hill, and what it held. Start with them, Batten decided.

Before he could check their whereabouts, a digit poked him twice between the shoulder-blades.

'Don't do that too often, Hickie, eh? Your finger's starting to come out the other side.'

'Sorry, sir. Priest-bloke. Over there.' Hick's finger jagged from Batten's shoulder towards the doorway, at an ageing figure in dark robes and an unmistakeable dog-collar. If it was supposed to be white, it had faded long ago to nicotine-yellow. 'He asked for you, sir. Well, asked for who's in charge.'

'What's he want?'

'Wouldn't say. To me. Asked for 'someone in authority.' Hick's lip curled with distaste. Not the first time today he'd taken a kick up the self-esteem. And no sign of a bacon roll to make up for it.

Batten sighed. 'OK, Hickie. Roll him in.'

When Kerry approached, Batten concealed his surprise. He expected a small, goofy cleric with pale skin and pimples. Kerry was tall enough to blot out the sun if he stood up straight. Age - or something - had given his broad shoulders a stoop. Batten imagined a large banana, in black robes. And completely bald.

As they shook hands, Batten saw the priest's head was recently shaved, and almost as ruddy as the face beneath it. Kerry caught Batten's glance of appraisal.

'Billiard Ball. What they call me at the school. I'm sort of Chaplain there. The staff I mean. I won't repeat what the youngsters call me.'

Smiling, Batten appraised the rest of Kerry. Size eight or nine feet, at a guess, and plenty strong enough to strap a light body to the cross-beams of a crucifix. If he had a reason?

'Inspector...Batten?'

'That's right, sir.'

'I wonder might we have a word, in private?'

The narrow confines of the skittle-alley weren't designed for privacy.

'My church, perhaps?'

The church suited Batten, since he welcomed a feel for 'the wider crime environment', which is what Area Superintendent Wallingford insisted on calling any building or open space near a murder. Priest and policeman strolled across a traffic-less road, up an incline and were soon passing through the lychgate to the vestry of All Saints.

Eleven

'I cannot offer refreshments here, Inspector. I do apologise,' said Kerry, indicating the Spartan surroundings. They sat on hard chairs either side of a chest which Batten assumed contained vestments, not bodies. A faint smell of damp filled the room. Next door, in the church itself, furniture was being moved by what sounded like a convocation of elephants.

Kerry ignored the noise.

'If I may come to the point, Inspector? My hill. I need it returned. Today is Good Friday, and for centuries our parishioners have climbed Crown of Thorns Hill in a witness walk to commemorate Christ's... crucifixion. And processed back here to the church, for worship. This year is no exception.'

It is now.

Batten shook his head, adding a shrug of apology.

'Not possible, Reverend. I'm sure you can work out the reasons for yourself.'

Sadness darkened Kerry's face. His banana frame seemed to bend even more as he walked over to a heavy wooden cupboard on the far wall, unlocking it with an ancient key. Returning, he placed an old ledger on the chest between them.

'This is All Saints' Easter Book, Inspector. Or the most recent one. The others are antiques, valuable, and locked away. Each book represents roughly a hundred years, and for each year there is an entry for Good Friday. Names of officiating clergy and dignitaries, the order of service, drawings by the children of the parish. Latterly, photographs, press cuttings. Our traditions go back to the 14th Century. Had you the time, you would struggle to detect a single Easter when the witness walk is not recorded.'

I'm often the bearer of bad news, Batten wanted to say. I'm like a priest.

But Kerry was steaming ahead.

'Throughout the First World War the Parish persevered: women, youngsters, a few old men, but up Crown of Thorns Hill they climbed regardless, and somehow raised the heavy cross in commemoration. And during World War Two, the same. We even have a press cutting of the 1941 ceremony, when a dogfight took place above the hill, in God's blue sky. It was not Spitfires and Messerschmitts which won the day, Inspector, but the Cross. In defiance.'

Batten nodded. In his professional role, he met a lot of defiance.

'The Church has always persevered, Inspector. This year, with the cross too heavy for our...ageing congregation to carry, I prevailed upon two stout worthies to erect it, yesterday, in advance. It is in place, and ready for our witness walk.'

'I'm aware of that, Reverend.' The 'two worthies' were Mike Brean and Chas Janner. He could have told Kerry their probable shoe-size. 'And I do respect the strength of your traditions, believe me. But your hill today is a crime scene. Fingertip searches, forensic sweeps, mapping the entire peak and its approaches - none of this will be over soon, and the hill will be taped off for some time to come. I wish I had a kinder Easter message for you.'

As if to punctuate Batten's statement, the rumble and scrape of furniture fell silent. Reverend Kerry's own silence might have been prayer, but it failed to deflect Batten's words, or mould hard reality into the comfort of ritual. The silence was shattered as the furniture-moving elephants resumed.

'Preparations,' Kerry explained. 'We add more pews on Good Friday, in hope of great attendance. We always have. Pews, I mean. And, yes, hope.'

Batten stood, Pontius Pilate from the CID.

'My hands are tied, Reverend. Alternative arrangements will be necessary. Or a postponement? I'm truly sorry.'

He turned to go, but found himself face to face in the doorway with a tall, heavy-set man, ramrod straight, furniture-moving sweat on his brow and a frown on his face.

'Ah, Leonard,' said Kerry. 'This is Inspector Batten. Leonard Tull, our Churchwarden, Inspector.'

If Tull reacted to Batten's nod of greeting, it was blink-and-miss-it. Batten didn't care. Tull's name conveniently appeared on two 'general suspect' lists. Was the Lord providing?

'As it happens, Mr Tull, I was hoping for a word. Can we...?'

'I have much to do, Inspector. Much. As Reverend Kerry has surely explained?'

Tull glared at Kerry. Kerry ignored him, closed the Easter Book, locked it in the heavy cupboard, and departed without a word.

Despite the religious setting, Batten rolled out another professional lie. 'This won't take long, sir.'

Leonard Tull got so far up Batten's nose it felt like a huge worm had slithered into his nostril.

Good job I've got the flu, thought Batten. *I can sneeze him into a hankie.*

As the big Churchwarden lumped and hissed across the vestry, huge worm seemed a fair description.

Kerry's seating arrangements were not acceptable to Tull. Ignoring them, he picked up two heavy oak chairs and flicked them either side of a chipped table by the rear window. Batten spotted the lower slope of Crown of Thorns Hill through the leaded pane. The Churchwarden's long legs crouched astride his wooden saddle, as if keen to gallop from the room.

'Well?' said his body, 'I haven't got all day!'

Batten made him wait. He knew plenty about impatience, its ups and downs, its uses. He'd spotted the hearing-aid, parked discreetly behind Tull's right ear. It has uses too, if needs must.

'I have the Good Friday service to prepare, Inspector,' said Tull, in a too-loud voice. He neither smiled nor explained himself.

'As I've just informed Reverend Kerry, sir, a postponement may be necessary. Under the circumstances?'

'Frequent attempts have been made to postpone Our Saviour, Inspector. He still manages to pervade.' Tull's lips flicked upwards and instantly down again, in a brief sour smile. 'Would you have us postpone Him till Good *Saturday* perhaps? I think not.'

Batten appraised Leonard Tull, another churchman who assumed he could usher a flock of worshippers up Crown of Thorns Hill, when taped off, and full of SOCOs and forensic evidence. Did Tull and Kerry ever compare notes?

'Well, sir, if it must be today, where will you hold it, in this instance?'

Mr Tull pointed over his shoulder at the hill. His sharp finger paused in mid-air and rapped sharply on the table when he saw Batten's raised eyebrows.

'The church, then, and only the church. In this instance.' He gave Batten two eyebrows of his own.

'A case of 'the Lord will provide'?' asked Batten, in a quieter voice.

Whether he heard it or could lip read, Mr Tull swatted away the jibe with a tetchy look at his watch.

Now we can start, Zig.

'Was it concern for the Good Friday ceremony which inspired you to view the proceedings on Crown of Thorns Hill through your binoculars, sir? This morning.'

Tull gave Batten a stare. Aggressive-defensive eyes. How many times had he sat opposite a pair of those?

'I am a curious person, Inspector.'

Batten let the irony tremble in the air.

'And of course a concerned one. There was without doubt a problem, with the cross, at the hilltop. I attempted to ascertain its nature.'

'And did you, sir? Ascertain?'

'I saw desecration, Inspector. I saw horror, godlessness. I saw and felt - still feel - assailed, abused. Insulted.'

'Insulted by what, sir? Forgive me if I ask the obvious.'

Tull gave Batten a glare with not an ounce of forgiveness in it.

'I am called a conservative, Inspector, by some.' Tull glanced at the doorway Kerry had stepped through. '*My* belief is the holy cross should be simply that - a wooden cross, a pure symbol of the resurrected Christ. Other religions choose to substitute the cross for a crucifix, adorned with an image of Christ's body, but as a Protestant with a deep sense of tradition I find such practice idolatrous.'

Oof, thought Batten, I think I'm being told off.

'The resurrected Christ is the salvation of Mankind - and my, my, how deeply Mankind requires salvation in this 21st Century of ours. So, to see a cross, with a naked...*puppet* appended to it. And appended crudely. And *female*? Are you a religious man, Inspector?'

Batten wished people would stop asking him that. When he investigated tractor theft, farmers didn't ask if he was a John Deere aficionado. He gave a non-committal shrug.

'It would be simpler to understand my position if you were,' Tull said, with what felt to Batten like a touch of the smugs.

He retaliated.

'I imagine, sir, when you ascertained there was a...*puppet* dangling from the cross, your religious feelings moved beyond insult and into, well, into human sympathy? Sympathy for the dead?'

Tull's right hand moved to swipe away the jibe, but his left hand had the sense to prevent it. 'Naturally, Inspector. But I feel no need to speak the obvious.'

Batten had met many a Leonard Tull in his time. Self-assured arrogance. A moral calling, but a cold heart. He wondered how far a man like Tull would be go, to achieve his aims. Whatever they were.

'You've been involved in the Good Friday procession before, sir?'

'Involved? I have offered to *manage* it, Inspector. Six times, have I offered. Every year, in the six years I have been at All Saints. To no avail.'

'Sorry to hear it, sir. But since you're clearly a man of some strength...' Batten let the thought linger. '...I was wondering why you didn't offer to carry the cross up there yourself?' Batten jabbed his own finger at the hill. 'I'm pretty sure you'd have no trouble *managing* it?'

Leonard Tull dismounted from his chair-cum-saddle and stamped wordlessly across the vestry - not to the heavy cupboard on the wall but to an old gunmetal filing cabinet. With one flick his fingers were in the top drawer and out again in a blink. The back of his hand zapped the drawer closed. Remounting his chair, Tull flipped a pale green folder onto the table. Without a word, he spun it so the heading faced Batten.

'Church of All Saints, East Thorne', it said. And beneath the insignia, 'Churchwarden: Duties and Boundaries.' Tull tapped an impatient finger on the final word.

Batten opened the file, before Tull could invite him to. After skimming through the gist, he homed in on the giblets. Slowly. Tull twitched in frustration, overactive eyes ogling his watch, a stainless-steel monster with a hurry-up second hand you could see from Mars.

'How do you feel about this, sir?' Batten held a long finger on the very specific list of boundaries. 'If it were me, I'd feel a bit...excluded? I'd want a bit more involvement in...I suppose I'd call it the planning side. And more involvement in the *ceremonials*, if that's the correct word?'

'The 'liturgy' describes it more accurately, Inspector. But the simple truth is I do not carry the cross on its witness walk to the peak of Crown of Thorns Hill because Reverend Kerry - All Saints Church, I suppose I mean - has its own restrictive view of the *ceremonials*. As a result, strict limits have been placed on the liturgical - and, yes, the developmental - involvement of officers such as I. In utter disregard for the strength of my faith in the untapped potential of All Saints.'

To Batten's relief, Tull paused to dispel old air and rasp in a new breath.

'Had I my way, a strong river - no, no, a *sea* - a sea of faith would surge forward. *Surge*, Inspector. New parishioners would flood into the church, filling the pews, filling the air with hymns and hallelujahs.'

'And filling the collection plate, presumably.'

'Even God has expenses. But, yes.'

Batten thought Tull was done, but there was more.

'My way, however, is altogether too *modern* for some. To them, I am a conservative and a moderniser simultaneously.'

Batten wondered if Reverend Kerry was one of the 'some' - or the only one?

'*New* parishioners, sir? From where?'

'Why, from the *new*, Inspector. New villages and villagers, new towns even - Somerset has need of them. New homes. New schools. Rejuvenated farms and factories, shops and services. Not all is austerity. New people may find God anew if they are shown the way.'

'All Saints must advertise, you mean?'

'All Saints must *inspire*. But to do so, All Saints must first be *visible*.'

Batten thought of the soaring hamstone tower dwarfing the village of East Thorne. Visible enough already. And the body-draped crucifix on Crown of Thorns Hill, sickeningly visible this morning. He had no doubt it would be visible in the newspapers, today and for days to come. On TV, too - he had watched the Outside Broadcast vans arrive. A naked female, crucified? On Good Friday? The press and media would devour it.

Might a man like Tull go so ridiculously far, in a quest for 'visibility'?

Batten was snapped back into the now by the Churchwarden's drumming fingers, which screeched to a halt as their owner leaned forward in his chair-cum-saddle to shoot two hard eyeballs at Batten.

'I have much to do, Inspector.'

Batten realised why he disliked religious zealots, of any country, creed or persuasion: their dismissal of the need to explain, their blind self-certainty. In Batten's world, the baselines were ambivalence, deflection, doubt. Or plain old lies. Evidence was weighed up. If weak, the Crime Prosecution Service shook their heads, and filed it.

He wanted to say to Tull, *Your Crucifixion, the original one - it's been a cold case for two thousand years. The one on the hill above us, it's brand-new. I need to find the perpetrator. Starting now.*

'To be continued, Mr Tull,' was all he said, voice a whisper.

He got up and left, not caring whether Tull heard him or not.

As he headed back to the incident room in The Rising Sun's skittle alley, Batten peered up at Crown of Thorns Hill. A SOCO was atop a ladder, untangling blue plastic sheeting from the claws of the single thorn-tree at the peak. A second colleague footed the ladder. A third carefully folded the sheet into a mammoth evidence box.

Batten considered climbing up and asking if anything significant had been found, but his mobile hadn't rung – and Connor always made sure it did, if urgent evidence emerged.

He'd gone off hills anyway.

And as for trees...

Twelve

Nina Magnus dashed from the Vestry back to her little Toyota, still parked on picket duty at the foot of Crown of Thorns Hill. A frozen-faced Mike Brean was slumped in the passenger seat, as cold as he was white. PC Jess Foreman was fond of Magnus, and being a wise old monolith, he winked at her car, at Mike, and at her.

I'll cover for you, he mouthed. *If you're quick.*

A relieved Magnus turned the ignition and ferried Mike home, driving faster than a cop is supposed to.

'Mike, you're probably in shock, but I've a thousand things to do. Stay under the duvet. Keep warm, and rest, OK?'

Mike Brean nodded. But when she moved to give him a goodbye peck, his strong carpenter's fingers clamped onto her arm.

'Ow! Mike!'

Despite her cry of pain, he didn't release her, but pulled her down on to the bed.

'Mike! Don't be ridiculous! I've got to *go*!'

His nails gripping her arm throughout, Mike Brean told DC Nina Magnus everything.

East Thorne's Community Shop was never this busy, this early, on a Friday morning. When DC Eddie 'Loft' Hick volunteered for food duty he hadn't expected to queue. Worse, the shop didn't sell bacon rolls. He settled for six micro-waved meat pies and since the microwave only held two at a time, the first batch would be cold by the time the last batch was warm. He earmarked the last batch for himself.

'Fetch your own, next time,' he'd tell his colleagues if they complained.

After a few seconds, Hick realised queuing had advantages.

'Bad business, this,' said a snooty man with a bone-handled walking stick.

'They'll be renaming it, the ch-church,' replied his stuttery companion.

'Renaming the church? What in hell's name are you spluttering about?'

'N-no. The church will have to rename *it*.'

'Has this queue moved even an inch? Rename what?'

'D-don't think so. Rename G-good Friday.'

'What? Just call it Friday? That'll simplify the church calendar, no end. You nutter.'

'B-Bad Friday. They'll have to call it Bad Friday.' He pointed upwards at Crown of Thorns Hill. 'You said so yourself. B-bad business, you called it.'

'Tuh. Bad for some. Not proving bad for the shop, is it?' He jabbed a finger at the long queue. 'And when The Rising Sun opens its doors, well, stand back or be trodden on.'

'I saw T-TV vans roll up. We'll be in the papers too.'

'Put East Thorne on the map.'

'Yes, the b-bad map.'

'No such thing. Not these days.' The snooty man lowered his voice. 'We'll be on one of those tourist Murder Trails. They have one in Dorset, at West Bay. Taking trippers round Broadchurch sites, and making a mint. And Broadchurch was only pretend. *We're* real.'

'Too r-real for my taste.'

'And for Reverend Kerry's. See his face this morning? Beetroot.'

'M-maybe whisky's gone up.'

'The church'll be on the map though. There's always a bright side. Our new churchwarden, he'll be rattling the collection plate and rubbing his hands.'

'Wouldn't that make him d-drop it?'

The snooty man ignored the question 'Are you going this year?'

'You mean, on the w-witness walk?'

'*Yes*, you nutter. If there *is* one. Will they let the likes of us up the hill? Good Friday or not?'

'Who?'

'*Who*? The police!'

'Ah. Suppose not. Oh, we're m-moving.'

The queue nudged forward a foot or two. DC Hick shuffled closer when the snooty man lowered his voice.

'It'll boost the property prices. All this.' He flicked his stick at the hill. 'No such thing as bad publicity.'

'You s-said.'

'Welcome news for those developers, at Turks Lane. Wish I had three hundred houses to sell, with free publicity on TV. Wouldn't surprise me if *they'd* done all this. Isn't it called *marketing*?'

'S-steady on. No houses there yet. Maybe never. You went to the public meeting, d-didn't you?'

'Went? I sat to you, you nutter. Public meetings won't stop 'em. When do they ever? Bulldoze us out of the way, you'll see.'

'Can't bulldoze what they d-don't own. Can't d-dig up Turks Lane while folk still live there.'

'*Now*. Give them a month or two. And plenty publicity to get buyers excited. Those bulldozers, I bet they're switched on and ticking over. Like this queue, at last.'

Hick's order was ready. He was torn between a warm pie and more gossip. Cold pie made up his mind, and he headed for the door.

The snooty man said, 'been queuing so long I can't remember why I came.'

'You n-nutter', said his companion, as the door closed.

Mal Muir's Easter weekend at home was one long interruption. He batted the Siamese cat off his lap with his left hand and fumbled for the ringing mobile with his right. He had two Siamese cats. And two phones.

This was the private one.

On the rare occasions it rang, the voice of Richard Pardew, ostensibly Muir's financial adviser, summarised the progress of certain 'investments' - in coded language, for safety's sake.

'Mal, I trust you've been informed of certain developments at a certain village of commercial interest to us both?'

'Unavoidably, Richard. Those 'certain developments' have attracted considerably more attention than I was led to believe?'

'Now, now, Mal. 'Investment' is never an exact science, as well you know. Let's say certain personnel handling the...fringes of your portfolio may have exceeded their brief, mm?'

Muir glared at the phone. Pardew had a way with understatement.

'So how do you propose rescuing my portfolio, Richard? You do *have* a plan?'

'Working on it, Mal, working on it.'

'And you interrupted my brief holiday to tell me that?'

'Phoned to wish you Happy Easter, Mal.'

A terse 'puh' was the reply.

'*And*, should certain 'regulatory forces' come a-calling, to check you'll maintain the usual discretion?'

'I don't require a reminder, Richard.'

'Good man. So, business confidentiality, Mal. Let it be our watchword.'

'As long as our other 'colleagues' make it theirs, Richard?'

'My phone will be hot with persuasion, Mal, rest assured.'

The Siamese cat jumped up when the phone went down. Muir stroked it, *business confidentiality* on his mind. How many times had he fallen back on phrases like that?

'*Ouch!*' he yelled, as the cat's claws found their way past the fashionable tears in his jeans, and into flesh.

'WHY DIDN'T YOU SAY SOMETHING BEFORE?'

Nina Magnus couldn't remember if she'd ever shouted at Mike Brean. She wasn't the shouty type.

'If we weren't together,' she added, 'I'd bloody arrest you for wasting police time!'

Mike's eyes said, you're the one who does this for a living, not me!

'NOBODY *ASKED!*' he shouted back.

'You're not dumb and blind, Mike. You can see how pressed we are. Did you want us to drag the village up the hill so a naked corpse could jog a few memories?'

'Her hair's different,' Mike mumbled. 'It was years ago. And if I ever expected to see her again it wasn't like...*that!*' The strength seemed to have left Mike's arms, and the best he could manage was a tired wave at the hilltop. 'Nina, for a living, I make things out of wood. I can't do what you do.'

Magnus had days when *she* struggled to do what she did. Days like today. She took a breath. 'Years ago? How many?'

'Get your note-book out, I'll give you a statement!' He cancelled his comment with an apologetic hand. Mike and sarcasm weren't bedfellows.

'Eleven years,' he said. 'I was all of eighteen! And it's embarrassing. Anyway, she's changed.'

'Different hair, you said.'

'And less of her. And a tan. Her body used to be...pale.'

'OK, Mike. OK. Just how certain are you?' Magnus needed more, before she told Batten. 'Eleven years is a long time.'

'When I say I was eighteen, I mean exactly eighteen.'

'What, your birthday?'

Mike Brean managed an awkward nod. 'She liked me. We always got on. Rebels, in different ways, pair of us. It was my birthday booze-up.'

'And she was there?' Nina Magnus was assessing the age of the corpse on the crucifix. Mid-thirties, they guessed. 'Bit old for you, Mike, I'd have thought.'

'Exactly twenty-four. It was her birthday too, same day.'

Nina Magnus ticked off another brownie point. Victim ID. Exact date of birth. An image flashed into her head - of Batten beaming ecstatically.

But a counter-image chilled her.

Information source? she heard Batten ask, and heard herself filling in the embarrassing blanks. She imagined poor Mike, in an interview room, recounting his personal history, to strangers. Some of hers would come into it too, no doubt, documented for public consumption. Working for CID had downsides.

Then, clang, a penny dropped.

'Are you saying it was your first time?'

Mike's white face flushed deep red.

'With her, that night? Your first time? Is that what you mean?' Magnus was half-cop, half-lover, providing the words so he wouldn't have to. She didn't say, 'you lost your cherry to a corpse?'

'My birthday present. S'what she called herself. And at eighteen, who turns down a present like that? I'd had a drink or three, you know, warmed the blood. Bit clumsy, to be honest, doing the unwrapping. Nobody teaches you, do they? Not that there was much to unwrap, being an August night. I managed to mumble a thank you, after. Said I wasn't much of a birthday present for her. Being my first time. *Yes.*'

'But not hers?'

Mike shook his head. 'I told you. She was a rebel, was Lish.'

'*Lish?*'

'What she called herself. Alicia. She didn't like her name. Didn't like her folks, her school. Didn't like university. Didn't like her life.'

'She liked you, though?'

Mike Brean's smile mixed fondness with sadness. 'She went backpacking again, a few months later. I offered to go too.'

It was Nina's turn to smile.

'Yeh, well, I was all of eighteen.'

'And massively experienced,' Magnus added.

This time they both smiled.

'She turned me down, thank god. I remember what she said. 'I call it backpacking, Mike, because I'm packing my bags and not coming back.' And she didn't.'

'Beg to differ, Mike.'

'Well, eleven years. Heading for Thailand, she said. I never saw her again, I swear.'

Magnus was doing the jigsaw. Cop, lover. Lover, cop. 'Where would she come back *to*, since she obviously did?'

Embarrassment coloured Mike's face. They'd slept in her bed, at her cottage, on his birthday night.

'To number 4, I suppose. And it must've been recent. I would have seen her in the street. You know, walking down it, instead of...' His eyes flicked at the hill.

'Number 4?'

'Sorry. 4, Turks Lane. Where Chas Janner lives. Used to be her parents' house. They died, ages back, and there's only Lish. Far as I know she still owns it. Owned it. Rented out now, through an agent. Well, Chas pays his rent to one.'

'So, would Chas have known Alicia? Or met her?'

Mike shrugged. 'Not sure. She'd left before he moved to East Thorne. I'd never dream of discussing...her...with *him*.'

Nor with me, Magnus thought.

'Chas happens to drink in the same pub. You've met him. Half the time he's on a different planet. We're hardly bosom pals.'

Chas Janner was not one of Nina's bosom pals either. Something edgy about him, she thought, on the rare occasions they'd exchanged a word in

The Rising Sun. She gave Mike Brean's big back an affectionate rub.
And ticked off more brownie points:

Victim ID.
Date of birth.
Biography.
Address.
Likely travel timeline.

And an awkward coincidence - for Chas Janner. He was clocking up appearances in 'areas of interest'. Magnus checked her notes.

Chas Janner:
Cider worker/Orchardman?
Helped erect the cross on Crown of Thorns Hill, Thursday evening.
Seen focusing binoculars on the crucifix, Good Friday morning.

She added, 'rents 4, Turks Lane, a house owned by the victim?'

Alicia Heron must have returned to England with some sort of luggage, Magnus told herself. Could it still be at number 4? Maybe with the clothes 'Lish' was wearing? And her keys? Her phone?

If so, the extra coincidence would elbow Chas Janner into a cell. Get a team over there, right away, Nina.

First, she finished gutting poor Mike.

'It was the tattoo, was it? That clinched things?'

Mike Brean shuddered at the memory-shock, of a blue-winged blemish between navel and groin. His clumsy fingers had traced its outline, that birthday night. And at sunrise today he saw it once more, eleven years on, through powerful lenses.

He cursed the binoculars, wished he'd never bought them, wished he'd never sharpened the focus on the bright blue tattoo. It flew at his eyes, wings rising from dead flesh the colour of wax.

'Bluebird of happiness. That's what it was. She said it was her mum's favourite bird. Lish gave it to herself as a birthday present. Tattoo man swore it'd bring her luck.'

Magnus allowed Mike his moment of sadness, before wrapping up the interview, ashamed to admit what it was.

'Alicia...?'

'Heron. Lish Heron.'

Openly now, Magnus scribbled 'Heron' next to 'Alicia' in her notebook.

Mike stared up towards Crown of Thorns Hill.

'She flew away,' he said.

Nina Magnus stroked Mike Brean's burly shoulder.

And hit the speed dial on her mobile phone.

Thirteen

Though his office was closed on Good Friday, Lesley Willey had no choice but to drive in and check his messages. With his bank balance more scarlet than red, even the smallest morsel must be pursued.

If he could only concentrate.

He flopped onto his swivel chair, mind clicking and whirring with the randomness of a fruit machine - apples, pears and lemons spinning into debts and bills and unpaid tax. Pulling the mental handle again, he tried to replace the debts with pound signs and 'financial inducements', the fruits of his role in persuading Turks Lane's owners to sell to a certain buyer.

His mind spun once more: the new housing development sales to come his way...the increasing commission as families moved in, moved out, moved in... the company rental contracts 'eased in his direction' - these would revive his business, he knew, if he could just keep it going, for a month, two, three.

But the slot machine in his head juddered to a halt. Sweat stippled his brow as different 'inducements' sliced into his thoughts - not apples, pears and lemons now but skulls, all skulls: the 'visits' from *that man*, in the underground car-park, late at night, the man's face hooded, he must have followed him, waited, in the half-dark...

'*Speed things up,*' the man had hissed. '*Clear?*'

To Willey, no, not clear at all - but the knife crystal clear, the faint glint of the man's knife, so near to his eye he feared for his sight. And next time, the hissed demands, for keys, master keys to Turks Lane, and, once delivered, thinking, I'm done now, I'm safe.

No, he told himself. You're not.

He rushed to the door and dropped the deadbolt. And when had he started to sweat? He never used to sweat. But a glue of fear had clamped his shirt to his skin.

Lesley Willey was expert at fear. Rubbing his eyes, he tried to switch off the slot machine in his head, to stop the skulls becoming three sharp knives.

Listen to your messages, and go, hissed his voice.

Before his finger reached the answer-phone, his mobile rang. Not his agency mobile. The other one. He stared at it. If not for the fear plastering his back and neck, he would have let it ring. Had he been a strong man he would have thrown it to the ground, stamped on it, smashed it to dust.

But he was Lesley Willey.

He answered, knowing full well whose cultured voice would whisper in his ear. This voice had no knives.

It warned him, just the same.

Eddie Hick's neck was clammy with the sweat of hard slog. He yanked at his tie to loosen it, even though it was always loose. Dangling below his collar, it looked like something the hangman left behind.

Despite the narrow confines of the skittle-alley, Magnus sat two chairs away. She liked 'Loft' Hick, but kept a chair between her and his elbows.

'Nice work, the pair of you,' said Batten, re-scanning the fresh evidence his DCs had uncovered. Magnus managed a nod of appreciation. She'd gutted Mike Brean, and her tight face showed how much it was costing. Batten immediately set her to work at the murder board - hoping to distract her. His concern was a waste of time. Magnus knew why he'd 'forgotten' to add Mike Brean's name to it.

A shower of pie-crumbs drowned Hick's response to Batten's praise.

'Could be nothing, Hickie, but could be plenty,' Batten said, in response to Hick's' eavesdropping experience in East Thorne's Community Shop. 'And this housing development's common gossip next door, you say?' Batten jabbed a thumb at the adjacent pub.

'Harry Finn, the landlord, he seems to know the score,' mumbled Hick.

'You know what to do, Eddie. Hit the phones. Get it followed up. The developers. The Council Planning Office. Find out what's being considered, and where. Who wants it and who doesn't.'

Since it was bank holiday weekend, Hick considered asking Batten if *he'd* considered offices were closed, and the staff on leave with their feet up. Unless they worked for CID.

'And find out who owns the other houses in Turks Lane, right? I'll follow up on Chas Janner.'

Batten hadn't got out the door before the phone rang. Hick listened, grunted, and twitched his arms in his boss's direction.

'Sir? Area, sir. They're insisting on a Duty Sergeant. To help coordinate...this.'

Hick flung a hand at the desks and phones and laptops. Magnus was adding lines of enquiry to the Murder Board. 'Under way' was scrawled next to many, but others had yet to begin.

'What shall I tell 'em, sir?'

Sweat dripped from Hick's chin onto the phone. Batten gave him an avuncular pat on the back. Hick's efforts were a holiday stop-gap.

'Cheer up, Eddie, a judge didn't just ban bacon rolls. You're doing a cracking job. But it's way above your pay grade.'

'Huh. Area agrees.'

'Once someone else gets stuck in, Eddie, you'll be out and about. Detecting. Isn't it what you prefer?'

Hick's head waggled a maybe. Or just twitched. It could be either.

'Right, sir. I'll tell 'em to send a Sergeant.'

'No, don't do that, Eddie. Put them on hold. I've a better idea.'

Stepping outside, away from eyes and ears, Batten took out his phone and stared at it. After a deep breath, he made up his mind, and dialled.

Di Ball answered.

'He's washing ten pounds of Welsh mud off the dog,' she said.

Batten had met Gus, a black lab who looked dirty even when clean. Di knew Zig Batten as well as she knew the dog, and sliced through the hesitation.

'Does Chris need to come to the phone, Zig? I can tell why you're calling.'

'When did you learn to read minds, Di? Fancy a job on the force?'

'Already got one, Zig. I'm on Switchboard today, aren't I?'

'Sorry for disturbing your Easter.' The Balls were in wet Wales, across the Severn Bridge - but not an hour's journey, the way Chris Ball drove.

'Well, as it happens, Zig, I'm staying here regardless. No desire to be in praying distance of East Thorne. Saw it on the news. A horror show. As for ruining Chris's break...'

'How is he? You know...'

'Oh, thirsty. For cider. For change.'

'Change forward? Or change back?'

'Zig, I should bang your two heads together. I really should. He's even talked about applying for your Erin's old job!'

Erin Kemp had moved from her job as Business Manager of a local cider farm, to the headier heights of the Somerset Produce Agency. Her role as a food and drink ambassador included trumpeting the county's produce overseas. Lately, Batten saw less of her. If Ball left the force to manage a cider farm, and Erin stayed in her new role...he'd need to make appointments to see either of them.

'Chris'd drink the profits, Di.'

'He'd do a fine job, admit it. He knows cider backwards, and manages awkward folk all day. Awkward folk like you, Zig Batten.'

'Tell me he's not serious, Di. Please?'

'Shouldn't he tell you himself?'

She let the offer hang.

Batten's wounded relationship with Chris Ball carried scars. Ball's headstrong decision last year, to 'lose' embarrassing evidence, still lingered in the awkward air.

Yes, the evidence was superfluous, and only harmful to the innocent.

Yes, it would have sliced into Erin Kemp's young daughter, Sian. To her, Sergeant Ball was 'Uncle Chris'. And Uncle Chris hadn't let her down.

In truth, Batten the Man was pleased to see the grubby pieces of paper disappear. Batten the Detective was a different matter. Worse, Ball burnt the evidence in Batten's own woodstove.

'Why couldn't you use your own bloody fire?' he'd yelled at Ball. 'Every time I light mine, I smell the smoke of corruption. You bloody yokel!'

Ball had offered to resign. Batten said he'd keep quiet if he didn't, but shop him if he did - and jeopardise his pension. Batten meant it, for the sake of what's right.

And because he'd struggle to replace the best on-duty Sergeant he'd ever worked with.

And miss evenings out with an off-duty friend who could read his mind.

Chris Ball stayed.

But so did a sharper edge between them.

It was Di Ball who broke the silence.

'Well, Zig? He's finished shampooing Gus. Are you going to ask him? Or leave him here in Wales, helping a clean dog detect fresh mud?'

Fourteen

Standing in the orchard with his back against the gnarled trunk of an old apple tree, Batten gazed across the narrow road at the four dwellings of Turks Lane.

In the morning light, he could have been staring at an old photograph. All four cottages were hamstone-built and 18th Century - maybe earlier, if their roofs were anything to go by. Andy Connor would probably tell him, without being asked.

As a group, the houses were a perfect demonstration of the life-cycle of thatch. Batten assumed the spruced-up Number 2 had been re-done with profit in mind. Its double roof sported the tell-tale pale-gold colour of brand-new thatch, with the thatcher's personal mark, an apple in this case, etched into it. The roofs of 1 and 4 were darker, worn but serviceable.

By contrast, number 3's was ancient, the thatch mottled-black and thin, its crown pock-marked and sunken. When the heavens opened, Batten guessed, whoever lived there would struggle to stay dry.

In the shade of the orchard, he scanned his notes.

Number 2 was twice the size of the others - clearly two original dwellings knocked into one. It stood empty now, framed by a monster 'For Sale by Auction' board. Batten notes said it was an executor's sale. He shrugged. One less occupant to interview.

The board sported an Agency's name: Willey and Associates. Batten had bought his own Ashtree cottage from Lesley Willey, without warming to the man. Where Estate Agents of a certain kind were concerned, he agreed with Woody Allen - you could become ill just by sitting next to one. He didn't look forward to sitting next to Lesley Willey again.

The next page told him Kenneth Leckey - Chairman of the East Thorne Orchard Preservation Society - lived at number 1, a smart, almost militarily-neat cottage. The pristine front garden was a green paean to ecology, bristling with flowery enticements to bees, butterflies and anything else with a taste for pollen. Batten blew his red nose, in defence.

Number 3's roof of past-it thatch belonged to Andrew Holt and his daughter, Biddy. 'Handy Andy' earned his crust as the local handyman, scratching an income from bits of gardening, cleaning and house repair, and by maintaining the other three properties in Turks Lane.

Why can't he maintain his own? Batten wondered.

For now, Batten focused on the nearest cottage, Number 4 - owned by Alicia Heron, rented out to Chas Janner, and looking far too pretty to be a crime scene. He reminded himself crime couldn't care less where it takes place. The rental agency was also Willey and Associates. Batten winced at the thought of questioning Lesley Willey twice.

Leaving the orchard behind and approaching the front gardens of Turks Lane, he saw it was a narrow cul-de-sac, though with the house numbers reversed. Number 4 sat at the open jaws, Number 1 at the closed end. His team had produced an access map, but he ignored it for now.

In his mind's eye, he saw a car arrive at Alicia Heron's cottage - without needing to drive past Numbers 1, 2 or 3. How easy would it be, he asked himself, to bung a lightweight corpse in the boot and drive off, unseen?

Drawing closer, he saw the problem.

No parking was allowed in the narrow lane, only just wide enough for a car. For those unable to work out the reason for themselves, a sign directed them to a lay-by, thirty yards back, just off the main road. The bulbous end of the cul-de-sac served as a necessary turning circle.

You're at Number 4, with a corpse dressed only in a loin-cloth. How do you get rid of it?

Park in the lay-by, out of view of the cottages, stroll into Turks Lane, pick up your handy corpse and struggle thirty yards back to your car, carrying something not remotely like your gym-bag? While crossing your fingers nobody sees you?

Or do you drive into Turks Lane, load up - somehow – and do a tight turn at the end of the cul-de-sac, passing every front window on your way in, and again on your way out?

Or use another route?

He walked quietly into Turks Lane, to find out.

Upstairs, behind a curtain, in the cottage next door to Alicia Heron's, Biddy Holt silently watched the tall man with the moustache wander down her street.

Independent Living Centre, closed for Easter. Just volunteers there today. Too strict, the volunteers. Don't like them. Sneaked away. Easy to sneak. Just pull up your hoodie, and go. Biddy liked wandering off.

Wander everywhere, searching for Mummy. Seen Mummy's face in Daddy's photographs. Search all over East Thorne, trying to find her. Will find her, one day.

Daddy out, looking for work. Daddy's job is to look for work. The tall man with the moustache, has he come to give Daddy work? No. Tall man disappeared-invisible now.

Cross the upstairs landing and peek from the bedroom window, at the back, but no sign. Does he play hide and seek, the tall man? The other man does, with a hoodie like mine. But I'm best at hide-and-seek. No-one ever finds *Biddy*. Hide-and-see, Biddy calls it. I'm best at hide-and-see.

Tiptoe downstairs so the tall man won't hear, to a special hiding place in the pantry. Too big now, grown too big to hide beneath the table there. Close the door and sit, in the dark, on the stone floor, disappeared-invisible.

Big gloved fingers. Count to ten.

But

Nobody

Finds

Me.

After peering into an empty Number 1 - Ken Leckey's house - Batten wandered past the turning-circle at the end of Turks Lane. His way was blocked by a tall hedge, with a narrow gap in it. Beyond the gap, he could see the faintest path, curling up through undergrowth towards the hilltop.

Possibilities?

The official route, favoured by dog-walkers and Prof Connor's army of SOCOs, snaked up the hill directly behind All Saints church, but it wasn't visible from here. Reverend Kerry would have slogged up it on Good Friday afternoon – were it not a crime-scene and had his cross not acquired a naked corpse.

The gap in the hedge leading to the unofficial path was too narrow for a car - and certainly not for the 4x4 demanded by the terrain. Too narrow even for a quad bike. Two burly men manoeuvring a heavy cross would have struggled, he thought. But someone squeezing a small corpse through the gap?

A forensic team scuttled towards him down the path, hampered by a deep covering of shrub, and no shortage of brambles.

'How long?' he asked the nearest SOCO, his CID shorthand immediately understood.

'We're done. Now, if you like - but stay to the left of the tape, yes?'

Batten nodded a thanks. The path piqued his interest. He'd explore it, once he'd checked in with 'Prof' Connor, whose van was up on the kerb outside the wide-open door of Number 4. Chas Janner might be the registered tenant, but he'd yet to make an appearance.

Where *was* Janner? Batten wondered.

On his holidays?

On the run?

Dead?

Even if he turned up, Janner wouldn't be laying his beard on a pillow in Number 4 tonight, Batten would bet money. With luck, he'd end up sleeping in a cell. Janner's rented house was a beehive of forensic staff.

Batten signed in outside the front door, and hovered.

'Anything yet, Andy?' he called.

Connor appeared, holding up a cautionary hand. 'Not quite finished in the hallway, Zig. My lesser minions are still foraging. Follow the tape down the alley and use the back door. We've finished there.'

Batten did as he was told and was soon leaning his long frame against a well-worn kitchen table.

'Interesting, Zig. We *might* have a locus for you.'

Batten kept his mouth shut.

'Not so much what we're finding in the hallway, at the front, but what's missing. I'll show you, once the lasses and lads finish up, but I see your eyebrows can't wait.'

'They never can, Prof. The gist will do.'

'The gist is a rug, Zig. Or the lack of one. There's shade-marks on the flagstones, which tell me something measuring six by four covered it. We found enough carpet-fibre to suggest whatever did was moved - and recently. A loose rug, my guess. Whole downstairs is flagstones and rugs. Not a fitted carpet in sight. The rest of the house is clean. Recently vacuumed. It gets done every Thursday, apparently. But the hallway - and only the hallway - is littered with fresh rug-fibre. Interested now?'

'I was before, Prof. I hang on your every word.'

'Sarky Yorkshire git. Go sit on your thumb while I juggle my bag of tricks. Might have juicier data for you, if you grant me five minutes to ponce up my prestidigitations.'

Instead of sitting on his thumb, Batten took in 'the wider crime environment', with the rear path to the hilltop still on his mind. He'd never been able to wait patiently for anything, without a fishing rod in his hand. And not for what Andy Connor, in his mock-professorial way, had begun to call 'data'.

Beyond the long back garden of number 4, between fence and hill, lay a narrow track protected from marauding deer by what looked like a ha-ha. Drawing closer, he saw it was a small brook. He opened the rear gate and strolled through.

The steep sides of the brook were bridged by an improvised gangplank of old timbers, just about safe enough to cross. The other cottages had stronger bridges. Number 1's, where Ken Leckey lived, was beefy enough to support a rugby team.

Risking a shoe-load of wet mud, Batten crossed the rickety bridge and strutted along the track. It curled towards the end of the cul-de-sac, till it reached the hedge he'd stepped through moments before. Sure enough, as he grew closer, a second gap in the hedge led him to the steep path winding through shrubs and trees up to the rear of Crown of Thorns Hill.

All four dwellings, Batten saw, had access to the path from front gardens, and from rear.

Though keen to hear Andy Connor's findings, a remembered line from a Robert Frost poem nudged him along the road less-travelled-by, and his curious feet followed the path as it twisted and turned towards the hilltop. He climbed into thicker woodland, and climbed again, staying outside the police tape but switching his mobile phone to video to record his route.

These modern times, Zig.

A tinkling sound of water drew him on, and he pushed his way through undergrowth till he came to a spring, bubbling up from rockier ground and pooling against the chance dam of a fallen tree. The water was deep here, but looked clean enough to swallow. Despite his thirst he was still too urban to risk it. And the police tape reined him in.

Above the spring, the thickets gave way to tree stumps and tangles of shrub, and he was surprised to see - above him in the distance - the rear of the white police tent still capping the hill, as if challenging the spiny claws of the lone thorn-tree. The path was a smudge now. He cursed it, too stony and firm, he felt sure, for useful footprints.

Looking back, four thatched rooftops blinked up at him from the lane below. The view from their doors and windows was screened by a mask of woodland.

'Another route for a body to reach the hilltop,' he muttered to himself. 'Out of sight of witnesses, too.'

He swept his phone camera over the view, for later, and with a second curse retraced his steps to Turks Lane.

'I said five minutes, Zig, not fifty. Or can't you Northerners speak Somerset?'

'Sorry, Prof. Exploring the wider crime environment.'

'Cuh. You're starting to sound like Wallingford. Book yourself in for therapy, quick.'

'Come on, spill the beans.'

'Despite you keeping me waiting?'

Connor's teasing pause set Batten's eyebrows off again.

'I'll tell you what we *haven't* found, Zig. Female clothes. Not a sniff. No suitcase. Nor a mobile phone, a purse, a make-up bag, a watch - nothing. And if Ms Heron opened this door with her own keys, well, we haven't found her keys either.'

'I'm overwhelmed with your bounty, Prof. Fast forward, will you, to the ends of her fingernails in an evidence bag - and tell me they're teeming with the culprit's DNA.'

'Nope. No nail clippings. And not because we didn't look.'

'Have you *any*thing?'

'Blood, Zig.' He let the word sink in. 'A tiny trace. Need to be at the lab, but it's recent. And I know what you're thinking. Chummy who lives here cut himself shaving. Because everyone shaves in their hallway these days.'

Batten smiled. According to witnesses, Chas Janner's beard hadn't seen a razor this decade. Connor knew. But a strapped-on light-heartedness kept you sane.

'The culprit's not a cat, is it, Prof? Who's brought in something red, dead and nasty? There's an entire orchard across the way, to hunt in.'

Connor slapped his forehead in mock-realisation. 'If only I'd thought to test it, Zig, the blood.'

'Human, then?'

'As you and me.'

'Except we're alive,' said Batten, stifling a sneeze.

Connor peered at the scarlet beacon of Batten's nose.

'One of us is,' he said, and went back inside.

Fifteen

'What do you mean, they're all at work? On Good Friday? It's the Easter holidays!'

Magnus almost reminded Batten *she* was on holiday. Till she remembered he was too.

'Handy Andy - Mr Holt, sir, at Number 3 - if he hasn't got work to do, holiday or not, he's off in his pick-up touting for it - can't afford not to. And he's never had a mobile phone in his life, so we're having trouble tracking him down.'

'His daughter?'

'Biddy Holt, sir. A sort of unofficial Day Centre this morning, and All Saints Church this afternoon. For the Good Friday service. The one no longer taking place up there.' Magnus pointed at Crown of Thorns Hill. 'Andrew Holt should be back for it, around three, according to Reverend Kerry. If not, Kerry 'keeps an eye on Biddy' - his words.'

'Ken Leckey, at Number 1?'

'Away, but not work. Orchard Preservation business, voluntary - so he said on the phone. In Gloucester. He left last night and stayed over. Back later today.'

'What time last night?'

'Eight-ish, so he claimed. We're checking.'

Batten blew out his breath. 'Prof' Connor's discovery of a probable crime locus was wafting in the wind, like the blue plastic sheet flapping and cracking on Crown of Thorns Hill when Batten arrived this morning – or was it a thousand years ago?

He glared at the four picturesque thatched cottages, every single one of them empty.

'So we've a crime scene, here in Turks Lane - the primary locus, sure as eggs is eggs! We've blood traces at the victim's house, but not one bloody resident available for interview?'

'Sorry, sir. Doing our best.'

Batten waved a hand in apology, his nose twitching and his stomach rumbling.

See, Zig, multi-tasking again.

'Is the pub still open?'

'It's called The Rising Sun, sir. Always coming up. Never sets.'

'The Rising Sun it is, then, to feed a cold with a rapid sandwich. Ring me, should a witness deign to materialise.'

Whenever Batten walked into a pub, he half-expected the incumbents to cock their heads and give him a stare. Part of being a cop, he told himself. Half-way through the door he almost stopped and turned around. It'll be full of journalists, he guessed. With cameras. And voice recorders.

But The Rising Sun was quiet.

At a table by the window, two ladies-who-lunch had their entire focus on a bottle of Sauvignon Blanc. Three old men played cribbage in an alcove by the fireplace. Three flat pints of cider waited for someone to win. Nobody gave Batten a second glance.

'Mr Finn?' he asked a landlord-looking man wiping the bar.

'Inspector...Batten?'

'I don't think we've met, sir, have we?'

'Villages, Inspector. News travels. Tall Northern policeman with a moustache? Right?'

'Been called worse.'

'Both of us. I've been called Flash Harry a time or two! But I'm plain Harry Finn. A drink?'

Batten checked his watch. Two-o-clock, and not even a breakfast coffee to his name. 'Can you do me a sandwich?'

'Take away?' asked Finn 'Or eat here?'

Batten paused. 'Here, please, at the bar,' he said, with what he hoped was a hint. 'And a coffee? Black, no sugar.'

'Thought you'd be ordering hot toddy,' said Finn, pointing his duster at Batten's red nose.

Cheeky sod. 'When I get home, perhaps.' *If I ever do.*

The landlord bustled off - on size eight or nine feet, Batten noted. Empty tables echoed in The Rising Sun. He made up his mind to visit of an evening, to see if the place filled up. If it didn't... Three pumps sported crests of different local ciders. Sergeant Ball would gladly join him, on his return.

Or maybe not.

A ham and mustard sandwich the size of a house-brick appeared on the bar, followed by posh coffee - silver tray with cup, saucer, compulsory biscuit, and a silver cafetiere.

Pointing to the sandwich, Finn said, 'we do rustic and we do delicate. I had you down as rustic. Delicate is what the ladies order'. He jabbed a thumb at the two ladies-who-lunch, nibbling away at crust-free bread and salad garnish, to soak up the Sauvignon.

'Rustic is fine', Batten said, casting his eyes over Harry Finn and taking a long bite of breakfast. He was used to persuading a witness to turn dour silence into ready speech, but the skills were redundant here. Finn was a talker, Batten could tell.

Or just nervous?

'I thought the pub would be packed with journalists, given what we found on top of your hill.'

'It is', said Finn. In response to Batten's quizzical stare, he pointed at the ceiling. 'Your lot already nabbed my Skittle Alley, so the gentlemen of the press commandeered the Events Room instead. Wi-Fi and a bar, up there. Cat, the wife, she's sweating behind it.' Finn looked up at the ceiling as footsteps echoed above. 'That'll be Cat's dainty feet. She's keeping them fed and watered – behind a painted smile. One of 'em even tried his luck, she says. Attractive woman, Cat. Never seen drink downed so fast and frequent. You should get one of your lads to stand by with a breathalyser, hahah!'

'Commandeered the room? For a fee, you mean?'

'A man's got to live, Inspector. Don't suppose you work for nothing?'

Well, I am right now, Batten could have said. 'And what are they thinking, your journalist friends?'

'Wouldn't exactly call them friends. Paying guests, more like. And we'll read what they think, in the papers, soon enough. One of the London bods said his headline was, 'A Thorne in Easter's Flesh', but his Editor pulled it.'

'What's it going to be? "Village Very Cross"?'

'Buh-boom!' Finn's duster gave the bar a redundant wipe. 'Not everyone's cross though, are they?' he said with a wink.

Don't hold back on your sense of decency, Batten wanted to say. He bit into his sandwich instead.

'I mean, All Saints Church'll get something worthy of the word 'congregation', this afternoon. And a collection plate worth the name, too. Make a change, believe me. I usually get the Sunday service afterglow in here - twenty souls, if I'm lucky, queuing for a Sunday roast and a half of cider. But this afternoon, bank holiday traffic permitting, just you watch - they'll be scrapping for pews at church and for tables in here as a chaser. I'm serving food all day, to capitalise. And it'll be bottles of wine, not halves of cider.'

'So *you're* not cross?'

'I said. A man's got to live. Can't sell a service if there's no-one to sell to. East Thorne needs people - young 'uns with salaries, not oldies with pensions. Don't care where they come from if they bring full wallets and wave 'em at *me*. Your rustic sandwich - tasty, isn't it?'

Batten chewed and nodded. The food was excellent, the coffee better. Perhaps The Rising Sun had something worth selling.

'Me, I'm pinning my hopes on this big housing development, over yonder.' He pointed beyond Turks Lane, at the distance. 'You must've heard the rumours?'

Another careful nod. 'What about you? Where did you hear them?'

Finn wiped the clean bar. 'I'm sure you've been in a pub before, Inspector. People come in for a chat, don't they? And every subject under the sun pops up.'

'Under The Rising Sun?'

Finn chuckled out a false laugh. 'Buh-boom! And, of course, a landlord's job is to listen.'

Mine too, Batten thought.

'Any people in particular?'

'In particular?' The clean bar began to shine as Finn's duster buffed away. 'A stranger or two, lately. Showing an interest, shall we say? What kind of village is East Thorne? What's it like living here? Amenities in place? Amenities we'd like, if we had the cash to pay for them? You get the picture.'

'Doesn't sound accidental.'

Finn tapped his finger against the side of his nose, and chuckled. 'Nor to me, Inspector. Nor to me.'

'Strangers, you said?'

'Not Somerset. Maybe London? Only too happy to serve them drinks - especially when they start buying big rounds for the locals.'

'Why would they do that?'

With mock-surprise, Finn said, 'because we're bloody lovely, of course!'

Batten smiled. Harry Finn wasn't 'lovely'. But he was rustically handsome. With muscles.

'Far as I'm concerned, they can bulldoze half the county, as long as they build plenty of houses - and the houses are filled with people, and the p-'

'Have full wallets, yes.'

'Which they empty into my till! Hahah! Another?' Finn pointed at Batten's almost empty plate.

'Wrapped, please? To take away?' Batten wasn't sure when he'd next get a chance to eat. The landlord disappeared, as did the ladies-who-lunch. Through the window he watched the backs of the three cribbage players wander slowly home. The only thing filling the pub now was a silence punctuated by journalistic footsteps from the room above. He wished he could wander home too.

'There you go. And a takeaway coffee, on the house, since you seemed to enjoy it.'

Rarely did Batten accept 'hospitality'. It could be misconstrued.

'Very kind of you. Yes, excellent coffee.' He paid his bill, but loitered. 'You said, 'not everyone's cross,' about all this.' He indicated the nearby hill, topped now by a white police tent. 'Who is, then?'

Harry Finn gave Batten the look he reserved for idiots. 'Well, Reverend Kerry's not too chuffed, is he? I doubt we'll see him in here tonight – and that'll be a rarity. I mean, poor sod, Good Friday, and this is what he gets?'

'A nasty way to publicise Easter?'

'Damn right.'

'You lent Reverend Kerry some plastic sheeting, I understand? And some baler twine?'

'Well, I lent it more to Mike Brean, on Kerry's behalf. They wanted to wrap up the cross, on the hill. Idiot me, I said why d'you want to wrap up a cross? Aren't you getting Easter mixed up with Christmas? Kerry gave me an eyeball, and explained the obvious - in a whisper, too! Didn't want it to *be* a cross yet, he said - not a day early...And he told me to keep my voice down. Get it back, will I? The plastic sheeting? It's off my log-store.'

Batten shook his head. 'Best use something else? For the foreseeable? As for the baler twine...'

'Oh, ten-a-penny. Can't walk past a gate-post in Somerset without bumping into orange twine. I gave Mike an armful of used lengths. We've a boxful, till your lot took it away. It was an orange box, buh-boom! Many a time, in here, I've seen it holding up a punter's baggy trousers. Somerset braces, my Cat calls baler twine.'

'Is that what your press boys are calling it?' Batten jerked a thumb at upstairs.

'Them? Humph. Bend words out of iron pokers, that lot. It'll be 'Somerset nails', or something worse.'

'Tasteful.'

'What is? Your ham sandwich?' Finn squeezed out another forced chuckle. 'All the same, Kerry apart, it's what I'm saying - no such thing as bad publicity. Puts the village on the map, doesn't it? Photos in the papers, telly vans filming away? And what do people see?'

'They don't see a body, Mr Finn - we covered it before the cameras got here. And for decency's sake.'

At the mention of 'body', Finn's duster screeched to a halt. He gazed upwards, towards Crown of Thorns Hill.

'Poor Lish,' he said. 'Poor Lish.'

As quickly as it stopped, his duster once more attacked the spotless bar. 'No, no, not a...body. Of course. No... But they see East Thorne, right? And hills, trees, gardens, and des-res hamstone houses with thatched roofs - and the happy landlord of The Rising Sun.' Finn pointed upstairs once more. 'Let's say Cat's giving our media men a tasty discount for a photo or two?'

Batten wished he'd paid for his takeaway coffee, while noting Finn's reference to Alicia Heron. So far, Mike Brean was the only person to call her 'Lish'. Just how well did Finn know her? And how did he know she was the body on the cross? Or was Flash Harry yet another East Thorne resident with a pair of strong binoculars?

Just as well he's a ready talker, Batten mused. He'll be talking plenty more, soon enough.

'East Thorne might be notorious today, Inspector. But, tomorrow, we'll be *famous*. The ghouls will turn up for a stare, yes, but they'll ring my till. And once the ghouls turn into tourists and the new houses are ready, we'll be a choice place to live, right? Punters'll fight to buy. And fight for Sunday roasts and big rounds of cider, in here, hahah!'

As Batten swallowed the last of his sandwich, his old mentor, D.I. Farrar, came to mind.

With crime, Zig, first thing you ask is 'cui bono' – and if it's all Greek to you, look it up!'

Cui bono? Who benefits? The list of beneficiaries was growing.

But growing more ridiculous?

Yes, he told himself, press and media coverage of English idylls and unspoilt countryside might put a quiet village on the map, and pique a prospective house-buyer's interest. Yes, it might bring new wallets to the pub and shop. And put the prices up - welcome news for developers and for collection plates. Would East Thorne end up like West Bay and Bridport, compulsory stops on a *Broadchurch* murder-mystery-tour?

But nobody kills and desecrates for publicity, good or bad, to fill churches, or sell houses, or induce tourists to plonk their bums on barstools.

D.I. Farrar's remembered Northern vowels cut into Batten's thoughts: *I've seen way too many bodies, Zig. And not one o' the buggers got murdered for any good 'reason' at all.*

Sandwich and free coffee in hand, Batten trudged to his car, a sudden change of air triggering a fresh sunrise in his pomegranate nose. Without warning, a high-decibel sneeze overwhelmed his arms and hands. The cardboard cup shot into the air, spun, and hovered - till gravity reclaimed it.

Hot black coffee splattered on his socks and shoes.

No sooner had his soggy feet trudged back into Turks Lane than Magnus approached, waving her phone.

'Possible development, sir. Just this second, a blue Renault pulled off the main road, heading this way.'

'Tell me it's Chas Janner, and he's giving the Holts and Ken Leckey a lift to their front doors?'

'Sorry, sir. Only one occupant.'

'Well, better than nothing.' Batten rasped out a sneeze. 'Whoever it is, the welcome committee is me, germs and all.'

Sixteen

Never smoke your own product, Chas Janner told himself, too often.

But after the weirdest Thursday night he could remember, he'd broken his own strict rule and selected a single pouch from his stash. He didn't deal skunk, the strong stuff. Tricky in court if you're nabbed dealing skunk. But he kept a small supply 'for personal use.' Smoking it was blissful, a release. Shouldn't have smoked the whole lot though, not on top of strong cider. He often said so, but when it came to ignoring his own advice, Chas was an expert.

Which was why, after hiding his takings, he smoked the second pouch too.

He wished he'd listened to his own advice now, because hammers and drumbeats rang and slammed inside his skull. Tiny drills jigged along his veins where the blood used to be, and when he tried to recall what happened on Thursday night all was a grey tangle of curled-up question-marks. Parts of him were still on cloud nine. The rest was cloud.

Should he even be driving?

Yes, because one rough night on the mattress in his secret lock-up was plenty. Enough of a struggle getting himself into his Renault and driving to East Thorne. But after spotting the police cars, and, worse, someone's idea of a crucifixion on Crown of Thorns Hill, what could he do but drive straight back to Yeovil, gather up cash, stash and scales, and hide them at Plan B, well away from the beady eye of the fuzz.

Now, more than ever, he needed a shower, and food, and clothes smelling of something other than cannabis. He couldn't recall when he last changed his socks but they felt like dead fish inside his boots. Driving past Mike Brean's workshop, he thought about dropping in and saying, 'my shower's broke, Mike, any chance I could use yours?'

But he didn't know Mike well enough. And his cop girlfriend might be there...

Cops.

Chas had enough experience of cops to know if he stayed away they'd come looking. And find him. And be doubly suspicious. No choice but to turn his battered blue Renault into the lay-by near Turks Lane, lock it, and stroll innocently towards number 4, jangling his house-keys.

And instantly wish he hadn't.

Cars weren't allowed to park in the narrowness of Turks Lane, but all the same it was a car park today. A police car, an unmarked Ford and a white van sat askew on the pavement, clogging what passed for a road. Before Chas even reached number 4, a tall man with a moustache thrust a warrant card at his face.

Coffee first, for god's sake, he wanted to say.

From experience, he knew he'd be wasting his time.

Keep your distance if you can. Let the smell of last night's dope blow away on the breeze.

Too late. He saw the tall detective's nose twitch, and a single eyebrow go up. For a ridiculous moment Chas wished his own eyebrow could do that. And wished he was invisible and deaf, because the tall man's lips were spouting words Chas had heard before.

'Mr Janner? Could me and you have a little chat?'

Chas Jenner hated police cars, even unmarked ones. And a Ford Focus?

Better than a cell, he said to himself.

'Might have been,' he said to the one called Batten, for the second time.

'I'll ask you again, Mr Janner. Were you at number 4, here, the cottage you rent, at any time yesterday evening? And did I mention my allergy to the phrase 'might have been'?'

Stalling for time wasn't cutting it for Chas. He could think of no better answer than the more-or-less truth. Or part of it.

'*Yes*. But I came in, and I went out.'

'Came in when?'

'After me and Mike Brean had planted that sodding crucifix, up on the hill. We had a quick pint, then I went home. I told Mike, never again. And if a certain bald git of a priest pesters me next year, he knows where he can stick his dog-collar.'

'Very interesting. But, in answer to my question, I'd like a number please. With 'o-clock' at the end of it.'

Janner tried to give Batten an eyebrow, but only succeeded in moving his whole face upwards. It made him stare like a frightened ghost with a beard.

'Came in about half-seven, I suppose. *O-clock*. After planting that cross.'

'And you went out when?'

'I dunno, it was dark. About eight. Went back to The Rising Sun, for another pint. You haven't made cider illegal, have you?'

If Sergeant Ball was here, Batten thought, your cider-sarcasm would be threatening behaviour. 'You left The Rising Sun at...?'

Chas's first 'appointment' last night was 10pm. He could remember, because cash-in-hand was involved.

'I had a couple of pints o' cider. So what's that? Half an hour?'

It was three pints, the strong stuff, Batten knew, and 9pm when Janner left, according to Harry Finn.

'And you went where, sir?'

'Where?' Janner licked his coffee-craving lips.

Trapped.

What could he say?

Well, Inspector, I tootled over to Yeovil in my motor vehicle, in disdain of the breathalyser, to do my evening deliveries, don't y' know. Eighteen bags of rather fine stuff, at thirty pounds a pop, and no questions asked. I know it was unforgivably remiss of me, but afterwards I did smoke a soupcon of my own product. And a soupcon more...

No way was he owning up to that. Jail-time, for dealing? No thanks.

He would have to gloss over the deliveries, tell this tall cop he went for a wander - he often did after cider - and ended up bedding down in his lock-up...Let the fuzz have a crack at proving otherwise. If they searched the lock-up, and wrinkled their noses like know-it-all cops do, he'd own up to smoking a touch of wacky-backy for his personal use. Safe enough tale to spin?

But how could he gloss over the rest? Assuming he remembered it right?

Well, Inspector, no sooner had I opened my own front door than I walked straight into a lippy little woman with a sun-tan and a cabin-bag, jangling a loud bunch of keys in my face.

'Who the hell are you?' she asks. 'And what are you doing in my house?'

*'I think you mean '**my** house,' I said. But she swore she was the owner and jangled her keys in my face again. She could've tunnelled out of a loony bin for all I know. Never seen the lippy cow before in my life. Feisty little tart, and no stranger to a set-to, which is what we had.*

I think.

'If you don't leave this minute,' she says, 'I'm calling the police!'

I remember her saying 'police' – not my favourite word. At what point I shifted from fight to flight, I couldn't say. It's still a blur. I was under pressure. Too many 'deliveries' to do. And cash-in-hand is cash-in-hand.

He wouldn't mention the deliveries, or the cash.

I stormed out. I think. Next I remember I'm cooling down with some anti-reality baccy, in my lock-up. But what with the dope, and the cider, I fell asleep on the cruddy old mattress I keep there - which is why I need coffee, and a shower, and my bed, in my house, if I've still got one. Other than that, Thursday night's a blur...

Chas Janner shook his head to clear it. His vision cleared too, and that Northern copper' face came into sharper focus - unsmiling, closer now, eyebrow raised. Chas knew in a blink he hadn't a snowball's chance in hell of doing tonight's deliveries, because the copper's lips were moving, repeating a question Chas barely heard.

Inside his skull, the wispy grey mass of question-marks began to uncurl and straighten, becoming exclamation marks, in *italics*, in **bold**. The dots beneath them joined up in his head and he re-lived this morning's woozy drive into East Thorne, the early streets full of shocked villagers, buzzing with rumour, pointing grim fingers at Crown of Thorns Hill.

And Chas pulling into the lay-by near the church, and peering upwards through the windscreen, and scrabbling in his glove compartment for his foldaway binoculars, and scanning the hilltop and, yes, the crucifix thing was still there, but different.

And, hell's bells, there she was, that same lippy woman.

Same, but different.

Naked-different. Dead-different. Crucified-different.

Crucified?

On the same cross him and Mike had dug the footings for?

For God's sake, Chas, try and remember what you did on Thursday night!

Because that bastard copper's eyebrow is pointing to heaven, and his moustache is closer still, so I can see the red skin on his nose and smell the coffee on his breath, and he says...

'And did I mention my allergy to the phrase, 'I can't remember?'

'Are we charging Janner, sir?' Magnus asked.

'Yes, Magnus, we're going to swab our skin and clothing, yours and mine, and submit the swabs as evidence of his cannabis possession. My nose feels like someone's stuck a joint up each nostril. Even the car stinks of it. If I get stopped by the police, they'll arrest my Ford Focus for possession.'

Magnus almost smiled.

'Improved your cold, sir?'

Man-flu! he wanted to shout.

'Nothing like progress to improve a copper's mood, Nina?'

Magnus bit her tongue, her mood having some way to go. 'Janner's a specific suspect now?'

'Damn right. His story's got more holes than a golf course. We'll hold him for 24 hours. Inspector's discretion, blah-di-blah. If the blood Andy Connor found at number 4 turns out to be the victim's, we'll have cause a-plenty for Mr Janner to continue polluting his cell.'

Before Batten could say more, the All Saints Church clock intervened.

Boom...Boom...Boom.

'Everybody in place?' Batten asked.

'All ready, sir.'

'Right. Three-o-clock, and I'm late for church. Janner can sweat till after the Good Friday service.'

Seventeen

Though the service had begun, he nevertheless played decoy, entering the church by the side door and walking slowly to the rear. He didn't kneel. He didn't pick up the hymn sheet lurking in his pew. Inspector Zig Batten sat down and scanned the congregation, but not from disrespect. If duty to God had been part of his make-up - and it wasn't - duty to Alicia Heron came first today.

East Thorne may have been a small village, but the church was two-thirds full. Eighty-four worshippers had preceded him along the revised pilgrim's way, and he wondered how many were here for God, how many for Rumour.

To the congregation's dismay, this year's Good Friday 'witness walk' was a makeshift affair, the route avoiding the now-sunlit peak of Crown of Thorns Hill, and half-heartedly circling the golden exterior of All Saints before ending in the anti-climax of a grey-brown interior lined with pews which had seen better days.

For most, the Good Friday service remained as significant the religious rite it had always been, and Batten watched them kneel and stand and sing with the power only true belief can arouse. For a few, the tingle of prurient rumour seemed a stronger draw.

These few, however, were disappointed.

Kerry was the first to admit, afterwards, the service was unusually mundane. When the time came for his Good Friday sermon, he did what he had never done before: he hesitated, stumbled over his words, losing his place in a text his own hands had typed. Only the sharp, sneering eyes of Leonard Tull spurred him on.

I will not give that man the satisfaction, Kerry told himself. And with a glance towards Heaven, he carried on.

The ceiling of All Saints church was high and wood-beamed. Usually, Kerry's clergyman-voice made it echo and ring. This year, Good Friday or not, his words lacked zeal. The heart had been sucked out of him and he could feel the echo in his chest. More than once during the service he stared beyond the altar at the permanent wooden cross, seeing only the desecrated version which the police had removed - *no, uprooted!* And from the peak of *his* hill.

Should they offer to return the sullied cross, would he want it back?

'I did my best, for the best of reasons', he silently told his God.

A few heads turned to stare at the lone figure of Inspector Batten, but neither Kerry nor his congregation spotted the plainclothes team discreetly watching the church fill and empty.

DC Hick reminded himself how lucky he was to be living in less godly times.

'Eighty-four and a priest is plenty,' shrugged Hick, who'd be doing much of the follow-up. How many hours it would take, he dreaded to think. The slow stream of worshippers mingled, chatted and dispersed, feet crunching on gravel, hands clicking open the lych-gate and holding it, unnecessarily, for the person behind.

Hick spotted Batten amongst them, failing to look inconspicuous - or not bothering to try. As if by magic, his Inspector appeared next to the wiry stick of a man several inches shorter than Batten's six foot.

'He can move on grease when it suits him, can the Northern Fork,' mumbled Hick to himself. 'And there's Andrew Holt - if his mug-shot's anything like. Answer his questions, mate, sharpish, or you'll get the eyebrows.'

As Holt and Batten spoke, Hick remembered the questions his Inspector had intoned to the team, this very morning.

'Right. First of all, cars. Which crop up on CCTV tapes, in police logs or witness statements? And if they don't, why not? Next, parishioners. Which are villagers, which not? Which have been interviewed, which not? Where do they fit in the timeline? Any gaps? And whether parishioners, witnesses or just passing through, find out which of the buggers knew the victim...And which are pretending they didn't!'

The final question on Hick's list was redundant in the case of Andrew Holt, who'd lived in the cottage next to Alicia Heron's for the best part of forty years. He helped the Herons move in, he told Batten, and still maintained the house and garden - for the rental agents now.

'Under the circumstances, sir, I'm not sure the churchyard is the best place for us to talk?' Batten pointed at the gravestones, some upright, some leaning, and a mournful few already horizontal, in harmony with what lay beneath.

Holt wrinkled his brow.

'I should get back to Turks Lane, Inspector. For Biddy, my daughter. She has...limitations, a lengthy church service being one of them. Kind ladies of the parish take turns to see her home, but she may wander. Not because she dislikes the church - far from it. Indeed, Reverend Kerry is perhaps her closest friend. Her concentration span, however, is not yours or mine.'

Waving his car keys, Batten said, 'perhaps if I drive us to Turks Lane?'

'Drive?' said Holt. 'We can walk there in three minutes.'

I don't think so, said Batten's face. His feet had walked it, downhill, uphill and along, past pub, shop, houses, gardens and school. Ten minutes at least. Fifteen if you stop to sneeze every fifty yards.

'Ah, you won't know the short cut,' said Holt. 'I didn't, till Biddy showed me. Let me show you.'

Crown of Thorns Hill looming above them, Holt guided Batten to a faint, stony path beyond the churchyard, striding past a compost bin towards what looked like the dead-end of a yew hedge. He slipped through a hidden gap onto a thin track just wide enough to squeeze down. Batten followed Holt's shoulders through the trees and undergrowth on the hill's lower fringe, away from the church and towards Turks Lane.

As promised, they arrived in mere minutes. Holt seemed to collide with an unkempt hazel-tree before chicaning into an invisible gap. Batten followed, and to his amazement emerged behind the cul-de-sac leading in one direction to Holt's cottage, and in the other to the rear track up Crown of Thorns Hill.

Well, well. May have to review initial thoughts about access and vicinity?

Andrew Holt led the way across the rickety bridge over the brook, and into his rear garden, ushering Batten into the back door of number 3.

'Handy Andy' might be his nickname, but Batten could see little evidence of handiness inside Holt's cottage. Clean flagstones in the hall, but cracked and deeply worn, the paintwork a faded grey, and the staircase so dry a whole vat of polish would fail to feed it. A dado-rail did little more than frame the scuffs and rips in the ancient lincrusta below.

In his own setting, Andrew Holt also needed hydration. Batten had never seen a man so desiccated. A dusty shirt dangled off his bony frame, and the skin on his hands and face was flaky and loose, as if half-way through trying to sandpaper it smooth, he'd thrown in the towel. Late 50s, was he? Or twenty years beyond?

The instant Holt closed the door, heavy steps clumped down the dry stairs. Isn't Biddy Holt deaf? Batten wondered.

'She senses strong vibrations,' explained Andrew Holt. 'Doors opening, doors closing, heavy footsteps. The tremor of raised voices. Sometimes even the kettle, when it rumbles on the stove.'

Biddy Holt stood in the hallway, her body blocking it, grinning curiously at Batten - knowingly, he could have sworn - and signing to her father. Holt semaphored back, and her face offered Batten something like a smile. She made a vague sound, and her white-gloved hands signed a sort of wave which he assumed was 'hello'. All he managed was a vague wave back. When Holt signed more instructions, she clumped back upstairs.

'Biddy was born with a catalogue of problems, total deafness only one of them,' Holt explained. 'She can make certain sounds, but she's never been able to speak. Awkward. Along with her other...limitations. She does her very best, which is all we can ever do. But her world is not yours and mine, Inspector. Please understand.'

'Um, the white gloves?'

'Yes, specially-treated. And hypo-allergenic. They help to contain her skin problems. One thing on top of another.'

Batten said nothing, but hadn't failed to notice the vacancy in Biddy Holt's face and the awkwardness of her lumpen movements. Physically, she was a fully-grown adult, but...

Vague lines from a poem flashed into his head. Something about God randomly deciding not all human dough shall have yeast? Was that it? Instantly, he understood the bony desiccation of Andrew Holt.

Biddy Holt had sucked him dry, worn him away to a thread.

'Please, Inspector.' Holt guided Batten to an armchair in the cottage's living room. Its tired upholstery summed up the rest of the house.

'I'm sure there's no need to explain why I'm here, sir,' Batten said. 'Considering today's turmoil. In Turks Lane, I mean. Not to speak of...'

He twiddled a finger at Crown of Thorns Hill. The gesture was becoming invaluable, now the news was out.

'Pure horror, Inspector. The village is in shock. Poor Dominic Kerry...Please God we never witness the like again. And poor Alicia. I've known her since the family moved in, next door. Well, since *she* moved in.'

'You met the parents?'

'Met, yes. Knew? No. They were here so little. I worked for them. I am - *used* to be - the handyman-gardener-cleaner for all the houses in Turks Lane.' He glanced at the faded furniture. 'Apart from this one,' he added, with half a smile. 'I've tried to put off the thought, for decency's sake, but losing another client is a blow to what I laughably describe as my income. Our income.' He nodded at the ceiling. 'My employment is being terminated, house by house.'

Batten nodded. Number 2, with its 'For Sale by Public Auction' board would soon be off the map. And now, Number 4 too. How would Handy Andy manage if Turks Lane was 'developed', and his employment - his cottage, even - was terminated completely?

Batten pointed to Number 4.

'When did you last clean Alicia Heron's house?'

Holt's face clouded over. 'Yesterday, Inspector. Every Thursday afternoon, in fact. I hoovered, dusted, scrubbed. Floors, furniture, sinks, bins, and toilet. Manual work.' He stared at the red scratches scarring the backs of his hands, as heavy footsteps clumped overhead. Giving the ceiling a glance, he added, 'a limited vocation, dictated by circumstance.'

'And everything was present and correct, when you left?'

'Why, yes.' Holt frowned. 'Why would it not be?'

'Just getting my ducks in a row, sir. I imagine you did the front hallway last? Before you locked the door behind you?'

Again a frown. 'I do the rear hallway last, Inspector. I use the back door, you see. My workshop, where I keep everything, is in my garden at the rear.'

Batten nodded. Too soon to ask Holt about a missing rug.

'And you still look after Mr Leckey's house?'

'Just. I'm paid to do more cleaning, true, since Mrs Leckey departed. But Ken tackles the DIY himself now, and the hedges and flower beds. Keeps him occupied, I suppose.'

A departed Mrs Leckey went into Batten's mental notebook, for checking. 'I thought his orchard preservation work kept him more than occupied. Is that why his wife left?'

Holt said nothing, but his vacant hands twitched as if signing an answer. Batten clocked the coincidence of two absent wives, at two neighbouring houses - three, if Alicia's dead mother was included.

'Did you see Alicia Heron, on Thursday evening?'

'Poor Alicia. Poor girl. But, no, no. I didn't.'

'But you might have seen her arrive? Heard a car?' He would get round to asking if Biddy Holt sensed its vibrations.

'I had no idea she was coming back - to England, I mean. Perhaps she arrived when Biddy and I were upstairs, at the back of the house? No easy task getting Biddy into the shower, picking up her discards, changing her gloves, easing her to bed - assuming I've actually located her and persuaded her to come home. She likes to wander off, at a whim, and surly pouts are not beyond her.'

Holt was describing the ritual of reining in a tantrum-heavy child at bedtime. But Biddy Holt was a full-sized thirty-something, if she was a day. Batten was glad to have no children of his own.

'You said, "at the back of the house". Did you see anyone in the back gardens? Or on the track behind?'

'I'm afraid not, Inspector. See for yourself, tonight perhaps, with the sun gone. The track is unlit. And the hedges between each cottage are deliberately tall, for privacy. I should know. I clip them twice a year. Well, I used to.'

'Could Biddy have seen something, front or rear - something you missed, I mean? Or... *felt* something?'

Holt caught Batten's eye, and shrugged out a rueful half-smile.

'*Felt* something...Ah, if only I knew what she *felt*. Not what you mean, I suppose.'

All Batten could do was open his palms and point ten fingers at the sky in apology.

'I was thinking she might have *sensed* a car door slamming? Or footsteps?'

'She would have told me. Signed, I mean. Signing is her enthusiasm, her connection to a world the rest of us take for granted. The staff at the

ILC say she has lightning fingers. She signs much as girls her age chatter about trivia.'

Did Holt habitually describe his adult daughter as a 'girl', Batten wondered? And what sort of trivia had he in mind?

'Sorry, the ILC?'

'The Independent Living Centre. The title is ironic to a fault, Inspector. Biddy is catered for at the ILC, most days, God bless them. If she wasn't, *I* would have no means of independent living. She calls it the I'll See. Deliberately perhaps, who knows?'

'ON the theme of independence, sir, could it be she saw or sensed something, but didn't tell you?'

'What a welcome change that would make. If you had to sign seven days a week, fifty weeks a year, you would understand how exhausting it is - and why she and I tend to sleep long and deep.'

'So she didn't?'

'It seems not.'

Unsure if Holt was being naturally protective of his Special Needs daughter, or something else, Batten kept his powder dry. Biddy Holt would be interviewed by a specialist officer with signing skills - if she ever returned from bank holiday leave.

Batten peered through the window as the sun emerged from a gap in the cloud, lighting up the untidy greenness of Holt's garden. He would have enjoyed sitting in his own, this bank holiday. The man-flu had been dwarfed by circumstance.

Holt let Batten out through the front door, into Turks Lane, opposite the long vista of apple trees.

'Lovely, isn't it, Inspector?'

'Indeed, sir. I'm not a local, as you will have guessed. But I've learnt to enjoy the sight of a Somerset orchard.'

They both admired the first stirrings of apple-blossom.

'Renewal', said Holt. 'Without exception, every year. Leaf, bud, blossom, fruit, and fall.'

'Not if the orchard is uprooted, sir?' asked Batten, as they gazed across at the trees.

'The orchard is threatened, Inspector, but not yet destroyed. I still believe in its survival. I attend church because I have faith. I have faith in

Nature too. I watch Biddy smile as she wanders between the lines of trees, enjoying the changing cycle of the seasons. It gives her hope. Or perhaps I just hope it does.'

With a smile half joy, half sadness, Holt said his farewells.

When Batten looked back at this thin, dry stick of a man, the gap in the cloud disappeared, and the sunlight too.

Upstairs, from the hall window, Biddy Holt watched the policeman with the moustache stride down the garden path. Long legs he has, long legs, Mr Top Detective. Said hello to him, watched his lips, but he doesn't hear. Talked to him all the time, in my head, but he can't hear me.

Find Mummy, I tell him, find her, bring her back. Detectives do, they find things.

Doesn't hear me, though. Biddy has no voice. No voice, no voice, they say. Kerry signs what he says about me, to other people. But Biddy better than Kerry. Biddy best.

Daddy signs, but tired. Too tired, he says to Kerry. I'm Tired. Tired is his favourite now.

No voice, they say. Biddy has no voice. Why have these words, then? In my head? All these words? What for?

See so many things. Not hide-and-seek but hide-and-see. Biddy-invisible, so hide-and-see. And telling every day but only in my head, where nobody hears.

Kerry, and Josie at the I'll See, they don't hear. Hear Biddy's fingers, yes, but don't hear Biddy's voice.

So, shan't tell them.

No voice, but secrets, all the same.

Secrets
Biddy
Won't
Tell.

Eighteen

The skittle-alley door burst open, narrowly missing the back of Batten's head.

'Success, Hickie?' he asked, without turning round.

'Yup. Tracked the bugger down, sir.'

Hick was searching for the taxi driver who ferried Alicia Heron to East Thorne, on Thursday.

'Trying to escape, was he?'

'Nah, sir. He's on holiday. Like we're supposed to be.'

'Spit it out, DC Hick.'

'Sir. Taxi-man picked her up from Taunton Station. Dropped her in East Thorne, 7.35. Last night,' Hick said, proudly. He confirmed Alicia Heron's flight and train times from London, and the earliest she could have reached her cottage in East Thorne - assuming she didn't stop off en-route.

'Very precise, Eddie, well done.'

'Nah, sir. She asked for a receipt, and the taxi-man does 'em on a pad. He showed me the carbon copy - date, time. price, pick-up, destination.'

'Where in East Thorne did he drop her?' Batten wondered if she stopped off to meet Harry Finn.

'You'll never guess.'

A sharp glance told Hick his boss didn't intend to try.

'Parking lay-by, sir, next to Turks Lane. But when she booked the cab, she gave her address as *Number 4*.' Proud of himself, Hick perched on the edge of his desk without knocking it over. '4, Turks Lane, sir. House Chas Janner rents. And right opposite that orchard, too. The one they want to dig up. Coincidences, eh?'

Batten nodded. More bad news for Chas Janner. 'What was she wearing?'

Hick flicked open his notebook, smug, a magician pulling a white dove from a top-hat.

'Classy leather jacket, blue,' he read. 'Blue jeans. But pricey, the taxi-man thought. Foot wear, he couldn't remember, but she'd had her nails done. He clocked them, when she paid. Like his wife's, he said, when she's back from the nail bar. Except Alicia Thing's were sort of a creamy silver, *and long* - exact words, sir. *And...*' Hick paused for effect.

'Haven't got all day, Hickie.'

'Well, sir. How's a white blouse sound? You know, a white shirt thing.' He let Batten add one more coincidence to the list.

'Silk?'

'I asked him, the taxi-man. The blouse, I said, was it made of that rough cotton stuff? You know, to see his reaction. "Rough?" he says. "Not bloody likely. Silk or better," he says. "I should have charged her double-fare. She was wearing the price of my cab!"'

'Luggage?'

'A little cabin case. A wheelie. Taxi-man bunged it in the boot with one hand. He said when he drove off, she was trundling it towards Turks Lane.'

Hick closed his note-book with a casual flip, but spoiled the effect by dropping his pencil and scrabbling on the floor for it.

Batten gave Hick's prone shoulder a pat, and went for a spin in his office chair, because it helped him think...

A taxi receipt wasn't the only thing missing. Feather-light or not, where was Alicia Heron's luggage? Not at number 4 - Andy Connor searched every possibility. No clothes, handbag, keys, phone. Nothing.

Who took them?

Where are they now?

And why did she get her nails professionally done, then crudely clip the ends off?

If *she* did?

He was pretty certain her white silk shirt was in an evidence box, duly recorded.

As for Alicia Heron herself? Batten, Hick and the whole team knew where she was, only too well.

She and her bluebird of happiness.

Evening was approaching by the time Batten arrived at Mike Brean's house. When Batten stepped into the kitchen, Mike was scrawling his signature on his full statement.

The handwriting wasn't the neat italics of Nina Magnus but would have been a tidy script had the pen not shook in Mike's hands. They still shook, if less jaggedly, when Batten sat down opposite the big carpenter at a handsome table in a room growing darker by the minute. Batten wondered if Mike had made the beautifully-crafted table and chairs. If so, he had a skilled pair of hands.

In contrast, his statement was barely crafted at all, being a loose string of memories and vague dates, none of them telling the police much more than they knew. His more-or-less alibi, Nina Magnus in the flesh, was both relief and embarrassment.

'I wondered if you wished to add anything, Mr Brean?' said Batten.

A white face glanced up from the table. 'Your lot asked me. I told them, either I can't remember, or I don't want to. To be honest, I couldn't tell you which it is.'

'Soon, perhaps, you might?'

Mike's big shoulders jerked out a shrug. 'I feel knackered. But I daren't close my eyes. Sounds naff, I know.'

Batten shook his head. 'Neither naff, nor new, as it happens.'

'Not much help, am I?'

Witnesses in shock can be many things, Batten thought. *Get him talking.*

'You could help me get a *sense* of Alicia Heron, maybe? You know, in your own words?'

Mike Brean clenched and unclenched his hands, ten strong fingers slowly tapping the wood of the table top, as if playing a dirge on an invisible piano.

'I'd be biased. Anyway, you'll have dragged the juicy bits out of Nina.'

Batten had. 'All the same...?'

'A *sense* of Lish? Not sure I know. Nobody knew *all* of her. Reverend Kerry kept a lookout, in the school holidays, and after. They got on OK, so ask him. He filled in for the parents half the time. Always late back from Africa. Except when they turned up in two coffins.'

'How was she - afterwards, I mean.'

'I didn't really know her *before*. Too young, me. And she was here and gone, you know? I'd see her in the street, then not for months. She backpacked all over the place. I once asked her why she kept leaving and coming back. 'Because there's no-one to stop me,' she said. Didn't like being stopped, didn't Lish.'

Someone stopped her. Forever.

'Did you know she got done for skinny-dipping in the River Parrett, one summer? I was fishing, just upstream. She didn't care. Pretty shameless, was Lish. She only dived in because her bloke said it was a bad idea. I could hear them, arguing. If he'd said 'let's go for a dip', she'd have ignored him and kept her pants on.'

'Her bloke? Was this a regular bloke?'

Mike Brean sighed and shook his head. 'One bloke. Another. We were all 'regular' to Lish, in the moment. Even me, young as I was. She had, you know, an appetite. But class, too. Star-bright, was Lish. She liked underdogs. Till they tried to be overdogs. She didn't like being *told*. Her mum and dad were the same. After they died, I suppose she kept the faith.'

'An independent woman?'

'Own woman. Own reasons.' Mike Brean's fingers paused on the invisible piano. 'Nina's asked me ten times why Lish came back. I told her, it wasn't to see *me*. Not after ten years or more. Could only just remember what she looked like, even when...' Mike's fingers tapped faster, louder on the table, the dirge now a polka. It had nil effect on Batten's professional sense of doubt.

'If you weren't the reason she came back...' Batten paused, in case Mike Brean had missed the slight emphasis on 'if'. 'Did she come back to sell up? Sell her house, I mean?'

'What? So this *Serenity* lot can edge a step closer to knocking down Turks Lane? I have my doubts. I told you, she didn't like *overdogs*. And she knew Andy and Ken. They got on OK. Ken Leckey lived there before she moved in. Andy Holt, even longer. It was Andy and Ken who sorted out her parents' funeral, them and Kerry - and Kerry couldn't even go. No priests. Specified in the will.'

Mike shook his head. 'I didn't go either. Didn't know her well enough. *Then*. But you didn't have to, to see the state she was in, for all she pretended not to care. She wouldn't throw Ken and Andy's kindness back in their faces. She would've asked them first. She would. I'm sure.'

She couldn't have asked Ken Leckey, Batten thought, if he really *was* in Gloucester. But Kerry, and Andrew Holt...

Mike Brean's drumming fingers lurched to a halt on the table. As if the remembering had purged him, his eyes began to close. Slowly, his head dropped down like a piano lid, till it rested on the backs of his hands.

'I've had my fill of it,' he said, the tops of his eyes glancing up sadly at Batten. 'Go and ask *them.*'

He yawned, once, and his eyes snapped shut.

Time is a waterfall, Batten knew, and a torrent when murder's on the books.

His last memory of 'home' was juggling a bottle of aspirin, at sunrise. Now, he could smell the evening smoke from someone else's woodstove, and the streets were dark.

He guessed why Magnus was in no hurry to leave the makeshift police post, but the rest of the team were out on their feet. As for himself, he was relieved Ken Leckey was elsewhere. Tomorrow would come soon enough.

For the first time in a long day, he saw the skittle-alley of The Rising Sun in its true colours. At the end opposite the bar, ninepins stood in defiance, waiting for a heavy wooden ball to demolish them - once the portable desks and police computers were out of the way.

'No thanks, sir. Too dog-tired for skittles,' said Eddie Hick, with an unsubtle hint.

'I'd only just noticed the ninepins, Eddie.'

'What's to notice, sir? Lumps of old wood.'

'Lumps of old wood? What, like an orchard, you mean?'

'Suppose. Lumps of old wood. Sticking out the ground.'

'And that creepy thorn-tree, up there?' Batten pointed above him. 'Just a lump of wood?'

Hick shrugged. Or twitched. You could never tell.

'Or the cross? On Crown of Thorns Hill? 'You *did* see it?'

'Cross. Thorn-tree. Orchard. Just wood. Sticking up. Too tired to care, sir.'

Sometimes, Batten thought, 'Loft' Hick deserves his nickname. Because he really is full of crap. Batten gave in.

'Get off home, Eddie. And well done today.'

'Thanks, sir. Glad to.'

'Door-to-door still at it?'

'Sir. And more to do. You want me here, or at Parminster? In the morning?'

'Parminster. The police caravan's arriving in East Thorne first thing, so tell Harry Finn he can have his skittle-alley back. But we'll coordinate from Parminster.'

'We, sir?'

Despite his whinges to the contrary, Hick was sick to the back teeth of 'coordination'. His bones were too randomly connected. By contrast, Sergeant Ball was one giant bone.

'*We*, Eddie, yes. Earning our crust.'

Hick's shoulders slumped in disappointment.

'Doing an early morning collection from your greasy spoon cafe, tomorrow?'

'Sir.'

Hick's bacon sandwich supply service was a breakfast tradition at Parminster. Batten handed him a tenner.

'My usual coffee, please. And a bacon roll. With a fried egg. And brown sauce.'

'I'll keep it warm for you, sir,' promised Hick, redundantly. Batten always arrived at the copshop before him, rain or shine.

'Oh, Hickie?'

'Sir?'

'Get one for Sergeant Ball, too. No egg.'

'Ah. Right. Glad to, sir.'

Hick's shoulders rose. More bacon-roll brownie points chalked up with Batten.

And Sergeant Ball was coming back.

Easter Saturday

Nineteen

For the second day running, Batten was up at sunrise, woken not by a sneeze, but by duty.

From habit, he drank his breakfast coffee outside, leaning against his little rear porch, his shoulder abutting solid stone, staring across the wooded valley towards the distant bulk of Ham Hill. However many times he stood here, the hill grew no smaller, its long ridge like a giant sleeping man in golden garments, trimmed today with the fresh green of Spring leaves.

He wished *he* was the giant sleeping man, as his thoughts turned to the green of a different hill, this one topped by an empty white shroud. The body of Alicia Heron had been removed but the police tent and crime-scene tape remained. Grumble all they liked, East Thorne's early-morning dog-walkers would have to adapt their plans. He was adapting his, wasn't he?

Downing his liquid breakfast, he slammed the door behind him, and drove to Parminster.

Zig, did he call you 'sir'? Again?

In Chris Ball's Somerset twang, 'sir' always came out as 'zor'. Always. Even socially. 'Zor', not Zig, used to be Ball's everyday name for Batten.

'Thank you, sir,' Ball said, in answer to Batten's 'good to have you back, Ballie.'

When Batten produced a Hick-supplied bacon roll, Ball's two-pounds-of-sausage fingers hesitated over it. 'Is this for me, sir?' he asked.

All Batten could do was nod. He'd grown used to 'zor'. He would just have to get used to the alternative.

But how much *effort* was it for Ball to twist his tongue and teeth around 'sir'?

And why was he still bothering?

Batten shrugged away Ball's new formality because it *was* good to have him back. And, true to type, when Batten had sneezed half-asleep into Parminster CID at half-past six, his holiday-forsaking Sergeant had already been there an hour, 'catching up'.

Now, in the confines of Batten's office, both Inspector and Sergeant pretended 'sir' was normal, as they chewed Hick's bacon sandwiches, greasy fingers staining their documents with tell-tale fingerprints. We could be a training exercise, for Connor's forensic team, Batten thought.

Ball's skill at picking out what he called 'the giblets' of a case had journeyed back with him from Wales. 'Lines of enquiry' sounded tame, by contrast. In preparation for the morning briefing, they counted off the giblets on greasy fingers.

'Turks Lane residents, sir, alive, dead, and missing?'

'And these property development rumours. And Harry Finn, the pub landlord.'

'And the Church people, uncomfortable though it'll seem?'

'It's the church gives comfort, Ballie. Not us.'

Ball's thick finger counted one more. 'Thailand, sir - need to do some digging about what the victim did there?'

'Magnus is onto it. Mind you, if we weren't short-staffed I'd put her back on tractor-theft.'

'To keep her mind off the other giblet?'

'Indeed.'

'Mike Brean?'

'Unfortunately, yes. Ever meet him?'

'Had a drink with the pair of them, once. He seemed straight enough.'

Batten shrugged. They'd both met Mike Brean. But if everyone who seemed straight *was* straight...

'You missed a giblet off your list, Ballie.'

'Who, sir?'

'Lesley Willey - with or without his 'Associates'. He's the snivelling little Estate Agent who sold me my house, remember?'

Ball's fingers spread more grease on his notes as he flipped back a few pages. 'The Turks Lane auction sale - number 2 – it's on his books? Right, sir?'

'For starters. He manages the rental of the victim's house, too.'

'A direct link to Chas Janner?'

'Direct, indirect, upside-down, who knows? But before I tackle Janner again, I'd like a word with Lesley Willey.'

'*Like*, sir?'

'Point taken. I'll ask the snivelling sod if he knew Alicia Heron was coming back. And if he tries to lie through his teeth...'

In reply, Ball pulled an unpalatable string of rind from his bacon roll, and made it dance between his sausage fingers like a puppet.

Batten shrugged out a smile.

His Sergeant might have swapped 'sir' for 'zor'. But he was back - and his sense of humour too.

By contrast, Nina Magnus had misplaced hers.

She tapped on Batten's door, dropping a report on his desk as if it was an injunction. He flicked through it, as she waited, stone-faced.

'Did you put this together yourself, Nina? Or did a B-movie scriptwriter do it for you?'

'Team-handed, sir. All our own work. Well, hers, I suppose.'

Alicia Heron's biography was racy reading, but it did nothing to fizz up Nina Magnus, whose own private biog was now on public display. Batten didn't tell her he knew how she felt, from experience.

'Our victim got around, in her thirty-odd years.'

'Thirty four, sir. Thirty-five on August the...' Magnus paused. She knew exactly when Alicia Heron's next birthday would have been. It was the same day as Mike's.

'I'll leave it with you, sir.'

An unsmiling Magnus squeezed out of Batten's cubby-hole office, leaving him alone with three miserable sheets of paper summarising the ups and downs of Lish Heron's sharply abbreviated life.

Through his cubby-hole window, he watched Magnus's broad back slump down at her desk. Only if the quality of her work tailed off, would he intervene. They were both professionals.

He turned from the living to the dead.

Alicia Heron was born in Langport, the notes confirmed. Her parents were loners...*outsiders with radical tendencies*...evidenced by school reports on their refusal to dress little Alicia in the plain black skirt and white blouse demanded by the uniform code. Batten tried not to think of the white blouse which gave Alicia's corpse its only dignity.

He read on. *Friction at Parents' Evenings...Mr and Mrs Heron escorted from the premises after a violent disagreement with Alicia's teachers...a period of home tuition... a new, progressive school... Alicia suspended twice...then GCSEs...*

Batten scratched his head at the next paragraph... *enrolled at the Dabinett School for Girls.*

A *boarding* school? And private? And pricey?

He turned the page and saw why. Term-time, Alicia did her A levels as a boarder at Dabinett, while her 'outsider' parents swanned around Africa.

Magnus had summarised the details with neutral restraint, laying out names and places, dates and money-trails. A large house sold, a small one bought, in Turks Lane, East Thorne - *for school vacations, and return visits, and for Alicia.* The rest went on school fees and the Land Rover in which the free-spirit parents explored the world's largest continent, *'to discover themselves'.*

In Africa, all the parents discovered was a pair of coffins. Alicia woke one morning to discover she was an orphan.

Batten read on. An ill-attended double funeral, a civil ceremony, priests and hymns forbidden. No relatives turned up to mentor Alicia. Magnus's neat writing said, '*Dabinett School presumably took on a pastoral role? To be checked.*'

Whether they did or not, Alicia passed her A levels and ended up at University... boomerang years followed - brief stints at Turks Lane, squeezed in between backpacking trips to Bali, Vietnam, Cambodia, Thailand.

Why did she keep coming back? Batten wondered. To see someone? Who?

During one return visit, just as Mike Brean said, she acquired a police caution for nude swimming in the River Parrett.

If she swallowed some of the water, they should've given her a medal.

Eventually, Alicia Heron upped sticks for the duration, renting out her Turks Lane house via Lesley Willey and Associates. The rent - minus Willey's cut - paid for her Bangkok apartment, at least until she began to earn a decent living at a Thai fashion house he'd never heard of, and certainly couldn't pronounce.

Magnus had never heard of it either because '*to follow up*' was inked in the margin.

In the final section, the most interesting data was heavily underlined:

A patient at The Old Rowan Clinic, London, October, 2007
Director still falling back on 'patient confidentiality'.
Clinic had a rep, at the time, for abortions.

Below, a note said, *now definite.*

Batten imagined Magnus giving the clinic's Director a tough time before choking the information out of him. And maybe choking on it herself.

Tapping a pen on the harsh white paper, Batten asked himself why – *why exactly* – did Alicia Heron choose to have an abortion? Like it or not, there were other routes.

Marriage: happy; shotgun; or otherwise?
Single motherhood?
Adoption?

None of them screamed 'Alicia Heron', the independent woman who, in Mike Brean's phrase, 'didn't like to be stopped.'

With a swig of cold coffee, Batten got his casual sexism under control. He pencilled in some notes of his own:

Who was the father?
Was he the reason she came back to England?
*If not, who **did** she come to see?*
If no-one, why come back at all?

He read his jottings, but the only certainties were the question marks. He flung down the report.

And picked it up again, its ironies striking him.

The Good Friday cross was planted on Crown of Thorns Hill a day early, on Thursday.

In her report, Magnus had brought Alicia Heron back from the dead – a day early. If the three thin pages he weighed in his hand were a kind of resurrection, wouldn't tomorrow, Easter Sunday, have been more fitting?

And who had Magnus resurrected? The report did little to conjure up a 'sense' of Alicia Heron. Nor tell him why she died.

He flicked back, to Alicia Heron's educational history. No need to grit his teeth onto a plane to Thailand to reach Dabinett School for Girls. It was ten miles down the road, on the edge of the Blackdown Hills. Magnus had provided the phone number.

Batten dialled. After some well-spoken wrangling, a PA agreed the Headteacher would see him - briefly - on Sunday, 'before she leaves for a very belated holiday.'

Huh, he thought. At least she's having one.

Twenty

In the absence of cider, bacon was fuelling Sergeant Ball, and his presence fuelled the team at the morning briefing – aided by his reservoir of local knowledge.

With the victim's ID and address now known, Turks Lane was the focus.

'We're miles from Turkey, so why's it called Turks Lane?' asked Batten.

DC Nina Magnus could have told him. But she'd had enough of words, today. She and Mike Brean had slept badly, and the process of washing, dressing and scraping butter onto cold toast only revived last night's tensions. 'We never argue,' she'd told her friends.

It used to be true.

'Turks Lane's named after an apple, sir,' said Ball. 'A Turks Red. You slice into bright red skin, expecting white flesh, but the apple's red all the way through. A Bloody Turk, some call them. Quite rare now. You'll find a few in the orchard. At Turks Lane.'

Batten wished he hadn't asked. The photograph of Crown of Thorns Hill, its white police tent like a bloodless cherry, clambered down from the Murder Board and squirmed into his head. Red and white were his least favourite colours, today.

'Someone killed Alicia Heron because of rare apples? Smuggling them, was she?'

Ball batted away the deflection with a wave of his notes.

'Apples might come into it, sir, all the same. Given where Turks Lane orchard is, between the main village and this new development.'

The team scanned the map pinned on the board next to unpalatable photographs, incomplete timelines, and a list of names.

A thick arrow pointed to the four dwellings in Turks Lane.

A second arrow jabbed at the orchard opposite.

Beneath, *Serenity Developments?* was written, in felt tip pen.

'Do we know much more about this lot?' asked Batten, jabbing a finger at 'Serenity'. 'Were they serene, Hickie, when you tracked 'em down?'

'They were pissed off, sir. Bank holiday. Their office sounded like a ghost town. After an age, I got the number of some bloke called Muir, who said 'if strictly necessary' about ten times. You're pencilled in for this afternoon. Two-o-clock. This Muir bloke, and the boss. His name's...'

Hick scrabbled through a note-book peppered with yellow post-its. Ball helped him out.

'Piers Tyndale?'

Hick nodded, and let his Sergeant take over.

'Tyndale owns Serenity, sir. Mal Muir is some sort of 'consultant'. Not quite sure what he's for.'

A Batten eyebrow flicked north.

'I've crossed paths with Serenity. As a civilian, I mean, sir. They wanted to build houses on our orchard at Stockton Marsh. Hundreds of houses.'

Ball's home village sat next to an apple-orchard you could lose an army in.

'*Wanted* to?'

'They tried to buy the orchard, lock, stock and barrel, and the land surrounding it. For crazy money. I mean, double its worth. There was a public meeting, then three more. We all own the orchard, you see. Twenty-odd of us, in the village, we have a share. Serenity weren't best pleased. Not pleased one bit when we all refused to sell.'

'You should've held out for a fat cheque, Sarge. You could've retired.'

Hick lacked nuance when it came to village communities.

'And do what, Hickie? Listen to the roar of new traffic? Elbow my way into my own village pub? Drink foreign cider because the orchard's gone?'

Hick filled his big mouth with an imaginary bacon sandwich.

'Are you saying they've got previous, Ballie? These Serenity people?'

'Speaking as a citizen, sir, which was why I was there, I'd have to say Serenity just 'did business', like business folk do. They had a plan, and they carried it out. Or failed to, in this case. But if I had to speak as CID...'

Ball never used to be so pernickety, thought Batten. 'You do have to, Ballie. It's why you're here, instead of shampooing Welsh mud off a dog.'

'Then, yes. More than a hint of previous. The top cat, Tyndale, comes across as honest John, self-made man, we're all in this together - the usual stuff. Maybe genuine, maybe not. Saw less of him. He's not hands-on.'

'But this...Muir bloke. He is?'

'Mal Muir, oh yes. So hands-on he's got three hands. All slimy. And there were plenty like him. Might have been twenty-odd of us to deal with, but they weren't short-staffed. I suppose paying all their wages shoves up the price of each house. They soon sussed the weak ones in the village, worked on the maybes. Well-versed in divide and rule - a bit like us, sir, in all fairness. You know, 'if so-and-so sells up, and you refuse, you'll miss out on the profits - don't be a mug!' They upped their offer, three times. One or two nearly cracked.'

'But they didn't?'

'You know the village, sir.'

Batten had sampled the local cider, many a time, in The Jug and Bottle at Stockton Marsh. The hangovers lived in his memory. He guessed the names of the 'one or two' who considered selling. And guessed what kind of peer pressure persuaded them not to. He jabbed a finger at the map of East Thorne.

'Bit different here, though? This land earmarked for housing, they already own it. Right, Nina?'

Magnus nodded, at Batten and at the map. Beyond Turks Lane, a vast shaded area with 'Serenity Developments' was pencilled in.

'Serenity's bought up a fair chunk of Somerset, both on spec and to plan, so rumour has it,' said Ball. 'I think the polite term is land speculation.'

'What's the *im*polite term? Land-*grabbing*?'

'I suppose it depends what's done with the land, sir. And who for. Even a Somerset yokel like me accepts we need to build more homes. The Local Authority can't do all of it by themselves, can they?'

Nina Magnus thought she'd better say something, before the team forgot she could speak. Sergeant Ball wasn't the only one with local knowledge.

'Serenity own a big swathe of land, sir, yes. But they don't own Turks Lane. Not yet. And they won't, if the owners keep refusing to sell. I went to the public meeting here in East Thorne. It got a bit sour. Ken Leckey, who runs the Orchard Preservation Society, he had plenty to say.'

Mike Brean had plenty to say too, but Magnus kept quiet about it.

'No surprise, Nina. Ken Leckey *lives* in Turks Lane.'

'Yes, sir. And at the meeting, he thumped the table and said he always will. Ken's not a happy bunny.'

Batten sighed. 'A policeman's lot is not a happy bunny business, Nina. We're here to remind folk why we have laws.' He managed not to flick an admonitory glance at Sergeant Ball.

'Sir. But I can understand Leckey's position.'

'Me too. If the plans go through, Turks Lane's had it, right? Assuming your map is correct?'

'Turks Lane will get a visit from the bulldozer, sir, yes.'

Magnus could have quoted every yell and scream of objection at the chaotic public meeting. For now, she kept them to herself...

'The Romans planted apple-trees in Turks Lane - before it was even called that!...An orchard existed there before the church was built!...And one of the stonemasons who built it lived on the site of Turks Lane in 1398 - the parish records prove it!...How many centuries of tradition do you plan to destroy?...That orchard is awash with rare species!...Got something against Nature, have you? Got something against orchards? And what's in it for you? Eh? Cat got your tongue?'

Batten brought her back to earth. 'Feel free, Nina,' he said, nodding at the map.

'There's two options, sir, according to the planning application.'

Magnus drew two thick lines on the map, one red, one black. The red line ran from the existing 'A' road, ploughed through the four dwellings in Turks Lane and bulldozed across the apple-orchard in a wide curve, from one end to the other, till it merged with the shaded area headed 'Serenity Developments'.

In some ways, the black line was worse. It wobbled awkwardly beside the front gardens of Turks Lane, but left the houses intact, before resuming its course through the centre of the orchard.

Batten thought of his own Ashtree cottage, where he woke to birdsong, the lowing of cows and a fine view of Ham Hill. What would he do, he wondered, if he woke to the roar of commuter traffic, thirty feet from his bedroom window?

'Looks like the devil and the deep-blue sea, Nina.'

'The problem's Crown of Thorns Hill, sir, and its steep gradient, and the stream. The road has to skirt them - according to the plan they showed us - and there's only two places it can go. If it goes at all.'

She let her comment hang in the air. Batten's eyes danced between his notes, the lists of suspects, and the arrows on the map. He remembered loping along the track to the rear of Turks Lane, by its little stream. Above him, on one side, loomed the steep hillside. On the other, lay the cottages, with their level gardens. And beyond the gardens, an easy apple-orchard landscape, merging with the flat fields bought up by Serenity.

'Just how far has it gone, then, Nina?' he asked.

Magnus shrugged, still taciturn. Ball stepped in.

'From previous experience, sir, I'd say farther than Serenity are telling, legal or otherwise. Should I come along, this afternoon?'

Batten shook his head. He knew what to ask Piers Tyndale and Mal Muir. The plans for Turks Lane, and the opposition to those plans, were emitting distinct whiffs of motive. And this morning, when he renewed his acquaintance with Lesley Willey, he hoped for a stronger scent.

'No, you have a crack at Chas Janner. Your eyes and ears might pick up something I've missed. If Willey coughs up a connection, I'll ring you. And there's no shortage of work here, Ballie. You've not been back five minutes, and your desk's a paper volcano. Good job the Fire Brigade's not on holiday.'

Batten didn't see Ball's guarded smile. His mind was elsewhere, on land and homes, and the Agents who deal in them.

Twenty one

When Batten clicked through the door of 'Lesley Willey and Associates', the eponymous owner hurriedly closed his mobile phone and slid it into a drawer.

'Surprised to see you open for business on Easter Saturday, sir?'

Willey had little choice. Business was bad.

'Always ready to be of service to the great British public, Inspector. And to your good self, of course.'

Batten scanned the empty office. If Willey did have 'associates', they were hiding in a cupboard. Willey himself sat in nervous isolation behind an empty desk, with Batten opposite - not for the first time. Two years ago, Willey sold Batten his Ashtree cottage, after some dubious wrangling over the price.

The same 'investment opportunity' brochures still dangled from the same holders, above a grey carpet crying out for shampoo. Willey, even thinner than before, also needed a make-over - commercially and personally. Batten wondered how far business pressure was nudging him. And in what direction.

'I trust you are still enjoying your cottage in...Ashtree, Inspector?'

'Yes, sir. When I'm there.'

'Hahah, yes. I know the feeling. Work work work, yes. Lots of work.'

When Batten gave the empty office a second meaningful stare, Willey jerked out a nervous smile. Beads of sweat stippled his brow and rolled downhill towards his eyes, before a twitch of a handkerchief flapped them away.

'Number 4, sir? Number 4, Turks Lane?' Batten paused. The beads of sweat returned. 'You're the managing agent, if I'm not mistaken?'

'Indeed, indeed. A fine little cottage. Thatched. Central-heating. Front and rear garden.'

Batten raised a hand. 'I'm not trying to rent it, sir.'

'No, no, of course. Professional habit, hahah.'

'And it's already let?'

'Er, it is. Let, yes.'

'To a Charles Janner? You'll have the paperwork handy, I imagine? The rental agreement?'

'Er, yes, I do.'

Batten silently stared at Willey.

'Yes, of course.' Willey jerked to his feet and unlocked a filing cabinet. The drawer made a hollow sound as he fumbled through it. A buff folder slithered onto the desk and Batten spun it round towards him, without asking permission. He was a fast reader: a damage deposit chit; an inventory signed by Chas Janner, and by Willey on behalf of Alicia Heron; standing order details; rental terms and conditions...And a notice agreement.

'This is interesting, sir. I wasn't aware you'd given Mr Janner notice. Correct, is it?'

'Er, technically, yes. I mean, at the behest of the owner. Ms Heron.' Willey's high-pitched voice rose an octave higher. 'Ex-owner. I mean, if the rumours are...?'

'Shall we assume they are, sir? For the time being?'

Willey's head bobbed up and down, his business brain computing loss of earnings, executor's paperwork, a diminishing portfolio. Amongst other things.

'So you've been in touch with Ms Heron, sir?'

'Oh, more a case of she with me, Inspector. I manage the letting of her cottage - rent, insurance, repairs and the like – and if all's to the good, send a quarterly account.'

'And has it been?'

'Er, has what been?'

'Has it all been 'to the good'?'

'Oh, I see. Why, yes, of course. Until yesterday's...rumours.'

'She hasn't been in touch, sir? Other than to ask you to give Mr Janner notice?'

'Well, strictly speaking, it wasn't to give Mr *Janner* notice. To my knowledge she's never met him. In ten years or so, several different tenants have rented number 4, of which Mr Janner is the latest. To my knowledge, she never met any of them. She lives in Thailand, you see. I myself can't recall actually *meeting* Ms Heron more than twice, over a decade ago.'

'I'm not asking about *meetings*, sir, but *communications*, in all their glory. Emails, phone-calls, texts, skype, tweets. Parcels by courier. Special deliveries. Modern days and ways, sir.'

Willey looked either bemused or shocked. Batten couldn't decide which.

'So, I'll ask you again. Has Alicia Heron been in touch?'

'Watch the bugger's eyes, Zig', D.I Farrar used to say, when Batten was a young Detective Constable in Leeds. *'Because behind the bugger's eyes there's a tiny calculator. And if you look hard enough you'll see it, and if you listen hard enough you'll hear it – trying out calculations, till the bugger comes up with one he hopes will fool you. Burrit won't.'*

Lesley Willey was habituated to subterfuge, and more so of late. If a property backed onto the railway, he'd extol its 'superb transport links'. Right now, he'd happily back onto a railway himself, and let a train demolish him. What did Batten *know*? This morning's clean shirt was plastered to his back. He flicked a hankie at more beads of sweat on his brow. It wasn't his brow giving him away. It was all of him.

'In touch? Well, yes, of course...Recently, you mean?'

Batten gave Willey another stare.

'In touch, yes, to give notice. Nothing more. An email, as I recall.'

'And could you recall this email now, Mr Willey? For me to read? I assume you kept a copy, as per standard business practice?'

Willey tapped his index finger against his lips. 'Er, now, let me see.' Slowly, he unlocked a second filing cabinet, rummaged, and produced a thin folder with little in it. All the same, he scanned its contents before extracting a single sheet of A4 and reluctantly placing it on the desk.

Batten took his time reading it.

'I'm a bit puzzled by the dates, sir.'

'The dates?'

'Well, a confusion of dates, in fact.' Batten pointed to Janner's notice agreement and then at Alicia Heron's email. 'Ms Heron appears to have given *you* six months' notice, doesn't she? She says here she's terminating her contract with you, as managing agent?'

'Yes, yes. Our standard terms and conditions require six months' notice. All above board.'

'And beginning in January this year, to end in June?'

'Um, yes?'

'She intended returning in June? To Turks Lane?'

'Return? Er, well, one can only assume so, Inspector. Indeed, given she appeared to have no further interest in renting the property, I did naturally offer to provide her with my expert assistance in *selling* it.'

'Really, sir? Selling it to whom?'

'Oh, Inspector, we have lists and lists of potential buyers. All craving property, residential or investment. We are an Estate Agency, hahah.'

'And would Serenity Developments be one of those 'potential buyers', sir?'

Lesley Willey's entire face appeared to wilt at the mention of Serenity. He licked his lips. Twice.

'Oh, one of many, Inspector. Yes. One of many names. On a long list. Long.'

'Leaving that aside, for now, what was Ms Heron's reaction? To your offer to sell the property on her behalf?'

'Er, to my knowledge...I mean, as far as I am aware, she was considering it. One mustn't rush these things, you know. It is not yet June, Inspector.'

'Yes, sir, but she returned in April nonetheless. Earlier than you expected? Perhaps she was in a rush, even though you weren't?'

If Willey intended to reply, a vague twitch of his hands got in first, dispersing thoughts into the air as if they were bad smells.

'And speaking of June, I see in Mr Janner's rental agreement' - Batten waved the first piece of paper at Willey - 'you gave Mr Janner three months' notice, January to *March*.'

'Er...March, yes...Yes, you see, after a tenant leaves one needs time for cleaning, for repairs. For the paperwork. And suchlike.' Even Willey wasn't convinced.

'But what I don't understand - March having gone and Mr Janner's notice period having expired - is why he seems to think he lives in Turks Lane. He told the police he still does. Not telling porkies, is he?'

Willey twitched his fingers at the buff folder on the desk and his lips moved, but words once more failed to make it into the air.

To encourage him, Batten added, 'whether porkies or not, he won't of course be sleeping there tonight. Having taken up residence in a cell.'

Willey's mouth made an 'o', but still no sound emerged.

'I take it he was still 'renting' Turks Lane with your permission, sir? If he broke into your office and stole the keys, well, we have no record of you reporting it.'

'No, no, no, Inspector. Nothing untoward at all. No break-in. No, no. I seem to recall Charles having difficulty finding suitable alternative accommodation. Yes, probably so.'

'Couldn't you have recommended a rental agency, sir? Given him some of your expert advice?'

'Hahah, but, rentals, Inspector. Much demand, little supply. And Ms Heron understood - I made it clear, I mean – how the termination of our contract could cause difficulties in...er, rental continuity.'

Batten gave Willey his *how stupid do you think I am* stare. 'Yes, sir, but Mr Janner was already at number 4, wasn't he, and appears to have stayed on? No 'rental continuity' problems there, surely?'

Willey's voice became a clockwork toy whose spring was winding down. 'Well, more of a... private arrangement...To help him out, I mean.'

'Ah, so Mr Janner was staying at Number 4 by 'private arrangement' with *you*? Despite it not being your house? And without the owner's knowledge?'

A bob of the head.

'Free, sir?'

'Oh, you know. Expenses. Insurance...Costs.'

Standing up but not leaving was one of Batten's ploys. It worked this time. Willey stood up too, to diminish but not remove the height advantage. He glanced at the front door, but knew he had no chance of leaving through it.

'I think, Mr Willey, we should finish our discussion within the formalities of an interview room.'

Caught, Lesley Willey's calculator of a mind clicked and whirred. He had few viewings today, but he did have *some* - and he needed them. The three months unofficial 'rent' he'd diverted from Alicia Heron's pocket into his own was a help, but a tiny one.

'Is that strictly necessary, Inspector?' he asked. 'Perhaps we could...*discuss* in the privacy of the rear office?' He pointed behind him.

'Depends how helpful you're prepared to be, sir.'

To decide, Lesley Willey had no need to spin his mental slot machine. The hooded man had done it for him, late last night, in the underground car-park, a concrete tomb so dark it was almost black. A new hiss of warning this time - '*keep your mouth tight shut. Got it?*' The words spun round and round in Willey's skull, to the rhythm of the waving of the knife – its blade so close to his face he thought his trembling eye would burst. And the deep, deep fear. Fear. Willey was expert at feeling fear.

The tall Inspector frightened him.

But nothing like as much as the knife.

White-faced, Willey stumbled in silence to the front door, clicked the dead-bolt and turned the 'Open' sign to 'Closed'.

'I always try to be...helpful, Inspector,' he said, leading the way.

Yes, Batten thought. But who to?

After formally cautioning Lesley Willey, and 'requesting his presence' at Parminster, Batten rang Ball, as promised. Whether sir or zor, his good sense could be relied upon.

A proper Sergeant thinks you, Batten's best pal, Ged, used to say. *And you think him. Neither of you think about thinking. It just happens.*

This proved so, when Ball answered the phone.

'You're making him sound like a jumping bean, sir. Didn't give him a Northern glare, did you?'

'Didn't need to. Something was giving him the Willeys before I arrived.'

'Something?'

'Something in addition to petty fraud, I mean. He's right to worry about losing his reputation, if he's got one. But he made my feet tingle, big-time, and it's not just prejudice.'

'Can he throw any light on Thursday evening? Don't suppose he wandered over to Turks Lane to collect Janner's rent, and decided to crucify Alicia Heron instead?'

'Janner's rent's currently finding its way into Willey's back pocket, in cash. Ask our dope-head why he agreed to such a novel method of rent-collection, will you? Even petty collusion will add to the pressure, and you might get a chunkier giblet out of him.'

'I'll put my fingers down his throat if you like, sir, and pull.'

Batten's grim chuckle was answer enough.

'As far as Willey's alibi goes, he says on Thursday evening he stayed open till six, had a bite to eat and took himself off to some place called *Spinners,* in Yeovil. Do you know it?'

'I do, sir. A private club. They call it 'gaming', but they mean gambling.'

'Well, he claims he's a member and he signed in, around half-eight, so send someone to check.'

'Won't be our first visit. We raided it, years ago. New ownership now, and from what I hear they're keen to keep their licence. Likely above board.'

'Willey was only too keen to stress what a genteel place it is. Swears he broke even, left at midnight.'

'CCTV, then. We'll check. And see if debt's involved.'

'There's more. Willey says all mobile phones have to be switched off and handed in, for obvious reasons. The punters get them back when they leave. Have to sign for them, Willey claims. Check that too, will you?'

Ball saw the significance. 'Because if Alicia Heron rang him on Thursday evening, she'll have been disappointed?'

'Or pleased as punch, who knows? He swears he hasn't seen her for donkey's years. All the rental arrangements for her cottage are done by email – and there's precious little of it. I bet his filing cabinets are padded out with old copies of *Estate Agents Monthly.*'

'When all's said and done, sir, Willey's not giving us much, is he?'

'Early days, Ballie. And I haven't mentioned the inventory.'

'Inventory of what?'

'Alicia Heron's cottage. Contents, fixtures and fittings. Tenants have to sign, and it goes on file, for when they want their damage deposit back. Mr Willey voluntarily provided me with a copy.'

'Voluntarily?'

'After a terse reminder of the shit he's in, yes. Not as boring as it sounds.'

'Glad to hear it, sir.'

Batten manufactured a long pause, to remind Ball how it felt when he did the same.

'Rugs, Ballie,' he said, eventually.

'Rugs?'

'One rug, in particular.' Batten quoted from the inventory. "A handmade rug, silk and wool, depicting a standing heron and a bluebird in flight. Six feet by four. Downstairs front hallway." Willey's handwriting's worse than Eddie Hick's but I think his scrawl says, "in fair condition."'

Ball shuffled through the paper-chase of his desk for Prof Connor's initial report and ran his finger down the page. 'The rug Andy Connor says is missing? That's shed fresh fibres on the hallway floor?'

'We'll assume so, till the Prof says different.'

Both men fell silent. Though the logic was simple, they struggled with the image of someone 'probably' bundling Alicia Heron's body into a hand-made rug, and carting both rug and body out of number 4, Turks Lane.

Who?

And did this same 'someone' hustle Lish Heron's rug-wrapped body up Crown of Thorns Hill, in the dark, to desecrate Good Friday's wooden cross by dressing it with her corpse?

Hell's bells, why would anyone do that?

'So, Ballie, raise the topic of rugs would you, when questioning Mr Janner?'

'My pleasure, sir,' said Ball.

He put down the phone. And cracked his knuckles in anticipation.

Twenty two

Holiday. Boring. Biddy Holt bored.

Independent Living Centre closed today. Biddy calls it the I'll See. Closed today and the others gone nowhere, but I don't care. Not telling them my secrets, why should I? Never tell me theirs.

Count to ten, and count again, in the hiding-place, Daddy's shed this time. Big knives on the wall, and a grinder-thing, to make them sharp. Mustn't touch the sharp knives, mustn't. Nor the torches, nor spill the oil. Daddy out looking for work and Kerry is churching. Nobody can find me. Top Detective is disappeared-invisible, searching for Mummy, and the hoodie-man, too, disappeared-invisible.

Can't see me, but I see them. *Hide-and-seeeee.*

Peek through the window in the shed, but nobody there. Sneak into the back garden and hide against the hedge but still no sign of the other man, with the hoodie like mine, who hides in the dark in the trees on the hill, where Kerry saves Jesus at Easter for all our sins of the world.

No frogs today in the brook just mud, so play with the catch on the garden-gate, click it, click it till it makes a song like birds in the trees under the hill, till my fingers hurt but mustn't scratch, no.

And bored again. So, across the brook and through the hedge to the secret path I show to Daddy. And to the church but watch out, yes, watch out for Tull. He only hides to catch me, shoves me, locks me out the Vestry with his scowling face, like the faces on the gutters, at the church.

Keep clear of Tull but see if Kerry will hide or seek.

Is Kerry churching?

Or

Something

Else?

Some days, Batten's Ford Focus was a conscious joy to drive. Other days...

Now, both hands gripped the wheel but steered the car nowhere. Batten's journey from the dubious charms of Lesley Willey's office was blocked by a giant refrigerated meat van, delivering supplies to the posh

Parminster butcher's shop he never shopped in. Was the butcher exacting revenge, by blocking the one-way street?

At least it cleared Lesley Willey from his thoughts.

The van's heavy doors swung open and two carcasses were dragged from its maw by two bruisers in white coats stained pink-red with blood. It brought Sonia Welcome's mortuary to mind.

Reborn on the shoulders of their guides, the carcasses walked themselves into the butcher's shop and the two men emerged, empty-handed. The first man pushed a button and, with a hum, a motorised rail swung more pink and white sides of pork and beef from the rear of the van to the opening. As they trundled closer, the carcasses dangled and swayed in a non-existent breeze.

Batten failed to stop an image forming as the meat was unhooked, lifted down, and carried inside. Alicia Heron's dead carcass, dangling and swaying from a wooden cross on Crown of Thorns Hill battered its way into his skull. Absurd orange baler-twine sliced into her arms and legs.

He rubbed his eyes, dragged his fingernails through his hair from forehead to nape, but the image remained, drilling into his retinas and screaming a harsh, repeated scream of *Why? Why? Why?*

Opening his eyes to shed the image, he saw dead space between his car and the receding rear of the butcher's van.

Why? Why? Why? screeched the car-horn behind.

Despite a misted windscreen, Batten turned the key and lurched away, waving a hand at the long line of frustrated drivers.

'Sorry', he mouthed.

He flicked on the fan to clear the screen.

But Alicia Heron refused to go away.

At least when Batten finally loped into Parminster CID, Ball had the kettle on. HQ was a sparse, ugly building at the best of times, made bearable by a Groundhog Day of coffee and tea. Hick dreamed of an Italian coffee-maker, plugged in where the communal printer sat. For Ball, a keg of cider would do.

'What d'you make of Chas Janner?'

'He needs a wash, sir. And after sitting two feet away from him, so do I.'

Batten pretended to sniff. 'You're just this side of tolerable,' he said.

'Have a wash later. First, the giblets.'

Plonking his long body into his swivel chair, Batten breathed in caffeine, and listened...

Chas Janner's first impression of Sergeant Ball could be summarised in one word: width. Ball blocked out the view, not that the interview room was much to look at. He'd never seen paint the colour of sewage before, and he sat on a metal chair so hard the dents were impressed into his arse.

For the second night running he'd managed snatches of sleep on a lumpy mattress. He wanted his home comforts, in his own home. Till he remembered he didn't have one. What he did have was Sergeant Ball. There was no space left for much else.

When Ball said 'discrepancy' for the fourth time, Janner knew he was trapped in a bottomless pit.

'I could use a cuppa tea,' he told Ball.

'And what would you use it for, Mr Janner?'

'No, to drink...Any chance of one?'

'I'm going to have one myself, by and by. You could join me.'

Janner glanced up hopefully.

'After we've clarified a discrepancy or two.'

Janner looked down again, as Ball's sausage fingers came together to form a pyramid. To Janner, the pyramid could have been Crown of Thorns Hill. Ball gazed at his hands in satisfaction, before folding his fingers into a giant fist, and proceeding to crack his knuckles, one by one.

'I don't suppose you embroidered it yourself, did you?' Ball asked, when his knuckles quietened down.

'*What*?'

'Embroidered it. The rug. The one from the hallway, at number 4. Where you lived. Till recently.'

Half of Janner's face screwed itself into a question mark. What's all this about a *rug*? said his face.

'A simple enough question, sir.'

'Embroidered a rug? Course I didn't embroider a rug. I wouldn't know how. Would *you*?'

'Oh, no, not me, sir. But if I had an embroidered rug, I expect I'd remember what I did with it. Can *you*?'

'Are you talking about that rug from the hallway?' He just managed to stop himself blurting out, *not you as well!*

'Am I, sir?'

'Well, if you are, it was just a *rug*.'

'Oh, a rug has many uses, sir. Many. When did you last see it?'

Janner knew the answer. He'd spilled cannabis resin all over the bloody thing, ages ago. Scrubbing just made it worse. A Wednesday night, it was. The damn rug stank and he couldn't get rid of the smell. Andrew Holt came in to clean the place, every Thursday. Couldn't risk Handy Andy sniffing around and speaking out of turn. So the rug had to go.

'The rug with the birds on?'

'A heron, sir. And a bluebird, yes.'

'Right, I remember now. Spilled oil on it. Engine oil. I was going to top up the car but I dropped the can. Went all over the rug, made a right mess. Couldn't get it off, so I binned the rug. Months ago.'

'Binned it? Where?'

'In the *bin*. Where else? Ask the dustmen where it is, not me. Anyway, I replaced it. Same size, same colour, more or less. Take it off my damage deposit. Who cares? Unless you're arresting me for not embroidering the new one?'

Does coffee go cold twice as fast when a suspect makes no sense?

Batten pushed his half-full cup aside.

'You took him a bit further, I take it? Our Mr Janner?'

'Forward, back, along, and round the houses, sir. But two things I couldn't shake him on.' Ball held up a pair of sausage fingers. 'One: he swore he damaged the embroidered rug an age ago, and replaced it. Two: he swore the replacement rug was still on the floor when he left.'

'What did Andrew Holt have to say about it?'

'He said one week the bluebird rug's in the hallway, and next week it isn't. A week later, when he comes to clean, another rug's there. Plain blue, same size, no birds on it.'

'And this was when?'

'Months ago, he says.'

'Wasn't he curious? About the missing rug?'

'He says him and Chas are ships in the night. Different clocks, different planets.'

'I think I can guess which planet Janner's on,' muttered Batten. 'They're not both telling porkies, are they?'

'I'll check. Holt seemed puzzled to be asked.'

'This is...weird. I can understand Janner lying about the new rug being there in the hall when he left.'

'Oh, I can too, sir. Particularly if he really did wrap a corpse in it and smuggle it out of number 4. But - '

'But why insist he binned the original rug in the first place? What's the point? It neither helps his story nor harms it.'

'Sounds irrelevant to me too. Which is why - '

'Which is why you think he *did* replace the rug. Come as no surprise if he'd dropped a lit reefer on it and burned the bloody wings off the bluebird.'

'I rang Connor, sir. About the rug. He'll get back to us if there's a story in the fibres.'

'A story with an ending, I hope. Be a big help if we knew which damn rug we were looking for. Assuming Janner's telling the truth.'

Uncomfortable with 'Janner' and 'truth' appearing in the same sentence, they scratched their respective heads.

'Ballie, does *your* coffee go cold when a suspect makes no sense?'

Twenty three

'Perpetual motion! Perpetual motion, Zig!'

D.I. Farrar used to describe murder cases so, and Batten couldn't disagree. His day was a whirl of asking, hearing, reading, delving, planning, thinking – and sneezing. Now he was driving too, into the almost empty car-park of Serenity Developments.

The office building looming above him was a grandiose pile, four floors of blue lias stone, striped with decorative brickwork and punctured by long swathes of tinted glass. Its porch could house a family. Batten parked his Ford Focus alongside a Lexus and a top-of-the-range Range Rover in a bay marked, 'Reserved for Senior Management'.

'Screw that,' he muttered as he failed to shove open a pair of glass doors tall enough to accommodate a giraffe.

A sullen flunkey with 'Security' written on his chest tapped on the glass, jerking his thumb to the left. Batten clomped to a side-door and the flunkey doled out a Visitor badge. A shiny lift rolled him to the top floor and, stepping out, he almost collided with a short, tanned man in a magenta sweater and jeans, made doubly expensive by the deliberate holes in the knees.

'Inspector Batten? Do come through,' said the man, opening a solid teak door. Batten followed him into a holiday-empty office, hushed further to silence by a carpet deep enough to swim in.

'Mal Muir,' said the man, offering his hand. Batten shook a limp rag of skin and bone. 'Pardon the attire. Supposed to be on our hols, this weekend,' Muir said, with a faint hint of annoyance. 'Had to cancel my round of golf at Willoughby Park.'

Huh, I've had to cancel my whole weekend, thought Batten.

'I was expecting to meet Mr Tyndale?'

'And you shall, Inspector.' Muir swirled a hand at the open door of a cloakroom. 'But might you need to freshen up first?' he asked, as if Batten should take a shower before meeting the boss.

'Just Mr Tyndale please,' said Batten in his politest get-a-move-on voice.

Muir's response was to tease open a second hardwood door, with

'Piers Tyndale' emblazoned on it, in gold lettering. He ushered Batten into a suite taking up most of the top floor.

Either Piers Tyndale had more time to dress or kept nothing informal in his wardrobe. A hymn of praise to the suit-shirt-tie, his tall body seemed to merge with the expensive cloth which covered him. He shook Batten's hand with the smooth, strong fingers of a man who had never laid a brick but might easily crush one.

'Inspector. Do sit.'

Tyndale pointed to a trio of chairs by a metal and glass table, framed by a semi-circle of manicured olive trees in stainless-steel planters. Batten took in walls of polished stone, dripping with exquisite prints in copper frames. Picasso? Paul Klee? Kandinsky? If not originals, they were of such quality Batten was tempted to believe it.

The Danish leather recliner seduced his backside the moment he sat down. As far as he could tell, it was a 20th Century antique, and genuine. On the table, two half-empty espressos scented the air with rich coffee aromas. The entire office was a palace of temptation, but neither Muir nor Tyndale produced a cup for Batten.

'Mal. Do join us,' said Tyndale, and both men eased down opposite, giving Batten a close-up of their well-coiffed hair. Well, well, he thought. Easter weekend, on leave, got the flu, and I'm squatting on a posh chair surrounded by perfectly clipped olive trees and a perfectly clipped pair of housing developers.

Tyndale's 'we're waiting' look inspired Batten to pore over his notes, making the pair wait longer.

'Thank you for agreeing to meet me, sir, despite the holidays. Both of you.'

Two haircuts dipped in acknowledgement.

'You'll know we're investigating a particularly nasty death in East Thorne, where -'

'Where we hope to begin a major housing development, Inspector, yes,' said Tyndale. 'And *soon.*'

'I'm afraid there may be a delay, sir, in view of the ongoing criminal investigation. The cottages in Turks Lane, and the orchard...' Batten let his words hang in the air.

Tyndale glanced at Muir. Muir nodded almost imperceptibly. Some kind of advisor, Batten decided, wondering which man pulled which strings.

'Turks Lane, yes, Inspector. Mal informs me it's some kind of crime scene?'

Here's a man too busy to switch on the news, thought Batten.

'Turks Lane may turn out that way, sir. And it would benefit the investigation if you could confirm what progress Serenity Developments has made, in, well, acquiring the orchard and cottages there? Important information can struggle to reach the public domain.'

The two men exchanged another practised glance. This time, Muir took the lead.

'I'm sure you will understand our reluctance to discuss private business decisions at such a delicately-balanced juncture, Inspector? Unless we are being unequivocally commanded to do so?'

Clever sod, thought Batten. Slap a court order on the table, and show your hand - otherwise, bugger off.

'And I'm sure you two gentlemen, as citizens, will understand the need to cooperate with a police investigation into an unusually nasty crime? Which happened to take place on disputed land you happen to have an interest in?'

Muir smiled. Batten imagined an oil slick.

'Where mutual interests coincide, Inspector, of course. All shall benefit from a case such as this being resolved. But business sensitivities remain. All development has objectors. And it is not in our interests to fuel the objectors' case by broadcasting delicate information. Further delays to our development will impact on very many stakeholders - in an area desperately short of homes. An area where you yourself live, I understand - as a citizen?'

Cheeky sod, Zig. And how does the little shit know where you live?

Tyndale raised a hand, reclaiming leadership.

'Thank you, Mal. I think we can safely assume the police are acting in the best interests of all.'

He flashed an affable smile, at the olive trees. Batten judged the time ripe for a more direct approach.

'For technical reasons, you'll appreciate we need to check the whereabouts, on Thursday evening, of all parties remotely connected to Turks Lane. You, Mr Tyndale?'

'At a dinner, Inspector. Rather more business than pleasure. The West of England Roofing Guild's annual dinner. I took my wife, who has yet to forgive me. There were sixty of us, 7pm till midnight, and it felt longer. My PA will send you a selection of names and addresses. Will that serve?'

Batten nodded. 'And you, sir?' He flipped an eyebrow at Muir.

'At home, Inspector. Just me, and two cats. I will send details also via Mr Tyndale's PA, yes? I expect some of the neighbours saw me drive in, around seven. If graced with X-ray eyes they will have seen me climb into bed for an early night. Piers works me rather hard, you see.'

After a schoolboy smirk, Tyndale pointed his haircut in Batten's direction. 'Perhaps I could show you something, Inspector, to emphasise our bona-fides?'

Muir's face disapproved of the suggestion, but Tyndale ignored him and reached for a trim metal widget on the glass-topped table. He pressed a button and a whirring sound came from what looked like an expensive wardrobe set into the wall.

The doors opened and, when Tyndale pressed a second button, a sort of hydraulic shelf slid noiselessly forward and made its robotic way towards them. Batten was reminded of the refrigerated delivery van at the butcher's, its mechanical rail whirring dead carcasses towards the doors. He hoped the shelf would stop before it socked him on the chin.

With a smooth click, it slithered to a halt, and he saw an architect's scale-model of a housing development - a vast one. Sweeps and rows of dwellings, large and little, chased each other along roads and pathways softened by neat lines of plastic evergreen trees. The garden designers had been busy, Batten saw, replacing with fresh greenery the orchards and allotments perhaps destroyed to make way for this New Jerusalem.

'East Thorne?' he asked.

'Goodness, Inspector, how premature. No, this is a sample project, but typical. Observe this section more closely, if you'd be so kind.' Tyndale pointed at a long, winding section of smaller buildings, set away from the main site and shielded from it by a high earth bank, generously forested with more plastic trees. 'Social housing, Inspector. Affordable housing. Ten percent more of it than I am required by contract to provide. *My* choice, not theirs.'

He threw the same finger upwards at what Batten assumed was officialdom.

'Imagine what ten percent of a full-scale development might come to, should it be translated into hard cash. A conscious loss - to profit, to investment, to shareholder dividend, to R&D - but a conscious gain to those on the housing waiting-list.' Tyndale leaned towards Batten, for emphasis. 'And I choose to carry the loss,' he said.

Muir chipped in. 'Strictly against my advice, of course.'

'Mal is reality-control, Inspector, and an expert. But the bottom line is mine to decide. And sometimes I choose to dress up harsh reality in its Sunday best. I clambered up from the lower rungs of the social ladder, and the roof over my young head looked down on the grubbier side of life. I do not allow myself to forget it.'

If he leans any further forward for emphasis, Batten thought, he'll fall off his bloody Danish chair.

'Why should the lower rungs be badly housed, when the upper rungs have wallets capacious enough to subsidise them? And why should the lower rungs face even longer delays - whether caused by Planning or -'

'By Police?' said Batten.

'As you say, Inspector. Delays obstruct house-building for all, and for all budgets. Particularly irksome for those at the lower end, given the shortage of affordable housing.' Tyndale leaned further forward still. 'I am keen to convert this lack into plenitude. And, let me remind you, Inspector, not all developers are.'

As Tyndale leaned back in his seat, Batten sensed genuine zeal - while reminding himself he heard lies at least as often as he heard truth. A fresh silence descended.

Is Tyndale waiting for applause? Batten wondered. Or a medal? He probably won't wait long. Investors and cronies will make sure he gets his day at The Palace, and his photo in *Somerset Life*, one arm round a proud spouse, the other holding his little padded box of ribbon and gold, for services to humanity. Batten didn't begrudge him the journey one bit.

Assuming he hadn't crucified anybody along the way.

'From your silence, I assume I have not convinced you, Inspector.' Tyndale's face became that of a child who'd bent the handlebars on his new bike.

'On the contrary, sir, you describe a worthy mission. But 'affordable housing'. If I was to speak purely as a citizen, I'd have to say I'm troubled by that phrase.'

Muir and Tyndale wrinkled their foreheads.

'This word 'affordable'. Why the need for 'affordable'? Why not 'housing', full stop? Isn't shelter the most basic requirement for human survival? Last time I looked, wasn't *shelter* the bottom rung of Maslow's Hierarchy of Needs? And shelter is your primary business impulse, I would have thought? Isn't shelter what you do here?'

Batten waved an arm at the art-worked walls, tinted glass and high ceiling. The two men followed the arm, but said nothing, which Batten took as an invitation to continue.

'I'm gratified you're doing more than planning rules require, of course. But your social housing, just how *affordable* is it, for the many? Here in Somerset, we have long waiting lists for council flats. I see homeless people on the streets, some of them evicted from houses they *used* to be able to afford. Mortgages shoot up, don't they? Rents too. And pressure builds, as I'm sure you're aware.'

The two men managed non-committal nods, wondering where all this was going.

'In my job, I deal with folk who wouldn't know what citizenship tasted like if you rolled it into a sausage and forced it down their throat. But even the best citizens can get desperate. Don't you think?'

Muir sneaked a glance at his watch.

'And desperate citizens might even turn to crime? You know, as a way of solving their housing problems?'

Batten let his meaning sink in. Tyndale kept his spoilt child face, but Muir picked up the drift sharply enough.

'I can assure you, Inspector, the East Thorne housing development does not have 'problems.' And even if it did, the two citizens perched here would hardly resort to crime to solve them. Would we?'

No, Batten thought, but might you pay someone to do it for you? He pointed at the widget on the table. 'If you press another button, sir, will a well-developed model of East Thorne slide out of a cupboard, just like this one?'

Tyndale caught up and, for a brief 'I'll show *you*' moment, his finger twitched. Pretending to reach for his cold espresso, Ed Muir subtly nudged his hand aside.

'East Thorne is still in the planning stage, Inspector. Why would Piers or I waste money by tempting fate?'

'Why indeed, sir. And when *will* East Thorne become a scale-model in a sliding drawer?' He chose not to add, 'so we can assess your methods of acquiring the houses and orchards - and people - of Turks Lane.'

In answer, Muir reached down and pressed the original button, and the sample model whirred back into the wall. When he pressed a second switch, the door slammed shut. The noise jerked Piers Tyndale to his feet.

'When a final planning agreement is signed, Inspector,' Tyndale said. 'As you must surely be aware? Till then, we are all in the twilight zone.'

Muir stood too, to emphasise the meeting was over.

Batten climbed out of the seductive leather recliner, his body reluctant to be upright, but his mind glad. *I'll be seeing you two again*, his face said.

Crossing the car park, he reminded himself the only person in the twilight zone was Alicia Heron. Tomorrow, he hoped Dr Sonia Welcome would tell him precisely why 'Lish' was being stored in a Pathology Lab, in a refrigerated drawer that didn't slide open at the touch of a pricey finger on a widget.

This dark thought on his mind, Batten drove back to Parminster, unaware of other drivers on different roads, with dark thoughts of their own...

Kenneth Leckey listened to BBC Radio Somerset as he plodded down the M5, staying within the speed limit all the way. An obscene parody of a crucifixion made sure his own village of East Thorne topped the bill on the radio news, for the first time in living memory.

No such thing as bad publicity. Last night, News at Ten showed the village in all its splendour - till the camera switched to a crime-scene tent atop a beauty spot helpfully called Crown of Thorns Hill.

In some ways, radio news was trickier, teasing the imagination as the reporter's voice struggled to find a balance between scandal and religious respect. Leckey weighed up one against the other, before stabbing a finger at the off button.

With much planning to do, he needed the silence.

Already alone with his thoughts, Andrew Holt chugged his old pick-up along the single-lane farm tracks skirting East Thorne, eyes flicking left and right like a metronome. No sign of Biddy. For a lifetime, she had 'wandered off', searching for Mummy, unable to understand why Mummy would never be found. Or refusing to?

Weary of his own searches for Biddy, he wondered how much petrol he had wasted, how much pollution his engine had poured into the air these last twenty years and more.

She was not at her usual haunt, the Church of All Saints, nor the Independent Living Centre, nor the village hall. He'd scoured the orchard, but no sign. At least he wouldn't have to search on the hill, still taped off and guarded by uniformed police.

You should never have taught her to play hide-and-seek, he told himself. *She's become an expert.* Aloud, he added, 'but at least she's expert at *something*.'

He pulled his pick-up into the lay-by near Turks Lane and prayed, with true faith, Biddy had found her way home.

Ten miles away, a dark-blue BMW crept to the rear car-park of a nondescript office building, and Lesley Willey got out, a hand-written letter gripped in his shaking fingers. He was supposed to seal it firmly in an envelope and slide it through a door marked 'Richard Pardew, Investments Adviser.'

'No digital traces please, Mr Willey,' Pardew had warned him. 'Handwrite your notes, keep no copies, name no names, and make it brief.'

Once more he had done as instructed, summarising the halting progress of *our housing investments*, but without naming Turks Lane. Willey assumed Richard Pardew was an intermediary. He slid a pen from his pocket and scribbled a rider on this week's note, for the eyes of whoever made the decisions.

'Am having major problems with our 'plumber'. Not responding to requests.'

About to seal the note in its envelope, Willey remembered the hooded 'plumber' in the darkness of the underground car-park, remembered the knife, close to his eye, the hissed threats, the demand for spare keys to the cottages of Turks Lane.

'I don't have keys to them all,' he'd lied. But the knife came closer, the mints-and-cigarette breath closer still.

'That handyman got the cleaning contracts from you, didn't he? And he has master keys? And I know you, you little shit - you've still got copies. So don't piss me about.' The knife had touched Willey's cheek, an inch below his eye. 'Or *do* piss me about, if you're happy to wave goodbye to an eyeball.'

Willey had handed over the keys, praying for an end to it. But later, in the same underground car-park, the same man reappeared, with the same knife, the same breath, and a warning this time – *keep your mouth shut!*

And then the visit from the police. Willey had said as little as possible to the Northern Inspector – but how much longer could his mouth keep doing so? How much longer must he look over his shoulder, and avoid dark streets?

With uncharacteristic boldness - or was it desperation? - he broke Richard Pardew's rules of secrecy and scribbled again, this time in plain text.

'Your plumber's gone too far. The police are questioning me. I'm closing down my investment.'

The sealed envelope slid through Richard Pardew's door, and Lesley Willey stumbled back to his BMW. He loved driving his car.

Today, it felt like an old jalopy, the steering-wheel one long shudder in his hands.

Twenty four

After the quicksand-carpet of Piers Tyndale's office, Parminster's plastic flooring felt solid and safe - till Batten focused on unanswered questions on the Murder board.

His old pal, Ged, at Leeds CID, used to welcome a juicy murder, or pretend to.

In policing terms, Zig, he'd say, *it's the FA Cup. And a nasty murder, it's the Champions League!*

Not for Batten. He stared at the photographs of a crucified Alicia Heron. If his future days were spent detecting nothing but stolen sheep, would he care?

On the 'Suspects' board, the Chas Janner column sported real evidence. The others - circumstantial bits and pieces. Felt-tipped pen in hand, Batten scanned the names.

All Saints Church
Reverend Kerry
Leonard Tull, Churchwarden

Turks Lane
Kenneth Leckey, Chair of ETOPS
Chas Janner [in custody]
Andrew Holt, handyman
Biddy Holt, his daughter

The Rising Sun
Harry Finn, Landlord

Serenity Developments
Piers Tyndale, Owner
Mal Muir, Adviser?

Others
Lesley Willey, Estate Agent

Batten stood back from the board, staring again at faces, names, dates and timelines. He added *Cat Finn*, with a question mark. When he'd nipped back to The Rising Sun, she turned purple and gave him a dragon-glare at the mere mention of 'Lish' Heron. 'Too busy', she'd snarled, and stormed upstairs.

He was tempted to move Lesley Willey to the Serenity column, but any link to Tyndale and Muir was speculative still. He compromised, by connecting all three of them with a red line. For balance, he added another question mark. Their names made his feet tingle, if on a low setting.

If it's not ruled out, it's still ruled in, he told himself, glancing at the gap beneath 'Others'. Just as he raised his pen to add the missing name, Nina Magnus slumped through the door. No habitual smile, for the second day in a row.

She scanned Batten, his eyes on the 'Others' column, and scanned his red pen and redder face. He clutched the felt-tip in his fingers, a smoking gun. *Weak leadership if I put it down*, he thought.

In the awkward silence, Magnus grabbed a pen of her own, and beneath 'Others', pointedly added 'Mike Brean'. With an unsmiling stare, she flipped the pen onto the desk, scooped up her notebook and hustled out the door faster than she'd hustled in.

Batten felt the heat rise in his face, cheeks scarlet now. *Man-flu*, he told himself.

Chastened, he hit the paperwork.

Uppermost on the pile lay Alicia Heron's biog, which Magnus had helped produce. It lay open at the offending page. He had clocked right away the awkwardly plausible connection doing nothing for Nina's mood, but had danced around the issue when she was in earshot.

Or chickened out?

If we weren't short-staffed, he reminded himself, she'd be off the case altogether.

The biog said Alicia Heron had an abortion at The Old Rowan Clinic in London, in October, 2007. And she had given her naked self to Mike Brean as a 'birthday present' in August that same year. What self-control Magnus must have needed to compile her neat report, its bland language noting the possible link between one August night and one October day?

Not proven, he told himself. *But if it's not ruled out...*

Detective Constable Magnus boiled with unaccustomed anger as she parked her Toyota in the lay-by near Turks Lane. Not the only time she'd parked here, she recalled. And she should've told Batten. She should tell him now.

But didn't her hot blood need to cool down first?

Before she could decide, PC Foreman tapped her on the shoulder with other information Batten needed. Scowling, she punched the speed-dial on her mobile phone.

Thinking Magnus was ringing to apologise, Batten began to mutter, 'no problem, Nina'. Instead, she passed on Jess Foreman's news in a curt monotone.

'Apparently he parked, unlocked his front door, sir, and went in. But before PC Foreman could intervene, Mr Leckey emerged in shorts and trainers, and jogged off into the undergrowth. Local wisdom says he's a distance runner. PC Foreman insists on calling him a white Mo Farrar.'

PC Foreman? thought Batten. What's wrong with plain old 'Jess'?

'Distance, you say?'

'Yes, sir.'

'We'll give him an hour. How's the deep search of number 2 going?'

The empty cottage between Holt's and Leckey's needed to be 'eliminated from enquiries.'

'DC Hick has made a start. I'm about to assist. Sir.'

DC Hick? Assist?

'Well, assist away, Nina.'

'Sir.'

When Magnus abruptly ended the call, Batten shook his head. He failed to understand people sometimes. Erin would have smiled and said, *sometimes*? Her name brought with it images of home, green eyes and closeness. Sergeant Ball's knuckles on the office door chased them away.

'I hear Ken Leckey's back, sir.'

'Back and gone, Ballie. Jogging. He'll jog home, soon enough. Plenty to do in East Thorne first. And, by the way, you're driving.'

Ball's hands on the wheel of Batten's Focus meant he couldn't crack his knuckles. It gave Batten reading time, too. The bumph on his lap was longer than Nina's face and a Russian novel combined. He flicked through to Ken Leckey.

'ETOPS, Ballie. Remind me?'

'East Thorne Orchard Preservation Society, sir. Ken Leckey's the Chair.'

'You know him?'

'Only by reputation. When our Stockton Marsh orchard was threatened, we asked advice from Orchard Trusts all over. Leckey's advice was part of the whole.'

'Sound advice?'

'Seemed to know his stuff. Although...'

That reticence, Zig. It never used to be there.

'Although what?'

'I suppose at Stockton Marsh we went about things, you know, quietly. When one or two wanted to sell to the developer, it was a word in the background to persuade them otherwise. A quiet word.'

'You mean a veiled threat?'

'Veiled, sir. Not threat. We appealed to their sense of community.'

'But Leckey's advice was different?'

'More direct, I'd say. Demos, media coverage, even civil disobedience. It was all placards and press releases with him. Where we opted for subtle, he was advocating...noise.'

'How far would he go to encourage *noise*? A crucifixion?'

Ball stopped himself saying, *if it's not ruled out...*

'He did come across as a schemer. And his own home's under threat, whereas mine wasn't. Ask him.'

Batten would, whenever Leckey's loins jogged back to Turks Lane. While waiting, he got Ball to drop him near All Saints Church.

To ask a favour of Reverend Kerry.

As Batten approached the Vestry, a tableau unfolded. Too far away to hear, he watched Leonard Tull, the Churchwarden, manhandle a sullen-faced Biddy Holt out of the Vestry door, only for an equally sullen-faced Reverend Kerry to appear from nowhere and ease her back in.

The two men stood on the threshold like a pair of stags, vying for supremacy. Words were exchanged - short, sharp - before Leonard Tull turned on his heel and stomped off, unsmiling, in the direction of the church. Kerry calmly went inside.

Well, well, Batten thought. These two are becoming more interesting every day.

Tapping on the Vestry door, he went in.

An old-fashioned chart was draped across an easel, and Biddy Holt peered at, as Kerry pointed to several highly speculative depictions of figures from the Easter liturgy. Batten noticed an affinity of spectacles, as priest and pupil stared through pebble glasses at the chart. Kerry mimed 'one minute' to Batten who leaned against the wall, watching.

When Kerry pointed at each figure in turn, Biddy Holt tried to fill in the blanks, her fingers slow now, struggling. Batten recognised Pontius Pilate, Mother Mary - even Judas, a tellingly devious look on his face. Typical, he thought. Trust a policeman to focus on the villain. And why can't every villain have a face as obviously guilty as the Judas depicted here?

'Inspector, said Kerry. 'Apologies. An impromptu Bible class, for Biddy.'

Batten pitched right in. 'It seemed Mr Tull objected to Biddy's presence, Reverend, unless my eyes deceived me?'

Head tilted to one side, Kerry glanced thoughtfully at Batten. 'Patience is a virtue, but it passes Leonard by. He prefers his needs to be instantly met.'

'Patience doesn't pass *you* by, though?' Batten indicated Biddy Holt, puzzling over the images on the chart.

'In my Father's house there are many mansions. Why should Biddy receive less attention for being a little…different?'

He smiled at Biddy, she at him, and Batten immediately understood why Andrew Holt said Kerry was her best friend. The ageing priest's hands jiggled signs Batten couldn't fathom.

'I am just reminding Biddy who you are. People tend not to. They take for granted the everyday social habits of interaction and memory, as if they are available to all. Not the case, alas. Biddy signed back to you - 'hello'. Like this.' Kerry demonstrated the waved 'hello' he'd seen before, and Batten repeated it to Biddy Holt. It drew a strange smile as curved as a banana, and she signed again.

'I think Biddy is calling you 'Mr Top Policeman', Inspector. Be flattered.'

The only other sign Batten could remember was 'thank-you'. He tried it, and Biddy Holt smiled her strange smile at him, eyes wide and glowing. Kerry's hands flashed and she returned to the Bible charts, flipping them backwards and forwards, trying to understand.

'She likes you, Inspector. And, believe me, she doesn't like everyone.'

She doesn't like Leonard Tull, Batten thought.

'When did you learn to sign?' he asked.

'Ah, too long ago to say. I had deaf and dumb parishioners, like Biddy. Three or four. And it was hard for them. The charts Biddy is studying, they came with me from my previous church. Out of date perhaps, but no more so than stained-glass windows - the Church's first visual aid, all those centuries ago.'

'No Power-point display for you, Reverend?'

'Far too modern. Or perhaps I am powerless and pointless? The Bishop employs what he insists on calling 'visuals', from a laptop, onto a screen. Here, though, a chart of images works well enough. And for Biddy, better, I think. Easy to flip back for a second go. Or a third.'

Kerry pointed at a folded chart with a purple cover. 'We've finished Lent – whose colour is purple. Now we have Holy Week, and Easter.' He pointed at Biddy's chart, the white trim seeming to light the Vestry. 'The colour of Easter is white, Inspector. White for purity, for resurrection, innocence, light, joy. And whatever others might think, white for the Biddy Holts of this world.'

It was a white blouse that Batten saw, a white police-tent, the golf-ball whites of Nina Magnus's eyes - and white carcasses of meat, tinged with red, manhandled into a Parminster butcher's shop. He shook the thoughts away.

'I wanted to ask a favour, Reverend. A delicate one. It concerns Biddy, in fact.'

Kerry cocked his head to one side, questioning.

'Our specialist signing officer is away on holiday...'

'Ah, you would like me to assist with Biddy? But you do know her father's command of signing is far superior to mine?'

As delicately as he could, Batten explained why Holt's presence was inappropriate. 'A temporary measure, to move us on. The specialists will re-visit any information we glean. And you'd also be in the role of responsible...'

'Adult?' Kerry caught the irony in an instant. 'Indeed. The mystery of being both adult and child simultaneously. For the precocious genius - a Mozart, for example - an adult mind in a child's body is marvelled at. But for poor Biddy, with her child's mind in an adult body...' Kerry shook his head. 'One of God's many mysteries.'

'One I've never understood, I'm afraid.'

Kerry's head tilted again as he considered Batten. Then he strode across the room and tapped Biddy Holt on the shoulder. A burst of sign-language passed between them and, presumably in answer to Kerry's request, she slowly removed one of her hypo-allergenic white gloves. Beneath it, her stubby bare fingers were ugly puckers of hard flesh, streaked with cracked red rivulets of what Batten assumed was psoriasis. He found himself recoiling, even though, as a policeman, he'd seen far worse.

'Touch Biddy's skin, Inspector. Shake her hand. Please.'

With reluctance, Batten did as Kerry asked, his tentative fingers gently touching Biddy's palm, while her hand squeezed his with happy pleasure. Her skin was cooler than expected. Softer, yielding, despite appearances. She flashed her banana smile.

'What you are feeling is the simple warmth of humanity, Inspector. The pulse of life. Nothing more, nothing less. Did you know touch has a memory? Mm? Your touch is remembering what it feels like, not to be perfect, no, but to be human.'

Batten nodded. Point taken. He swallowed the lesson as tactfully as he could. Biddy Holt struggled back into her glove, smiling all the while, before signing to Kerry.

'Biddy wants to tell them at the Independent Living Centre how she shook the Top Inspector's hand. Is it allowed, she asks?'

When Batten nodded, she clapped her hands together, opened the Vestry door and hovered on the threshold.

'She may wander off, Inspector. To show everyone she meets how she shook the hand of the Top Inspector. I will gladly help you, of course. Biddy trusts me and will behave herself.'

'Appreciated, Reverend. Before she wanders off, perhaps?'

Kerry looked at his watch. 'I have twenty minutes or so, will that suffice?' When Batten nodded, he beckoned to Biddy. 'I am due to oversee a pensioners' lunch, Inspector, and Biddy is my unofficial helper. Today, lunch will be about hands. She will 'demonstrate' shaking yours, to one and all, whether the pensioners like it or not...'

After twenty minutes, Batten was exhausted. The fragmentary process of asking, signing, replying and translating took deep levels of concentration. He thought of Andrew Holt, who did this daily, and had done so for thirty years.

Biddy's answers teetered on the edge of helpful. Batten sat up when she claimed she saw Kenneth Leckey walk down Turks Lane on Thursday evening, a bulky bag in his hand.

When Kerry paused to counsel Batten, the brief return to everyday discourse was a relief.

'Remember, Inspector, my knowledge of signing has limitations. And remember you have entered an alternative world, Biddy's world. I suspect she really did see Kenneth, because she knows him. But 'Thursday evening' could merely means it was getting dark. Whether it was seven-o-clock or nine, is a different story.'

Story.

That's what Batten was sensing. He was watching a story, heard in translation.

And stories are not the same as facts.

'Biddy's broken world deserves some lassitude, Inspector. She compensates, freely sometimes, by developing structures of her own.'

'Structures?'

'Simple ones. For example, hide-and-seek. She can shape her day by hiding, sometimes for hours, if the mood takes her. She almost always wins because few have the patience to seek her out. All the same, winning at something bolsters her self-esteem, so I encourage it. I shall ask her.'

His hands flashed again, and the cautious reply was translated.

'I think she is saying hide-and-seek is not one of your strengths because she hid from you yesterday and counted to ten but you never spotted her, so she wandered off, to search.'

'Search? For what?'

Kerry gave Batten another of his curious glances. 'More who than what, Inspector. She searches for her mother. It is Biddy's daily task. Andrew didn't explain this to you?'

Batten shrugged. Andrew Holt said little about Biddy, and even less about the absent Mrs Holt.

'Andrew rarely talks of Elisabeth. She departed young from God's earth. There are photographs of her in the house, still. Mostly upstairs - where only clergy and doctors are encouraged to go. Biddy has one in a frame by her bed. It was taken when her mother was ill, so is rather a pale imitation, alas. If you were female, Inspector, Biddy would have given you a long, hard stare by now.'

'And gone away disappointed?'

'Indeed. She will be forever disappointed - in *this* life.' Kerry indicated the white chart, dangling from its easel. 'The miraculous birth at Christmas, Inspector, Biddy follows to some degree. But when the Easter liturgy turns to Death and Resurrection, can you imagine how attractive such concepts are to her? Despite their enigma? While I struggle to explain the difference between symbolic and real, Biddy simply prays for her mother to be reborn.'

Batten thanked his lucky stars he wasn't a priest. Being a cop was bad enough.

In the pause, Biddy Holt's fingers danced at Kerry.

'I think she's saying she hid from the black police lady...and from Mike and Chas with the big cross.'

'She saw Brean and Janner carry the cross up the hill?'

After another exchange, Kerry said, 'she did. But as the cross was at Andrew's, being varnished, it's anyone's guess exactly what she saw and when. Making sense of her logic is often guesswork.'

'I need to ask her about Alicia Heron.'

Kerry nodded. 'I doubt Biddy will remember. Alicia left too long ago. And for obvious reasons, Andrew did his best to keep Biddy indoors on Friday morning. She deals with...disturbances rather badly, I'm afraid.' His fingers asked Batten's questions and decoded the response.

'She calls Alicia the poor lady on the hill. Andrew's description, I think.'

'But did she see Alicia? On Thursday evening? Or any other time?'

More signing flashed between Biddy Holt and Kerry, followed by a long pause. Kerry's face became a puzzle, and when his hands signed again, uncertain twitches replaced what before had been smooth. He reminded Batten of Eddie Hick.

'Forgive me, Inspector. Biddy's...nuance has confused me.' Uncertain twitches resumed. 'Tired on Thursday,' she says. 'Too far. The hill too far.'

'Too far for what?'

With reluctance now, Kerry signed Batten's question. Whatever the answer, the response was terse.

'Too far away to see? I wonder if her thick spectacles embarrass her. I'd rather not probe.'

Batten nodded. The specialists would probe, soon enough. He again took in the pebble lenses of Kerry and Biddy Holt.

Kerry checked his watch, suddenly keen to end the three-way exchange.

'We must go, Inspector. The pensioners await.'

'Thank you, Reverend. If I need to...?' He let the request hang. His unwitting fingers were almost trying to sign.

'If necessary, Inspector.'

And they were gone.

A deep yawn released the tension in Batten's jaw. Glancing across the churchyard to Andrew Holt's hidden short-cut to Turks Lane, he thought of re-discovering it. Perhaps he'd bump into a sweaty Ken Leckey on the way. Put off by the image, he made for his car.

The steady rhythm of shoes on paving stones brought Kerry's words back to him. 'Touch has a memory'. Wasn't it from a John Keats poem? One of his English degree tutors had been a Keats fanatic. He tried to remember how it went.

Touch has a memory. O say love,
What can I do to kill it, and be free...?

Was Kerry trying to tell him something?

About Harry Finn? Mike Brean? Chas Janner? Did one of them - or someone else - remember the touch of Alicia Heron? And kill the memory, to be free?

If it's not ruled out...
He reached his car.
It bleeped at him.

Kenneth Leckey's trim cottage sat at the end of Turks Lane. Its house-number, a giant 'One', was carved into an apple-wood nameplate in the shape of a tree. Subtle, thought Batten.

As Ball tapped on the door, Batten peered back at the sinuous path they had plodded down, a tapestry of intertwining stems in every shade of pink, blue, white and yellow - tulip, peony, daffodil, iris, primrose, hyacinth, pansy. Here and there a crocus, or was it cyclamen? Budded stems lurked, aching for summer and nodding in envy at the orchard opposite, where a few flickers of apple-blossom were beginning to emerge.

Batten wished he was a bee.

In contrast to his garish garden, Leckey himself was a colourless man. He stood in his open doorway like a steel reinforcing bar, thin but strangely powerful. No detection skills were needed to tell he was a runner. The shorts, vest and trainers announced it. And the sweat. Judging by his wiry build and Mo Farrar muscles, Batten guessed he was more than your average weekend jogger trying to rein back the beer-gut.

'I was about to take a shower, Inspector,' he said.

Silence often worked better than speech, Batten found. He said nothing.

'Well, come in, but give me a moment to at least grab a towel.'

Waving the two detectives to a sofa, Leckey disappeared. Batten took in the masculine walls, a few scenes of rural nostalgia jarring against the athletics photographs in black and white. If Mrs Leckey had ever made her mark on the decor, no trace remained. Over the hamstone fireplace, in pride of place, hung a framed award. Batten got up to see.

For Services to Rural Conservation, said the heading. *Kenneth Leckey, Chair, East Thorne Orchard Preservation Society* was proudly emblazoned in the centre.

'And rural habitats desperately need conserving, Inspector. Do you not think?' asked Leckey, returning with a sweaty towel curled round his neck.

Batten imagined Erin Kemp's soft voice in his ear: 'Now pop that soiled towel in the washer, Zig, if you'd be so kind? And don't forget the detergent. And to switch it on.' He ignored Leckey's tone, moving instead to alibis and histories, and Alicia Heron.

The responses were terse, grudging. Batten could have been a dentist, extracting teeth.

'So did anyone see you leave on Thursday evening? Around 7.30pm, I think you said?'

A dismissive shrug was the reply. 'How would I know, Inspector? I wasn't seeking an alibi. I had no need of one, not having committed a crime.'

'And you drove to Gloucester?'

'I did.'

'For any particular reason, sir?'

'For many particular reasons, Inspector. Friendship being the primary one. I *do* have friends.'

'Like-minded ones, I would imagine?'

'Is there any other kind?'

For help, Batten looked at Ball. None came. Instead, Batten moved to the question of housing development, the topic instantly igniting Ken Leckey.

'Were you aware, Inspector, I have had three visits from that odious prick of an Estate Agent?'

'Mr Willey?'

'Mr Willey? *Mr Inducement.* The very best sale price. A 'special bonus'. A favourable resettlement. Assistance with removal costs, with Stamp Duty. Etcetera. You get the picture, I'm sure.'

'And why should Mr Willey offer all that, sir?'

Ignoring Batten's forced naivety, Leckey opted for a look with 'you cretin' stamped all over it. Ball remained poker-faced.

'Mr Willey has little reason *of his own* to offer me anything, Inspector. But whatever he may say to the contrary, he is clearly an agent of Satan. I do beg pardon. I meant to say 'Serenity'.'

Batten wanted to tell Leckey how cleverly he did the smugs. Instead he asked, 'any evidence, sir?'

Throwing his arms theatrically at the walls of his cottage, Leckey said, 'you are sitting in the rather obvious evidence - this very building. Defiantly standing in the way of what profiteers insist on calling *progress*.'

'Defiantly, sir?'

'I shall not be swept aside, Inspector. Not I. I shall not be stopped.'

Like Alicia Heron, Batten wondered? She didn't like to be stopped, either, according to Mike Brean. Especially by *overdogs*.

'This is one cottage, sir? Aren't you a bit out on a limb?'

'One cottage? *One*? Do you think for a moment Andrew Holt will uproot himself and Biddy, and sell to those people? Check your facts, Inspector. And I doubt the fate of poor Alicia's house has yet been decided? Who knows, we may even outbid Serenity when number 2 is auctioned off.'

'We?'

'A combined effort from the purses of our ETOPS members. And those of other affiliated Orchard trusts.'

'Would some of those affiliates be located in Gloucester, perhaps?'

The shrewd question was rewarded with a sneer. 'Near and far, Inspector, will you find Orchard Trusts. I seem to recall your Sergeant here being a member of the one at Stockton Marsh?'

Ball's ruddy complexion turned redder, but he let Batten do the talking.

'And as a collective you hope to compete - financially, I mean - with Serenity Developments?'

'We do. We *will*. To Serenity, we are 'anti-progress', because we represent those who *conserve* rather than destroy. But we shall prevail.'

Good luck with prevailing, thought Batten, his visit to Serenity Developments in mind. He could still hear the motorised whirr as the scale model of a huge, meticulously-planned housing scheme emerged from its lair and slid towards his chin, as if on grease.

'And across this very lane is evidence anew of the battle between those who conserve and those who destroy,' said Leckey. 'The Turks Lane *orchard*. And beyond the orchard, more evidence still - the fields, farms and hedgerows bought up by Serenity *Developments!*' He spat out the final word as if it was poison. 'If you are experiencing difficulty in joining up the dots of evidence, then think of the dots as a *road*, Inspector. A road that, if built, will sweep aside all and everything in its path! Now, was there something else?'

Sergeant Ball raised a hand. Appropriate, thought Batten. Leckey's cottage was beginning to feel like school.

'On the plans, sir - the ones given out at the public meetings here - isn't there a fall-back position?'

It was Ball's turn to receive a smug stare. 'We would expect nothing less of these people,' spat Leckey. 'If they cannot have the houses of Turks Lane, they will try to usurp the orchard alone, and divert their pernicious road where living trees grow.'

'But wouldn't that be worse? For you, I mean?' Ball said. 'If the road skimmed past Turks Lane and only replaced the orchard, you'd end up with a highway at the bottom of your garden. You'd have noise and dirt and diesel where apple blossom used to be.'

Blowing out his breath, Leckey leaned towards Ball. 'Your erroneous assumption, Sergeant, is the orchard *will* be 'replaced'. Not if ETOPS has anything to do with it.' Flinging his arm at the window, he added, 'this orchard is awash with rights of way and one protected species after another. For example, I don't suppose you are familiar with a rare plant species called Oenanthe pimpinelloides, Sergeant? Either of you?'

In case he hadn't patronised the two detectives enough, Leckey spelled out the Latin name. He got as far as 'P.I.M.P' before Batten raised a hand in surrender.

'Best assume not, sir. For efficiency's sake.'

'Oenanthe pimpinelloides is a flowering plant, a vague relation of the carrot, I'm informed, and rare. Dense white flower heads. Occasionally pink. Beloved of pasture, and of orchard habitats - which serve to preserve it for insects. And for *posterity*. *If* the orchards themselves are preserved, rather than butchered to make rich people richer.'

Leckey paused for his message to sink in.

'You may know Oenanthe pimpinelloides by its marginally more common name perhaps?'

Batten wondered if he'd strayed onto the set of Gardeners' Question Time. 'Enlighten me,' he said, gritting his teeth.

'Our friend Oenanthe is also known as the 'corky-fruited-'

'Water dropwort,' added Ball, teeth way beyond the gritting stage.

'Ah. The corky-fruited water dropwort is familiar to you,' said Leckey, disappointed.

'Yes, sir. I know orchards well, and what lives in them,' said Ball.

'Then you also appreciate their significance, and their dire need of preservation?'

'I do, sir,' added Ball.

Leckey shifted his glance back to Batten. It had a triumphant air, a lawyer with friends on the jury. But Ball hadn't finished.

'And for houses too,' Ball said, pointing at Leckey's beamed ceiling and hamstone walls. 'Old houses, like this one, for those who love old houses.'

A smirk from Leckey was premature.

'And new ones, for those who prefer the new,' continued Ball. 'Don't all houses begin in the ground, sir, new or old? Just as trees do?'

Kenneth Leckey yanked the sweaty towel from the back of his neck and whipped it across the room and through the kitchen doorway. It landed in the open maw of the washing machine.

This man has a strong arm, Batten noted. Does he practise? He also noted the wooden block of kitchen knives sitting on the worktop.

'Only if the ground is plentiful, Sergeant,' Leckey replied. 'But the ground is being swallowed up, eaten away. Do you know how many orchards we have lost in the last sixty years?' He paused for effect, casually leaning against the fireplace, next to his framed award for services to rural conservation. '*Too many!*' he snarled.

We'd better wind this up, Batten thought, before he switches on the Power-point display. But Leckey's thin veneer of patience had cracked. He strutted towards the front door and dragged it open.

'So, *gentlemen*, perhaps now you will appreciate the efforts of ETOPS, and other doughty groups such as mine? If you need me, I shall be in the shower, for exactly five minutes. After that you will find me constructing banners and placards in the village hall. Goodbye.'

As Batten and Ball made their way down the bee-friendly path, Leckey poked his head past the door-frame to ram home his point.

'There will be no road driven through Turks Lane, Inspector, nor through the apple-orchard of East Thorne. Tarmac will never replace these cottages and trees. The bulldozer will be forced to bulldoze *me*!

Serenity *Developments*? Humph, they will have to carry me out in a box!'

Batten prayed it wouldn't come to that.

From the window of number 2, next door, DC Nina Magnus watched Batten and Ball shuffle away and head for their car. A sweaty Kenneth Leckey was standing in his porch, arms folded, as if seeing them off the premises.

Magnus wished she could leave too.

The search itself was a waste of time. Number 2, the double-sized cottage with the *For Sale by Auction* board, had the familiar smell of damp and old dirt, common to empty properties. The only trace of unofficial occupation was a long-dead dormouse. Otherwise, the place was the same as when Magnus last crossed its threshold, months ago.

She didn't mention this to Hick. Instead, she listened to the nag-nag-nag of her professional mind and grabbed her phone.

'Hickie?'

'Uh?'

'I'm just going to make a call. Cover for me, will you?'

'Call? Of nature? Try crossing your legs.'

'*Phone* call, Mr Loft.'

DC Hick shrugged and continued searching.

Magnus gritted her teeth and jabbed at the speed-dial...

'WHY THE BLOODY HELL DIDN'T YOU TELL ME?' yelled Batten down the phone.

Because I didn't want to get yelled at! Magnus didn't say.

'Sir, it's been mad. And what with Mike and everything.' She blew out her breath. 'But standing in Turks Lane just now... Last time I was here, the sign wasn't. Soon as I stepped inside, I remembered. And had to say.'

Despite predicting your reaction.

'I'm heading for my office,' said Batten. 'Since you can't be there *yesterday*, be there bloody fast!'

Twenty five

A night in the cells didn't improve Chas Janner's mood. Had he known more nights were in the offing, his gloom would be deeper still. But exhaustion helped him sleep, and sleep cleared some of the fog from his memory.

That rug! The lippy cow went on about that bloody rug! More worried about the bloody rug than me being in her bloody house.

He propped himself on the hard bed and recalled more of Thursday night...

'Where's my *rug*? What have you done with it? Where is it? It's always been here. *Here*! It's in the inventory. The inventory you must have *signed* before you moved in!'

Alicia Heron pointed at the hall floor, covered now by a cheap rug very different from the one she'd draped there, lovingly, all those years ago. 'You shouldn't even be in my *house*! And if you want to see your damage deposit again, you'd better produce my *rug*!'

What could Chas say?

Yes, Miss Lippy Cow, cannabis resin does tend to leave nasty stains on a rug. It made a right mess of yours. And the smell...Well, I had to get rid of it. But don't you worry, I bought a replacement. This one, here. A bit plainer, yes, but it keeps the chill off these flagstones. Same size, same colour - more or less. I'd like to say I searched for a rug embroidered with herons and bluebirds, but, frankly, I couldn't be arsed.

He shrugged his giant shoulders at her. She's just a smudge of a person, he thought. She could fit down a drainpipe.

'Are you *listening*? My *mother* made that rug! She wove it herself and I helped her. The best wool, the best silk. Six months it took. Six months! It has a heron at one end, and a bluebird at the other. That rug is *special*! So what have you done with it?'

And around in circles they went.

Rug, rug, rug.

Get out of my house, house, house.

When it became police, police, police, Chas realised his shoulders had tightened up.

He began to say, 'I'm staying. I've got a rental agreement.' Then he remembered he didn't. A back-hander, the private deal he'd done with Willey.

Yes, yes, Lesley, of course I'll vacate before the owner comes back. June, you say? Yes, yes, cash, no questions asked. No problem!

But the lippy-cow-owner was early. And feisty with it.

Cash.

Willey and Janner were fond of cash. But what clinched it was the thought of tonight's cash, and tonight's deliveries, waiting in Chas's lock-up for darkness to fall.

'*Stuff your rug and stuff your damage deposit!*' he told her.

He could earn that in a weekend. And find somewhere to doss, for a day or two.

'And I know the law, *lady*. You touch my possessions, any of them, and *I'll* have *you*! Change the locks for all I care. You've still got to let me in to move what's mine - so I'll be back. And if you think I'm wrong, go ahead and ask the *police!*'

And he grabbed his coat, phone and keys and slammed the door.

Last he remembered, wasn't the lippy cow glaring up at him, fists on her hips?

Till Friday morning, that is, when he saw her again, from his car, through binoculars.

On that crucifix.

Dead.

He could almost feel the binoculars' shiny coating in his hand - till through a crack in his broken memory another shiny-coated object tumbled into his skull: his baseball-bat. Hidden in the boot of the car, under an old blanket. Handy, a baseball-bat, for persuading lippy punters to quieten down and pay up.

Should never have left it there!

Chas Janner stared at the sewage-coloured walls of his cell, and slumped forward on the hard mattress. Burying his throbbing head in two giant hands, he waited for the sound of a key in a lock, and for the questions to start again.

About baseball-bats this time.

While foggy Chas Janner stewed in his cell, Batten worked on the fog surrounding his other 'suspects'. The paper-chase on Ball's desk carried an avalanche warning, so Batten kept his distance while pumping his Sergeant for local knowledge.

'Seems to me, Ballie, these Somerset villages of yours magnets for problem daughters. Don't tell me, on top of Alicia Heron and Biddy Holt, we've a load of Missing Wives and Mothers as well?'

'No, no, sir. Mrs Heron you know about. And Mrs Leckey's living in urban bliss in Newcastle, if the door-to-door is accurate. She divorced Ken Leckey a couple of years back. Got fed up of playing second fiddle to a protest march. And to apples, earth, fire, air and water, I suppose. She found herself a new first fiddle, a catering manager from up North. We're checking.'

'Didn't bump into a Mrs Holt while she was up there, I don't suppose?'

'There really *was* a Mrs Holt, sir, but not for long. Never recovered from the shock of bringing poor Biddy into the world, by all accounts. Died young, alas.'

'From what?'

Batten watched Ball scrabble through his paper mountain, without knocking it over. *Lord knows how he ever finds anything.*

'Dysentery, sir.' Ball waved a post-it note in triumph. 'Complications from…bacillary dysentery - but don't ask me what that is. Caught it in Thailand, says here.'

'Thailand? What was she doing in Thailand? Any connection with -'

'- I know, sir, I know. We're checking.'

'Dysentery? I didn't know you could die from it. You sure it wasn't despair, dismay, or demoralisation. Or something else beginning with D.'

'She died all the same, sir. Before Biddy was even three years old.'

'Flaming hell. Andrew Holt's looked after Biddy for thirty years? Poor devil. On his own?'

'Bless her, sir, but I imagine Biddy's a bit of a passion-killer - assuming her dad tried to find a new partner.'

'How does the poor sod keep going?' Batten recalled the dry stick of a man he'd interviewed.

'Doesn't have much choice, does he?'

'No, I mean finance-wise.'

'He's Handy Andy, sir. He touts for work, and folk trust him, so...There's his Turks Lane contracts - what's left of them. He has a giant compost heap, too, and sells it, three quid a bag. Pukka stuff, Jess Foreman says.'

Batten thought of the compost he should be spreading on his own neglected garden, this *holiday* weekend.

'And he's the church cleaner,' said Ball, his local knowledge a boon.

'Who looks after Biddy, while he's earning?'

'She goes to an Independent Living Centre, mid-week. A minibus does the rounds. At weekends, if she hasn't wandered off she helps her dad. Proud to, apparently.'

'Helps him? How?'

'I'm not a church-goer, sir, but when I had reason to visit All Saints - a spate of thefts, not long ago - I remember seeing her slide up and down the pews on her backside, sitting on a duster. I assume it works. Personally, I can't remember the last time I dusted anything other than a fingerprint.'

'Why won't Andrew Holt sell the house, Ballie? If Serenity Developments are offering to pay over the odds, shouldn't he be asking to see the colour of their cheque-book? You've been to his place. Best way to improve it would be to knock it down.'

'He spends six days a week maintaining other folk's places, sir. Can't have much left for his own.'

'No-one as badly shod as the cobbler's children, eh?'

'S'right, sir. And by all accounts, Biddy Holt scribbles all over the bedroom walls. I'm told he doesn't bother re-painting them now.'

'But if he's been offered way above the cottage's value? Why not bite their hands off?'

'And go where, sir? He's living in a house with a garden, close to what he's always known. And what Biddy's always known, more to the point. There's people around him who'll help. Specialist college nearby. Kerry and the church. An orchard opposite.'

'You're making him sound like you, Ballie. A dyed-in-the-wool local yokel.'

'Somerset does that, sir. Stay long enough, it'll do it to you.'

'Only if I drink the cider.' The thought of drink changed Batten's track. 'Does he patronise The Rising Sun? Andrew Holt?'

'Once a blue moon, according to Harry Finn. And Cat Finn doesn't like Biddy going there. She's funny about *any* kids being in the pub. Andrew goes to hardware and charity shops, garden centres, church, and bugger all else. Once a year, he gets two weeks respite care, and he disappears. I know, sir - find out where. On the list.'

Batten scowled at the word 'list'. The one on his own strewn desk was longer than Eddie Hick's shirt-tail. Near the top, he'd scrawled 'Orchard Preservation.'

'You're the orchard expert, Ballie. Is Handy Andy a member of...remind me?'

'ETOPS, sir. East Thorne Orchard Preservation Society. And yes, he is. But works too many hours to be an active member.'

'You sure?'

Ball rubbed his nose with a sausage finger. It helped him think. 'Not completely sure, to be honest.'

'Then you know what to do, Ballie.'

'Yes, sir. Put it on the list.'

Twenty six

To smooth the waters, Magnus arrived at Batten's cubby-hole carrying two takeaway cups. She placed Batten's carefully on the tiny lozenge of his desk not swamped by paper.

'Double espresso, sir, black, with a splash of hot water. No sugar?'

Batten stared at the cardboard cup. 'A bribe, is it?'

'A bribe, sir, yes. Best I could do at short notice.'

'Hmph. What's in yours?'

'Hot chocolate, sir. I know I'm chocolate already, but lately I've not been feeling too hot. Topping up.'

Batten allowed a tiny grin to bend his lips. He liked Magnus, as a detective and a person.

'I should strangle you.'

'Don't, sir. It's against the law.'

'Tell, Nina.'

She did, embarrassment and all...

'I've been in number two before, sir. At Turks Lane. Six or seven months ago, as a punter. Me and Mike are - were - looking to buy a place together, maybe in East Thorne, and my shift patterns mean I can sometimes view properties midweek. Turks Lane only went on our list because it was empty, and I must've viewed a dozen houses around then, all of them a blur.'

'I hope you mean all except one?'

'I do, sir. *Now*. I remember getting the brochure, and arranging to meet the agent at the house, but he rings to cancel, and wouldn't say why. Leave me a set of keys, I say, and after a bit of push and pull, he agrees. I go straight round to pick them up.'

'Pick them up from Lesley Willey?' Batten clocked another coincidence.

'From Willey and Associates, yes. Willey's not there. Some minion makes me sign for the keys and I drive to Turks Lane. When I arrive, there's someone parked in the lay-by - a punter, because when I walk past, I notice he's reading the same glossy brochure as me. I think, get in first, Nina - and I do. I use the key, and lock the door behind.'

'Don't tell me?'

'Yes, sir. Not been there thirty seconds when I hear a key in the lock and the other punter walks in, from the car, waving his brochure. Chunky bloke with a full beard, dark suit, short on smiles.'

'"You do know the owners have taken it off the market, don't you?" he says. I didn't even know who the owners were, but the does.'

'"It's going up for auction now," he tells me, "so you're wasting your time."'

'I tell him I'm perfectly capable of turning up at an auction and making a bid, and I wander into the kitchen to have a closer look. He comes after me.'

'"You do know you have to stump up 10% of the final price on auction day? And if you can't stump up the rest within 7 days you lose your deposit – you do know?" he asks. I'm getting that tingly feeling you sometimes get in your feet, sir, yes?'

Batten nodded. If his feet ever stopped sensing crime, he'd pack in CID and re-train as a chiropodist.

'So, I do my girlie act, all naive. Gosh, really, I didn't know, blah-blah. And I tell him it doesn't say so in my brochure. He grabs it and has a stare.'

'"That's an old one," he says, and shoves my brochure back at me. He flashes his own version and points to the small print on the back, under Auction Terms and Conditions. While he's doing it, I'm carefully easing my brochure into my bag, taking care not to smudge his fingerprints - just in case. I tell him 10% isn't a problem, assuming I like the house, and I head for the sitting room.'

'"Whatever you bid, we'll bid higher," he says. He definitely says 'we', but he's wearing no wedding ring, so who knows what he means? I tell him, if I want it more, I'll bid higher too. 'Isn't that how auctions work?' I ask him.'

Batten's interest was so piqued, his coffee was going cold.

'I didn't want the house, sir - one of the reasons I forgot it. The ceilings were too low, for me and... But I did want to see his reactions. "You won't like it here," he says. His voice takes on a hard note, and I swear he gets bigger. "Very traditional here, this village. They won't like your sort." I ask him what he means. "It's a very *traditional* village," he repeats. "They like it the way it is, if you get my drift."'

'I could have told him I spend every other weekend in East Thorne. Could have said I play for the Ladies Skittles Team at The Rising Sun. I could have told him East Thorne is *traditional*, but not racist. Instead, I tell him I don't get his drift, no, and can he spell it out, pretty-please.'

'"Are you thick?" he says. "It's a very *white* village. How much spelling out do you need?"'

'I ask him, does he mean the village will ostracise me if I buy this house, because I happen to be black?'

'"You're not buying it," he says.'

'I tell him I might, once I've had a look round, and I open the sitting room door. His hand shoots out and grabs my wrist, hard. 'Please take your hand off me,' I say, with forced politeness.

'"You're not buying this house!" he hisses, so close to my face I can smell his mints-and-cigarette breath and I'd swear his pupils were twice the size they should've been. I'll ask you, politely, I say, for a second time, to remove your hand. And, sir, if he had, I'd have put it all down to racial experience. But up comes his other hand. It clamps onto my shoulder and he starts to bundle me back down the hallway towards the front door. Well, you can imagine what happened next, I suppose?'

'I can indeed, Nina.' Batten knew Magnus was ex-Army, and combat-trained.

'I let him scuttle me along until his centre of gravity's more helpful to me than him, whip his arm up his back till his shoulder has to break or drop, and down he goes. He might have had a bit of help from my knee, to be honest. Strong lungs he has, because I hear the air whoosh from them as he hits the ground and rasps out more mints-and-cigarette breath - but at the carpet this time. I'm paraphrasing, but he says something like, "You black bitch, I'll tear your effing skin off! I'll turn you effing red!"'

'So, Nina, you declared you were CID, and made an arrest?'

'I should've, sir, I admit. But off-duty, with no witnesses? And if I arrested every muscle-bound racist who got in my face, I'd never do a day's work, would I?'

Batten nodded, postponing the lecture Nina was going to get.

'Whatever, I warn him I'm ex-Army as I open the door, but I keep his arm jerked back, in case of lingering ideas about retaliating. He's shorter than me but there's plenty of muscle in his arm, so he could've. I wish he had - for a face-full of pepper spray. But he changes his mind and scoots towards the lay-by. Gives me an expert glare of pure hate, though. I've had plenty, but this one... Anyhow, I track him, till he gets in his car and guns it down the road.'

'Car registration?'

'Yes, sir. At home. And his fingerprints. I didn't run any of it. Not a formal case.'

'It could be now. Run them, when you get a minute. Was he local?'

'London, sir. I'd bet money. Like he was off *Eastenders*. You know, where the actors shout at each other in cockney. Except it wasn't an act.'

'That all of it, this time?' Batten asked, softening his question with a smile.

'All of it, sir. Off my chest, onto yours.'

'Well. Hope you feel better.'

She did. Would getting things off her chest with Mike make her feel better too? Tonight. She'd try, tonight.

Batten watched her leave and downed lukewarm espresso coffee, breathing in its heady whiff.

And in the recess of his mind, he breathed in the heady whiff of motive too.

'You been working all weekend, Zig?' asked 'Prof' Connor.

Batten gave Connor an eyebrow.

'I guessed you had. Because you look like me. Us lot at Forensics, we don't sleep either, you know.'

'You bowled over to Parminster, in person, just to remind me?'

'I bowled over for this appalling tea,' Connor said, holding a steaming, cracked mug. 'And with hot data, to warm the deep-frozen cockles of your heart.'

Pulling out the only spare chair, Batten bit back a comment about Connor's penchant for calling his findings *data*. The banter was tongue-in-cheek, self-protective, and Connor knew it too.

'Blood, Zig, first of all. The fleck we found in the hallway at number 4. The victim's. Definite. No question.'

Batten nodded in thanks. 'Bad news for Chas Janner. Hope his cell's comfy.'

'But we didn't find much else, Zig, apart from rug fibres. Chris Ball said you'd developed a burning interest in rug manufacture. Said you might go on a course, to learn how to embroider little blue birdies onto rugs. In wool and silk.'

'Did he now?'

'Or maybe I misheard. Whatever, the fibres we found were common-or-garden polyester. Every single one. Not a sign of wool, silk, or anything else. If you ever turn up the polyester version, don't waste your time queuing up at *Antiques Roadshow*. More like *Poundstretcher*, if the fibres are telling the truth. You've gone quiet. Something I said?'

'Thinking.'

'Bad for you. Makes you look tired. Have I mentioned cannabis resin? Faint traces, in the cracks in the flagstones, downstairs hallway.'

'Where the rug should have been?'

Connor nodded.

'Any traces of engine oil?'

'Nope.'

'Chas Janner swears he spilled engine oil on the rug - a wool and silk rug. Embroidered. Like his story.'

'Whatever. No engine oil.'

'Anything else?'

'Yes, orange baler-twine. The stuff securing the tarpaulin to the cross. All from Harry Finn's box of bits at The Rising Sun. We matched the cut ends, one to another. All frayed and worn. Except where recently cut - and re-tied, of course.'

'Cut? Not undone?"

'Cut. Which is why we've got the knots. Severed, with a bladed implement, extremely sharp.'

'So somebody sliced through the baler-twine and re-used it? To...' Batten didn't need to borrow Sonia Welcome's finger twirl. Connor knew what he meant.

'Afraid so, Zig. Yards of it. Plenty enough for that poor slip of a girl.'

The two men shared a moment of silence.

'There were a few strands of twine still on the tarpaulin. They show the same cut marks. Just the one blade, I'd say.'

'Which makes the chances of it being one person a tad more likely,' said Batten. He imagined an unknown hand clutching a knife and slicing away plastic sheeting to reveal the bare wood of the cross. And gathering up loose strands of baler-twine, for a grislier purpose.

'Is it time for your nap, Zig, or shall I tell you about the knots?'

'Sorry, Prof. Reef knots, weren't they?'

'Yes, and considering they must've been tied in the dark, quite a set of reef- knots - all beautifully precise, almost identical.'

'Somebody obsessive?'

'Couldn't say, Zig. Maybe whoever tied them was a sailor, dreaming of the sea. Or military, and disciplined. Or something else.'

'Where's this get us?'

'That's your job, Zig. Mine's to tell you the few bits of twine still attached to the plastic sheeting were held on with reef knots, too – but these were looser, and the odd granny-knot thrown in. Probably the way a mere mortal like you would tie on a plastic sheet.'

'So these knots were tied earlier - by Mike Brean and Chas Janner?'

'Not by Janner, Zig. We fingerprinted Brean and Janner, for elimination, and the only partials on the knots came from Brean's big fingers. Nothing of Janner's, except on the sheet. Found some of Harry Finn's prints – on the sheet and the twine. And Mrs Finn's. How you choose to interpret such data is your business.'

'Since the Finns provided the sheeting, Prof, and the baler-twine, you'd bank on their prints cropping up.'

'Well, Zig, maybe they banked on it too, eh? Cat Finn switched from angel to axe-murderer when we tried fingerprinting *her*. Just saying.'

Connor swigged more tea and pulled a face. 'I'm going to confiscate whatever's in this mug and test it for poison.'

'Anything else?'

'Oh, well, we found a signed confession, in a Tupperware container, hidden behind the fridge. Aren't bloodstains, fibres, cannabis, cut-marks and reef-knots enough for you?'

'No other prints? In Alicia Heron's house?'

'Loads of those, too. But apart from hers and some useless smudges, all the prints belong to Chas Janner, who lives there, Andrew Holt who cleans the place, and your squirmy Estate Agent who I suppose collects the rent.'

'He collects rent, alright. Straight into his pocket.'

'He was a bag of nerves, too, when they fingerprinted him. Nearly jumped off a cliff when the lads said 'for the purposes of elimination'. Is he on pills?'

'He's on sufferance. No rogue prints?'

Connor shook his head. 'We searched close and hard, Zig. Be assured. Oh, nearly forgot, do you remember we took casts of the footprints, on the hill?'

'Yes, Prof. I'm not senile.'

'Well, what I said at the time. Two big-footed beggars and a smaller foot. Can't be certain for the courts, but maybe a size eight or nine. And on top of the bigfoots.'

'So someone who turned up after they'd gone?'

'Ah, Zig. Naughty. Could be someone who was there all the time, but moved a bit slower. Again, in a courtroom, I couldn't swear either way.'

'You've been such a big help,' Batten said, with a smile.

'And what do I get for my pains? Appalling weak tea in a cracked mug full of bacteria. But, I shall return - once I've finished comparing notes with the luscious Dr Welcome. How come she's working all weekend too, but manages to be twice as luscious as you and me? How does that happen?'

'Our beauty's on the inside, Prof. Hers is inside and out.'

'Feel free to tell her tomorrow, Zig. She's expecting you, at Pathology. If it were me, I'd take champagne and a picnic rug, and an old-fashioned wind-up gramophone, playing *I'll Be Your Sweetheart!*'

Connor laughed his way out of the door, leaving a crisp report on the desk.

Oh good, Batten thought. More paper.

He carried on, eyelids growing heavy as one page became another.

He gave up, and let the car drive him home.

Twenty seven

As soon as Batten pushed past his front door, the landline rang.

Expecting Sergeant Ball's voice bearing bad news, he softened and exhaled when Erin Kemp spoke. Feet still in his shoes, he flopped onto the sofa. He hadn't told Erin about the murder case, but she knew anyway.

'You telepathic, all of a sudden?'

'With you, Zig, being telepathic wouldn't go amiss. Just *tell* me, in future. Unless you don't need support, *all of a sudden*?'

'I didn't need to tell you. I knew you'd find out.'

'I didn't *find out*, Zig. I switched on my phone. A news-bomb, like yours. They do have wifi in Spain, you know. And did you imagine religious scruples would persuade the Spanish media to ignore an Easter crucifixion, at a place called Crown of Thorns Hill?'

Batten had no such illusion. But he didn't want to fill their precious long-distance call with talk of murder.

'If you want religion, Zig, Spain's the place. And at Easter, multiply by ten. East Thorne made the Spanish news all right, double-quick. Topped off by a tut of disapproval.'

The instant he heard Erin's voice he wanted to be in Spain, even if it meant flying. She wouldn't be returning soon - his diary said so.

'So, yes, Zig, I'll promise to avoid the news if you promise to clear your head. Do you still have daylight over there?'

'Some,' he said. Through the window, early evening sun carved shadows on Ham Hill, slumbering on its long back in the distance. He'd driven home before dark because he was falling asleep at his desk. 'Why?'

'Why? Because even from Spain I can hear steam hissing in your stubborn kettle-skull. Let it out. Put your boots on. Walk. I'd dearly love to walk with you, but I'm too far away.'

Yes. Too far away. Too far away, again.

'The Spain people, they're taking us on a walking tour of Cordoba. A selling tour, really. Everyone's selling. Why don't you walk too? Hike to Ham Hill, and pretend I'm with you.'

'Too far, this evening.' He was only just home. She was right, though.

'I'll walk a bit of the Parrett Trail instead. Let out the steam. Watch the river flow and pretend you're beside me.'

'Promise you won't walk upstream, Zig, with East Thorne on your horizon? Please don't refill your skull with thorns? Promise?'

'No, no', he said. 'I'll go Martock way. Promise.'

They said their goodbyes, and he pulled on well-used boots. Outside, Erin's words still in his head and the path soft with new Spring grass, he began to walk downstream, in harmony with the glistening water.

His well-used boots though - or was it something cantankerous inside him - refused to allow it. At the first bridge, left foot and right conspired to cross to the far bank and reverse their track. Upstream, his boots went, against the river's flow, drawn towards East Thorne where the white police tent still perched on Crown of Thorns Hill like a bloodless cherry.

After half a mile, by a wooded drove, a swathe of bright orange stalks lined the track. Whether dogwood or willow, they were the colour of baler-twine. As he peered closer, a buzzard the size of an umbrella flapped up from the orange clump on giant wings, momentarily shocking him. In its beak, he saw the red remains of a kill, and wondered if he would bother to eat tonight. His stomach dropped down the food-chain, whenever murder rose up.

At the next stile he turned towards a sluice gate, the river boiling and foaming towards him, blue-grey droplets spiralling into the air. Early Spring blossom softened the faint acid scent of white water, beautiful and disturbing, equally.

Further along, the river's detritus stuck to tangles of reeds like flies on fly-paper. A pair of fallen tree-trunks sliced into the stream, the first deflecting the flow back on itself, the second pushing it along, faster still. He thought he saw a large white sack jammed against the first tree but, drawing closer, the white sack took on a more ominous shape. Against his wishes, he recognised the shape of limbs.

Stomach, gut and throat all lurched together when he realised what it was.

Trapped in the fallen branches, whitened, bloated, hopeless, was a body. For an instant he felt a nauseous taste in his craw, foul and familiar, and the same old question: does the job seek you - or you the job?

He grabbed his phone and was about to ring Parminster when the white sack shifted in the water, its human flesh slowly morphing into the body of a long-dead horse. The banks were steep here, the river swift. A sodden grey tail and mane swished in the iron-blue stream, two front legs pushing at the fallen tree as if for leverage. Tomorrow, he would report it to Sergeant Ball, more informed than he about countryside protocols. Ball's contacts at the River Authority would do what needed to be done.

Batten envied them. Would he gladly remove a putrid horse from a river, stench and guts and all, if the payback was never again setting eyes on a crucified corpse?

To deflect the question, he turned away from birds of prey and dead horses and clambered over the next stile.

A straight track between two tall thickets faced him, framing what at any other time would be a fine long view. Sunset was colouring Crown of Thorns Hill, and on its peak, even at this distance, the unmistakeable shape of the white police tent pricked his eyes. As he stared, the changing evening light slowly turned its cold whiteness a deep blood-red.

His eyes rebelled.

Erin Kemp's soft voice whispered in his skull, and he cursed himself and his wayward boots for not listening. On one side of the track, the hissing river swirled and foamed. On the other, he could hear traffic from the nearby road.

A barbed wire fence and tall tangles of shrub snaked between him and the tarmac, but without a thought he did something he had never done before. He kicked down the nearest fence-post, the wood snapping like a gunshot, and he stepped over the wire, replacing it as best he could from the other side. Bursting through the hedge, brambles snagging his waterproof and scraping his hands, Erin's voice in his ear faded and a policeman's voice emerged.

'Damage to property', it said. 'Failing to observe a bye-law. Wilful trespass.'

'So, arrest me,' he snarled, clumping off with a scowl. Crown of Thorns Hill burned behind him as he tramped faster and faster away from it, blood-red peak diminishing by degrees as he slogged back on the hard roadside, feet pointing home, away from the beauty of the evening river. The unfamiliar echo of boots on tarmac rang in his skull all the way to Ashtree.

He locked the front and back doors, and leaned against the kitchen worktop.

'You need to eat,' his stomach said. But his feet rebelled again, striding past the fridge, and hauling him upstairs to bed. In moments he fell into the depths of sleep.

But not for long.

Red-beaked raptors, dead horses, and the bloodless cherry of a white police tent flowed like a river through his dreams. The dark silhouettes of a crucifix and a dying thorn-tree finally roused him from sleep.

He lay awake, almost till morning.

Easter Sunday

Twenty eight

6.30am.

No lie-ins, on a murder-case.

Batten didn't remember driving to Parminster, nor confronting the files on his desk. Sift, sort, prioritise, he told himself. Keep calm and carry on, in the service of the great British public.

Ball had beaten his Inspector to the office by twenty minutes, and amid the fly-tip of his own desk was carrying on too.

'Easter Sunday, sir.'

'Is it? Anything useful come in?'

'Bits and pieces, and what you've already got.' He waved the victim's biography, and continued to reduce it to bullet points, for the morning meeting. 'She's done a decent job, has Magnus. On the victim, I mean. But reading Alicia Heron's life, well, it's a bit like ...'

'A bit like she's been resurrected?'

'I suppose I do mean that, sir, yes. Sorry.'

Batten was thinking the same.

'Let's agree, then, Ballie. No jokes about resurrections, today? Alicia Heron's not coming back, Easter Sunday or any other day. And I've had my fill of death *and* religion.'

'Suits me, sir. Never warmed to either.'

As the two detectives returned to their paper mountains, the CID office door banged open, handle clattering against the wall. Without looking, they knew who it was.

His favourite cafe closed for the holiday, DC Hick's arms were unencumbered by coffee cartons and bacon rolls. This new freedom increased his scope for colliding with doors and furniture, and his wayward boot duly splattered the waste-basket's contents across the floor.

Hick followed, spiralling himself through the room past a blockade of sharp-edged filing cabinets, till his desk recognised his body and re-claimed it. His arse flopped into the sitting position, randomly coinciding with a chair.

'Easter Sunday, Sarge,' Hick said, swivelling round. 'Any sign of a resurrection?'

Last to arrive was Nina Magnus.

Since her own excavations into the life of Alicia Heron, she'd been running on clockwork, refusing to deal with the joined-up dots in her own puzzle. Now, she read the bullet point summary Sergeant Ball had prepared for the team. Bullets, indeed, she thought. The connection she was pretending not to make, Ball had re-emphasised for her.

This morning, breakfast with Mike was a series of grunts, punctuating the otherwise silence - till Mike grabbed his coat and stomped off to his workshop on the far side of East Thorne.

'It's Easter Sunday!' she'd shouted after him. No reply.

Climbing into her Toyota, she considered moving back to her flat, at least for now. She'd given up saying *I'm just doing my job, Mike.*

So far, he hadn't said, *try doing it somewhere else!* Not Mike's way at all - so far.

Magnus spent her journey to HQ cursing murder, corpses and crucifixions. As soon as she read Ball's bullet points, the curses began again.

In cool, neutral language, Ball noted Alicia Heron was Mike's 'birthday present', one balmy August night, when he was 18 and Alicia 24.

Huh, thought Magnus, we've all seen 'Lish' *naked* now.

The next bullet point noted the coincidence of Alicia Heron's abortion, which took place that same October.

'Don't jump to conclusions, Nina,' she told herself. 'You're a detective, not a scandal sheet.'

But her mind niggled away, and when she switched on her laptop the bullet points re-appeared in the case update. She tackled the long snake of jobs on her desk, but Alicia Heron's visit to The Old Rowan Clinic laddered itself to the top.

'*Did Mike know he was the father*?' asked the voice of her emotions.

'Who else did Alicia sleep with, around then?' asked her police brain.

'*Did Mike use a condom,*' said her first voice.

'DNA?' asked the second.

'*Who paid for the abortion*?' asked both together.

When Batten emerged from his office, she almost pleaded to be 'placed on other duties', despite being steered away from roles involving

Mike Brean. Not the roles of housemate and bedfellow, though. Some decisions she alone must make.

But you said you'd make a decision yesterday!

Disquiet must have crept into her face because Batten was asking, 'everything OK, Nina?'

Mind off Mike Brean, please, she told herself. Focus on Alicia Heron instead. Trouble is, when you do, it comes full circle to Mike.

'Oh, struggling along, sir.'

Batten nodded. He'd experienced the impact of murder on his personal life - and on his partner and her daughter too - in a previous case.

'Murder tunnels into those left behind,' he'd told Ball – without expecting his Sergeant to remove some of the pain by burning some of the evidence. He shook off the memory.

'I was wondering, Nina.' He tailed off. Magnus had the face of someone who's lost a million quid and found a bent coin.

'Sir?'

'I was wondering about Hazel Timms. About seeing how she's fixed. What with us being short of bodies?' His sigh and head-shake claimed responsibility for careless words.

Magnus didn't smile. DC Hazel Timms was on extended leave, and if she felt half as bad as Nina, extended leave was the best thing for her.

'She's just buried both her parents, sir.'

Batten knew. Alicia Heron buried hers at eighteen. Biddy Holt, a thirty-something child, was still searching for one of hers. He didn't say this to Magnus.

'We had a coffee, last week.'

'Any better?' asked Batten, without hope.

Magnus shook her head, to dislodge the memory of Hazel Timms, ashen-faced, her pale fingers stirring and stirring a froth-coated coffee but drinking none of it. 'You'd not be doing her a favour, sir. Nor them.' She waved at the rest of the team, ploughing through the mire of a murder case, with little energy to spare for a troubled colleague.

He nodded.

'I expect we'll have to work harder, sir,' Magnus said, spotting Batten's circuitous reminder that she wasn't pulling her weight. He's right, sod him, she told herself, and got down to it.

But tonight, said her silent voice, there'll be no more postponements. Mike Brean and I will have a serious discussion. About condoms, an abortion, and the real reason 'Lish' returned to East Thorne.

And afterwards, either Nina will stay over, or Detective Constable Magnus will leave.

While his team got stuck in, Batten drove through late morning brightness to the fringes of the Blackdown Hills. Even without satnav, he couldn't fail to spot Dabinett School for Girls in the distance, perched on a bare hill, as if for safety.

Alicia Heron's alma mater was a stern-looking building with turrets – perhaps to defend the maidenly virtues of the pupils. The staff, too, he mused, following a tweed-clad aide of indefinable years down a corridor lined with portraits of one gowned sage after another.

He paused to glance at the brush strokes of the most recent, before being escorted into a Victorian museum masquerading as an office, where the stern portrait in question stood up from her pristine desk to shake his hand, embossing her fingerprints into his palm with a nutcracker squeeze.

A crisply turned-out forty-something, Mrs Welford-Daniels filled the power zone of her office much as her portrait filled the ornate frame on the corridor wall.

She waved Batten to a hard chair - more used to the tight bottoms of intransigent pupils, he imagined - before sliding herself onto a much softer seat behind a desk you could land an aircraft on. An antique silver inkwell glinted like a sunlit mountain amid an entire army of knick-knacks - all laid out in a tight grid formation.

The only out of place object in the entire room was Batten.

Mrs Welford-Daniels settled ten elegant fingers on the armrests of her chair, before easing them onto her desk as if it was a banquet table, and pudding was about to be served. Batten had met her type before. In the absence of a knife and fork, she'd struggle to eat a banana.

Her steely antennae picked up his non-deferential cast of mind, and she sprayed her forty-something eyes across him, as if smoothing his rusty rough edges in one easy, lubricated movement. He flashed his own eyes back. It may be rust, they said, but it's *my* rust.

Silently, he renamed her Mrs W-D40.

'Ella - my aide - has furnished the information you requested, Inspector.' Her fingers flicked at the corridor and wafted a thin sheet of paper towards him.

Batten read it in seconds - dates, subjects, exams. Not much of a resurrection.

'Concise', he said.

'A virtue, Inspector. Here.'

'Could you add a little colour, maybe?'

Mrs W-D40 had smoothly anticipated this.

'I have spoken to staff members, on your behalf. Alicia was in the Upper Sixth when I took over.'

She said, 'took over' as if it was a coup. Might have been, Batten thought.

'Their comments must of course be viewed anecdotally. You have the verifiable data.' Again she flounced a hand at the thin paper. 'It appears Alicia did not fully adhere to the school's ethos, nor manage her exit with quite the smooth formality of the rest of our girls.'

Batten's interest perked up.

'Expelled, was she?'

Mrs W-D40 baulked at this.

'We do not 'expel', Inspector,' she said, in a voice that could slice cheese. 'Coax, nurture, polish. Ex*tend*. But never ex*pel*. Alicia left...a little earlier than usual. She was something of a headstrong young lady. An only child, and given to outbursts. Her personal tutor described her to me as "a hot flame in a small frame." Telling, perhaps.'

'Telling what?'

She paused for several seconds, before remembering the subject in question was deceased and thus safe to discuss.

'Inadvisable liaison, Inspector.' She paused again, distaste colouring her face. It was the only thing that had managed to, so far. 'Inadvisable liaison, with inadvisable *males*.'

'Staff members?' asked Batten, aware he was over-stepping.

She gave him an armour-piercing glare. '*Village* members, Inspector. Despite extensive pastoral guidance, Alicia was prone to excessive...urges. And indulged herself. With the local village youth.' Mrs W-D40 said 'youth' as if it was a disease. 'Reluctant though I am to throw stones, I'm afraid to say 'youth' proved insufficient to Alicia. It seems she developed a taste for what modern magazines call *mature men.*'

'Seems?'

For the briefest moment, shadows of embarrassment clouded her porcelain face.

'There was...involvement...with a male almost twice her age. I'm told he was the landlord of The Blackdown Arms. In Raincliff.'

'Raincliff?'

'The next village. A sort of dormitory village, for...workers.' Mrs WD-40 fussed a Kleenex across her lips as if to soak up a bad taste.

'Told by whom?'

'By my predecessor, Inspector. She, poor woman, not me, was called into action. He, the landlord, also performed occasional duties here, at the school. He provided the bar for us, at our Annual Fete, for example. It - he - was rather too close to home. My predecessor rescinded his employment. And, in view of the moral obligations of the school, informed his wife.'

'Really? What was her response?'

'I was not present, Inspector,' Mrs Welford-Daniels reminded him tersely. 'I am *told* his wife turned purple with anger, while appearing unsurprised. The pair of them moved on shortly afterwards. Please do not ask me where. I have no idea, and no wish to have.'

'But do you recall their names?'

'My recall is excellent, Inspector. I may prefer to forget Alicia Heron, but where the well-being of the school is concerned, memory is my metier.'

Fed up of pulling teeth, Batten waited in silence with his eyebrows raised. After five seconds of ice, Mrs WD-40 emitted a low hiss. 'The landlord's name was Finn. Apparently known in Raincliff as *Flash Harry.*' Mrs W-D40 squeezed the two words past her cultured lips with distaste. 'Dear me, for one of our girls, a seventeen year old, to...*liaise* with such a creature, it beggars belief. His wife's name, I never knew.'

Batten knew though, surprised as he was. Cat. Cat Finn. And I'll be having a word with her, sharpish, he thought. And reacquaint myself with Harry Finn too. Because after the pair of them 'moved on' from Raincliff, they shipped up as landlords of The Rising Sun - in East Thorne, where Alicia Heron lived.

And died.

And where she and Harry Finn continued *liaising*, perhaps?

Batten's feet tingled.

'She was a free spirit, was she? Alicia?'

'Free? Goodness me, Inspector, the liaison was sordid enough in the first place. It was not further sullied by money changing hands.'

For a moment, Batten thought Mrs W-D40 was cracking a joke. Her un-cracked face said otherwise. Batten re-grouped.

'Whether free spirit or not, she managed to pass her A levels?'

'She passed because the school exceeded its educational expectations in her regard. I accept we may have fallen short on the pastoral side. Having coaxed her through her exams, her tutors naturally assumed she would stay on. Our brightest girls do. For Oxbridge entry. We have a long, successful tradition.'

Batten had walked through portraits of it, in the long, successful corridor outside.

'But she refused?'

'She rejected the offer of support, Inspector. Stubbornly. She applied to the University of Bath. For reasons of style, rather than scholarship, in my view. We failed to dissuade her. As, indeed, did her parents. Something of a wayward family altogether. You will have considerable difficulty corroborating these facts with her mother and father. Alicia had yet to begin her degree when they shook off the mortal coil.'

At least Mrs W-D40 was confirming something Batten knew. A fatal car crash, while scooting through Uganda on their 'self-discovery' trip. Alicia Heron was the one family member left alive to do the burying.

'So, at Bath she -?'

'Read Foreign Languages, Inspector, if memory serves. Does one 'read' such a subject? 'Speak', perhaps?'

With civilised reluctance, Mrs Welford-Daniels floated from her chair to an expensive-looking computer in the far corner of the office, an interloping new-technology-dunce, banished away from the tight traditions of the 'old' school. She glided onto another soft chair and clipped the 'on' key round the ear with a brisk finger, before punching several more. Batten was glad she wasn't punching him. The screen lit up and she perused.

'I was correct, Inspector. Human memory once more outdoes the machine, hmm? Yes, Modern Languages. And, typically, having studied Western tongues, she chose to move East...to Thailand, of all places.'

'Doing...?'

Mrs W-D40 peered at the screen with distaste. And at Batten too.

'Something unspecified, in the Thai fashion industry.'

'Did she re-visit the school? After university, I mean? I imagine your girls often do?'

'Alas, she chose *not* to. We would have recorded it. Nor did she return to England for her graduation - how sullen. She appears to have 'commuted' between England and Thailand, before her permanent move 'over there.' To work for emerging fashion houses, it says here. Before you ask, which ones is an unknown. I am merely telling you what my machine is telling me - it being the school's policy to record the career trajectories of our alumni. Even when their direction is dubious.'

She made to stand but glided her cultured bottom back into the chair.

'In the light of school policy, it may be apposite to insert Ms Heron's...well, to finalise her records.'

Mrs W-D40's fingers clenched above the keys like a pair of claw-hammers.

'Now. What did she die of?'

Twenty nine

From a hideaway amongst the thickets skirting Crown of Thorns Hill, high above the rooftops of Turks Lane, Biddy Holt counted slowly to ten, and ten, and ten.

Wait and wait, hide-and-seek, but not a soul. Instead, play hide-and-see.

Police lady gone, the black one. Not Mummy, because in Daddy's photo Mummy is white, always white. White like Easter, Kerry says. White like Biddy. Except for the red parts on Biddy's hands. And on her legs, sometimes, if she scratches. Mustn't scratch.

Biddy bored.

Go to church? Yes. To church.

All who go to church, Kerry says,

Shall

Be

Saved.

In a wooded clearing on the fringe of another hill, Ham Hill, the crowd gathering for the Easter Sunday Egg Hunt spilled over onto the track. More than one irate jogger was forced to skirt around the noise and confusion.

Clamours of children babbled, making almost as much noise as their vicarious mums and dads. Some youngsters impatiently jiggled the ears of their Easter bunny outfits. Others, dressed as chicks, their yellow onesies sporting improvised feathers and cardboard beaks, pulled at parental arms with impatience.

'Oh! *Ohhh*! Where's Katie?' cried a yummie-mummie.

'She's with Edward,' said her husband, fondling his hipster beard.

'Edward's *there*!' said the wife, pointing. 'Katie's not! I *knew* you'd let her wander off. Can't you manage a simple task? Kate! *Katie*!'

The hipster-dad peered through his Buddy Holly glasses. 'There she is!' he said, much-relieved.

With a scream that could curdle an un-laid egg, little Katie emerged from the trees, Easter bunny costume askew and a few desultory twigs embedded in her fake fur.

'Katie!' said her mother, fussing. 'Just look at you! Where have you been? Stop crying and tell me where you've *been*!'

'M-m-m-monster!' screamed Katie, pointing at the trees. 'Monster! *There*! In the woods!'

'There's no such thing as monsters, Katie. And certainly not in the woods. Just fabulous chocolate eggs to find. Don't you want a *fabulous* chocolate egg?'

'Monster! *There*! *Monster*!' screamed the girl, till hipster-dad wrapped her sobbing frame in his arms.

'*I'll* look after Katie', said the mother. 'You go and look in the woods.'

'There aren't any monsters in the woods,' whispered the father. 'Kate's being Kate, as usual.'

'Go and look anyway!' said his wife, dropping her voice. 'Pretend! And say all the monsters have gone.'

'You told her there's no such thing as monsters!'

'*Just do it*!' snapped mum, rolling her eyes and pulling twigs from Katie's costume.

'Come on, Edward,' said the hipster, and father and son loped into the trees in a futile search for ghouls. 'You pretend to look there, and I'll look down here.' He poked about where the undergrowth was thicker.

'Nothing, dad!' shouted Edward.

'Nothing here, either!' dad shouted in reply.

Nothing but a patch of ground, flatter than the rest. And a feeling. A feeling of being watched. But seeing nothing.

'You're getting as bad as Kate,' he mumbled to himself, and wandered back.

'All gone!' he told his tearful daughter, while giving Edward a nudge.

'Not a monster in sight,' said the boy.

Katie's sobs receded. 'But there *was* a monster,' she whispered to mum. 'There really *was*. In a mask. In a hood. I saw it. I *did*.'

'Course you did, Katie.' She pointed across the clearing at a new stir of excitement. 'But see, *see*, the Easter Sunday Egg Hunt - it's about to begin. Shall we hunt down a yummy chocolate egg, just for you?'

Katie nodded. Chocolate was scrumptious.

She'd seen it, though, the monster, behind the trees. In a hood, a mask. Watching.

Despite driving back from Dabinett School on empty roads, through a green-blue billow of woods and sky, Batten's journey was a blur.

Alicia Heron and Harry Finn zinged to and fro in his skull, joined at intervals by Cat Finn and Mike Brean, the four names spinning into a melee from which only questions emerged. He drove into East Thorne wondering how best to tackle Harry Finn and his 'purple with anger' wife, his mind made up for him when he spotted the unmistakeable bald figure of Reverend Kerry ease open the doors of The Rising Sun, and step through.

Parking in a side-road, Batten followed Kerry into the pub, lunch his excuse. Kerry sat at the end of the bar where 'the men' congregated, though alone today, a double-whisky in his hand as Batten sidled up.

'Inspector. You too have a second Headquarters. Welcome.'

Batten nodded in response to Kerry's raised glass, and at Debra, the barmaid. He ordered the known quantity of a ham sandwich and, after a moment's thought, a small whisky. It would do no harm to get into step with the tall clergyman, since both Cat Finn and Flash Harry were quick-stepping in and out of a packed restaurant, carrying plate after plate of Sunday roasts. As predicted, ghoulish media coverage had popularised the place.

With unusual patience, Batten turned his attention to the good Reverend Kerry. When the whisky arrived, he chinked Kerry's glass, sipped, and settled on a strategy.

'I need this,' Batten said. 'I've just been talked at, by Alicia Heron's old Headteacher.'

'Ah, you entered the hallowed grounds of Dabinett School for Girls, and escaped alive?' Kerry tapped himself lightly on the brow. 'Oh dear. A faux pas, under the circumstances. Forgive me.'

'Isn't forgiveness your department, Reverend?'

'Then I shall try to forgive myself.'

The two men sipped in silence, till Batten's sandwich arrived. 'Not eating, Reverend?' he asked.

'Taking in calories nonetheless,' Kerry replied, with a wave of his half-empty glass. 'And did she enlighten you? The Headteacher? As I recall, Alicia had little time for her ministrations.'

'Alicia talked to you about Mrs Welford-Daniels?' he asked.

Kerry gave Batten a sidelong look, a slight twinkle behind his pebble lenses. 'Not by name, as I recall. The school changed its staff more often than I change my socks. Teaching, humph. In these modern times, one thankless task after another. For the clergy, too. And the police, perhaps?'

'Well, you and I don't enjoy tasks like…this, do we?' Batten borrowed Sonia Welcome's illustrative finger-twirl, his hand pointing up at Crown of Thorns Hill.

'Poor, poor Alicia. I have prayed for her. With my entire soul, believe me.'

Lost in thought, Kerry downed the rest of his whisky. When Batten nodded to Debra, the glass was quickly re-filled.

'Too kind, Inspector. I shouldn't really, though my Easter Sunday duties are fulfilled for the day, liturgically speaking. This year's Easter service lacked the joy and glory common to the occasion, truth be told. Under the circumstances, we should drink to Alicia, perhaps?'

Again they touched glasses.

'When did you get to know her?' asked Batten.

'Oh, when the family moved here, I suppose. When Alicia was, what, sixteen, and a boarder at the hallowed school you escaped from. I knew her only in the vacations, of course.'

'And the parents?'

'Ah. They are another matter. Being here so little. You're aware of their explorations in Africa, I take it?'

Chewing a mouthful of sandwich, Batten allowed Kerry to fill the silence.

'At first, Alicia's parents flew home in the holidays. I overheard them, once, whining about the cost of flights. Then, when Alicia was seventeen, they telephoned to say their Land Rover had skidded into a ditch, and they were too bruised to travel. Well, it felt like a pack of lies. Her father, who wouldn't put ten seconds aside for religion, had the gall to telephone me. *Me*! Could I "keep an eye on Alicia, on this unfortunate occasion?" The occasion, Inspector, was Christmas.'

'And did you? Keep an eye?'

'Of course, insofar as Alicia wished me to.'

'How far would that be?'

A steely look flashed behind Kerry's glasses. 'A flock is a flock,

Inspector, and whatever rumour may say, I will do anything for mine. I still practise my vocation.'

We both do, Batten thought. I'm practising mine right now.

'Alicia helped me serve the lunch we provide each Christmas, for those who would otherwise spend Christmas Day alone. Never has irony felt so profound.'

'Did she get used to fending for herself?'

Kerry shrugged. 'Perhaps. Or pride prevented her admitting otherwise? She never admitted it to me, at least. Soon, the parents barely bothered returning at all. A few days after Alicia's eighteenth birthday, they were dead.' Kerry took a longer pull from his glass. 'I still have them on my conscience. You see, when their Land Rover *did* end up in the fatal mud of an African ditch, I struggled to mourn.'

'Under the circumstances, you can be forgiven.'

A sad chuckle croaked its way past Kerry's dog collar. 'You have definitely strayed into my professional domain now, Inspector.'

'Perhaps our two domains have something in common, Reverend. Isn't the Law a kind of salvation?'

Raising his glass in mock salute, Kerry smiled. 'To salvation, then.'

'Did Alicia talk about her parents?' Batten asked.

'Rarely. If she was angry, hurt, lost - or unforgiving - she did not unburden herself. She hardened. Yes, the absolutely correct word. Once university claimed her, the church ceased to be of interest.' Kerry glanced at the reflected light glinting on his whisky. 'And when I say, 'the church', I of course mean 'me'.'

Batten watched Kerry's dog-collar twitch as his prominent Adam's apple gulped sad thoughts back down his throat.

'Others in my broad flock may have mentioned my visits here, to The Rising Sun?'

Was Kerry referring to Leonard Tull, Batten wondered?

'Well, in her university vacations, Alicia and I might occasionally coincide at this bar, more or less where you and I are sitting now. But her interest in the spiritual had waned. Her focus was on the flesh. Of others, I mean.'

'Any particular 'flesh'? Of others?'

Kerry paused, to pat his ethics into shape.

'I'm prepared to confirm or deny any information you may have. But if you require me to kick rumour down the road like a tin can, I politely decline.'

'Harry Finn?' Batten asked it quietly, though both Cat and Harry Finn were a distant blur of plates and diners. From the expression on Kerry's face, Batten guessed he'd kicked an appropriate can.

'I know little of infatuation, Inspector. But, yes, there were signs of a...connection. Alicia didn't sit here because she wished to converse with *me*. Her focus was on the far side of the bar. The landlord side. Whether I approved or not...Perhaps in the absence of her parents she sought a father-figure? I am but a Reverend, you see, not a Father.'

A sad silence hovered.

'Mike Brean?' Batten asked.

'Ah. Dear Mike. Only natural, as a churchman I should have a soft spot for carpenters? Mike and Alicia were friends, yes, for a short time. She was much older. Five years, I think.'

'Six,' Batten said.

'Well. Just friends. Never the type of connection you perhaps have in mind.'

Batten left Kerry's thin slice of innocence untouched, knowing village rumour would destroy it, soon enough. Nina Magnus knew it too. He changed tack.

'Have you bumped into any of those Serenity Developments people? Any regular visitations from them, at the bar?'

His ethics challenged once more, Kerry cauterised the wound by draining his whisky.

'We are a divided community, where they are concerned. Some of our people gaze at the village horizon and see the beauty of orchards and hedgerows. Others see empty fields, ripe for new homes. Some are persuadable, some not.' Kerry read the silent question on Batten's face. 'Serenity Developments have never tempted my own flesh, perhaps because I relate to an ageing flock, in these modern times. New homes appeal more to the young, and the new. Nowadays, when the young and new enter the Church of All Saints, it is to admire the architecture.'

'But there have been 'visitations'?'

'Why would there not be? Investment carries risk, and I daresay

Serenity is no less risk-averse than other developers. For myself, I am able to enjoy the water of life with any stranger' - he clinked his empty glass against Batten's - 'while remaining what I am: not the finest example of a man of the cloth, but a man of the cloth all the same. Regardless of whose whisky I drink.'

A steely glint flashed from Kerry's eyes, for the briefest moment. Till his familiar face returned, red-veined and inscrutable. To emphasise his point he caught Debra's eye, dabbing his index fingers at Batten's glass and his own.

'Just for the Reverend, please,' Batten said.

When the golden glass was refilled, Batten waved away Kerry's wallet. 'Any particular strangers, where Serenity is concerned?'

Kerry sipped his whisky carefully before speaking. 'By profession, I am a flock-gatherer. So, inevitably, I notice new sheep when they stray into my fields.'

'New sheep? Or new wolves?'

'I am more comfortable discussing sheep, Inspector. Metaphorically apt. And a stray sheep or ram - with a cut-glass accent and a cut-glass suit - is an uncommon sight, here.' He pointed his glass at the nearby tables.

'But sheep and rams stray in, regardless?'

'A stop for a bite of lunch. A drink. A conversation struck up with the locals, eased by the bounty of a round or two. What's it like to live here? What would the village benefit from - if it had the cash to pay for it? Who are the movers and shakers? Who is in the know?'

'Subtle', said Batten, twirling the whisky in his glass, but not drinking.

'Subtle is as subtle does. Perhaps the police should interrogate suspects after tempting them with pints of cider. Give me the safer haven of whisky, any day.'

Batten wanted to say the police don't interrogate, they 'interview'. Then he wondered which he was doing right now.

'These stray sheep, did they return?'

'Some. Till other faces replaced them. Perhaps where large-scale development is concerned, the market-research departments are equally large. Perhaps a hoard of gossip-attuned inducers is despatched into the field, much as missionaries used to be?'

Were the missionaries from Serenity doling out more than pints of cider? Batten asked himself.

'You said your own flesh was never tempted? Whose was?'

Kerry rolled his whisky glass between his palms. 'Ah. You seek pure gossip now. Feel free to put your questions to Churchwarden Tull. He has skills in the art - honed by firing frequent arrows of tittle-tattle upwards to the Bishop. He may, or may not, unburden himself to you.'

At that, Kerry emptied his glass and placed it silently on the bar. 'Next time, Inspector, it will be my turn to pay. Should I temporarily forget, I trust the Lord will remind me.'

And he was gone, three double whiskies dulling his thoughts. Or quickening them?

Batten wasn't sure.

Crossing the road from The Rising Sun, a grubby-grey pick-up truck with a throaty exhaust almost ran Batten over.

'Accidental, I hope,' he thought, as another member of Kerry's flock steered the truck towards Turks Lane.

Andrew Holt's bony skull scanned left and right like a tennis umpire. 'Searching for Biddy,' Batten told himself. 'Who's searching for her mother. Who's somehow risen from the grave.'

Easter Sunday ironies in mind, Batten drove in silence to the Pathology Lab. To learn what Sonia Welcome had managed to resurrect from the stone-dead corpse of Alicia Heron.

Thirty

If Dr Welcome was annoyed at the disruption to her Easter weekend, she didn't show it. When Batten ducked into her neat office he was met by an attractive face, a soft handshake, *and* a coffee. The mere sight of her reminded him how much he missed Erin Kemp.

Which country was Erin visiting, in her new role as cheerleader for Somerset produce? Portugal or Spain, or both? To his shame, he'd forgotten. When he took in the attractions of Sonia Welcome, with no crime-scene suit obscuring them, his traitor-mind forgot Erin Kemp too.

'A welcome coffee', he said, not intending the pun.

Sonia Welcome had the grace to cover his gaffe with a smile, but he still felt like a schoolboy at a disco. Discos were 'clubs' these days, but *club* wasn't a word he warmed to, given what he did for a living. And given why he was here.

'My technician used to be a *barista*. He makes the coffee, not me.'

Batten nodded his appreciation. In the silence, he sensed she'd spotted him sizing her up.

'I assume you're not expecting a typed report, Inspector, on a holiday weekend. Some of your colleagues seem to think I wield a scalpel in one hand and a laptop in the other.'

Batten leaned forward expectantly, hands open. 'Verbal reports are fine by me.'

'You've come across contre-coup before, I imagine?'

'It's a TBI, isn't it?'

She nodded. 'I daresay Traumatic Brain Injuries are as much part of your job as they are of mine. Different perspectives, of course.'

'Boxers get contre-coup, don't they? From being punched?'

'They can, or not. But your victim was no boxer. Not even a bantamweight. In her case, contre-coup managed to bounce her brain from one end of her skull to the other. Double damage, if you like. First, at the site of the initial collision, the back of the head, and next to the frontal lobes when the brain shook. Fatal, in her case, poor love.'

'Let me get this right. A blow to the head - damage - then a sort of recoil, and more damage?'

'I prefer the term 'collision,' Inspector, because I found insufficient evidence to call it a *blow* - in the sense you mean.' Dr Welcome's smile only made it to her lips, this time. 'How convenient if I could say 'Colonel Mustard in the library with a candlestick'. But this is real-life.'

It was his turn to raise an eyebrow at the gaffe.

'Crass of me,' she said. 'Real-death. Let me clarify. I'm unable to swear your victim was deliberately hit, or if she suffered an accidental collision with an object or surface hard enough to take her life. If she was deliberately struck, the object in question was ubiquitously blunt. Not a candlestick, claw-hammer, spade, machete or house-brick. No palpable marks, no significant tissue damage. *Not* an edged implement.'

'What, then? A baseball bat or something?' A much-used baseball bat, hidden in the boot of Chas Janner's car, was with Forensics.

'You will groan at my reply. A case of definite, possible, or unlikely.'

Batten duly groaned. This time her smile was fuller. She sipped her coffee. Batten took a wary swig of his.

'First of all, the possible. Because, regardless of the severity of internal damage, there *is* external bruising. But was it from a fall, a collision, or a blow? All three remain in the equation, I'm afraid. And you can guess how easily Alicia Heron might tip - or be tipped - from vertical to horizontal. She weighed in at a smidgeon over 99 pounds. Enviably non-obese.' She spotted Batten's brow trying to do the sums. 'Seven stone one. Or 44.9 kilograms, if you voted Remain.'

'Thanks. But I could use a definite,' he said.

Another smile. Despite the evasions, Batten was pleased not to be sitting opposite Doc Danvers, with his protective veneer of riddles and irony. Sonia Welcome was a more pleasurable sight, though the long silver earrings dangling from her delicate lobes came as a surprise. He hoped she took them off before she...

'Let me first dispense with the less likely? If a baseball bat, it was not used with sufficient force to do palpable external damage to the skull, other than bruising. Also, no trace remained of paint, wood, metal, varnish etcetera in the bruised area.'

'No trace remained? But at some point, there *was* trace? So a baseball bat *could* have been used?'

'Ah, we are back to possibles, I'm afraid. But this particular possible needs to be qualified by the one strong 'definite'. You see, if traces existed, they may have been removed. Because the body was definitely washed.'

'*Washed?*'

'Yes. With water, but not with soap, detergent or bleach. We analysed the deposits on the skin. And when I say 'washed', in fact I mean almost totally immersed, prior to an unknown hand yoking the body to a crucifix.'

She sipped her coffee, letting the information sink in.

Immersed? In soap-free water? How? Batten recalled his journey to and from the houses in Turks Lane, through the rear gardens and along hidden tracks to Crown of Thorns Hill. Despite his hatred of lists, he compiled one - possible water-holes.

Four houses. Four bathrooms, at least? One bath, one shower in each? He cursed. They'd have to scour every bloody pipe and drain.

A cruddy stream, in the ditch behind each house. He didn't envy the poor sods who'd have to scour *that*.

Higher up, in undergrowth, a spring, feeding a brook, which trickled into the stream below.

Was brook or stream deep enough to immerse a seven stone corpse? Perhaps where the dam of a fallen tree had caused a pool to form?

He blew out his breath at his own log-jam of work.

'These deposits on the skin, from immersion? Likely to be domestic?' Salts could tell a tale, he knew.

'Mr Connor is re-testing, but he thinks *not* a household water-source.'

'So an *outdoor* source?' Crossing his fingers, Batten thought of the time they'd save.

'*Probably* an outdoor source. The significance is beyond my purview.'

It wasn't beyond Batten's.

'Someone tried to wash away blood traces – is that what you're saying? But cocked it up?'

Sonia Welcome offered a sympathetic smile. 'This is why I prefer written reports. Categories in sequence. Itemised findings. Logic and limitations. By contrast, the spoken word is *Teflon*, isn't it?'

'All the same...'

'*Possibly* is the best I can do. Immersion may have removed...whatever it removed. I can only comment on what remains. You spotted the minimal blood traces yourself, if I recall?'

He nodded. A skull job, he'd guessed.

'A further definite is the blood belonged to the victim. No evidence of an assailant's blood. None.'

'That's definitely definite,' he said, 'but less useful.'

'Which also describes the speck of red found beneath the victim's shorn thumbnail. Mr Connor agrees: chilli sauce.'

'Cuh,' said Batten. Airline food, maybe, on the flight from Bangkok? One more thing to check.

Sonia Welcome paused to sip her coffee, and change her tone.

'In addition to definite and useful, I'm afraid *distasteful* makes an appearance. You see, in contre-coup, internal bleeding is a factor. The body may not bleed, but the brain does.'

Batten failed to hear Sonia Welcome's new tone, still wondering why a killer would go to the considerable trouble of immersing a corpse, yet fail to remove all the blood.

'Couldn't Alicia Heron have simply taken a shower,' he asked, '*before* someone clobbered her?'

'More *Teflon*, Inspector. If she showered, how did she avoid both domestic water and soap?'

'And all this post-mortem?'

Sonia Welcome shook her head, her smile gone. 'You touch on a further area of uncertainty. On the *distasteful*.'

Batten's penny took longer to drop than it should have.

'What? She was *alive*? Some bastard washed her, and hung her, *alive*, on a cross?'

'I'm afraid it's a possibility. The nature of a fatal contre-coup is that death need not be instantaneous.'

'But might look like it? To an untrained eye?'

'It might. Even this trained eye can fix time of death only *between* 8 and 11pm. Given how long the body was outdoors, and given its...circumstances.'

Batten cursed murder, religion and - right now - pathology. His face must have shown it, because she waggled the coffee pot. When he declined, she ploughed on.

'Some blood seeping from brain to ear may have been removed by washing, yes, but the traces you saw on the body were visible because it is highly probable they seeped out *after* she was washed. And after she was... I refuse to say crucified. Not because I'm religious - which I'm not - but because it would be inaccurate.'

She topped up her coffee. Batten pushed his aside, shamed now for enjoying its rich flavour. It took revenge, swirling and swilling in his gut.

Leaning forward, Sonia Welcome tried to sweeten the pill. 'I can say with some probability Alicia Heron was at the very least unconscious when...' She twirled a finger, the same gesture she'd made on Crown of Thorns Hill.

'If we're back to probabilities,' he said, face darker than his coffee, 'might she have survived - if some bastard had called an ambulance, instead of dunking her in water and...?'

He twirled a finger of his own, aping Sonia Welcome, but in anger now. She gave a tiny shake of her head.

'Impossible to prove, in a courtroom. Now, in my office? Perhaps 50-50. Given the damage to the brain, the strongest likelihood is that from the moment of collision she was...how can I put it? If not yet dead, then dead to the world, while journeying towards fatality?'

Batten's mind was a blur - brains bouncing, pin-ball style, his own amongst them, and blood seeping from a half-dead ear, and *someone*'s hands lifting a still-warm corpse and - somewhere - washing it, for reasons obscure.

And, at some point, adding a shirt-cum-loincloth, tied in place by the cold absurdity of a granny knot. He saw bright orange baler-twine, yards of it, securing dead or dying flesh to a heavy wooden cross, in misty darkness, with nothing but an old thorn-tree for solace.

Sonia Welcome's golden voice snapped him out of it.

'Her fingernails were removed with nail-clippers, rather than scissors. Not particularly sharp ones, either. If you discover the clippers in question, we should be able to match them to the cut marks. Something useful, I hope?'

Was it? Batten didn't know, his head still bouncing, in sympathy with the victim's. To deflect the image, he scanned his list of questions.

Do clipped fingernails suggest knowledge of forensics? For a bizarre moment, he imagined 'Prof' Connor, bored with other people's crime scenes, deciding to create his own.

Clipped fingernails as mementoes? Did the killer take clippings as a trophy? And preserve them somewhere, as potential evidence? *All you have to do, Zig, is find them.*

Why wash a body? To remove blood? Or something else?

Or as a ritual act, removing nothing at all?

He hissed out a sigh, his face a giant frown. The laboratory resurrection of Alicia Heron's body was teasing, not telling.

Sonia Welcome's blonde hair had fallen across her eyes. She flicked it away, her silver earrings glinting in the light of the desk lamp. Noticing Batten's cold coffee, and the look on his face, she said, 'something stronger?'

An invitation.

An attractive smile.

Somewhere within him, the desire to accept.

But no time.

And no heart, now, for such things.

Thirty one

For a man with hands like blocks of granite, Sergeant Ball still took pains to tap lightly on Batten's cubby-hole door. And to hover on the threshold, instead of dropping straight into the one spare chair, as he used to.

'I didn't want to say it at the briefing, sir, because I'm not easy with gossip. But it may well be relevant, so...'

Eyebrows up, Batten waited.

'It's about the Chief Planning Officer. At the Council.'

'I've got a note about him somewhere, haven't I? Isn't he on my list?'

'Yes, sir. His name's Pride. Thomas Pride.'

'That's him.' Batten waited again.

'His interventions, sir. That's the gist.'

'Interventions? What kind of 'interventions'?'

'Well. Favourable ones. On Serenity's behalf. I was reluctant to mention him before because, at the end of the day, he has targets to meet. Housing quotas, and the like. No surprise if he takes a view where house-building's concerned, I don't suppose.'

Batten appraised his 'new' Sergeant: ultra-careful, unhappy to stick his neck out without insurance. He wished the old Ball would return.

'But?'

'Well, there is a 'but'. He's a bit too pally with Serenity. And Joe Porrit, from our Parish Council - you've met him, straight as a die - he has his suspicions. One of Joe's mates is on the ground staff at Willoughby Park golf club, and it seems Mal Muir and Thomas Pride play a fair few rounds together.'

'Half the business deals in England are fleshed out on a golf course, Ballie. Or over a glass of nectar in the nineteenth hole. Networking's not a crime.'

'I know, I know, sir. But according to Joe's mate it was Muir who put Pride up for membership. Rumour is, he got it free. And still does. And, not long after, he turned up with a brand-new set of clubs, and a brand-new trolley.'

'Even so.'

'And a brand-new Mercedes estate, sir?'

Batten sat up. 'Are you suggesting Serenity's paying?'

'I'm suggesting the possibility.'

'But Pride must've declared all this? He's a public servant.'

'It's not in any register I could find. Though the contribution Serenity paid into the Council's Community Fund *was* made public, when our Stockton Marsh orchard was under threat.' Ball let this snippet sink in.

'Contribution? Talk numbers, Ballie.'

'£100,000, sir.'

'Oof. Presumably it was given back? Since you and your bolshie cider-pals refused to sell the orchard to Serenity?'

'It wasn't given back, sir. It stayed in the pot. For goodwill, maybe? Or for next time? Or because it really *would* have looked like a bribe, if Serenity had asked for its return.'

'Mm. And used for what?'

'Discretionary, sir. Tree-planting? Traffic calming? Playgrounds?'

'Not sure I see the problem, then.'

'There might not be one. Except, Serenity paid another £100,000 'contribution' into the Community Fund, two weeks ago. And the only large-scale housing development currently awaiting full planning is...'

'East Thorne?'

Ball's ginger head nodded. 'I'm only raising it because, at Stockton Marsh, Thomas Pride made one or two, well, *particular* interventions, if you get my drift. He didn't sound overly neutral, when he stood up at the public meetings.'

'But you said it yourself, Ballie. He's under pressure. Building houses is part of his job. Nobody's building enough. And Government quotas aren't optional.'

'Ways and means, sir. You had to be there, at those meetings. The bias was pretty brazen. It's not just the controversy over Section 106. Of the Town and Country Planning Act - a dog's breakfast of legislation, well-intended or not. But some of these big developers, they've got consultants swarming round like flies on a dead sheep. To put pressure on Councils to say 'yes', they pay top whack for these so-called 'viability reports', wrapped in barbed wire and written in smoke - but no Council has the staff or time to unpick the rigmarole.'

Threats to his own village orchard still fresh in his mind, Ball had dismounted from CID and climbed on his civilian hobby-horse.

'Sorry, sir,' he muttered. 'Got carried away.'

Batten was glad to have his Sergeant back, but within limits. 'After we solve this murder, Ballie, maybe you can re-educate me about Section whatever-it-is of the Something Act, yes? I'll even buy you a pint of cider, to go with it.'

Despite the mention of cider, Ball hovered.

'Ballie. If you're suggesting Thomas Pride is corrupt, bring evidence. Even then, this is Fraud, not us. If Pride's politics offend you, vote for the other side next time. OK?'

'Yes, sir, but you see, I was wondering. What if *you* talked to him? Pride knows me, from Stockton Marsh, and he'll not be well-disposed, since we blocked the development he was pushing for. And left him with a hundred grand's worth of egg on his face.'

'Why should he be well-disposed to *me*?'

'No, what I was thinking is, you can be...you can be a bit *direct*, sometimes, with witnesses? Direct to order, I mean? A chat with Pride, you might shake the tree, see what drops?'

Batten stared at his Sergeant, 'new' in approach, but drawing shamelessly on old knowledge.

'He'll not be around just now, Ballie. The whole world's on holiday - apart from us.'

'No, no, sir. Pride isn't. There's a budget crisis, at the Council, see, and most of them are in tomorrow, holidays or not, for emergency meetings. Deciding what services to cut.'

'And me questioning him while he's stressed out by a crisis...'

'...Might loosen the tree a tad more, sir, yes.' Ball cracked his knuckles. 'I'm glad we're seeing eye-to-eye.'

'Stop your knuckles firing gunshots, Ballie, and I'll think about it. No promises. Tomorrow, maybe. Shut the door after you, OK?'

Watching his Sergeant's broad back depart, Batten allowed himself a wry smile. 'Crystal' Ball could still see into him. Serenity Developments warranted close inspection. Might the Council's Chief Planning Officer be the magnifying glass?

He picked up the phone and, with tomorrow in mind, left a deliberately vague message for Thomas Pride.

Then burrowed back into the paper mountain.

Door-to-door statement summaries covered Batten's desk like a pile of cold spaghetti, beige, sauce-free. He was almost glad when DC Hick rattled the cubby-hole glass.

'Sir. *Sir!*'

'It's not time for your tranquilliser, Eddie. Go away.'

'No, sir. There's trouble, sir. East Thorne.'

'Batten groaned. 'Says who?'

'Says Jess Foreman. There's some sort of demo going. Those 'Save Our Orchard' lot, and that ETOPS bloke.'

'Ken Leckey?'

'Him, sir. Jess says there must be three hundred of the buggers, and they're not all locals. Rent-a-crowd, he says.'

The reason Ken Leckey went to Gloucester? Batten wondered.

'We'll have to do something, sir. There's three hundred bolshies yelling in the street by All Saints Church. Because the TV cameras are there, Jess says. That stone-faced Churchwarden, he's given Jess an earful, and now he's in a stand-off with the demo people. The media's loving it. Could turn nasty.'

'Does Sergeant Ball know?' asked Batten, pushing aside the paper-spaghetti.

'He's by your car, sir. Waiting.'

Surprised once more by Hick's efficiency, Batten grabbed his jacket and reluctantly headed for the car-park.

First a desecrated Good Friday. Now, a loud demo amid the peace and restoration of Easter Sunday. He couldn't blame All Saints Church for complaining.

He just wished they'd complained to someone else.

East Thorne's main street was swamped by Viking invaders. Bristling beards and broad shoulders marched backwards and forwards as one, the Perpendicular Gothic of All Saints Church a cynically-chosen background.

'Save Our Orchards' placards jabbed from the phalanx like a shield-wall. If not for the modern dress, it could have been a scene from *Game of Thrones*.

'*ESS-OH-OH!*' chanted the crowd in shrill unison.

'*ESS-OH-OH!*'

'ESS-OH-OH!'

PC Foreman wasn't lying. Protesters were here in their hundreds, a deafening, well-coordinated mass, gleefully filling journalist note-books and TV cameras alike. News at Ten will get value for money tonight, thought Batten. Had Ken Leckey deliberately taken advantage of a news-light Easter Sunday? And because he knew the media would be camped in East Thorne?

Turning to ask his Sergeant, Batten confronted a silent Buddha, awkward neutrality plastered on his face. As a leading member of his own village's Orchard Trust, Ball sat in the passenger seat, impassive.

Batten had barely stepped from his car when Leonard Tull marched across the road towards him. The Churchwarden's presence was no surprise, but where was Reverend Kerry?

'Inspector! I trust you have come to-'

'ESS-OH-OH!'

'ESS-OH-OH!'

'ESS-OH-OH!'

'Get *in*!' shouted Batten to Tull above the noise, and the two men clambered into the back of the Ford Focus, doors closed, windows up.

'Horrified, Inspector. *I am horrified*!' Despite the noise outside, Tull's voice was twice as loud as it needed to be. 'I trust you have come to *arrest* these *hooligans*?'

'I may or may not disapprove of their choice of place and time, Mr Tull, but I can't arrest them for exercising their right to free speech. Assuming they stay within the bounds of legality.'

'Legality? You call this *legal*?'

'Not me personally, sir. I was referring, for starters, to Article 11 of the Human Rights Act. I'd be pushed to argue the crowd is restricting the church's rights and freedoms, despite the noise. They may be near the church, but they're not *in* it. And there's no religious or blasphemous element to their demonstration – unless I'm missing something?'

'But it is Easter *Sunday*! Have they no shame? You must at least be able to move them elsewhere? Back to where *some* of them came from – which isn't East Thorne! I am formally requesting you move them, on behalf of All Saints Church.'

'Is that the request of Reverend Kerry too, sir?'

Tull curled his lips into a sneer. 'The good Reverend Kerry is sleeping through the entire episode.' With that, he humphed from the car, slamming the door behind him.

Batten wondered if Kerry had wind of Leckey's plans in advance and swallowed a few lunchtime whiskies to neutralise himself. He climbed out, and Ball reluctantly followed. As soon as their feet touched the ground, the rent-a-crowd chants swelled to a crescendo.

'ESS-OH-OH!'

'ESS-OH-OH!'

'ESS-OH-OH!'

'I'll do my best to quieten them down, sir,' Batten shouted to Tull, above the din. 'But they're not blocking traffic or trespassing on private property, so please don't expect a miracle.'

Tull sneered again, perhaps at 'miracle'. Through gritted teeth, Batten hummed The Kinks' song about village green preservation societies, before clumping across the road towards Ken Leckey.

The Chair of the East Thorne Orchard Preservation Society was a cat with the cream. Batten remembered their previous encounter, at Leckey's cottage in Turks Lane. He'd never seen a middle-aged man so thin but so full of apples, health and fresh air. Today, surrounded by a swarm of muscled protesters, Leckey seemed to have put on weight.

Batten opened his mouth to speak.

'ESS-OH-OH!'

Raising a polite hand to quieten the chanting crowd had no effect. 'I've got the message, Mr Leckey,' Batten shouted. But the chants increased.

'ESS-OH-OH!'

'ESS-OH-OH!'

'Do excuse them, Inspector,' Leckey shouted back. 'They've rather lost their faith in the law. Would you like me to turn down the volume?' He said it with a dollop of the smugs.

Batten gave in with a nod, and a single flick of Leckey's hand returned the street to silence. The same hand flicked at the nearest banner.

'S.O.O, Inspector. Our crusade.'

'*SAVE OUR ORCHARD!*' was block-lettered onto dozens of placards, emblazoned on T-shirts, scrawled onto hand-made canvas banners strung on railings, trees and one parked car after another. The TV cameras were lapping it up.

'I think I got the point some time ago, Mr Leckey,' was all Batten could manage. He nodded at the cameras. 'I think they did too. But isn't it time to move things along, for decency's sake?'

'Decency? *Decency?* What's decent about the destruction of an orchard, or the demolition of dwellings centuries-old? And all so the bigwigs can inflate the dividends of their shareholders - who wouldn't know an orchard if it clubbed them on the back of the head!'

'Mr Leckey-'

'You'll do all you can to block *us,* and allow *them,* I suppose? Because they wear expensive suits and silk ties? Apples and democracy - who cares? Rural destruction and corporate greed - provide a police escort!'

'Let me tell you my position, Mr Leckey. Crime is crime. Whoever commits it. And I'll politely ask you to remember.'

'Well, Inspector, demonstrate, and I might.'

'You appear to be the one doing the demonstration, sir.'

When Batten pointed to the mass of bodies and placards, the deafening chants screamed out again, a cacophony now.

'ESS-OH-OH!'

'ESS-OH-OH!'

'ESS-OH-OH!'

Leonard Tull's thin patience snapped. He wrenched a placard from its owner's grip and was about to brain the nearest demonstrator when the sausage fingers of Sergeant Ball clamped onto it.

'Now, now,' said Ball, pointing discreetly at the cameras. 'A Churchwarden doesn't want to appear on the news demonstrating violence, does he, sir? Think of the embarrassment if we were obliged to arrest *you.*'

Tull leaned down towards Ball and hissed, 'in which case, *you* do something!'

'Leave it to the police, sir. Not a request, by the way.'

With that, Ball strode past the chanting phalanx of placards towards Ken Leckey, drawing him away from Batten into the relative quiet of the churchyard. After a brief exchange, Leckey strode back to his supporters - and the cameras - to announce they would march to Turks Lane, placards, banners and all, where the beloved orchard awaited them.

To Batten's amazement, they formed up and moved off in seconds, *ESS-OH-OH!* diminishing by degrees as they marched away. Leonard Tull folded his arms, but neglected to thank Sergeant Ball.

'How'd you manage that, Ballie?' asked Batten, when the noise levelled out.

'Well, sir, what with the light starting to go, I thought I'd remind Ken Leckey the cameras would soon stop rolling, and it'd be a shame if Turks Lane orchard didn't make it onto the evening news. He seemed to agree. And the TV crews were pleased as punch to follow.'

Batten could only smile at more of the old Sergeant Ball seeping through.

'Shall I drive us back to Parminster, sir? To get on with our proper job?'

'Our proper job's in East Thorne, Ballie, right now. You tag along behind Mr Leckey, and keep an eye. A bit of judicious questioning, if the opportunity arrives? He's a schemer, for sure.'

'Not expecting me to walk back to Parminster, are you, sir?'

'I'll meet you here. Half an hour. Or I'll be in The Rising Sun. Doing my proper job.'

As Batten and Ball went their separate ways, a hooded figure, concealed in deep undergrowth on the fringe of Crown of Thorns Hill, also 'kept an eye' on Ken Leckey. Through binoculars, the figure watched the swarm of protesters march away, placards jabbing skywards, before turning the glasses on the two detectives. When Ball strode off in Leckey's wake, the hooded figure ghosted off.

Too many police in East Thorne right now. But thin on the rural ground elsewhere.

Another place, another day.

Thirty two

Villagers, media and rent-a-crowd had swarmed off to celebrate an orchard, leaving peace to descend on The Rising Sun. Cat and Harry Finn would be hard-pressed to block more questions by pleading 'too busy'.

When Batten stepped through the doors, Harry Finn was nowhere to be seen. Mrs Finn was, but after one look at Batten she grabbed a duster and zipped it up and down the nearest brass beer-pump as if it was a magic lamp.

Last time Batten pushed through the doors of The Rising Sun, Cat Finn had turned purple and disappeared in a puff of smoke. Batten's face told her it wouldn't work this time. The pub was three-quarters empty.

'Somewhere quiet?' he asked.

She semaphored to Debra, the over-friendly barmaid, who semaphored back. The exchange reminded Batten of Reverend Kerry and Biddy Holt. He followed Mrs Finn into a cramped, pitch-black store room smelling of stale beer. The room's ambience wasn't improved when she punched a light switch by the door. In the absence of anything else, they squatted on a pair of upturned beer crates, she with her arms folded so high and tight across her chest she looked like a reluctant Cossack dancer.

'I know you're busy, Mrs Finn. You know what I need to ask. So, can we cut to the chase?'

She managed one word. 'Harry?'

'Harry, yes. And Alicia Heron.'

'Huh. Just her?'

'Yes, just her.'

'Won't take long then. I thought it'd be the rest of his women too. I mean, you're a policeman. You'll have dug up the rumours. They don't call him Flash Harry for nothing.'

'In truth, Mrs Finn, the rumours were unavoidable. I prefer facts, though.'

'Well, note-book and pencil out, and write quick. Fact Number One: Harry screwed everything in a skirt, everything willing, I mean, soon as we moved to Somerset. We had a country pub in Raincliff, in the

Blackdown Hills, before we came here. *Harry* said the countryside bored the pants off him - literally. Some excuse, eh?'

'Fact Number Two?'

'Fact Number Two: Alicia Heron was one of the skirts. The last one, as it happens.'

'The last one? Why?'

'Why? Because of Fact Number Three. Me putting a stop to it!'

Batten didn't think Cat Finn could fold her arms any tighter, but she did.

'You mean you warned her off?'

'I warned *all* of them off. With mixed success. Warning *Harry*, that's what worked. If I hadn't switched *him* off, you'd be talking to an empty room. I'd be grazing in pastures new.'

'Would I be jumping the gun if I said Mr Finn strikes me as a man whose switch is, well, more *on* than off?'

For the first time, Cat Finn produced something close to a smile. 'Harry's switch is always 'on', true enough,' she said. 'Has its advantages, in a marriage. But Fact Number Four is he used to switch it on *outside* our marriage too - and for that Heron trollop in particular. She used to drink in our pub at Raincliff, her and those girls from some posh school near there. Liked to mingle with a bit of rough, I expect. Underage, more than likely. Arrest me, why don't you, for serving them.'

'Maybe later.'

Mrs Finn almost smiled again.

'Could've knocked me over with a bar-cloth when we moved to East Thorne, and I find the little trollop actually *lives* here! She'd better not be why we moved, I told Harry. I've got limits, and I told him that too.'

'Was it? She, I mean. The reason Harry moved here?'

'Not even Harry has that much nerve. My stinking luck, that's all. The other trollops, well, I could grit my teeth and tolerate them. But her? Wasn't just her cheek-bones. Young, with it. Fifteen bloody years too young. And a Harry-magnet. We'd only been here a fortnight and he's dropped his pants for her *again*.'

'I thought you'd switched him off?'

'For *them*, yes. I make sure he's always switched on for *me* - and only for me. *Now*.'

'Now?'

'Fact Number whatever-it-is - and it might make you blush. Harry got a final warning, one hot night. He tried to make it up to me. In bed. It's Harry's way. I knew he would. So, I'd popped a kitchen knife in my bedside drawer. A nice sharp one, too. We're in the throes and I fumble for it. Harry thinks I'm fumbling for a toy. You're a man of the world, I expect. You know how it is.'

Batten didn't, but his false nod must have been convincing, because Cat Finn kept talking.

'As soon as he feels the cold steel against his organ-pipe, he turns into an Eskimo, despite the heat, and when I press a bit harder, well.'

Threatening behaviour, thought Batten. Or tried to, his head cringing with alternatives.

'What Harry didn't see - what with him being, you know, distracted - was I'd turned the kitchen knife around. It was the blunt side, the cold steel back, that's what he could feel. But it did its job. I told him, there'll be one 'skirt' and one skirt only in our life from now on. *Mine*. I didn't ask his opinion. Take it or leave it, I said. Or I might have said take it or *lose* it? I forget.'

'But Harry didn't forget?'

'Not once. Not in all those ten years since *she* buggered off.'

'Eleven years,' Batten said.

'Whatever. Ten or eleven, Harry's been good as gold. If he hadn't, he'd be walking funny, and he's not. I think you get my drift.'

Your drift is crystal clear, Batten thought. *Don't mess with me*, it said, *I have knives*. Trying not to squirm on his groin-crushing beer-crate, he changed tactics.

'Alicia Heron still drank here, though?'

'We run a pub. In case you hadn't noticed. No choice but to serve her.'

'And chat?'

'Bar talk.'

'Harry talk?'

Cat Finn gave Batten a stare. When he stared back, she knew he'd keep asking.

'I told you. I warned all of them - her in particular. *Once*.'

'Once?'

'Only needed to be once. If Harry told her I meant business, or if she picked up the gist from 'the other skirts', I wouldn't know.'

Another stare, harder. This lady can take care of herself, Batten thought.

'And is there a when and a where?'

'Isn't there always? Not long before she buggered off to Thailand. And good riddance. I thought it was ten years ago, but you say eleven. We had a brief, private chat.' Cat Finn unfolded an arm and stabbed a finger at Batten's beer-crate. 'She sat there, as a matter of fact. Didn't take long.'

'You got your point across?'

'Put it this way, she left a full glass on the bar. And she'd paid for it.'

'She ever come back? Before Thailand, I mean?'

'We run a *pub*, Inspector.'

'So Harry would have served her, too? Spoken to her?'

'Bar talk *only*. 'Ice and a slice, Alicia?"

'Not 'Lish'?

'*No*. Not after his warning. Harry's not stupid. He's got eyes. He can spot when a kitchen knife's missing from the rack. I told you, if he hadn't behaved himself, he'd be walking funny. And he's not.'

'What about after she left? Any long-distance contact?'

Cat Finn reverted to her earlier mode. Mouth tight. Eyeballs like lances.

'No *need*. As I said, she got my message, loud and clear.'

'I meant Harry. Did he have any further contact with Alicia?'

'Why would he *dare*?' Mrs Finn's arms unfurled, as if searching for a weapon. Batten could almost feel a kitchen knife slicing through his nether regions.

'I'm just doing my job, Mrs Finn, thoroughly as I can. *Was* there any contact, afterwards? I'm sorry to ask this, but, for example, did any money change hands?'

'Money? For *what*?'

She held his gaze, he hers. Before, her eyes had screamed self-assurance. Now, they were pools of confusion. If Harry Finn paid for Lish Heron's abortion, perhaps he forgot to tell his wife.

The wife in question rose so briskly from her beer-crate it tumbled over with a thud. She ignored the noise - and ignored Batten too. But did he detect a glimmer of awareness in her eyes?

'I've a pub to run,' she said, and whacked the door open, anger in her fist. 'Switch the light off when you leave.'

Her tight back disappeared, and Batten was left squatting awkwardly in the grubby store room with only the smell of stale beer - and Cat Finn's version of how she'd dealt with Alicia Heron, all those years ago.

Was he burrowing down a rabbit hole where his other suspects were concerned?

Was the explanation simpler? Did Cat Finn renew acquaintance with Alicia Heron after an eleven year gap she'd assumed was permanent? Or did Harry do the 'renewing'?

And did one of them ensure permanence, once and for all, when 'Lish' made her unexpected return?

Once the late afternoon light began to fade, the TV crews climbed into their Outside Broadcast vans and drove away from East Thorne.

Ken Leckey had thanked rent-a-crowd and sent them off. He was now giving press interviews, gesticulating at the white-speckled orchard while leaning casually against the porch of his Turks Lane cottage, with its carved, tree-shaped 'Number 1' above the door.

Sergeant Ball watched from distance. Leckey enjoys being number one, he thought. Because he has a one-sided view of the world? Ball wasn't sure. And when he took in the pleasurable dots of apple-blossom, a one-eyed view of the world invaded him too.

He tried to remove it with a shake of his head, gave up, and trudged back to Batten's car.

Neither Batten nor Ball knew video clips of the East Thorne demo were currently trending on social media. Mobile phones were busy, and 'hashtag S.O.O.' seemed more than a last-minute invention - not least to Mal Muir.

His Easter Sunday was less than serene, as he - and a considerable Twitter audience - viewed the sylvan charms of one threatened apple-tree after another. Muir's lips tightened as placard after placard on stick after stick shouted 'Save Our Orchard!' Whoever uploaded the videos made damn sure to include plenty of shots of the 'Turks Lane' and 'East Thorne' street signs. When Muir turned on the sound, angry chants of mass protest vibrated against the walls of his silent house.

No sooner had he closed the phone than his second phone rang, the private one.

Richard Pardew's over-jolly voice and familiar coded language, chirped at Muir's ear.

'Mal, I trust you're hale and hearty, despite a *frisson* or two on Twitter?'

Muir's grunt was Pardew's answer.

'Now, Mal, the fund we discussed - the *significant* fund in your portfolio? Urgent attention required, I'm afraid. You know how these funds work - strike soon and sudden, before the opportunity departs? Why don't we meet for an early dinner, mm, in view of the urgency? Your golf club, still serves a decent plate of food...?'

When the waiter slid dishes of salmon and avocado onto their private table and toddled off, the two men resumed their coded exchange. Pardew's summary was no less alarming for its journey through shell-company safety zones.

'I just don't understand these types, Mal. For no reason at all, they forget to follow instructions. Or make up their own. I've frozen all the relevants, but where the pesky beggar has absconded to, well, ask the man in the moon. Vanished. Not answering his phone, not picking up messages. Even sent a trusted aid for a gander, hoping to juice the beggar up, but there's a distinct absence of presence. Your chap is in the wind. Or *somewhere*. A concern, without doubt. Action required, I'd say.'

'We are talking about the same fund?' asked Muir.

Pardew handed Muir a slip of paper. No need for either man to say the name out loud. Safety first.

'Yes, this one, Mal.'

Two names were written there: the name of the 'fund', and the name of the 'handler' - Ryan Brand. Pardew's shady team of handlers were recruited from specialist backgrounds, and controlled through a web of shell companies. Muir never met a handler face to face. Deniability was a sound precaution. He tried to remember Brand's file. Thick-set? Dark-hair and beard? A walking gym-membership? Londoner? That was him. Ex-Mercenary, too, and not one to mess with. Wasn't he the one who'd had a warning? For drugs? Hell's teeth, if he's *on* something and gone rogue...

'What's his specialism?'

Pardew thought of himself as a 'progress-chaser', and each 'handler' as a plumber with specialist skills - useful for unblocking certain drains.

'Oh, you know, Mal.' Pardew dropped his voice. 'Able to 'invest' himself, unseen, past a locked door, with or without keys? Military background in 'concealment and surprise'. Inhabits the more robust end of the spectrum. Compared to some.'

The forkful of salmon in Muir's mouth tasted slimy and coarse. Busy connecting dots, he almost forgot to swallow it.

'You've suspended the account, you say?'

'Oh, yes. We'll keep our lawyer friend on the payroll, as a precaution, but otherwise - a touch of dry-cleaning. Once we track down the absconder.'

'These rogue traders can do damage, Richard. Bad for your reputation, I would have thought.'

'True, Mal. And possibly for yours, should there be any...leakage.'

'And will there be?'

'That's not something we can know in advance, I regret to say. If you recall, a strong warning *was* issued, some months ago?'

'Seems it wasn't strong enough.' Muir leaned across the table. 'Seems this 'fund' is accruing the wrong kind of *interest*. Did one of us make an error of judgement, Richard?'

Brow crinkled, Pardew passed the buck with a shrug of his hands, and a casual untruth. 'My role is largely advisory, Mal.'

Muir tapped his fork against his lip. His temples throbbed. The salmon and avocado on his plate were as pale and green as he felt. Stabbing his fork at Richard, he dropped his voice to a hiss. 'At least assure me a...mediator is in place? For damage limitation?'

'Ye-es.'

'Well?'

'In this instance, the mediator has...limitations of his own. Is proving next-to-useless, I'm afraid.'

'Hell's teeth! Give me the details.'

Richard twiddled a finger at the slip of paper. 'On the back, Mal, for your convenience.'

Muir leaned towards the fading light spilling onto the table. Beyond the window, the golf course was disappearing, flag by flag, behind an incoming tide of darkness. He read the reverse side of the flimsy paper soon to go up in flames.

And winced.

The next-to-useless mediator was Lesley Willey. His attempts to 'induce' the residents of Turks Lane to sell had been underwhelming. His chances of curbing a rogue Ryan Brand were nil, or less. Marginally worse than *my* chances, thought Muir, if Brand has gone feral. He re-read the name of the 'fund'.

Turks Lane.

Mal Muir stabbed his fork into the greasy avocado, and crushed the piece of paper in his fist.

Thirty three

Back at Parminster, Ball and Batten swopped the outdoor smugs of Ken Leckey for the indoor pong of Chas Janner, who still looked as though the interview room had shrunk around him. Is Janner's beard twice as prickly as yesterday, Batten wondered, or am I just knackered?

'I keep saying *I don't know*,' said Janner, 'because *I don't know!*'

Janner refused to change his story. And refused a solicitor.

'*Why? I don't need defending from what I haven't done!*'

Ball glanced at Batten, who glanced back. They were close to believing Janner's tale. Or bits of it.

'Have you noticed, Mr Janner, how the significant elements of your case all begin with 'B'?' asked Batten.

'*What?*' said Janner? 'What are you on about?'

'Well, there's the blood, you see. The blood of the victim, in your hallway. Though you keep saying you *don't know* about that.'

'Because I *don't*! How many more times?'

'And then there's the baseball bat. The one in the boot of your car. Pity you don't have a BMW, instead of a clapped-out Renault.'

'Or a Bentley,' Ball chipped in.

'Yes, or a Buick. Or a Bugatti.'

Chas Janner groaned. He wanted to go home. But he didn't *have* a home.

'You don't look like a baseball player to me. What do you think, Sergeant? Does Mr Janner play baseball?'

'We should ask him, sir.'

'*Already told you I don't*! The bat's just *there*. I've got an old picnic blanket in the car too, but I don't do picnics!'

Batten nodded, but only at the picnics.

'Then of course there's the missing bluebird. On the missing blue rug. Which you say you spilt engine oil on. Even though there's not a trace of engine oil on the flagstones – not even in the cracks between them. Your cleaner must work miracles.'

'No, no, sir, if the cleaner - Andrew Holt, I mean - if he worked miracles he'd have got rid of the cannabis too. Which also has a B in it.'

'Thank you, Sergeant.' Batten paused. 'Anything else I've overlooked? Anything else beginning with 'B'?'

'Well, there's Inspector Batten and Sergeant Ball, sir. But I sense Mr Janner's a bit bemused by us. Because he's bored perhaps. And past his bedtime.'

It's past all our bedtimes, thought Batten. But no bugger's going home.

'Let's turn to your alibi, Mr Janner. Did you know alibi has a B in it...'

It wasn't far off midnight.

To stay within bounds, an insomniac duty solicitor was produced. He was as relieved as the police when Janner coughed.

Not to murder, though. Or crucifixion.

'I told you, I came back from The Rising Sun - and don't ask me again what time because I don't *know* - and there's this lippy cow standing in my hallway, rattling a bunch of keys. *Who the hell are you*? she says. *And what are you doing in my house?* I'd never seen her before in my life. She could've escaped from a loony bin, for all I know. And she might have been dressed like a classy bitch, but when it came to the F word she wasn't backward in coming forward.'

'Frightened you, did she? On account of her being a giant and you being so small? Don't make us laugh.'

'Half-a-pint she might have been, but she gave me a gallon of lip.'

'Which got under your skin, didn't it? So you introduced her to your baseball bat!'

'*No*! It was in the car! Just in the *car*. *She* was in my bloody *hallway*.'

'And after you'd tapped her on the back of the head with your bat, you rolled her up in a handy blue rug, with or without its bluebirds and herons, and strapped the corpse to a handy cross on Crown of Thorns Hill. You knew the cross was there. Because you'd just erected it!'

'*No!*'

'Did you know she might still have been alive? Or couldn't you care less?'

'I told you! Last time I saw her she was *plenty* alive. And going on about a bloody rug she and her bloody mother made. And threatening to change the locks. And telling me *don't come back, or else!* On and on and *on!*'

'Which is why you had to stop her? Had to shut her up?'

'I shut her up by *leaving*! Leaving my own house, with all my gear in it. I warned her, touch any of it and I *will* have you. You two know the law - so tell me who's in the right, eh? She can't touch my stuff - that'd be theft.'

'She didn't touch your stuff, Mr Janner. You made sure she couldn't!'

Chas Janner's face turned from red to purple. 'When I closed the door, she was in the hallway, fists on her hips and face like a gargoyle! And *upright!*'

Janner tried to be upright too. The insomniac solicitor eased him back down into his seat and asked for a recess. Feelings mixed, Batten switched off the tape.

The wall-clock ticked past midnight.

'Easter Monday, sir,' said Ball, plonking two more coffees on Batten's desk.

'What a relief. I was fed up of Easter Sunday. And who needs sleep?'

The two men yawned, in unison, without noticing.

'What d'you think, Ballie?'

Ball paused, but not from caution. 'Dunno, sir. Even with blood traces in the hallway, it's circumstantial. And all the witnesses are blind and deaf.'

Batten nodded. 'Got to admit my tingling feet have calmed down. But Janner's alibi's holier than All Saints church. Even if he left while the victim was alive, there's a distinct absence of why and where to. If he says 'a pub crawl in Yeovil' one more time I'll throttle him.'

'Thursday night, odds on he was dealing, sir. Cannabis keeps cropping up, and not just in my nostrils.'

'And Janner can't stump up an alibi, because his only witnesses were buying dope from the niffy sod? What about his lock up? Anything?'

'There's the smelly mattress he swears he bedded down on, and a few traces of weed. But no supplies, no equipment. Wherever stashed, he's not telling. And if he says 'for personal use' one more time, *I'll* throttle him too.'

Sipping coffee, Batten tried to get his ducks in a row. 'No surprise he's denying murder, Ballie. But why won't the evidence shake him? Blood.

The cross. A baseball bat. And coughing up to a ding-dong with the victim, same evening she was killed?

'I don't get it either, sir. Mr Average would've cracked like an egg by now.'

Batten drank more coffee. It was strong, black, and tasteless. 'Arse over tip, Ballie. His energy's focused on denying a bit of dealing, when the charge sheet says murder and crucifixion. Janner's not even in the Fourth Division.'

Knuckles rattled the office door, and DC Hick's pale wraith of a face ducked in. Hick's fingers twitched on the door-frame as if, too tired to speak, he'd turned to signing instead. His hands reminded Batten of Reverend Kerry's, pausing, strangely awkward, while translating Biddy Holt's story from signs to words.

'Yes, Eddie?'

'Sir. Duty solicitor wants to know the score. What do I tell him?'

Batten looked at the clock, and at Ball, who shrugged in response. Janner's detention limit was ticking away.

'Tell him to go home, Eddie. Tell yourself to go home too. Your face looks like it's been dipped in a bag of flour.'

Hick rubbed a finger over his face to check. When it came up clean he gave a grateful nod, and departed. Ball got to his feet.

'If it's not Janner, sir, should we spread the net?'

'Plenty in the net already. Let's take a last gander at the murder board.'

Sergeant Ball sat astride a chair as if it was a horse, reminding Batten of Leonard Tull, who'd done the same on Good Friday, in the vestry. A thousand years ago.

The names on the murder board were no easier to stare at.

'If Janner's telling *something* like the truth, are we looking for a motive in the wrong place, Ballie?'

'I'd be happy to find one anywhere, sir.' To emphasise his point, he cracked a knuckle.

'Two crimes, is it, maybe? Not one?'

'Murder, followed by a crucifixion, you mean?'

'Two separate crimes. Maybe?'

'By two separate people?'

'Maybe, again.'

Sergeant Ball lumped his ample body from his chair and tapped a finger on the map of East Thorne.

'She was killed in Turks Lane, sir? We're comfortable with that?'

'*Comfortable*?'

'Well. With the evidence.'

'Yes, but not with the distance between Turks Lane and the top of that bloody hill. She didn't fly there on bluebird wings, and perch herself on a cross, did she? So, who helped her along, if it wasn't Janner?'

'And why?'

'Why, indeed. We need to eliminate some of our suspects from this damn list.'

'Including Mike Brean, sir?'

Ball's ambivalence was badly hidden.

'*Sergeant*, Mike Brean has history with the victim. And he knew where the cross was - because he planted it. Might be uncomfortable for Nina, but we don't give preference to one of our own. *Do* we?'

Ball reddened, but jabbed a finger at Mike Brean's timeline. 'Nina's shift finished Thursday evening at eight. She arrived at Mike's place in East Thorne - knackered, she said - just after half-past, and Mike was making dinner for the pair of them -'

'But he left the pub before half-past *seven*. Over an hour unaccounted for. And he could find the top of Crown of Thorns Hill in a blindfold.'

'He says he went straight home. Peeled the potatoes.'

'Wouldn't take over an hour.'

'Well, in my case it would, sir, but leaving that aside...'

'Leaving that aside, we still have dead time. And Mike Brean could flip a 99 pound body onto a cross with one hand, if he had good reason.'

'My point exactly, sir. Does he?'

The murder board stared back at them now. A grim arrow linked two dates. The hot August night when Mike Brean's 'birthday treat' was Alicia Heron. And, eleven weeks later, the cool October day when her pregnancy was terminated. It was Batten's turn to stride over and tap a knuckle on the board. Ball's face screwed itself into a knot of doubt.

'But Mike was eighteen, sir. If the baby was his, he'd have mixed emotions, I don't doubt. But with his whole life ahead of him, wouldn't he be relieved?'

'Only if we take his word for it. And I don't. For precisely the same reason I don't take the word of Harry Finn - nor his missus. They stay in the frame, Ballie, along with Mike Brean. First thing tomorrow, get the team *triple*-checking, OK?'

Ball's nod triggered a yawn like a chasm. Through the window, the car park was shrouded in darkness and April mist.

'Maybe it's time we went home, sir.'

'No maybe about it, Ballie. Tomorrow, we'll take a final run at Janner. If we blank, *then* we'll spread the net.'

'In that case, Happy Easter,' Ball yawned.

'You too, Ballie. See you tomorrow.'

'Today, sir. It's today, now. Easter Monday.

Easter Monday

Thirty four

Dog-tired.

But sleepless, too.

The ambivalence of policing, Batten told himself, scraping at stubble with a new razor, and nicking himself in the process. Driving to work, even earlier than planned, red pinpricks of blood dotted his chin like chickenpox.

Hints of daylight took his mind off blood and razors - till a memory of sunrise on Good Friday clicked into his thoughts. With images of a corpse-hung cross and a looming hill in mind, he turned off the Parminster Road almost without thinking - drawn to East Thorne, and an unplanned return to its crime scene.

Crown of Thorns Hill almost burst through the windscreen as he drove in. Though the cross and corpse had been removed, the old, gnarled thorn-tree was silhouetted against the dawn sky like a broken umbrella.

Coasting up the main street, he was surprised to see he was not alone in sleeplessness. Framed by the lych-gate of All Saints Church, two more early birds confronted one another, though not in friendship. Nor were they admiring the ancient hamstone beauty of the church. Two pairs of arms gesticulated. Two sets of shoulders tightened. Car window down as he approached, Batten heard two strong voices squaring up.

'If *I* had organised the planting of the cross on a holy hilltop, *I* would have made a less embarrassing job of it! And yesterday, *you* were absent again, in All Saints' hour of need! Where were *you*, on our holiest Easter day, when a rabble marched and chanted, *here*, where Christian dead lie buried! Had it not been for *me*, would the police have even *turned up?*

Leonard Tull's over-loud voice was clearer than a church bell to Reverend Kerry, whose calming hand gesture reminded Batten of the Pope, in St Peter's Square.

Wrong denomination, Zig.

And wrong effect.

'What must our Bishop have thought, when he saw All Saints,

swamped by protesters, on the Television news? An Easter church under threat, and not a *clergyman* in sight!'

Kerry dropped his futile arms to his sides. 'I imagine the Bishop thought, "thank God for Leonard Tull." I'm sure you took advantage of my absence, Leonard, and gladly. No?'

Tull's crimson face seemed to open, but before words thudded out, he saw Batten approach. Kerry also turned, and the trio stood for a moment, three Magi in search of a star.

'Wrong place, wrong time, and wrong volume?' asked Batten, waving a hand at the quiet streets of East Thorne. 'Would it be an intrusion if I asked you to take your differences inside? Where the Christian dead won't hear?'

Tull glared at Batten, but stood his ground. Kerry gave the faintest of smiles, and strode towards the Vestry.

'After you, sir,' said Batten. He waited, in silence, till the stubborn Churchwarden turned on his heel and followed.

Hell's teeth, Batten thought, I've become an arbitration service to a pair of feuding Ecclesiasts, when I'm supposed to be revisiting a crime scene. Unless there's a connection?

Reverend Kerry nodded when Batten politely suggested they postpone their 'discussion'. Kerry's parting act was to point to his living quarters and, in a low whisper, ask Batten if he would like coffee. Since Kerry seemed to have something on his mind - and Batten's breakfast had yet to happen - he held up five fingers and nodded back.

Tull's alibi for Thursday evening had interesting gaps, and Batten could just about tolerate five more minutes with the unsmiling Churchwarden, slumped on a hard chair in the traditional manner this time, arms squeezed across his chest as if to keep them from Kerry's throat. Or from Batten's.

The Vestry was a cheerless room at the best of times, but the radiators were clap-cold and the place like the inside of a fridge.

'Yes, *yes*,' Tull said. 'My alibi, though why I should need one is still a mystery, is as previously recorded. Why would I need to change it?'

Batten decided Tull could work that out for himself.

'Choir practice, you said, seven till eight-thirty?'

Tull sighed out a nod of assent. His presence had been confirmed by the Choirmaster. "Leonard is hard to miss," he'd said. "His voice borders on sacrilege."

'And after, you walked home - alone, I think?'

'I did. Your people wrote it *down*.'

Batten knew what else they wrote down. On Tull's five-minute journey, not a soul saw him go by.

'My *people* also wrote down what you saw, on Thursday night. Sticking to it, are you?'

'Sticking to it? Sticking to it? I said I *thought* I saw something, in the shadows, behind the church, as I made my way to the lych-gate.'

'According to your statement, it wasn't something, but some*one*.'

'I thought it may have been Andrew. Mr Holt, I mean. He and that daughter of his sometimes use the hidden short-cut, behind the church.'

'The short-cut to Turks Lane?'

'Or *from* Turks Lane. Since I merely *thought* I saw him, I am naturally unable to say in which direction he was moving.'

'But it might have been Andrew Holt?'

'Or someone of similar height. Too dark for certainty. I was tired. I did not loiter. I went home.'

'And you live alone?'

'When I made my statement, a mere four days ago, I lived alone. And would you credit it, I still do.'

Batten preferred a touch of irony to Tull's snide anger, despite the counsel of Ged, his Northern police pal. 'Irony, Zig? Just sarcasm for intellectuals.'

There was nothing intellectual in Tull's sullen response. Nothing good-natured either. What's he like in *church*? Batten wondered.

'So from around ten-past nine you were at home, alone?'

'And still alone when I went to bed, at ten, Inspector. Or has an early night now become a crime, without the Great British Public being informed?'

Not a crime, no, Batten thought. Not unless you slipped out your back door, unseen, in your jim-jams? And toddled over to Turks Lane, to biff Alicia Heron over the head? And/or string her up on a handy wooden cross? So you could finish off Reverend Kerry? Or put the church of All Saints on the map?

223

He opened the door for the unsmiling Churchwarden, glad to see the back of him. His musings about Tull were self-indulgent.

From distaste, though, he wanted them to be true.

Weak instant coffee in Kerry's Spartan kitchen wasn't the breakfast Batten had in mind. He clocked the empty whisky bottle jutting from a waste-bin, and the pile of dog-eared books dangerously perched on a sideboard.

While Kerry measured out a life in coffee-spoons, Batten read the titles. *Robinson Crusoe. Your Health in Retirement.* Last year's *Cricketer's Almanac.* He noticed *The British Sign Language Companion* amongst them.

By the time Kerry placed two pale beige coffees on the kitchen table, early morning sunlight was tinting the windows. Batten craned his neck to look past the curtains at the sky.

'Think of the morning light, Inspector, as symbolic of Christ. Today underpins our belief in Salvation, because Easter Monday is traditionally when Christ returned to Earth.'

Batten wanted to ask if, when Christ traditionally returned to Earth, he traditionally brought strong Italian coffee with him, but Kerry hadn't finished.

'And did you know, in the Eastern Orthodox tradition, Easter Monday is called 'Bright Monday'?'

Shaking his head, Batten sipped his too-bright coffee, thanking his lucky stars he had Sergeant Ball for a sidekick, not Leonard Tull.

'The day's begun with sunlight,' he said, but it doesn't seem to have shone on your Churchwarden. Did he develop a dislike for you, Reverend? Or was it the other way round?'

'Ah, Inspector. I dislike no-one. Leonard, I fear, arrived at All Saints with a burning ball of anger in his heart. Nothing quenches it.'

Not even whisky? Batten wondered, as Kerry blew on his cup.

'You should know, in the past Leonard trained for the priesthood. But failed to graduate. In response, he developed a strangely exacting view of how a clergyman should behave. And it appears I come up short.'

Batten's eye fell on the empty bottle sticking out of the bin. Kerry also gave it a sheepish glance.

'In fairness, Leonard has a case. It may be equally fair to say I still see the Church as my vocation, whereas Leonard sees it as his *property*. Perhaps he should work not for God, but for a developer.'

Perhaps he does, Batten mused.

'But I shall soon retire. And the present will become the past. Churchwarden Tull will fade into history.'

'Maybe they'll make him Bishop.'

A wry smile crinkled Kerry's face. 'I shan't be praying to my God for that to happen.'

Swallowing more beige coffee, Batten turned to Kerry's reason for inviting him in.

'Too much has happened, Reverend, this weekend. Wouldn't you say?'

'I would. Alas.'

'And while I don't want to rub salt into wounds, Mr Tull does perhaps have a point? About your absence on Easter Sunday? When All Saints became the backdrop to a demo putting East Thorne on the media map? For the second time in three days?'

'Ah, Inspector. I told your colleagues where I was.'

'True, yes, but incomplete, if you don't mind me saying? You told them you were *here*. It's less clear what you were doing.'

'I can only repeat what I said. I was communing with my God, in private. After a lengthy commune with the Devil.' Kerry cast another glance at the empty bottle in the waste-bin, twitching his hands against the arms of his chair as if signing to himself.

The movements became a reminder of Easter Saturday and Kerry's curious halting pauses as he translated Biddy Holt's signed story into words.

Perhaps accurately, perhaps not.

Batten wandered over to the dog-eared pile of books, picking up *The British Sign Language Companion*. 'What if I took a wild guess, and said your private communing might have something to do with this?'

Kerry's pebble-lenses squinted at the title. And squinted at his feet.

'I will not say, "I don't know what you mean." To do so would trigger the need for a further commune with my God.'

Clasping his hands together - in pain rather than prayer, Batten thought - Kerry fell back on silence.

'I think you should just tell me the facts, Reverend. Isn't truth the core of your profession *and* mine?'

'*But I do not KNOW the truth!*'

Batten's eyebrows went up at the suddenness of Kerry's reaction.

'Maybe not. But you know *something*, and you know it isn't right. Not right with Biddy Holt? Not right with your 'translation' of her story for me, the other day?'

'I told you, I am not an expert at signing. I was very clear. Why do you think I keep a copy of *The British Sign Language Companion* to hand? I make mistakes. I need to check the...nuance, sometimes.'

'And after I'd left, what did the nuance say, once you'd checked it? Was it different to what you told *me*?'

This time, it was Kerry who got up, returning *The British Sign Language Companion* to the bosom of its dog-eared friends.

'You must understand, Inspector, Biddy has major difficulties with language. With its very essence. Her world is not yours or mine. Hers is a world of hiding and seeking, secret fantasies and unhappy confusions. The so-called *normal* world categorises Biddy as having Special Needs, when what she really *needs* is to feel *special*. Instead, she is ignored. So, she makes a fresh world for herself, in her own special way. And translating her world is a journey without a map.'

'Nevertheless...'

'*Nevertheless*, there was a...strange nuance, yes. *Yes*. She has been different, these last few days. I put it down to the foul desecrations, up there on *my* hill, and the foul desecration of Easter itself. Deeply disturbing, for all, but more so for Biddy. Her own understanding of Easter is entirely *special*, for all my attempts to instil some orthodoxy. You, I'm sure, have no difficulty understanding Easter as a time of symbolic death and resurrection - for those who tread the path of Christianity?'

A nod.

'But does *Biddy* understand? On the path she treads, the symbolic is her right shoe, and the real her left. They frequently collide. You are aware that when Biddy wanders off, she does not do so aimlessly, as my Parishioners seem to think, but to search?'

'For her mother. I'm aware.'

'Her mother. Elisabeth. Her mother long-dead. Do understand, then, why Easter is acutely special for Biddy. At Easter, for Christians, a death leads to a resurrection?'

'Yes.'

'So why not a special one for Biddy? Why not a new Elisabeth?'

Batten needed stronger coffee than this beige soup from a stale jar. His internal logic baulked at Kerry's meanderings.

'You said you put Biddy's 'strange nuance' down to the desecration of Crown of Thorns Hill. Are you telling me you've changed your mind?'

Kerry blew out a long, sad sigh. 'In all conscience, I must tell you I have. I *think* Biddy knows more than she is saying. She signed some curious things - which, yes, I had to check. And perhaps I was economical with what *might* be the truth. Biddy takes on a particular posture, a particular expression when she feels special - you must have noticed, when she shook your hand?'

Batten shrugged.

'And when I asked her about 'the lady on the hill', her special look was there. She corrected me. I think she signed, 'No, she's with the angels. She's the Jesus lady."

'The *what*?'

'The Jesus lady. Who saves all the sins of the world.'

'Meaning what?'

'I'm unsure. As I said, what you and I take for granted, Biddy can confuse. Is Alicia 'the Jesus lady'? Does Biddy hope the resurrection of the Jesus lady will somehow save us all? Or 'simply' bring back her mother? I do not *know*.'

That's two of us, thought Batten. He regrouped. 'Let's simplify, shall we? Does Biddy mean the lady was 'with the angels' because she was dead?'

'Perhaps.'

'And she knows the lady is dead because you told her? Or Andrew Holt did?'

'Neither of us, Inspector. And quite deliberately.'

'So how did she know? So soon, I mean.'

'I cannot say. Biddy has become more secretive, of late.'

So have you, Batten thought. He tried to watch Kerry's eyes, strange behind the thick glass of his spectacles.

'How far can Biddy see?' he asked.' I mean, what's her long vision like?'

Kerry nodded a sad head at Batten's implication. 'Yes. It is not the best. She and I share the affliction.'

'So she wouldn't be able to see 'the lady with the angels', or the Jesus lady - or whatever - from a fair distance away?'

Kerry's head dipped again. 'Alas, you and I are of the same mind.'

'She had to be closer, didn't she,? To know the lady was with the angels? Or that there *was* a lady?'

'If your interpretation is correct, yes.'

'So she was on Crown of Thorns Hill? Before the police arrived? Perhaps even on Thursday night?'

'I fear so. I do. She wanders where she pleases.'

Batten tried to visualise Biddy's shoe-size.

'Does Andrew Holt know? Know she was up there?'

'Andrew?' Kerry paused. 'He will have tried to speak to her. I do not know with what success.' Kerry kept to himself his decision *not* to ask Andrew Holt. Even a deliberate ignorance can be defended.

'But surely you could speculate?'

'Inspector, even if Biddy was a dictionary, instead of a *person*, her lexicon is not yours and mine. I can tell you what I think she signed to me, that's all. She did not remember Alicia. Ten years is a long time in Biddy's world. She could only call her, 'the lady with the angels,' and while her precise reason for such a name was beyond me, her disappointment was not.'

Disappointment?'

'*Yes*. 'Lady with the angels not Mummy,' she signed, all the while shaking her head at me. 'Not Mummy. Not Mummy.' Kerry involuntarily twitched his fingers, perhaps signing the very words he was speaking.

Glancing across the room at *The British Sign Language Companion*, Batten cursed his own lack of expertise.

'Rarely is Biddy's face so readable. This time, her pain was a canyon. I could see into its depths.'

'I'm sympathetic, Reverend, but I fail to see why you couldn't tell me this on Saturday.'

Kerry fell into a fresh silence. His right hand clasped his left, his left his right, in a repeated rhythm, one hand struggling with the other.

'Because there is *more!* And more discomfiting. I can make no excuses for my absence during the ETOPS demonstration, but the weight of knowledge I am carrying is at least a reason. My duty and my conscience have been at war, and it is a war without a victor. Whatever I tell you, there will be only the defeated. But I cannot hide it - even if I do not *know* its meaning.'

'Just tell me, Reverend.'

Kerry's fingers continued to clasp and unclasp, a conscience on display.

'Inspector, I'm almost sure Biddy signed, 'Helped Daddy. With the lady with the angels. On the hill. Helped Daddy. Cared for Daddy by helping.'

'Helping him with what?'

'I do not *know*. It could mean innocent things.'

Did Kerry *want* to know, Batten wondered? He reminded himself a priest is not a policeman.

'But I bet you and Andrew discussed it?'

'I chose not to. And I still do.'

'To protect him?'

'*NO!* To protect *HER!*'

The bare room rang with the power of Kerry's voice. Then all was quiet again.

'Poor Andrew. He is her one true protector. Without Andrew...'

'You do realise I have to take this further? And not only with Mr Holt?'

'My *conscience* knows it! Is that not enough?'

Kerry rubbed his bald pate with both hands. Behind his pebble glasses, Batten thought he saw moisture.

'My apologies, for raising my voice. And for any delay I may have caused. All I will ask is what I ask my parishioners. In the churchyard, please do not walk on the graves.'

Difficult, Batten thought. I walk on graves for a living.

'You chose not to speak to Andrew. But you must have spoken again to Biddy? Signed, I mean?'

'Biddy is unavoidable, to the few souls who sign. Yes, of course.'

'And?'

Reverend Kerry's long-fingered hands appeared to wash themselves with invisible soap and water, thumbs rubbing at the palms, left, right, left again.

'She signed the same unchanging message. Over and over.'

Reluctant to shout in frustration at a man of the cloth, Batten shrugged his arms and hands at Kerry, trusting him to pick up the signed request: *spit it out!*

'She said, 'won't', Inspector.'

'*Won't?*'

'Over and over. I took her into the church itself - she understands how holy and truthful a place it is - and I asked her again.'

Kerry shook his head at the memory.

Blood from a stone, Zig!

'Her eyes peered at me, in that special way. 'Promised Daddy,' she said. Won't tell. Secret.'

'Secret?'

Kerry nodded. 'One word, and not another since. 'Secret."

Thirty five

DC Nina Magnus rarely arrived first at Parminster HQ.

Today she did.

Alone at her desk, she shook Alicia Heron from her mind, till the day's case-load thwarted her. A pre-booked conference call to Alicia Heron's Bangkok employer stared up from the page.

Top-of-the-list, though, was a different task: the letter, nestling in the palm of her hand, like a new-born Easter chick.

She and Mike Brean spent last night sitting at the hand-made table in Mike's kitchen, failing to notice how hard the chairs had become. Dinner sat in the fridge, uncooked. An unopened bottle of Malbec and two empty glasses loitered on the worktop.

'I've never thought of anyone else but you, since the day we met, Nina. More than two years, now.'

It was the same for Nina Magnus. But she wasn't ready to tell him.

'Not even Alicia Heron? Not once?'

'When I saw her - there, like that...' Mike gestured in the vague direction of Crown of Thorns Hill, but refused to turn his eyes towards it. 'I couldn't help thinking about her *then*, could I? For god's sake, she was my first time!'

'What about before?'

'Is this an interview?' Mike asked. 'Do I need to accompany you to the station?'

'Mike, you're being unfair. I have responsibilities to my job, just as you do. When do you ever walk past dodgy woodwork without saying 'Tut'?'

'Hardly the same.'

'No, Mike. Our jobs are hardly the same.'

'So, swap me for someone with the same job as you? Is that what you want?'

'Not my choice alone, Mike. What do *you* want?'

Mike sank further into his chair, his muscles tight - the same tightness he'd experienced on Good Friday morning, staring wide-eyed through binoculars at a dead Lish Heron. And later, squashed in Nina's car at the foot of Crown of Thorns Hill, feeling useless.

He liked being a large man. Liked Nina's robustness. Lish was small. But large, still.

'What *I* want...what I want...is to show you something. I've wanted to, ever since Good...'

Good Friday morning stuck in his throat.

'I didn't, because it's painful. Personal. Not sure I can explain it even to *you*. As for *them*...' He waved in the vague direction of Parminster HQ.

Magnus folded strong black fingers round his white hand. We're both strong, she wanted to say. So *be* strong. She kept her counsel and let Mike decide for himself. In silence they sat, till faint moonlight crept into the room.

When Mike made up his mind, his hunched frame rose from the hard chair and headed for his 'den'. Nina heard him rummage, heard more silence, heard him return, and winced when he switched on a lamp.

In his giant hand he clutched a thin blue piece of paper.

Isn't that an old-fashioned air-mail letter? Nina thought. The kind where you write in the middle and fold the edges over to form an envelope? Do people still use them, these days?

Mike stared at Nina across the table, gently opened her fingers and placed the almost weightless letter in them. Tenderly, he closed her fingers over it.

'In all these years, only two people have read this,' he said. 'Me, and the person who wrote it. You'll be the third. If you choose.'

Nina's eyes danced between the letter in her hand and Mike, who was struggling into his coat and scrabbling for a door-key.

'I'm going for a walk,' he said. 'If you read it, and you're still here when I get back, we'll both know what we want.'

And he closed the door behind him.

When a bleary-eyed Batten eventually shuttled from East Thorne to Parminster, it was no great shakes to follow his Sergeant across the car park. But both were surprised to see Nina Magnus at her desk, a cold tea by her elbow. Batten was still standing when she tapped on his door.

'Bright and early, Nina? Thought you weren't due in till eight?'

'Whatever, sir. Can I...?'

The clock said 7.35. A shrug from Batten said, 'why not?'

Magnus sat down, placing an evidence bag on the desk. Batten watched as she carefully removed a feather-like oblong of blue paper. He hadn't seen an air-mail letter in ages. Do people still send them?

'You didn't have to write, Nina. My door's on hinges.'

Unsmiling, Magnus unfolded the thin paper, ten years old. She teased out the creases and pushed it towards Batten.

'Mike Brean's given me permission to show you this, sir. Before we record it as evidence. I suppose. You needn't worry about prints, but the content...' She glanced across the desk at Batten, uncertain what he'd say.

'You sure about this, Nina? Once I've read it...'

She told Mike much the same, last night, before he'd 'gone for a walk'. Now, she said, 'I'll leave it with you, sir, either way,' and returned to her desk.

Uncertain, Batten eased it to one side while he grappled with the problem of Andrew and Biddy Holt. All the while, his stomach wished Hick's greasy-spoon cafe wasn't closed for the Easter break. And wished for an Easter break himself. The sneezing fits had downgraded themselves to a mere Force 4 on the Beaufort Scale. Strong enough, though, to sneeze Andrew and Biddy Holt higher up the suspect list.

It was 8am by the time he picked up Mike Brean's letter, handling the flimsy blue paper with care.

The instant he saw who'd written it, he sat bolt upright at his desk.

I don't write letters, Mike. I used to get little blue letters from mum and dad, from Africa, and they put me off for life.

But I'm writing to you now, in case the village rumour machine ticks over. Villages always have whisperers, don't they? It's one of the reasons I'm in Thailand, and not coming back. They can whisper about me all day in East Thorne, who cares?

You'll care, though. Because the whispers will tell you I was pregnant, not long before I left. And had an abortion. And it happened not long after we spent our birthday night together. A bit drunk, the pair of us, weren't we?

You were so lovely, Mike. I wish I'd been as tender as you at 18. But I wasn't. Not even at 16, if I'm honest. We had different role-models, you and me. But I can't have you worrying, so I'll tell you straight off.

The baby I was carrying was never yours. Don't be upset if I'm blunt - that's me all over - but you weren't my 'one and only', were you? I'm sure we both knew, when we staggered out of The Rising Sun that birthday night?

But I need to apologise. It wasn't the whole reason - and believe me, please - but a little part of why I enticed you back to Turks Lane was to make himself jealous. Himself on the other side of the bar.

And it worked - briefly, at least. I fell pregnant not long after. Yes, with himself - but only because I chose to. My decision, not his. And if I ever fall pregnant again, it'll be my decision too.

*I'm not callous, please don't remember me that way. But, yes, it was a test, to see if he'd go through with it, see if he'd come with me, to Thailand. Him, me and the baby. Well, he bottled it, didn't he? Paid for my trip to some posh clinic in London, rather than upset **her** behind the bar.*

I always knew he'd bottle it, for all his promises. But something inside me had to be sure.

In any case, since I'm being blunt, on our birthday night there was no way I was letting your little swimmers get anywhere near my eggs! I didn't have to try too hard, did I, because you went off a bit fast, what with me being your first? Don't worry. My vanity persuades me it's because I'm such a siren!

But I still enjoyed lying there, with you, curling myself into your big body, feeling safe, wrapped up in a giant teddy-bear. I felt protected, Mike. A rare feeling.

This letter's blue, like my bluebird - but you needn't be. You'll make a tender lover for someone, soon enough. I've had plenty of practice, so please believe me when I say bodies learn easy and they learn fast.

Hearts, though, they're the way they are, I suspect. Yours is a good one.

Please give it to somebody who deserves it more than I did.

Fondly,

Lish x

Examining the flimsy paper back and front, Batten saw what Magnus had already spotted: the return address was a box number. Whatever the letter's sentiments, Alicia Heron was inviting neither dialogue nor visitors.

For now, Mike Brean's name on Batten's list slipped below two others: Harry Finn, and his angry wife, Cat.

Beyond the cubby-hole window, Nina's broad shoulders tightened as she tapped keys and made notes. It was not her shoulders, but the look on her face which disturbed him when she'd stuttered into his office, first thing, her eyes staring into the awkward no-man's-land where public and private worlds collide. And where the intimacies of her life with Mike Brean were on display.

To her implied question, he would have to reply, 'I'm sorry, Nina. Embarrassing or not, the contents of this letter could relate to the case. It will need to be recorded, in evidence.'

Another voice hissed at him, the cold voice of rules, codes of practice, regulations. Batten had turned blue with anger last year when Ball, to safeguard the innocent, burned a handful of evidence - unimportant though it was to the death in question.

In Batten's head, regulations battled with fellow-feeling as the same cold voice hissed, '*That letter needs to be recorded **now**!*'

A memory butted in, of his early days at Police Training College. An over-sized trainer pulled him aside one day and said, 'you'll never learn to be a fucking policeman, Batten, until you fucking-well learn to fucking swear!'

'I suppose by the same rule, sir,' Batten had replied, 'you'll never learn to make love?' He'd walked away, leaving the man to figure it out for himself.

Now, as the cold voice-of-duty nagged, Batten stared at the flimsy blue letter. He should hand it to Sergeant Ball for logging, right away. Through the window, Magnus was tapping fast fingers on her laptop.

'*Fuck it,*' he mumbled.

Replacing the letter in the unmarked evidence bag, he slid it into a desk drawer. Just for the time being, he told himself.

Then he turned the key.

Nina Magnus ploughed herself into the job.

The printer, as if to frustrate her, chugged out useless car registration details. The real name of her Turks Lane adversary was proving hard to trace. She still thought of him as 'Art' - Anonymous Racist Thug.

And 'Art' he remained. The car she'd seen him climb into was rented by a company 'no longer trading'. The driver was an imaginative Mr Jones. She showed the results to Sergeant Ball.

'Fingerprints?' he asked. 'On the brochure?'

'Sent it off, Sarge, in case there was DNA. Waiting.'

'Isn't everybody, Nina? Hickie's waiting for his greasy-spoon cafe to open. Chas Janner's waiting for a solicitor to sign him out. And I'm waiting to sift through more porky-pies. You're not waiting for something to get on with, are you? If so...' He patted the pile on his own desk.

'No, Sarge. Plenty of jobs.'

'Well, then,' said Ball.

And Magnus got on with it.

Thirty six

The downside of not placing Mike Brean's letter in evidence meant Batten had to deal with the contents himself. Not that he didn't fancy a fresh encounter with Flash Harry Finn and his tight-lipped wife - but when?

Not yet!

The schedules on his desk glared at him, a consequence of workforce 'rationalisation' and a countrywide shortage of detectives.

Oh, and murder, he reminded himself.

The first name in this morning's diary was Thomas Pride, the Council's Chief Planning Officer. If Pride spilled a bean or two it might inform his next interview of the day, at Serenity Developments. Maybe Piers Tyndale would serve rich Italian coffee this time. If so, would Batten drink it?

Flicking down the page, he saw there'd be no time for coffee. Since he doubted his Sergeant's neutrality whenever orchards cropped up, Batten had reserved the smug mush of Ken Leckey for himself. Lesley Willey, too, demanded another chat. Or would a visit to the dentist be preferable?

Whether from *schadenfreude* or simple revenge, Batten dropped Lesley Willey's file on Ball's desk. Along with a scribbled note.

Ballie – our sign-language interpreter's back from leave tomorrow, so when you've done with Willey, suss out Andrew Holt. And firmly invite him and Biddy Holt to Parminster. And if she requires the presence of a responsible adult, make sure it's not Andrew Holt or Reverend Kerry!

Batten gave his Sergeant's shoulder a satisfied little pat, and headed for his car.

Ball's reaction to Batten's 'bounty' was to flick Lesley Willey's file to one side, and turn instead to the Holts. But before he could grab his own car-keys, Magnus waved a note at him with one hand while covering the receiver with the other.

'I've got Thailand on the phone, Sarge. Incomprehensible, so far. But this snippet looks juicy.'

Ball read the neat message. Juicy, indeed. And unexpected.

He'd enjoy clocking Andrew Holt's reaction...

...The two men stood for a moment in Holt's garden, gazing beyond Turks Lane at the orchard, a first flush of blossom dotting bare branches. Spring was Ball's favourite season. Holt's too.

'How many trees, Mr Holt, would you say?'

'Well, five acres, Sergeant. And these trees are standards, not halves, so about forty to an acre? Two hundred trees, give or take.'

'Ah, not enough cider to fill a warehouse. So not a huge loss, if the orchard becomes a road?'

Ball plastered on a touch of levity, to disguise his own orchard-ambivalence. Holt's response was quiet-voiced and level.

'Always a loss, Sergeant, when even one tree disappears. Each tree is a life. And two hundred trees...'

You're a more careful zealot than Ken Leckey, thought Ball, continuing to plug away.

'But trees for roads, if the roads lead to homes, sir? Homes where folk can raise a family? Folk have to live somewhere, don't they?'

'Then why not in brown-field sites? How much ugly, derelict land must I drive past, daily, with little sign of development taking place? More expensive to buy and clear, I suppose. Whereas here' - Holt waved a bony arm at five acres of orchard - 'here, a single bulldozer can scrape the turf from the ground and uproot these trees in a day. Topple their trunks and crush them into matchwood, regardless of how much the orchard provides, and for how many centuries. And, heaven knows, regardless of its beauty.'

Ball had no need, he saw, to question Holt about his sympathies for Ken Leckey's views. He blocked out an image of the massive orchard surrounding his own village of Stockton Marsh. He'd voiced Holt's very arguments when it too had been threatened.

'And am *I* not 'folk', Sergeant? I need to live somewhere. And what of Biddy? Where will she live, if not in Turks Lane, familiar and safe? Is it a sin to fear displacement by incomers, roaring their engines along tarmac roads where ancient acres once thrived?'

'But change happens daily, sir. Wouldn't we turn to stone without the new?'

Holt stared up at the thin, black thatch on his roof.

'Give me the old, Sergeant. Why must it be destroyed? But, please, come in.'

From her dark hiding place on Crown of Thorns Hill, Biddy Holt watched Daddy show the squat detective into their house. Thick bushes and tree stumps here. And bubbles from the spring below, and clear water in the deep pool where the tree-trunk fell. Hide here for ten, count to ten, and ten, and ten.

No-One-Will-Find-Me.

Won't.

Small detective wants my secret. Comes to ask Daddy. But Daddy won't tell. Biddy helped Daddy. Not even Kerry knows. Biddy knows, but Biddy hides. Hides her secret. Hide-and-see all the Turks Lane secrets.

Won't.

Small policeman's go, his turn to ask. Top Detective came before, and had his go. Shook Biddy's hand. And the hooded man who hides, he had his go, because gone now.

Biddy hide. Secret.

Go meet the small detective. Shake his hand. But hide first.

And not tell.

Can they find me?

No

They

Can't.

By the time Biddy Holt searched her way across the brook and into the back door of number 3, Sergeant Ball had pocketed his notebook and, with an admiring glance at the Turks Lane orchard, driven away.

'Saw small policeman,' she signed.

'Mr Ball', Andrew Holt signed back.

'Shape like a ball. Can I shake his hand?'

'Gone home. Shake his hand tomorrow. Invited us to his police station.'

'For another go?'

'Yes. Another go.'

'Is Top Detective there?'

'Yes. Top Detective wants to see us. You and me.'

'Won't tell.'

'Won't tell what?'

'Secret.'

'What secret?'

'Won't tell anyone. Helped Daddy.'

'Yes.'

'Helped Daddy with the angels lady. Lady with the angels not Mummy.'

'No. She's not. Not Mummy. No.'

Every day, Andrew Holt saw the face of his young wife, Elisabeth, in his mind's eye. Every day, still.

'She's not Mummy, no', he signed, sweat prickling his skin. Not the familiar warm sweat of remembrance, but a cold, disturbing sweat. He stared at Biddy, at the threadbare house they lived in, stared through the window at the familiar long view of ancient trees, not knowing what to do or say, hands silent in his lap.

'Lady with the angels not Mummy,' Biddy signed. 'Is Mummy at the police station when we go?'

'No. I don't think she is.'

'Not going.'

'Top Detective invited us. We mustn't be rude.'

'Won't shake his hand. Already did.'

'That's fine. No need to shake his hand. But if he asks about helping Daddy?'

'Secret. Won't tell.'

'Sure?'

'*Won't.*'

Not even a crow-bar could prise a secret from Biddy, Andrew knew. But what will happen, he thought, when the Top Detective asks *me*?

'Put the kettle on, please,' he signed. 'Daddy tired.'

Biddy Holt's independent living skills proudly accomplished, her father slumped in his threadbare seat, staring at a mug of brown tea, dreading tomorrow.

Answering Sergeant Ball's questions about the orchard was almost a pleasure. Trees are easy to love. Trees bring peace. And the questions about Ken, Chas Janner, about Lesley Willey's attempts to induce him to sell - these he handled smoothly too.

But questions about Alicia Heron, they shook him. The same questions the tall Inspector had asked.

Did he see her, or hear her, on Thursday evening?

Did he know Alicia was coming back? Did he know *why*?

The same questions as before. Why was he not believed the first time?

And, at the end, the Sergeant's new questions.

Harder.

Our latest information suggests Ms Heron had agreed to sell her house. How might that affect you? Sir?

I'm not sure.

You were unaware of her decision?

I told you I was, before.

Where was Biddy, on Thursday evening?

Here, of course.

Did Biddy see or sense anything untoward?

I don't know.

Did she leave the house?

I don't think so.

Did you? Sir?

I already told you. Why don't you believe me?

Oh, but you've met my Inspector, sir. He's a stickler. Has to have his ducks in a nice neat row. If something's not ruled out...

So the squat policeman said, before 'inviting' him and Biddy to Parminster, tomorrow.

Andrew Holt stared at nothing. The tea Biddy made was still on the table by his chair, untouched. Thick, brown tea, greasy from too much milk, the only tea she could make, the tea she'd been making for twenty five years, the tea he hated and never drank.

Hearing her footsteps thumping up the stairs, he ducked into the kitchen and poured cold tea down the sink, as he did daily, running the tap so she wouldn't notice.

To protect her.

To protect her feelings.

Not that he was certain what they were.

Thirty seven

Batten didn't *hate* municipal buildings, ugly or not. But he spent long hours inside them, walled up, the air-con too hot, too cold, or non-existent. If it wasn't cop-shops, it was prisons, mortuaries, archives, all with the same claustrophobic smells. And a colour scheme selected for, or by, the blind.

Before, in urban Leeds, when friends asked 'if you weren't an Inspector, what would you be?' he struggled to answer. Now, in rural Somerset, he'd say a Park Ranger, a water bailiff, a conservationist. Someone who works outdoors.

Someone who inspects living things.

Today, indoors, trapped by dun-coloured walls, Batten grappled with a low-slung chair in the Council's Planning Office, tapping impatient fingers on his document case while the morning ticked away. Thomas Pride, the Chief Planning Officer, was eighteen minutes late, and Batten had a murder to solve.

When Pride arrived, Batten blinked aside the brusque apology – 'important meeting, significant business, couldn't very well get up and leave.'

More important than murder? Batten wanted to ask.

'Serenity Developments,' he said, returning the brusqueness. 'You've had dealings with them, I'm informed?'

'And with many, many others, Inspector.'

'But the recent events in East Thorne will not have escaped your attention, sir?'

Pride nodded, but said nothing.

'So, in the light of those events, I wonder what you can tell me about Serenity's plans for East Thorne?'

Pride paused, measuring his response. 'The initial planning enquiry provides a broad enough outline. Would you like to see a copy?'

Batten had a copy in his document case, as Pride surely knew. It wasn't much of a read.

'I was hoping for a more detailed assessment, sir. And perhaps a little background, on Serenity. The kind not included in a 'broad outline'?'

'I don't know what to tell you, Inspector.' Pride nudged the pens on his desk into a neat row. Batten thought the truth might be useful.

'Oh, I'm sure you do, sir, with your history. Twenty-eight years in Planning, I understand?'

If Pride saw Batten's words as a compliment, his face didn't show it. He wriggled a portly behind in his chair - taller than Batten's and perhaps as uncomfortable. Or not.

'Well. Important company. Strong pedigree. Superbly-managed. Piers Tyndale - the owner, as I expect you know - is something of a self-made man. But *well*-made, in my opinion.' In response to Batten's eyebrow, he added, 'he chooses quality sites. Builds quality homes, on time, and far exceeds his social housing quota - voluntarily. A planner's life would be less stressful if all developers did the same.'

'A saint, would you say?'

Pride's brusqueness returned.

'Business is business, Inspector. Don't saints, and indeed sinners, belong in the realm of religion? Business is...what it is. On the one hand, the profit imperative. On the other, human needs, environmental factors, government quotas, the planning process. Serenity, like others, inhabits the spaces in between.'

'Inhabits how?'

'Well, by being a large company, I suppose. Serenity stretches across the gaps, if you like. And does it better than most.'

'These 'spaces in between', sir. Who fills them?'

Pride puzzled his face into a frown. 'Goodness. Well, for example, researchers, geologists, consultants, focus-group organisers, and suchlike.'

'Not lobbyists? Or process managers? Or, I don't know what to call them - *inducers*?'

Thomas Pride looked at his watch. Batten waited for him to invent an urgent meeting.

'I am somewhat pressed for time, Inspector. Wall-to-wall today, you understand?'

'I sympathise, sir. Yes, we should arrange a more intensive interview.' Batten pretended to consult his diary. 'At Parminster CID? And being a murder enquiry, how would tomorrow morning suit? 7.45 am?'

With a squirm, Pride removed his spectacles and pretended to clean them. 'If strictly necessary, then of course, of course. But perhaps I can clarify matters to your satisfaction today?'

Back went the spectacles, and a more cooperative view emerged through cleaner glass.

'Let me put it so: Serenity works *with*, more than it works against. Homes must be built, but Local Councils simply cannot take on large developments. They are the realm of private enterprise, like it or not. And Serenity is more cooperative than most, from the planning perspective. *Generous*, in fact.'

'Generous, sir? Might such a word be a little awkward, within the Public Sector – which we both serve? What sort of generosity had you in mind?'

Pride appraised Batten across his expansive desk. And received an appraising stare in return. Tiny prickles of sweat began to glisten on his brow.

'*Legal* generosity, Inspector. The various provisions in the Town and Country Planning Act aside, it is not unusual for interested parties to, how shall I put it, bring something *extra* to the table? When a development is under consideration.'

'A sweetener?'

'I doubt the beneficiaries of our Community Fund would use such a word. Not with Council funding tighter than it has ever been. If Serenity and other firms offer to sweeten the pill, the Community reaps the benefits. To turn down healthy investment, in these modern times, would be *criminal*.'

Pride let the word hang like a challenge in the morning air. Batten let it dangle even longer.

'Wouldn't it depend on what Serenity expects in return, sir?'

'Legal generosity cuts both ways, Inspector. But let me assure you, our planning regulations are strict and scrupulously fair.'

The Chief Planning Officer earned another eyebrow, as Batten mulled over Sergeant Ball's reservations about Pride's partiality. In return, Batten earned the sight of more sweat on Pride's brow.

'Were you to press me, where Serenity is concerned, I may admit to a little occasional...*alacrity*. Once planning has been granted, I mean - not before. The planning process tends to grind slowly, and while speeding documentation along the road is small beer for a Council, it can be financially meaningful for a business. After all, time is money.'

Pride allowed himself a satisfied smile, as if *time is money* was a phrase he'd just invented. Batten was pondering '*alacrity*'.

'It's the road *towards* planning I'm more interested in, sir. And under the circumstances, the road towards East Thorne. I had hoped you might enlighten me.'

A puzzled look was all Batten got.

'I mean, have any...obstacles cropped up, where East Thorne is concerned? Any difficulties?'

'Goodness me, difficulties are quotidian. Daily. Timeworn.' Pride ran out of adjectives, so cleaned his glasses again. 'Disputed ownership of land, for example. Drainage issues. Reluctance to sell. Infrastructure delays. Public meetings. Access problems. A hundred others.'

'And how might a firm such as Serenity go about solving them, sir?'

As if the room was full of invisible grime, Pride's spectacles succumbed to more cleaning. If he's not careful, Batten thought, he'll change the bloody prescription on his lenses.

'Why, as other firms do, depending on circumstance. Um, the funding of local meetings, computer-aided presentations, generous offers of purchase and re-housing, free landscaping, the ping-pong game of for and against? Agreements are generally arrived at. You surely have some process awareness, Inspector?'

Damn right I do, thought Batten. From hard experience.

'But in a case where, say, the 'difficulties' remain difficult, sir, and only *dis*agreement is arrived at, might other 'processes' come into play?'

Like converting life into death, then crucifying the corpse, as a strong warning to the uncooperative?

'Inspector, I have neither knowledge of, nor involvement in what occurs before information lands on my desk. I am a planner. I interpret information and make recommendations to the planning committee, and *they* decide.'

More prickles of sweat glistened on Pride's brow. In lieu of his ultra-clean spectacles, he flourished his watch, and lifted his ample bottom from his chair.

Batten was glad to get up too, from his low seat. Having further to climb, it took him longer. He had reached the point where, in a more formal interview, Pride might consider making a phone-call.

'If we need to meet again, Inspector, so be it, but I really must go.'

Pride hovered at his office door, waiting to close it, the honest-broker-running-late. Batten watched his well-fed frame wobble away towards the lift. He knew he'd be taking a closer look at Thomas Pride.

Before the lift doors closed on him, Pride glanced back. The grim expression on his face suggested he knew it too.

Outside, Batten paused by the reserved parking bay, and pretended to make a phone call. The 'Chief Planning Officer' space was filled by a brand-new Mercedes Estate. Taking Ball's advice, he peered through the windows. Golf clubs, next to an electric buggy. And the woods and irons neatly wrapped in protective covers, all sporting the same logo.

Willoughby Park Golf Club, it said.

Batten wondered if Thomas Pride and Mal Muir just played golf together.

Or if they played at anything else.

While Batten scooted between Council Headquarters and the offices of Serenity Developments, Ball arrived back at his Parminster desk just in time for the phone to ring. Five seconds later, he wanted to throttle it.

'No, no, madam, of course I'm not saying you don't matter.' He was saying exactly that. 'The bottom of the pile? Certainly not.'

But she was. Every pair of eyes in CID was focused on murder and crucifixion, and this posh-voiced woman wanted Ball to send 'a detective' to a petty break-in at the *Community Angels* charity shop – which shouldn't even be *open* on Easter Monday.

'I did not say we were open, Sergeant! I said the *door* was open - because it has been forced, and the door-jamb splintered into pieces. Had I not been passing - on a rare day-off, I might add - I should not have noticed till tomorrow. When we *are* open!'

Stuff your *Community Angels,* thought Ball. I'm up to my armpits in Community *Devils!* His sigh must have made it down the phone, because he got another earful.

'I have been asking to speak to a detective for *hours*! My charity shop has a broken door, and I am surrounded by the kind of post-burglary chaos I am growing used to. I am also surrounded by Television crews and journalists, gawping like ghouls at Crown of Thorns Hill. Would you prefer it if I told *them* my story? Perhaps they will take notice - and their viewers and readers soon after? Yes?'

'You're in East Thorne?'

'I *told* you I am in East Thorne!'

She hadn't, and Ball saw no point in correcting her. But he could see tomorrow's papers and the local TV news - callous policeman dismisses 'little woman' in the face of 'proper crime'. Worse, the emotional baggage of 'charity' was involved. He could see 'Sergeant Christopher Ball', there, in print, the 'detective' who ignored a plaintive plea for help from the poor-but-charitable Mrs Community Angel.

The Chief Constable would crucify him.

So would Di Ball, who had volunteered in charity shops for a decade.

He put down the phone.

'*Hickie!*' he yelled. '*Tuck your shirt in. Got a job for you!*'

Thirty eight

Given Thomas Pride's evasions, and Lesley Willey's half-truths, Batten pleaded urgency to Piers Tyndale during a phone-call consisting largely of grunts, and a meeting was arranged.

The security guard was spotty and only just out of short trousers - holiday cover, Batten guessed - and working to rule. Batten had to sign in his car, sign in himself, sign a disclaimer, sign for his Visitor badge, all the time wanting to scream, *there's only you, me, and the boss in the entire building!* Serenity seemed an apt name for the place, today.

Three clipped olive trees still poked from their stainless-steel containers in Piers Tyndale's office, the Danish leather recliners empty, the electric cupboards firmly closed. It was so silent, Batten could almost hear the sound of Tyndale's after-shave sweetening the room.

'You're fortunate I could get here, Inspector. I should be dusting off the barbecue.'

Piers Tyndale waved at sunlight fighting its way through the tinted windows. He finished signing a slew of documents on his desk, apart from one, which he frowned at and pushed aside.

'*Good* fortune, sir, I trust.' Batten added a painted smile, because fortune had nothing to do with it. His team were doing their best to keep an eye on Tyndale and his crew. If an unscheduled Bank holiday meeting with, say, Thomas Pride popped up, the effort might be worth it.

'One always hopes for good fortune. But *un*fortunately Mr Muir cannot join us. Otherwise engaged.'

'Pity.' Batten hoped his white lie was convincing. 'But you and I take our opportunities where we can, sir,' added Batten, pointing at Tyndale's paperwork. 'I do appreciate you agreeing to see me.' He glossed over how reluctant Tyndale had been.

Tyndale's pen went down and his open hands pointed in the direction of the carpet. A less cultured man might have said 'get on with it.'

'It would help our enquiries no end if you could remove any…vagueness about your East Thorne development, sir. In view of lines of enquiry we have little choice but to pursue.'

'Vagueness, Inspector? In what way?'

'I'm thinking particularly of Turks Lane, sir. The four houses there. And the orchard, opposite.'

'And they are relevant? I'm not sure I see how.'

We should be doing this with swords, Batten thought. Two fencers, at the Olympic Games, trying to score. Or defend.

'Then I wish I had your success in avoiding the television news, sir. And the press, radio, and social media. Alicia Heron, the dead woman, owned number four, in Turks Lane. And almost certainly died there, before...' As shorthand, he borrowed Sonia Welcome's finger-twiddle.

'And Turks Lane has significance for the East Thorne development?'

'We'd be remiss, sir, if we didn't explore the connection.'

'You're not a man who believes in coincidence, Inspector?'

Damn right I'm not.

'Me, sir, I'm trained to believe in evidence. For example, I had a conversation with the Council's Chief Planning Officer, earlier today -'

'Thomas? I do know Thomas Pride, before you ask. Every developer in the county knows Thomas.'

'And we had an interesting discussion about...I don't know what to call them...inducements? An appropriate word? *Financial* inducements?'

Tyndale steepled his fingers, briefly admiring his manicure. 'I'm never sure if the public sector fully understands how the private sector works. Or if they *refuse* to understand? I don't make the unwritten rules of business. They've existed for centuries.'

So have orchards, Batten could have said.

'All developers must make their projects financially attractive - to interested parties. The rules of the game, yes?'

Meaning no, Batten managed a nod, following Tyndale's eyes as they glanced at the empty leather recliners. *Wishing Muir was here, Zig, to provide more slippery language?*

As if to prove he made his own decisions, Tyndale rose from his chair, crossed to a smoked glass panel in the wall, opened it, and pressed a button. Batten expected an elaborate architect's model of East Thorne to pop out, but what emerged was a shiny silver coffee-machine. Without asking, Tyndale concocted two espressos, their aroma filling the room. He placed them on the glass-topped table, by the recliners, and sat down.

'Mal swears it's the taste of Italy,' he said, sipping.

Without admitting his experience of Italy was a single brief weekend, Batten sat too, cautiously, the scent of rich black nectar tempting his nostrils.

Tyndale's question surprised him. 'Have you a house, Inspector?'

'Of course, sir. Haven't you?'

'I have three. I make no apologies. I have earned each one many times over, with long hours and perseverance.' He sipped more espresso. 'But your house. Do you know its current value?'

Batten nodded.

'Let's assume it is worth £500,000.'

'Let's not,' Batten spluttered.

'Humour me? On my day-off?'

A shrug. Batten's house was worth half that.

'What if, today, I offered to buy it, for its fair market value plus twenty percent? £600,000, for the sake of argument. An instant boost to your net worth of £100,000 - assuming your accountant is as skilled as mine.'

My accountant? I'm a bloody Police Inspector. I'm on P.A.Y.E!

'And what if I added a bonus, for an instant sale? Shall we say £20,000? A total windfall of £120,000, pretty well tax-free, if managed shrewdly?' Tyndale drained his coffee cup, with something of a flourish. 'Now, what might you do with £120,000? I do not in any way wish to demean, but I doubt you have such an amount lolling around in your account as we speak?'

Damn right I haven't. Batten let silence speak for him. For Piers Tyndale, it said silence betokens consent - here, in this palace of temptation.

Leaning back in his recliner, Tyndale appraised Batten, the questioner now being questioned. Silence is a mere pause in the temptation process, said Tyndale's eyes. A silent fish is tempted by the lure. Suspicion, resistance, refusal – all may kick in. But not forever. A larger lure is dangled. The fish bites, is hooked, and silently landed.

But Tyndale didn't know Batten was an angler, who knew a fish - and a lure - when he saw one. He pushed away his untouched coffee, sliding it across the glass-topped table.

'It doesn't matter what I might do, sir. Because I don't live in Turks Lane.'

Tyndale waved his free hand dismissively. 'I was speaking hypothetically. But my point is relevant. Whatever the significance of Turks Lane, and whatever...obstacles it may represent, my solutions are, and always will be, based on *reward*. Significant reward, in fact. With reasonable people, arrangements can be made.'

Batten recalled the negative tone of Alicia Heron's Headteacher, and Mike Brean's pithy summing up: *Lish didn't like to be told. She didn't like overdogs.*

'But Ms Heron, the deceased owner of number 4, made a habit of being *un*reasonable, by all accounts?'

'Inspector. I know almost nothing of Alicia Heron. I have never set eyes on her, nor spoken to her on the phone. Mal Muir or more likely one of his associates perhaps did. I do know Serenity made three offers to buy her property, each offer more generous than the previous one, in a genuinely business-like attempt to strike a bargain - '

'I'm not here because someone struck a bargain, sir. I'm here because someone struck a *skull*.'

It was Tyndale's turn to slide his coffee cup across the table. 'Not I, Inspector. Not us,' he said, voice a whisper. 'Unless you are saying differently...?' He allowed the unspoken threat to hover.

'Let me be clear what I am saying - *asking*. Given Alicia Heron turned down your offers, one after the other, did other '*rewards*' come into play?'

Tyndale ignored Batten's tone. '*None*,' he said, face curling into a wry smile. His voice became a low, smug whisper. 'Because she did not turn us down.'

Batten had trouble controlling his eyebrows.

'Ah. I assumed you knew.'

No, Zig. You bloody didn't! An out-of-date murder board popped into his head, *Turks Lane* underlined.

Number 2. *For Sale by Auction.*

Numbers 1 and 3. *Refusing to sell*, scrawled in black felt-tip pen.

Number 4, where Alicia Heron once lived and died. *Refusing to sell* - in mistaken blood-red ink.

Batten ate humble-pie.

'She agreed to *sell*?'

'She did.'

'When was this? And I mean *exactly* when?'

If it was old news, Batten might add 'withholding information', and 'wasting police time' to the pile of papers on Tyndale's desk.

'Exactly?' Tyndale pondered, blew out his breath, strode to his desk and picked up the phone.

Batten thought he heard it ring, but it might have been the sound of doubt echoing in his skull.

'Mal? So sorry to disturb your day...' The conversation batted backwards and forwards for a minute, till Tyndale replaced the receiver. 'Mal will ring me back. He has to find out. He isn't sure, *exactly*.'

The leather recliner, comfortable before, felt lumpy in the fresh silence. Batten struggled out of it and stared through the window at the empty car park. Piers Tyndale's tapping fingers must have energised the phone because it rang, loudly, and a second coded conversation began. When the receiver went down, Tyndale tapped a remonstrative finger at the unsigned document on his desk.

'Thursday, Inspector. At 6.30pm. An answer-phone message, which of course was not immediately picked up. It seems Ms Heron was on a train. Mal didn't deal with her directly.'

'So who did?'

'Business confidentiality, Inspector.'

Batten ignored the terse rebuff. Lesley Willey, Estate and Land Agent, was doubtless the oily go-between, who would plead business confidentiality too, at least for now. He juggled times and dates, while fathoming Tyndale's new glumness.

'Was it a verbal agreement to sell? Or written?'

Piers Tyndale slid into his chair and glared long and hard at the unsigned document on his desk. 'Alas, verbal.' He tapped the document again, as if chastising it. 'She was to sign the legal agreement this week. So we are led to believe.'

She won't be signing now, mused Batten.

If Serenity knew she'd agreed to sell, did other interested parties find out?

And did someone stop her, *before* she could?

Who?

Not me, Tyndale's face said, as he replaced Batten's untouched cup, and his own, behind the smoked-glass panel, with something of a hint. If Alicia Heron agreed to sell, the interests of Serenity Developments would best be served by keeping her alive.

But Batten's suspicious mind rumbled on.

'So when exactly did *you* find out? You and Muir?'

'Find out what, *exactly*?'

Batten ignored the sarcasm. 'That she'd agreed to sell. You and Muir didn't deal with her direct, and the answer-phone message wasn't picked up immediately - isn't that what you said? So when *exactly* did your anonymous go-between pass on the happy news?'

Tyndale, no stranger to project management, saw the import of Batten's question right away.

A triangle of time, information and motive closed in.

If Alicia Heron was still believed to be a threat on Thursday evening, Tyndale remained a suspect - Muir and Willey too.

In the deepening silence, Batten chose not to point out there's no such thing as murder-by-mistake. But he made sure to tap his size nines as loudly as the thick carpet would allow.

Piers Tyndale weighed the pros and cons of further smoke and mirrors. One side of his face twitched as he considered falling back on damage limitation. In Mal Muir's absence, he opted for the truth.

Face grim with implications, he said, 'we were told on Friday morning. Shortly after our intermediary picked up his belated messages.'

'Good Friday morning?'

'*Yes*. Ten-o-clock. *Exactly*.'

Thirty nine

Eddie 'Loft' Hick's day went from gloom to gloomier. His favourite greasy-spoon cafe was still closed. Now, he was being bumped off a murder case to scratch his arse at a petty break-in, at the *Community Angels* charity shop in East Thorne.

'I wouldn't send you at all, Eddie, if the place wasn't swimming in media folk grubbing for a story. But it *is* their umpteenth break-in, so there might be a pattern. OK?'

Both men knew the score. Staff shortages nudged petty crime to the back burner - except when the East Thorne's of this world are swarming with TV crews.

Hick grumped his way to his Jeep, gunned the engine, and soon pulled up outside *Community Angels*, its frontage obscured by a thin geezer in faded grey overalls, doing his best to repair a smashed door.

When the thin geezer turned around, Hick recognised Handy Andy Holt, chisel in hand, wood splinters on his work boots.

'Crow-bar?' asked Hick, staring at the splintered jamb, and trying to sound interested.

'It was the lock, last time,' said Holt, nodding. 'I had to replace it. At least this time the lock survived. Still a mess.'

Whether Holt meant the splintered wood, the shop, or Easter Monday, Hick didn't care. With a grunt, he stepped inside.

Her name badge said the manager was Evie Mellor, but since it didn't specify her age Hick was no wiser. She could be fifty-eight or eighty-five, he thought, as she answered his questions in a voice twice as bored as his.

'What can I say? They break in - youths, more often than not. They rummage. We empty the till every night so there's no cash to steal. They rifle through the bags of donations - mostly pointless because mostly old clothes. We fit a stronger lock - on advice from the *police*. Next time, they jemmy the door frame instead. If your lot bother to turn up again, they'll say "fit a steel door-jamb."'

Hick, about to offer such advice, twitched instead.

'So, what was taken?' he asked, with what authority he could muster.

Evie Mellor swallowed a sigh. 'Same as before. Trinkets from the display cabinet. Worth what, thirty pounds? For once, they didn't smash the glass. Several donation bags have been sliced open, but since we hadn't inventoried them, who can guess what's missing? A Picasso? The Crown Jewels?'

She paused, as the noise of Handy Andy's hammer started up again. Above it, she yelled, 'at least Mr *Holt* is charitable. *He* turns up, and works for free, without being asked. What a diamond. He collects for us, too, you know. As if he hasn't enough on his plate with Biddy. If only *more* people were *diamonds*, Constable.'

A squashed Eddie Hick couldn't know today's break-in was Evie Mellor's last straw. Five charity shops she'd worked for. Twelve burglaries. Enough is enough. Once this *detective* with his shirt hanging out disappeared, she intended giving notice.

Hick scribbled a few dyslexic jottings in his notebook. 'Theives used crow-bar and knife. Broken door-jamp. Value of prop stolen aprox £30, as per previous.'

He added 'LP' - Low Priority - thanked Evie Mellor, mumbled the usual, and left.

As Hick's Jeep gunned away, Andrew Holt slotted a steel strip onto the broken door-frame, and screwed it into place.

With Piers Tyndale's news fresh in his mind, Batten shuttled back to HQ. Rural policing means rural driving, and he spent long hours in his car, often glad of the thinking time.

Though the distances had been shorter in urban Leeds, he'd sat in traffic almost as often as he breezed along clear roads. Somerset had spoiled him, and when he did encounter a traffic jam like this one, he pretended it was a crook sending vengeance. A hefty tailback, and the road too narrow and steep-sided to turn.

Oh well, thinking time.

Across the valley, he could make out rows of red-tiled roofs in the West Ashtree housing development. Before buying his old cottage not far from here, he'd viewed West Ashtree, but the new estate was a fussy pile of bright bricks in the middle of nothing. It could have been the set of a TV soap. Old suited him better.

Did this preference for the old underpin his dislike of Piers Tyndale and Mal Muir? Or was it because their unelected, in-the-know power made his toes tingle? He gazed at the shadows and sun on West Ashtree's rooftops. Three hundred houses? More? Did Serenity Developments build that estate too?

West Ashtree.

East Thorne.

What next? North Oaks? South Poplar?

Tapping his toes at the traffic jam, he conjured up a new law – preventing housing developments being named after any tree destroyed in the building process. The thought disappeared when he remembered Sergeant Ball asking Ken Leckey, 'don't all houses begin in the ground, sir, just as trees do?'

The car in front revved its throaty engine and roared off, beneath a sun-dappled canopy of elms. Batten followed, West Ashtree growing smaller in his rear-view mirror, but looming larger in his head.

Eddie Hick's car jerked its way into the HQ car-park a safe ten seconds after Batten emerged from his. Hick looked as glum as his Inspector felt.

At the murder board, Batten grabbed a pen. If Piers Tyndale's information was true, and Alicia Heron *had* agreed to sell her Turks Lane cottage to Serenity Developments, the shifting sands of motive and suspects would shift again. He raised the felt-tip - and stopped.

Someone had beaten him to it.

A cough from Sergeant Ball made Batten turn, and a nudge of Ball's head at Nina Magnus made him turn again.

'We were just about to phone you, sir,' said Magnus, pointing at the corrected board. 'Not long ago found out.'

'Me too,' said Batten. 'I found out from Piers Tyndale. Who made me look like a plonker. Can't believe Alicia Heron agreed to sell to *Serenity*!'

Ball sat up in his chair. 'Ah, we didn't know that bit, sir. That's news. Andrew Holt was cagey enough when I suggested Ms Heron might sell. But if I'd known the buyer was *Serenity*...'

'Don't worry, Ballie. We've not finished with Mr Holt just yet.' He rammed the cap back on the felt-tip pen and turned towards Magnus. 'I had the distinct impression, Nina, Ms Heron thought developers were Satan's spawn. Any clue why she changed her mind?

'Only after the world's slowest phone-call, sir, with Ms Heron's Thai employer. I still can't pronounce her name, it's a foot long. Our victim accepted a partnership in the firm - a fashion house. Signed and sealed, the boss said. The deal meant Alicia had to buy in, though. Buy shares.'

'Shares? How many - I mean, how much?'

Magnus looked at Sergeant Ball, whose calculator was translating Thai Baht into sterling.

'Works out at a few quid over £280,000, sir,' said Ball.

'About what her house is worth?'

Ball shook his head. 'Even with a strong valuation she'd be well short - by about sixty grand.'

'What if you added 20% extra, plus a bonus for an early sale? That'd push the price towards something like, wouldn't it?'

'If that was Serenity's offer, it would indeed.'

'So she caved in to inducement?' Batten kept quiet about Piers Tyndale's attempt to induce *him*.

'Time pressure, sir,' said Magnus. 'Her employer wanted the agreement sorted. And who's going to cough up over-the-odds cash and fast paperwork for a quick sale? Not your average house-buyer.'

'But Serenity could. Which is why she flew back at short notice?'

'Partly, sir. The other reason's to do with the surety she'd signed over. To seal the partnership.'

'Let me guess. Her house deeds? For Turks Lane?'

Magnus nodded, as all three of them stared again at the murder board. Alicia Heron's motives may have been surprisingly venal, but at least now they were clear.

Motive, motive, motive, Zig.

'How did she take the bad news, Nina? Alicia Heron's unpronounceable employer?'

'Mixed, sir. I suppose she now legally owns number 4. And would you bet against her selling to Serenity at an inflated price?'

'Fat chance. Why mixed?'

'Because Ms Heron was only half-way through designing a new range. They'd already agreed a logo.'

Batten took another guess. '*A bluebird*?'

Magnus nodded. 'Her own brand, sir. Bluebird. As you'd expect.'

Batten stared at Lish Heron's photo. What *did* he expect?

Fresh red ink underlined more names now.

Ken Leckey.

Andrew Holt.

Harry and Cat Finn.

A dotted line, not in red but black, tentatively picked out Reverend Dominic Kerry, if only because of his allegiance to Andrew and Biddy Holt.

Sergeant Ball had added two question marks - against Lesley Willey and Serenity Developments. Batten scrubbed them out.

'Piers Tyndale didn't know she'd agreed to sell till Good Friday morning, Ballie,' he said. 'Neither did Mal Muir. And I'll eat my hat if it wasn't Lesley Willey who passed on the belated news. So on Thursday night, all three were in the frame. And still bloody-well are.'

With a faint smile, Ball said, 'you mean, *because if it's not ruled out, sir, it's still ruled in*?'

Batten flumped away to his office. A fine thing, he thought, when an Inspector breathes a sigh of relief because his Sergeant's started to take the piss.

Picking up the Thailand details Nina Magnus had left on his desk, he read the hand-written postscript in her familiar italics.

Btw, the DISAYA label on Alicia Heron's silk shirt, is Disaya Sorakraikitikul, a Thai fashion designer. Elegant, expensive clothes, apparently.

Batten blew out a sigh. Murder and DISAYA? When was murder ever desirable? Or elegant? Expensive, yes. Always.

He recalled the last chance he'd had to contemplate desire - when mishearing the attractive Dr Welcome read the label on an improvised silk loincloth. Briefly, he'd hoped her mind was on desire for living bodies, not dead ones.

Could desire be murder's bedfellow, in this case? Was Harry Finn's desire for Lish Heron powerful enough to lead him to kill?

Ask him, Zig, now.

Batten groaned at more driving. Good job you're Sergeant's covering your back, he thought.

And taking the piss again.

Forty

How many times have I been in The Rising Sun, Batten wondered, without ever just ordering a drink?

Once more, he found himself not in the comfort of the snug, but in the pub's store-room - even dingier than before. This time, it wasn't Mrs Finn who sat opposite Batten on an upturned beer-crate, but Harry Finn himself. And the only desire apparent on his face was a desire to leave.

'Can we hurry this up, Inspector? Cat'll be needing me, next door.'

No she won't, thought Batten, because Debra and the other bar staff are standing in. Cat's pretended to go to the cash and carry but really she's sneaked off to Cafe Nero for a latte with cinnamon syrup and a blueberry muffin. Won't be back for an hour. Debra the barmaid was more than over-friendly. She was an uncorked vat of information.

Batten began with a question whose answer he could guess.

'Easiest way to hurry this up is by being straight, sir. Alicia Heron: did she come back to East Thorne to see *you*?'

'See *me*? I wish.'

'And wishes sometimes turn into horses, in my experience. So, before I commandeer your phone records, can you swear I'll find no messages there from Alicia Heron? That what you want me believe?'

Harry Finn didn't care what Batten believed, as long as he went away. But Batten pretended his upturned beer-crate was super-comfortable, despite being a foot too short for his legs.

'Go back ten years and you might find a message, for what it's worth. And maybe a *Merry Christmas*. Knock yourself out,' said Finn, arms tight across his chest. Batten wondered if the Finns practised together, in front of a mirror.

'And what if I just go back ten *days*? Or sooner? A much easier time-frame for gutting your phone. Won't take us long.' Batten knew it would, but maybe Harry Finn watched too much telly, and didn't. Silence festered.

'One text,' snapped Finn. 'One. One text in ten years.'

Eleven, Batten could have said. He let Finn talk.

'She was on a train, on Thursday, coming here.' He threw an angry arm at East Thorne. 'Why do people have to tell you they're on a bloody train? Who gives a toss?'

Batten shared Finn's view, but his lips stayed as tight as Finn's arms.

'Didn't want me bumping into her in the street and having a heart attack. That's what the text said. And she was coming back so she could *leave*, if you must know. I thought, what a surprise, *not*. Time was, she'd come back whenever it suited her, just so she could bugger off again. I replied, and told her. *Not this time*, she said. *I'm selling up.*'

'Did she say who to?'

'Didn't ask and don't care. It wasn't the first thing on my mind.'

'What was?'

Flash Harry Finn morphed from ruddy-faced landlord to unrequited lover. His eyes grew dreamy. Batten wanted to squirm.

'Oh, old time's sake, I suppose. And fun times, mostly. One last drink, I texted back. Can't we have one last drink?'

'Just a drink?'

'Yes. *A drink*. That's all.'

'And did you?'

Finn shook his sad head. 'She never came. To the pub, I mean. Probably for the best. Cat would have seen her off, with bells on, if she'd been here. Might've seen me off, too.' Harry Finn's dreamy eyes grew moist. 'To be honest, I still don't know what I would have done.'

Batten's antennae twitched. 'You said, if Mrs Finn had been here? Where was she?'

Flash Harry came back to earth. 'Where? Pulling pints. At the bar by the skittle alley, mostly. Where your bods camped out, on Good Friday. Thursday night's the Merriot and District League. Cuh, they can put it away.'

'She was *mostly* pulling pints?'

Harry Finn gave Batten a look, till his penny dropped.

'Don't you dare. Don't you *dare*,' he said, marital loyalty returning. Batten ignored both stare and request.

'"Mostly in the skittle alley" - your words, not mine - means she wasn't always in the skittle alley. So where else was she?'

Finn shrugged. 'I can see you've never run a pub. You have to be everywhere – bar, cellar, storeroom, customers, kitchen. She'll have been in all of them. *Mostly - and all the time!*'

Just like she's at the cash-and-carry right now? Batten could have asked. And not munching a blueberry muffin in Café Nero? He returned to Alicia Heron.

'So you wanted to share one final drink with 'Lish'? Your only reason?'

'What do you mean?'

'I think you know what I mean, Mr Finn. You and Lish had history. Intimate history. And history's never over till the book comes out. Is it?'

More silence festered. Batten's upturned box was cutting into the back of his thighs, but he refused to squirm. Harry Finn was squirming enough for the pair of them.

'Cat doesn't know,' Finn said, his Flash Harry voice gone and a murmur replacing it. 'She doesn't know, not for sure. It has to stay that way.'

Finn was whispering now, eyes pleading, voice so quiet Batten almost said, 'for the tape, please, Mr Finn,' despite the dingy store-room walls.

'Doesn't know *what*?'

Finn's pleading eyes returned to their harder state. 'God, I couldn't do your job,' he said.

No, Batten thought, *you bloody couldn't*.

'Cat doesn't know Lish was pregnant, that's what! *Satisfied*?'

In a way, Batten was. Because Mike Brean's letter, locked in a desk drawer, was redundant now.

'Cat has no idea I stumped up the money. For the...you know.'

'For the what, Mr Finn?'

Flash Harry's eyes stared harder still. 'For the *abortion*. Satisfied? Cat doesn't know. Doesn't know it was my *child*, for god's sake! You have to promise you won't tell her. Please. If she finds out, poor Cat, it'd kill her.'

Batten could have told Flash Harry his 'poor Cat' might have guessed.

'She's more likely to kill *you*, wouldn't you say?'

'No, no, no. You don't understand. Cat, see, she can't have kids. And we try most nights, if you must know. Clear enough *I* can. But not with Cat. It's the reason I agreed in the first place. To get rid. Agreed to the *abortion*. It was the last thing I wanted. But when I saw what it'd do to Cat...'

'You're trying to tell me you didn't twist Alicia's arm?'

'Huh, you never met Lish, did you? Lish went first, decided first, always first. *Nobody* twisted *her* arm. All the same, what I told Cat, you know, where Lish was concerned it was only Flash Harry's sex-drive working overtime. Well, it wasn't true. And I wasn't just hankering after a bit of young flesh, either - you can think what you like, I don't care.'

You cared about the demise of the Finn dynasty, though, didn't you? Batten thought, as Harry Finn's arms unfolded, slowly wrapping themselves round his knees, as if caressing old memories.

'*I* know it went deeper. Lish was *flame*, you see. *Fire*. Forever burning. It always pissed me off when she left - and she knew it. That's why she left and came back so often - to test me. To test old Harry Finn. Didn't matter. Something of her always stayed behind, some of her flame, *here*.' He tapped his chest, where perhaps a heart resided.

To Batten's amazement, a tear dribbled down Finn's cheek, before he wiped it away.

Even the toughest nuts can dissolve in a swill of remorse, Batten knew. *CID soup*, old Inspector Farrar used to call such tears. When another escaped, Harry Finn let it fall onto the store-room's grubby floor. Batten broke out in pins and needles. Or was it the uncomfortable stool?

'So you still desired her? After ten years?' No point reminding Finn it was eleven.

'*I* desired *her*, yes. *Yes*. I'll admit it.'

'But she didn't desire you?'

Sad-eyed, Finn stared at nothing. When he spoke, his voice was a faint rustle of leaves.

'She texted back, said no, sorry, she wasn't coming back to Turks Lane because of me. Said she wouldn't have *time*. *Time?* How could she say that, after... She was coming back to sell her house. And collect her bloody rug. Said she should never have left it there.'

'Her *rug*?'

'The one with the heron and the bluebird. Her mother made it. About the only thing her mother left behind, apart from a pile of grief. Lish said she was sending it back, the rug, to Thailand. *Repatriating it*, her text said. For the *memories*.'

Against his better judgement, Batten squirmed on the upturned crate as Finn's illusions about Lish Heron crumbled to the floor. If Finn was one of her memories, he was well down the list, way below a time-pressured house-sale and an old doormat. And he knew it now. When he spoke, his gaze was anywhere but on Batten.

'She'd forgotten every word I said, all those years past. We don't have to do this, Lish, I'd said. But she says, *ah, changing your mind about paying for it, are you*? Don't talk like that, I told her, I'm serious. It's a child. Half mine. I'll find some other way, I said.'

'What, like selling your pub and moving to Thailand? That was your other way?'

For a moment, Batten remembered squatting on this same upturned crate opposite Cat Finn, as she spat out her story of sharp kitchen knives and threats to Harry's manhood. But it was Harry Finn speaking now, his voice no louder than a breath.

'I couldn't do it,' he said. 'Sell up. Leave Cat, I mean. I tried to make myself. But I couldn't. *I knew you wouldn't*, Lish says. She was half-laughing, half-crying. But I said, wait, I've a plan. Me and…me and *Cat*, what if we bring up the baby? *My* baby. Bring it up, here, in East Thorne? You can still be in Thailand, if you want? And when the baby's grown up, perhaps, you know, perhaps later, we can maybe let on who the real mother is?'

Is it the cider fumes in this pub storeroom? Batten wondered. Or have I climbed into a Mills and Boon novel?

'Well, Lish gripped my arm so tight, with both her hands - her eyes were soft at first but, oh, the grip on my arm, I could feel her nails, cutting into my flesh, ten red marks her fingers left. I can still feel every pointed nail, even now, sharp in my arm after all this time - and she says, *Harry, it's for me to decide, not you. I make my own decisions,* she says - and not just her mouth talking, but her nails, ten sharp voices digging into my skin. And I remember seeing her eyes change, grow hard, till they burned into me and she hisses, *I'll not bring another child into this world to be as lost and miserable as I was!*'

Batten let the silence hang.

Harry Finn tried to regain his composure, rubbing his arm as if he could still feel Lish's nails, as if she, and they, had never taken flight.

'I tried talking her round, tried convincing her. Had a hammer and tongs time a-trying, I can tell you. But Lish is Lish. *There's not one word more to be said*, she tells me. Next morning, carrying the only child I'll ever have, a child *half-mine*, she goes to the clinic. On her own.'

Finn pulled out a hankie, like a white flag, and blew his nose.

'I couldn't take her, you see. I couldn't. Because of Cat.'

Finn's cheeks were wet now, little pearls of pain dribbling down. Tiny drops mottled the arm he was still soothing with his free hand, the fingers a ruined parent and the skin an unborn child. In the dullness of the storeroom, the flowing tears drained the flash from Flash Harry Finn, who stared beyond the confines of his four grubby walls, across space, across time.

To Batten, he seemed to stare over East Thorne at the empty sky, way past Crown of Thorns Hill, to his lost child perhaps. And to the open sea beyond, where Thailand lay, futile, its population lighter by 99 pounds. Or, how had Sonia Welcome put it? 44.9 kilograms, if you voted Remain?

Interview over. But only for now.

Because when Batten closed the pub door behind him, it was neither Thailand nor Sonia Welcome on his mind.

It was fingernails.

Forty one

Sergeant Ball had one foot on his desk and one ear clamped to the phone when Batten strode past.

By degrees, Ball's foot slid from desk to floor, and his slumped frame sat up. Soon he was on his feet, bolt upright, torn between throttling the receiver and smashing it to a fine dust. Even a drive back to wet Wales, to a smelly Labrador, teeth clamped round a slobber-covered stick, would be preferable to what he was hearing.

The receiver clattered into its cradle, and Ball shuffled on automatic pilot to Batten's office. He stood in the doorway, his alphabet-face making speech redundant.

Still recovering from Harry Finn, Batten groaned when he caught Ball's eye. Being back in tune with his Sergeant had downsides.

'I guess you've guessed what I'm about to say, sir?'

A weary nod was all Batten could manage.

'Where?'

'In the woods, far side of Ham Hill'

Batten's stomach lurched. Ham Hill was a favourite place, full of fine walks and vistas, and a finer pub at journey's end. The lurch in his gut spread to his skull and he was reminded of the bloated body of a long-dead horse, swaying in the River Parret's flow, like a premonition.

At least he'd have an excuse for postponing his next appointment. Was even a corpse preferable to a Ken Leckey ETOPS lecture?

'Just what we needed, Ballie. Another body. First one must've been lonely.'

The thinnest of smiles shrugged onto Ball's face. Both men knew to lighten the load.

'There's a bonus, sir.'

Batten's eyebrow went north.

'Body number two. Seems it's still alive.'

At the peak of Ham Hill, in The Prince of Wales, an off-duty Jess Foreman was stretching his giant legs, fist gripping a pint of cider, when the dog walker burst in. She'll need more than cider, he thought, seeing her stark-white face.

Stumbling across the flagstone floor, she pleaded with the barman to call the police, her voice taut with shock. Without asking, the barman pumped a double-brandy into a glass with one hand, and crooked an apologetic finger at Jess with the other. Foreman was a regular. Even stark-naked, he'd look like a policeman.

Here we go: lost dog, lost phone, lost keys, thought Foreman. He finished his pint in one swallow. Off-duty, my arse.

Sixty seconds later, he rang Parminster CID.

Batten dashed along the same route followed earlier by Foreman, through undergrowth softened by veils of wild garlic flowers and blue-white wood anemones. Random flecks of premature bluebells - crisp English ones, not Spanish invaders - nodded as he sped past. Batten knew the trail. Ham Hill was a walker's paradise of woodland, open fields, streams, slopes, and long views over Somerset, provided free by Nature.

Today, unnatural sights confronted him.

Foreman had made sure the Paramedics trod carefully, and where told. Even so, 'Prof' Connor and his Forensics team were glum-faced when Batten arrived.

'Sod all to find, Zig,' Connor said. 'Unless the blood is from more than one set of veins, which I doubt. Let's hope for some trace on the victim.' Connor pointed to a bright yellow marker, only just visible through the trees. 'Over there's where our villain must've waited. The vegetation's flattened. By shoes with plain soles and heels - size eight or thereabouts. Good place to hide. You can see the track from there, but the track can't see you.'

'Deliberately chosen?'

'Well, Zig, he - or she - didn't drop in at random from outer space. Someone with a bit of knowledge. Of good places to hide, I mean.'

'Any sign of a weapon?'

'Still searching. Don't hold your breath. Whatever it turns out to be, I can tell you right now it's bloody sharp.'

Batten had glimpsed the damage done to the victim, when he'd peered over Ball's shoulder into the ambulance, before heading for the crime scene itself.

His mobile rang.

'Ballie?'

'Paramedics are finished back here, sir. Victim's stable. I assume you'll want a chinwag with all concerned, before the ghouls and boffins take over?'

Ball could be as rude as Batten about doctors and forensic staff, but not in earshot.

'Ten minutes,' he said.

The back doors of the ambulance were open when Batten arrived. Like a pair of theatre curtains, he thought, framing the spectacle – a heavily-bandaged man, sitting up now, within a stage set of lights, buttons and tubes.

'Yes. Yes. Seven days a week,' the man said, in answer to Batten's question. 'I always jog here. I keep fit.' His voice came out in spurts, a response to shock. 'I'm in training. Cross-country. Through the woods. There's a 10k, next week.'

Not for you, thought Batten. Not with a broken nose. And, god knows, the rest of it.

'Did you...?'

'See? Did I see? Felt, more like.'

The man's broken-nosed voice was high-pitched. The sound would be comic, under different circumstances.

'I'm jogging along, as ever, earphones in. Next second, there's a dark shape. Jumped out from behind a tree. No warning, it just punched me, punched me in the face!' Gingerly, an index finger touched a nose in need of a surgeon. 'I went down. You can imagine?'

Batten could. He didn't know a single cop, male or female, who hadn't taken a punch to the head.

'Then, in my daze, I'm being picked up, from the floor, and whisked away. You see, I thought I'd been found. Helped. Like the ambulance people helped. But it was him. The man who'd punched me!'

'Certain it was a man?'

'Certain? I'm not certain of anything! A mask over the face. Not a mask. A balaclava thing. Like skiers wear?'

Ball made notes. Batten nodded encouragement. The waif-like victim needed it, his runner's frame light and wiry, clothed only in trainers, shorts and a jogging vest. The heaviest things on his entire body were the fresh white bandages.

'Next I remember, I'm in the undergrowth. A thicket. Almost dark.' The bandages defeated his attempt to point towards the scene. 'Face to the floor. Something stuffed in my mouth. Couldn't scream. I'm pinned down. And that's when the...'

The victim shook himself into silence, eyes closing, refusing to re-live his nightmare. It would be re-lived soon enough, thought Batten, when the poor sod makes a statement. Or looks in a mirror. He was tempted to pat the bandages in sympathy, as he and Ball climbed out of the ambulance with a nod of thanks to the paramedics.

'Jesus Christ, Ballie. Just when you think you've seen it all.'

'I know, sir. Carved. Exact word the paramedics used. A knife - or something. Each leg, sliced, from shorts to socks. Arms the same, down to the wrists. Likely to be scarred, they say. If the cuts had gone deeper, blood-loss might have done for him. He was lucky.'

'Lucky? A lucky sadist bumps into the lucky victim he's tracked through the woods? And, lucky-lucky, lays his hands on a knife sharper than a scalpel, and thinks, well, stroke of luck, I can do a bit of human carving with *this*. Lucky, my arse!'

'I meant lucky the dog-walker found him, sir.'

Batten opened his clenched fists in apology.

'Sorry, Chris. But when the job takes a knife to you...'

He relived the imprints in the rough woodland track, the crushed wild garlic, its white flowers dappled with blood, and the snake-like trail where the victim crawled from deep undergrowth back to the path he'd innocently jogged along.

'If our unknown person wanted to make a kill, Ballie, the blade was sharp enough. So why not?'

Ball shrugged out the obvious.

'A warning. Marking the victim?'

'A bloody permanent marker.'

'But warning of what, sir? Exactly, I mean?'

'Exactly? You've written down the *exactly*.' Batten jabbed a finger at Ball's notebook.

Ball nodded at the details - at each connection, in black ink on a white page. At the coincidence of Ken Leckey's name, and his Turks Lane address. At the coincidence of Leckey's role in the *Save Our Orchards* campaign.

Ken Leckey, leader of the East Thorne Orchard Preservation Society, fresh from a highly visible demo against those who would destroy Turks Lane and its ancient trees - a demo in the papers and on TV. Yesterday.

And today, Ken Leckey, in the back of an ambulance, his carved flesh held together by dressings whiter than apple-blossom.

Ball underlined the connections with a thick black pen, as he and Batten watched the wheels of the ambulance roll away, leaving in their wake two flattened strips of wild garlic flowers - white, like unrolled bandages squashed into the ground.

Once PC Jess Foreman had called in the troops, he immediately joined the door-to-door enquiries, off-duty or not.

'Not so much door-to-door as tree-to-tree,' he told his colleagues. Half an hour later he phoned Batten again, arranging what at any other time would be a pleasant meeting at The Prince of Wales.

'Just tell the Inspector what you told me, Mr...er... Don't worry now. We won't keep you long.'

No, we won't, thought Batten, each tap of his foot a reminder of the tasks piling higher at HQ. The witness, sitting awkwardly on a picnic-bench outside the pub, had a hipster beard, expensive skinny jeans and Buddy Holly glasses, but looked like he could use a high-carb meal.

'Well, it wasn't today, in fact. It was yesterday.'

'What?' said Batten.

'I *did* tell your colleague,' whined the hipster, pointing sheepishly at Foreman's giant frame. 'I did say it was yesterday, at the Easter Sunday Egg Hunt. For the children.'

'What about it?' asked Batten, throwing a less-than-patient glance at Jess Foreman.

'Well, I'm not entirely sure 'what about it.' In fact it was Katie - Katie's our daughter - who sort-of raised the alarm. There was a man hiding in the woods, she said. A *monster*. In a hood. We humoured her, of course. She has flights of fancy. But when the police asked about *today*, you see - 'was anyone behaving suspiciously etcetera?' Well...'

'Did *you* see anyone?' Batten asked.

'That's just it. I sort-of thought I had. But if I'm honest it was more a feeling than a sighting. Am I making sense?'

No, you're bloody not, Batten wanted to say. But someone hiding. In these woods. In a hood. Yesterday - 24 hours before...

'I thought perhaps Katie had seen one of the joggers. There's often joggers here.' The hipster dropped his voice. 'I've occasionally seen one nip into a thicket, to, you know...'

'Urinate?' asked Batten.

'Well. If you must, yes.'

'But it wasn't?'

'There was no sign of any jogger when I went to see. Actually, I was only *pretending*, to placate Katie. And placate my wife, of course. But, there was a piece of ground, sort-of flatter than the rest. And I did have a strange feeling someone was there, you see. Watching me. Even if *I* couldn't see *them*.'

Once the hipster returned to the bosom of his family, Batten raised an eyebrow at Jess Foreman.

'I know, sir, I know. But I rang you because he's the third. Adult, I mean. Who thought there *might* be someone, yesterday and today, hiding in the woods.'

'On Easter weekend? Ham Hill's packed at Easter. You'd have to be on something stronger than cider to try hiding *here*.'

'Oh, there's always places, sir. The courting couples find 'em, believe you me. But you're making my point. If this is the same nasty as carried out what you saw up yonder, maybe *something stronger than cider* is involved. What I witnessed today looked crazy-dangerous to me.'

Wise old bugger, Batten thought, as he appraised PC Foreman.

'If I had time, Jess, I'd buy you a pint, in there.' He pointed at the buzz and bustle of The Prince of Wales. 'Since you're off-duty.'

'Appreciated, sir, but I'm staying on. Thought I'd give the team a hand. Don't like nasty beggars with sharp knives doing mischief in my woods. Plain wrong.'

Batten nodded. Plain wrong, indeed. 'Then I'll owe you one, Jess.'

Heading for his car, Batten wondered how many team hours of

unpaid overtime he'd softened with a pint or two, paid for with unpaid overtime of his own. He softened the thought by glancing past the pub's outdoor tables at the immense view of Somerset and Wiltshire beyond. Nearby lines of lynchets, the Medieval remains of ploughed terraces, led his eye towards the faint Iron-Age bump of Cadbury Castle, sitting on the horizon, inscrutable. In the far distance, more bumps whose names he didn't know punctuated the landscape.

If ancient man could build strings of hill-forts, he asked himself, across vast expanses of ground, using little more than antler-picks and effort, why are you struggling to solve a 'straightforward' murder and a 'mere' crucifixion?

Two hours ago, Harry Finn, Andrew Holt and Piers Tyndale topped of the suspect list. Now, the gold medal's been nicked by an unknown knife-wielding nasty who hides in the woods on the busiest day of the holiday weekend.

Shaking his head, Batten pulled his key from his pocket. When he pressed it, he knew his car would bleep at him.

It duly did.

Forty two

Off-duty at long last, Jess Foreman strolled back into The Prince of Wales and ordered a pint of local cider. His bar stool, just about strong enough to support his bulk, was an old tractor-seat, re-purposed. When his cider arrived, he re-purposed that too.

'You're like a big sculpture, Jess,' the landlord said.

'Me? Sculpture?'

'You know, leaning forward, chin resting on your hands? *The Thinker*, is that what it's called?'

The only reason Foreman's hands supported his chin was because his glass was empty.

'I suppose I *was* thinking,' he told the landlord. 'They take the mick, down at the station, because I sometimes get these hunches, see.'

'Not cider-induced, are they, Jess? Your hunches?'

Foreman glanced at his empty golden glass. 'Let's say it helps,' he said, smiling.

When the landlord moved away, the smile disappeared. His hunch was serious. These are my woods, Jess told himself. And I won't have a crazy-dangerous *someone* make mischief here. Someone losing control, on Ham Hill. *My* hill. My house is halfway down the slope. Or halfway up, when I'm at the bottom.

Despite being more often at the top, where the pub was, he knew Ham Hill backwards, knew the woods, the streams, the new and old quarries, the archaeological dig sites. And the jogging trails - which set off his niggling hunch again. He declined another pint, and let his hunch drag him away.

The Easter holiday crowds were a thin departing trickle now, the car-parks almost empty. Something closer to silence descended on the hill as Jess Foreman took his bulky body down stone steps into deeper woodland, towards the hidden thicket pointed out by the hipster-dad with the Buddy Holly glasses.

A flattened patch of ground was still visible – though not from the jogging trail. He pushed his way through shrubs and tree-trunks into the next thicket, into another, and deeper into the undergrowth, quietly delving into weeds and plant-debris with the stem of a broken branch. Despite his bulk, he could move with stealth when he needed to.

Something shiny glinted up from the woodland floor. Drawing closer, he saw a small glass phial, and another, freshly-emptied, broken at one end. So-called legal highs? Kids, was it? Hiding here? Playing high-de-high in my woods? Or had the phials contained something stronger?

One thing was sure, they hadn't been here when Connor's forensic team scoured the area. The Prof could find a blood-stain on a grain of sand in the Sahara desert, if he put his mind to it.

And Jess Foreman could explore a niggling hunch, with or without the aid of cider. Hazy sightings of an unknown stranger in the woods - more a shape than a person - were still being reported when Jess signed off.

What if the bugger's come back? It wouldn't be the first time.

He wrapped the phials in a clean hankie the size of a tablecloth, and moved quietly through more thickets, further and further from the track, to where a dark tangle of ivy clothed the trees.

And lo and behold.

Laugh all you like, he told his absent colleagues, but, see - this hunch has legs.

As did the body on the ground at Jess's feet. A breathing body. Jess watched the chest move up and down. An artificial sleep, he thought, tapping the hankie-covered phials in his pocket. Wary, he checked the comatose form for wounds, and for weapons. Not least for a sharp blade.

Nothing.

Hunch still a-tingle, he wished the shape on the ground would wake and run, so he'd have the satisfaction of clobbering it. But as colleagues joked, if Foreman so much as *tapped* a crook with his steel-plated fingers, it was tantamount to excessive force. In any case, the shape slept on. Or continued to sleep something off.

As a precaution, Foreman pulled out a set of cable-ties.

Then, for the second time today, he pulled out his phone, and punched the speed-dial for HQ.

'I know what I'd *like* to charge our anonymous smack-head with,' said Batten, as he and Ball peered at Interview Room 1's video screen. 'Other than possession.'

'When he was brought in, he said barely ten words to Jess Foreman, all of them foul,' said Ball. 'Jess thought maybe a London accent?'

'London, eh?' Batten recalled his conversation with Reverend Kerry, about smooth Londoners in suits, buying drinks for locals in The Rising Sun, and tapping them for inside information about housing needs. This man seemed a long way from 'smooth'.

'Might as well be from Mars, sir, for all his cooperation. He's carrying a wad of cash, but no credit card.'

'Which means we can't do him for vagrancy - and he probably knows it. Where's his cash from, Ballie? Someone's providing it.'

'My guess is the same as yours, sir.'

'Serenity?'

'One way or another. But still a guess. Nothing on his person to prove it. Because there's next to nothing on his person.'

'Most of it's inside him. But if he *is* the sod who knifed Ken Leckey, why the hell risk coming back?'

Ball shrugged. They both knew the answer. To boast. To prove he could. Because the scene becomes a magnet. Because he *enjoyed* it.

'The sheer recklessness, Ballie, and the drugs. Is he going off the rails?'

'Going?'

'OK. Gone.'

'Gone something, sir, apart from to sleep. Jess calls him the Babe in the Woods. Whatever he's on, he's swallowed too much of it.'

Whatever the man was on, it was wearing off.

The police doctor could only suggest 'an opiate of some kind.'

'Can he be interviewed?'

'I see no reason why not, though he uttered not a word to me. And my concern was his *health*.'

'Mine's not', mumbled Batten.

He and Ball watched their suspect on the screen.

'He's still refusing to give his name.'

Batten could only grunt.

'And no keys or phone. Not a single thing in his pockets with an ID.'

'Stashed somewhere, Ballie. Came prepared to be anonymous, the sod.'

'Brown boots, brown hoodie, brown coat, sir. Blending in.'

And the boots a size nine, Batten noted. 'What about his dabs? On the phials? Don't tell me the prints got smudged?'

'We're pestering the boffins, sir.'

'Be nice if they're the same dabs as on that Estate Agent's brochure of Magnus's. My feet'd tingle.'

'We sent it off. Still waiting.'

'Bloody bank holidays,' said Batten. 'What's keeping Nina? Need to see if she recognises matey in there.'

'She's at the hospital, gutting Ken Leckey.'

Unfortunate use of words, thought Batten.

'Should we wait for her, sir, and let Mr Smack-head stew?'

'Tempting. But I fancy a crack at the bugger. While my blood's up.'

In the tight confines of Interview Room 1, the muscles on the brown-coated man seemed to grow. The broad bulk of PC Foreman added balance. When Batten and Ball sat down and switched on the recorder, the walls moved in.

'Might as well give us your name. Your prints are chugging through right now. Only a question of time.'

Silence. Whoever the man was, he refused with a twitch of his head. Batten gave him a long stare.

'Since we don't know your name, and since you've decided to keep mum, I suppose we'll have to call you *Mum*. That OK?'

Silence. And the faint red glow of anger around the man's eyes.

Batten and Ball exchanged glances.

'For the purposes of the tape,' Batten said, 'and in the absence of a response from *Mum*, I am summarising the reasons for *Mum*'s presence here. While being arrested, *Mum* used a range of abusive words to address a Police Constable. Inflammatory words. Wherever did you learn language like that, *Mum*? Eh?'

Silence, this time punctuated by a sneer.

'And to add to *Mum*'s bad manners, she was in possession of some rather dubious substances of an illegal nature. When you cracked open a phial or two, did you have to put down your shopping, *Mum*? Were you having a hissy fit? Was your bra riding up?'

The sneer became hate. Lips moved. But reconsidered.

'And, worse, *Mum* was discovered in close proximity to the scene of a particularly nasty knife attack, which took place on the very same day. But a mere coincidence, eh, Sergeant?'

Ball peered at the macho-man.

'Possibly, sir. Maybe *Mum* was driven to knife-crime by the strain of cross-dressing. Maybe *Mum*'s not comfortable in male clothing.'

'Ah, of course. An insult to your femininity, eh, *Mum*?'

'I'll have you. Have the *pair* of you.'

Nothing else.

Eight terse words, hissed through a grid of teeth, and followed by silence – broken by a rap on the door. DC Hick's arm jerked a sheet of paper into the room - the fast-tracked fingerprint results.

'Blast! We'll have to stop calling you *Mum*. Your dabs belong to a bad lad called Ryan Brand. 35 years old, and ought to know better.'

'And no stranger to a cell, are you, Mr Brand?' Ball nodded at the sheet. 'Actual Bodily Harm. Intimidating a Witness.'

Brand sneered back at Ball, then turned his gaze back on Batten, the hate in his eyes a deep, dark red. He added one word to the proceedings.

'Solicitor'.

'Getting more like *Strictly Come Dancing* every day, Ballie! First we tap our toes waiting for a duty brief to foxtrot over to Parminster, then the bugger does a pirouette and tangos into the wings - while you and me tap our toes waiting for a posher version to waltz in!'

'Posh, indeed, sir. I bet my car cost less than his suit.'

The source of Ryan Brand's new brief was a mystery. His command of his role, no mystery at all. Not long after waltzing into HQ, the expensive legal-eagle polka'd out again, with Ryan Brand in tow, shrugging off the paltry cautions.

Batten wished he was a sheriff in a Western, six-shooter in hand, drawling, *don't leave town*. Without more evidence, Ryan Brand could fill himself with drugs, crucify the inhabitants of Turks Lane if he had a mind, and postpone the consequences.

'If looks could kill, sir, you'd be dead.'

Batten shrugged. Nothing new, Brand's red-eyed glare of hatred.

Forty three

'Zig, do you want the good news first, or the bad?'

'Prof.' Connor's phone manner was brisker than normal. Batten reminded himself Connor was supposed to be on leave, too, and it was late in the day.

'The good, Prof. I'm an optimist.'

'Huh, you think? Anyway the good news is we fast-tracked the fibres swabbed from Mr Leckey's teeth and gums. If you recall, someone kindly stuffed a rag in his mouth before carving him up.'

'Why's it good news?'

'Because it's better than the bad, Zig – which concerns the nature of the fibres. Bog-standard, so far. Could even belong to you, assuming you keep a duster in your kitchen drawer.'

'It was a duster?'

'Well, the fibres *suggest* so. We scientists are not allowed to overstep the logic of our trade, Zig.'

'Our assailant planned to buff up the crime-scene, Prof?'

'Despite a fingertip search, no mop, bucket or furniture polish was discovered, so I couldn't possibly comment.'

'You've been a big help.'

'Sarky Northern git. I won't tell you the new stuff.'

'If you don't, Andy, *you*'ll be the crime-scene.'

'Huh, make a change. First of all, rug-fibres. From Turks Lane. We found minute traces in Alicia Heron's hair, ears, eyelids - as you'd expect, despite the dunking in water. But we found traces in the victim's nasal passages. And, Dr Welcome confirms, in the lungs.' Connor let the information sink in.

'Hell's teeth,' said Batten. Both men knew the import. 'She breathed them in?'

'Must have, Zig. And you can't do that when you're dead.'

Spinning round in his swivel chair did nothing to reduce the bad taste in Batten's throat. 'Someone did wrap her in the rug? And cart her off?'

'Appears so. A cheap rug, too. 100% polyester. No trace of wool or silk fibres.'

'So it *was* the rug Chas Janner said he bought to replace the bluebird one?'

'You'd concluded as much, hadn't you?'

'Yes. And we know why we're waffling about it. So we don't have to contemplate some bastard wrapping Lish Heron in cheap polyester and hauling her up Crown of Thorns Hill - still alive!'

'Thanks for saying it, Zig. I'm happy not to.'

'You can stop now, Prof.'

'There's more, sorry. But it might be useful. I assume you want to hear?'

No. Batten didn't. 'Go on,' he said.

'Baler-twine, Zig. Bright orange, man-made, and cut by a bladed instrument. Since I'm addressing a lesser mortal, I'll refer to said instrument as 'a knife'. And not one of ours.'

'Again, already known, Andy. Stop pissing about. Please?'

Connor adjusted his tone, in response to a voice sounding more tired than he was.

'Cut-marks, Zig. Cut by a blade with a blemish – a tiny nick in the blade at the sharp end. I've multi-tested the strands now, and they all share the same tiny nick – a distinctive chevron where the metal's been damaged. The blade slices through cleanly everywhere, except for this one recurring blemish.'

Batten caught up. 'Any chance you can link the blade to *two* crime scenes, Prof?'

'All of a rush, still, but likely. The knife that scarred Ken Leckey's flesh nicked his sleeve and shorts too. And, more usefully, his socks. Same distinctive chevron in the cloth fibres. Chances of it being two different knives are tiny, statistically speaking.'

'Could it be a kitchen knife, or something like?'

'Now, now, Zig. My preferred term, 'a bladed weapon', is what I'll have to spout when addressing Your Honour.'

'I wish we'd got as far as a courtroom.'

'But if we do, I'll say whatever sliced through the baler twine on Crown of Thorns Hill sliced up Kenneth Leckey too. Just find the knife, Zig, and who owns it. Simple!'

Connor's forced levity rang down the phone, without lightening

Batten's mood. As far as sharp knives were concerned, he didn't need to tell Connor there was no shortage in the wider crime environment of East Thorne. Or tell him a surly, muscled lump called Ryan Brand was current favourite for ownership of this particular knife – for what it was worth.

Brand had been 'released under investigation'.

To freely walk the streets.

When Batten plonked his bum on the edge of Ball's desk and recounted Connor's news, the reply was a thoughtful stare.

'Sir. Not your fault she died,' Ball said.

'But we had to let Brand *walk*. I'm doing my job with one hand tied behind my back.'

'Wouldn't have made much difference, sir. Not with his posh lawyer. There's no evidence linking Ryan Brand to any kind of blade.'

'All the same, give uniform a nudge, over at East Thorne. If it is Brand, and he's still got a taste for opiates, who's to say what the bugger might do.'

'Ask me, he'll have taken his brief's advice and got as far away from East Thorne as his walking-boots'll carry him.'

'Depends what's gone down his throat or up his nose, since we last had the pleasure of his company. I've zero confidence in Brand taking *anyone*'s advice. So make sure uniform switch their brains to the 'on' position.'

Feet tingling, Batten lumped back to his office, Ryan Brand on his mind. Along with rugs and dusters, baler-twine, knives, and fingernails.

And motives clear as mud.

A dying sun toyed with the horizon as Richard Pardew rolled his Porsche into the deep shadow of a huge campervan. The car park of The Mason's Arms at Oddcombe, where he and Mal Muir had arranged to meet, was quiet now. When Muir parked his Lexus in the same shadow, Pardew climbed into the passenger seat. In less fraught times, he might have enjoyed the view beyond the windscreen, of old trees and new greenery.

But not this evening.

'I take it you've received the latest intelligence, about our friend Mr Brand?'

Mal Muir rewarded Pardew with a stony glare. He was in no mood for levity. 'Friend? Never *that*. Even before you let him turn rogue.'

'Just a figure of speech, Mal. Don't lose your sense of humour.'

Richard Pardew appraised Muir's stony look. Did Muir *have* a sense of humour?

'Richard, just tell me what you intend doing about Brand. I thought our lawyer *friend* was supposed to clean up, once he'd unhooked him from our stroppy Northern policeman?'

'Our lawyer friend managed to keep Brand's mouth shut, Mal, and remove him from the clutches of CID, so give him credit, eh?'

'Credit? On top of what we pay him? He's a leech.'

'A leech we trust, Mal.'

Muir's reply was a grunt.

'And Brand *was* useful. In an unplanned sort of way.'

'Useful? Is that what you call it?'

'I do, Mal. Count the chickens before you shoot the fox. His warnings to our Estate Agent *friend* may have been a tad gothic, but you have to admit they worked? Some minor legal issues will doubtless nip Mr Willey in the behind, but I'm damn sure he'll keep his mouth shut about the major ones - you being one of them. A result, I'd say.'

'Don't crow, Richard. You should never have used him in the first place.'

It was Muir's idea to use Willey, but Pardew didn't say so. '*Additionally*, our Mr Brand, despite his somewhat gory modus operandi -'

'Which was a magnet to the forces of the law!'

'Even so, Mal, the impact on our bolshie orchard expert *has* been effective. I'm told Mr Leckey is quite cut up about the whole experience.' Pardew chuckled at his own pun. 'I fully expect him to re-think his position. With a view to permanently leaving the area.'

'You *do* mean selling up?'

'And if he does, Mal, rest assured whoever buys his house will be *friend*, not foe.'

'Make sure it is. And the decrepit handyman, and his lump of a daughter? Any progress?'

Pardew paused. 'Mr Holt is remarkably resistant to financial inducement, Mal. A surprisingly tough nut, with or without Brand's skills of persuasion. Efforts will be redoubled. By different personnel, rest assured.'

'This Holt fellow must have a weak point, Richard. Everybody does, somewhere.'

Pardew considered *Muir's* weak points. Too many? Perhaps it was time Mal bowed out?

'In Holt's case, Mal, the some*where* is a some*one*. But leave that particular problem to me, yes? And worry not. Ryan Brand is history. Other plumbers will unblock the drain.'

Mal Muir changed tack. 'Kindly tell me where Ryan Brand *is*? *Yes*?'

Richard Pardew tapped his fingernails on the dashboard. Through the windscreen, the last fragments of sun were painting shadows on the landscape, all the way to the horizon. How best to say it? For once, Pardew settled for the truth.

'Mal. Ryan Brand has vanished. Hopefully forever. People do vanish, you know. *Yes*?'

Street lamps and darkness were at war by the time DC Nina Magnus left the hospital. A chastened Ken Leckey stayed behind, staring in a silent daze at his bandaged arms, his legs, his arms again. She remembered him from the heated public meetings in East Thorne, where he'd waved those same arms at planners and developers, in loud defence of orchards and democracy.

Poor sod, she thought, despite finding him hard to like.

Back at Parminster, she yawned at a recording of Ryan Bran, squirming on a hard chair like a Buddha with haemorrhoids.

'They have similar builds, sir,' she told Batten. 'But the ART I saw had hair.'

'*Art*?' asked Batten.

'Sorry, sir. Anonymous Racist Thug.'

'Well is he the same *Art* who tried to chuck you out of Turks Lane? Or not?'

Magnus blew out a breath. 'In a courtroom? Cross-examined by a defence lawyer who's just reminded me I saw him for two minutes, seven months ago? *Probably* is the best I'd do. The eyes are the same. Nasty. But my thug had a full beard and hair, and a black suit. This skinhead's beardless, and wearing outdoor brown. And whatever's inside him hasn't improved his complexion. So, *probably*, sir. Sorry.'

Ball gave her a supportive nod as she headed for the car park.

'Maybe when she and Mike Brean have, you know, settled down a bit, sir?'

Batten's exhausted nod was all he had left. A definite link between Ryan Brand and Turks Lane might have perked him up to face his office, where documents were breeding on the desk like bacteria.

'Maybe, Ballie. Lots of maybes. But only one definite.'

'What's that, sir?'

'Definitely time we got some sleep.'

Easter Tuesday

Forty four

While touting for work, Andrew Holt pushed empty *Community Angels* collection bags through every letter-box he passed. When next he drove through the same streets, he loaded the filled black bags onto his pick-up, and dropped them at the charity shop.

He'd been doing this, unpaid, for eleven years now.

This morning was different.

Because this afternoon he had to present himself at Parminster CID, with Biddy, and dreaded the thought. Still, charity is charity, he told himself, so he did his collections, as usual.

He didn't see the car, just heard its engine while tottering to his pick-up, arms weighed down by heavy plastic bags of old clothes. When he reached his truck, someone had dumped another sack there. Thick, grey, anonymous, no logo.

I suppose they didn't have a proper bag, he thought. No matter. Charity is charity. He leaned across to put it with the rest.

It moved.

As he jerked his hand away, the bag moved again. And again. He forced himself to prod it with his hand.

Miaow! said the bag.

MIAOW!

Shocked, angry, he opened it, jumping aside as the terrified cat hissed and spat before leaping from the pick-up, dashing across the pavement and fleeing into the nearest garden. Holt scanned the area, but the cat - and the car that must have brought it - were nowhere to be seen.

What remained was the bag. And something lumpy, within. Wary, he picked up the nearest weapon, a spade, and nudged the thick bag till it fell on its side.

That's when the head rolled out.

He leapt backwards in shock, acid and bile in his throat - till he saw it was the head of a child's doll. No body, just the head.

Both eyes had been removed.

It stared up at him, like a skull, a rolled up scrap of paper poking from the cavity.

Andrew Holt read the four short words, in crude block letters.

WE DO DAUGHTERS TOO.

Blood drained from his face, as the shock hit. He staggered against the truck.

Had he owned a mobile phone, he would have instantly called the police. But by the time he climbed behind the wheel and quivered down the road, second thoughts dug him in the ribs.

Tell the police *what*?

He still didn't know what to tell them this afternoon, at the station. And telling of a headless doll, a terrified cat, a veiled warning – twice as dangerous as saying nothing at all?

First, Alicia, yoked to a crucifix.

Chas, arrested.

Ken, sliced up like a carcass.

I'm the only one left, he said, with a shudder.

He read the words again.

No.

You're not.

WE DO DAUGHTERS TOO.

No names. No demands.

But Handy Andy got the message, all the same.

Forty five

DC 'Loft' Hick lumbered his way through gaps in witness timelines, one after another. Most resulted from witnesses forgetting when Thursday *was*, let alone what they were doing between 7pm and 11. At least his favourite cafe was open, and he had a double-strength latte and a bacon roll inside him.

When the phone rang, he was the nearest, so got lumbered with that too. He duly slogged to Reception to collect the announced visitor - only to stop in his tracks when her bright blue eyes and sharp cheekbones twinkled at him. Twenty-something, and better curves than Dr Sonia Welcome, he thought, in his unreconstructed way.

'E-E-Eddie Hick,' he said, shaking hands.

'Lorna Wilde,' she replied. 'DC Wilde.'

'L-like me. I'm a DC. Coffee?'

Eddie, he told himself, stop making everything rhyme. And stop looking at her lips. Get hold of yourself, man.

Hand sneaking behind his back, Hick got hold of his shirt instead, feeding it back into his trousers, while Lorna Wilde said no to coffee and yes to her meeting with Inspector Batten. Hick ushered her to Batten's office, this time colliding only with a pleasant feeling higher up his body than normal - about where his lost heart used to be.

'D-D-DC Wilde, sir. About the signage.'

'The sign*ing*,' said Lorna Wilde. 'But thank you, Eddie.' She twinkled another smile, to soften the correction.

'Stuck for work, Hickie?' asked Batten, as Hick loitered in the doorway.

'Sorry, sir. I'll leave you with Lor - with DC Wilde.'

You could cut yourself on her cheekbones, thought Batten. Hick has.

'He struggles to leave my office,' Batten told her. 'My magnetism.'

Lorna Wilde smiled again, inscrutably.

'We've a tricky job for you, but Area said you're something of a British Sign Language expert, yes?'

'I can handle the Somerset version, too, sir,' said Wilde. 'There *is* one,' she added, when his eyebrows went up. 'It has more oomph. BSL meets Charades, sort of.'

'As long as it works on our Special Needs witness.'

'We're tending to say 'globally-delayed' now, sir, rather than Special Needs.'

Batten couldn't force his eyebrows any higher.

'Well, her name's Biddy Holt and she's a globally-delayed thirty-three year old. And she's all yours.'

Lorna Wilde spruced up Interview Room 2 with cushions and a pair of throws from her car.

'To soften the environment, sir,' she explained.

Despite the added frills, Josie from the Independent Living Centre sat next to Biddy Holt more like a prison guard than a responsible adult. Biddy Holt's face seemed as closed as ever.

But when Lorna Wilde began to sign - fluent, exuberant - Batten realised the smile on her face reached down into her fingers too. He was conscious of being in the reassuring presence of expertise. Biddy Holt began to sign back, body language relaxing, suspicion replaced by something closer to eagerness, if not trust.

And the questions, with pauses for translation, clarification, delving. A far different process to the strangely broken attempts of Reverend Kerry, or the contained caution of Andrew Holt - whose ghost-white face hadn't smiled at all when an expert signer from the police turned up at his door to collect him and his daughter.

Batten asked first about Alicia Heron.

'Biddy signs her as 'the lady with the angels,' said Lorna Wilde. 'She isn't Mummy,' she says. Does that make sense?'

Batten explained, and the signing resumed.

'Not Mummy, she says again. Too dark.'

'The lady was too dark? Or the night?'

More smooth signing.

'Both, alas. Wait… Always dark at night, she says, but darkness shall be light…I'm not getting much further, sir.'

'Ask Biddy if she went out, Thursday. In the dark.'

'Not allowed, she says. Bedtime. And a secret.'

'What kind of secret?'

As Lorna Wilde's hands signed away, Batten could have sworn Biddy Holt's face took on a knowing look.

'Special secret...That's all she'll say.'

'Who else knows the secret? Please ask her.'

'Won't say...Curry asked. Curry?'

'She means Kerry. Reverend Kerry, from All Saints.'

'Ah, yes...Won't tell Kerry. Top Policeman wants to know...she means you, sir... And the one shaped like a ball. And the one with a hood. Won't tell, though.'

'A hood? Who does she mean?'

'On the hill, she says.'

'Crown of Thorns Hill?'

'Yes. The hill where Kerry saves Mankind on Good Friday afternoon...the hill where dark becomes light. Best if I keep translating literally, sir?'

'I assumed you were.'

'There's literal and literal. If you see what I mean?'

Batten thought he did, and thought of Andrew Holt, his life worn out untangling his daughter's silent world - uncertain what was literal, what was not.

'The SOCOs wear hoods? On their crime scene suits?'

'She's saying 'man', not men. But she may just be fixating on one particular SOCO...'

'Ask if this man wore a white suit.'

'No. Brown, she says. He plays hide-and-seek, on his own.'

'Ask if he has a knife.'

'Oh. She didn't like the question, sir. Wait... Not allowed near knives, she says. Knives bad. Daddy has sharp knives, in his workshop. And a stone. She means a grindstone. Not allowed where the knives are.'

'Perhaps she disobeyed?'

'She says no. Mustn't touch knives...Mustn't. Not sure if she did or didn't, sir. Says she does what Daddy tells her.'

What *did* Daddy tell her? Batten wondered. And if Biddy didn't take a knife up Crown of Thorns Hill, who did? He had one strong theory, at least. Could Biddy Holt pick out Ryan Brand in a video line-up, assuming the police reacquired him? And if she managed to, how much credence would her testimony have in court? He sighed his doubts away.

'Let's go back a bit. Ask if Daddy knows her secret,' Batten said.

'Won't tell. Won't.'

Batten watched as Biddy's shoulders came up, and her arms folded themselves across her chest. 'That's all, sir. Shall I try again?'

'Ask if she helped Daddy, on Thursday night. No, wait. Ask *how* she helped him.'

Kerry had been pretty sure Biddy helped him with *something*, and Batten was of the same mind. Biddy's arms unfolded, and she signed, stiffly now, to Lorna Wilde.

'Secret, she says. And again, sir. Secret.'

Next door, in an interview room bereft of cushions and throws, Sergeant Ball was renewing his acquaintance with Andrew Holt. Or had a ghost replaced him? I didn't think he could turn any paler, Ball thought, staring across the table at this whitened carcass of a man.

'So, you were nowhere near All Saints church on Thursday evening? And you certainly didn't climb up Crown of Thorns Hill? What you said before, I think?'

Holt's mind was on neither of those places. It was in his pick-up truck with a terrified cat, a headless doll, and a stark warning. It was in his threadbare cottage in Turks Lane, the kitchen sink stained by Biddy's thick brown tea, the only tea she knew how to make, the greasy tea he'd poured down it every day, for a lifetime.

'Sir?'

'Yes. Yes,' he said. They wouldn't keep asking, he knew, if they didn't know something. 'We're early-to-bed, me and Biddy. We need sleep.'

'Don't suppose either of you sleep-walked, sir, Thursday night?' asked Ball with a false smile.

Holt flashed a frown across the table. Perhaps he and Biddy had? In a dream. A nightmare.

'If we did, we wouldn't remember. Isn't that how sleep-walking works?'

'Oh, all sorts of strange things happen when folk are asleep, sir. You'd be surprised.'

And also when they're awake, Holt wanted to say. When they're working for nothing, for charity, and the surprise is the skull of a doll, and a warning like a needle in the heart.

At least Biddy's safe, next door.

But for how long?

And, next door, would Biddy keep their secrets? Or would they be dragged from her?

Ball was staring, harder now.

How long can I keep this up? Holt asked himself. And why am I putting Biddy through it? Am I protecting her? Or she me?

He made up his mind.

'I have to be with my daughter,' he said.

'And why so, sir?'

Holt paused, but pressed on.

'To give her permission.'

'Permission, sir? To do what?'

'To tell secrets,' said Andrew Holt.

A puzzled Lorna Wilde was asking Biddy how Mummy was supposed to come back to life when Ball's knuckles tapped on the door. He'd never disturb a delicate interview without reason, Batten knew.

Seconds later, Eddie Hick was scooting his new lady-friend away for a coffee-break, while Batten and Ball conferred.

'This better be good, Ballie. We almost got Biddy to cough.'

'Leave her be, sir. Daddy's beaten her to it.'

Forty six

Reverend Kerry should be doing this, thought Batten, not me. He was reminded of the confessional, at his Roman Catholic church, as a child.

I'm not a priest, I'm a policeman.

Or are they much the same?

It was much the same to Andrew Holt, white-faced against the brown-beige walls, solicitor on his left, untouched tea on his right, like the brown tea Biddy makes, the tea he never drank. He watched the tiny flickering lights on the voice recorder and spoke to them.

'Thursday night will haunt me to my dying day, Inspector. I'd spruced up the Good Friday cross - I promised Reverend Kerry I would. And after Mike and Chas carried the cross up the hill, Turks Lane was quiet as a grave.

'I never hear noises from Chas's place, next door. But a little later I did. Raised voices, a man and a woman, I was almost sure. It went quiet, and when I went round, the back door was wide open and all the downstairs lights were on. With Ken being away, and Chas never there, I was concerned. And I have keys, because of the cleaning, so I thought, well, I can lock up, at the very least.

'I thought I was sleep-walking at first, because there, in the spill of the light, was Alicia - an image I shall never be rid of. Alicia Heron, stock-still, in the rear garden, staring at the trees - no more than shadows - and at the dark shape of Crown of Thorns Hill. She turned round, and stared wide-eyed at her house. I swear to you, I had no idea she was coming back.

'She had different hair. Her skin was brown - from the Thai sun, I suppose - but it was Alicia. And so embarrassed to see *me* she scuttled inside. I followed.' Holt glanced at his tea but didn't touch it.

'And Alicia?' asked Batten.

'Despite the tan, she seemed to blush. But, oh, still direct to a fault. She told me she'd decided to sell, to *those people* - just blurted it out. I went cold. There, in her hallway, the hallway I'd dusted and scrubbed every week for as long as I can remember.

'Do you know what day it is?' I asked her.

'She looked at me as if I was mad. "Thursday," she said. "It's Thursday. It's no *secret*."'

'It's the day before Good Friday,' I told her. 'The day Judas sold Our Saviour for thirty grubby pieces of silver. The day of betrayal. That's what you're doing to us - to me, to Biddy, to Ken. Betraying us, for thirty pieces of deceit! *Shame* on you!'

'She just said, "My life's elsewhere. I need the money, to keep it that way."'

Holt's hands were shaking now.

'She didn't apologise. Not a word of concern for the neighbours who had helped her. We practically buried her parents - she was in no fit state, but she'd forgotten that too... It was more than I could stomach. The young, these days, they want the moon, and they want it on a stick! I shouted at her, *don't you think I could have had a life elsewhere? Don't you think I need money? But I cope. I work. I meet my responsibilities!*'

'"You shouldn't," she said. "You should live, instead." And she asks me, "Why don't you sell up too? Take the money. Money gives you *choices*."'

'Choices? *What* choices? I thought of Biddy, and her choices - or lack of them. I tried to explain, but Alicia turned her back on me, walked away. It was too much. Deciding our future, without a second thought, this slip of a girl! With her back turned she looked nothing more than a child!'

Andrew Holt's solicitor made a calming gesture with his hands. Batten was thinking, with Biddy's back turned she looked nothing more than an adult.

'I caught her by the shoulder, so she'd face me, so I could reason with her. But she's a slip of a thing, and the rug in the hallway, the cheap rug Chas put there - there's no backing on it. I should know, because it keeps getting caught in the vacuum cleaner. Well, her foot shoots out from under her and over she goes, onto the floor, head to the stones, only the rug between her and...hardness.

'I saw a trace of blood, on the rug. And Alicia wasn't moving. I checked her pulse but I couldn't find one. I tried to revive her - you must believe me. You must - I'm not someone who walks away!'

Batten thought of the thirty years Holt had spent wearing himself to a thread, not walking away from Biddy.

'Lying there, she reminded me of Elisabeth, my dead wife. *You can bring neither of them back, Andrew*, I said. *Who do you think you are? God?*'

Batten caught the solicitor's questioning brow, dismissing it with a tiny head-shake.

'I couldn't cope with her eyes, staring, the life gone out of them. To stop them looking at *me*, I covered her, folded the rug over her face. Nothing more than a child, I thought. Covering her seemed the only decent thing.'

Times like this, Batten thought, cover me too, let me not see or hear.

'You must understand, I'm in Alicia's house, her body on the floor at my feet. Have I killed her? What will happen to me? My God, what will happen to *Biddy*? I dashed home and up the stairs, but to my huge relief, Biddy was fast asleep. I dashed downstairs again, all in a panic. I didn't know who else to turn to, who to ask. I blundered along the path, I didn't even remember to bring a torch, my hands scratched to pieces by the brambles, on the path leading to the rear of the church, to find Dominic.'

'Reverend Kerry?'

'Yes. Our one true friend.'

'And what did Reverend Kerry do?'

'Nothing. He was nowhere to be seen. Neither in the vestry nor the church house. I peeked into the church but it was choir practice, and Tull goes, so Kerry doesn't. My heart sank when I realised he must be in The Rising Sun. I couldn't go there.'

'Because witnesses would remember?'

'Partly, I suppose. I go there so little. But, really, I was too shocked to be among revellers. Too ashamed.'

'So you came back to Turks Lane?'

'Yes, to do what Dominic would have told me to do - call an ambulance. I blundered back along the path. But when I reached Turks Lane, she was nowhere to be seen.'

'She?'

'Alicia. Gone! And the rug gone too.'

'Gone where?'

Holt struggled to reply, the details too painful, the consequences worse. As the voice recorder flickered, Batten eased him along.

'Alicia didn't go anywhere under her own steam, Mr Holt. We both know that. I think I can guess the answer, but tell me, please.'

Holt gave the saddest nod Batten had ever seen. Wet-cheeked, shaking, he told what he would have told Dominic Kerry. Had Kerry chosen to ask.

'I thought, what if Alicia was only stunned? What if she woke up and, you know, somehow staggered off? I wanted it to be true, but I knew it wasn't. The ridiculousness of it: she rises from the flagstones, gathers up a worthless rug and wanders off, leaving the doors open and the lights on, leaving her bag, her phone, her keys... I had to get rid of them.'

'We'll come to that, Mr Holt. We both know Alicia didn't miraculously climb to her feet.'

'No. She did not. In a panic, I rushed next door and ran upstairs, and my heart leapt into my throat when I found Biddy gone too. Grabbing a torch this time, I ran down the short-cut, looking for Biddy. All Saints is her haven. If my first thought was to seek out Dominic, might she do the same? I was half-mad, not realising I would have caught her up, or collided with her on her way back.'

'Biddy didn't go to All Saints?'

Holt shook his head. 'The track was empty and the church dark. And Biddy's never welcome in The Rising Sun. In a daze, I scoured her favourite wandering places, where she still searches for her Mummy. I scoured the orchard. I drove my pick-up to the Independent Living Centre, but no sign. I toured the dark lanes, shining my pathetic torch into the hedgerows where she hides. Nothing.'

'You didn't mention searching on Crown of Thorns Hill, sir.'

Andrew Holt stared down at his shoes. Hard truths stared back at him.

'No. I did not search there. Only later could I accept the harsh reality: I was not trying to find Biddy. I was escaping from her. And from what I knew in my bones she had done.'

'She?'

'Both of us. She and I. I knew Biddy could only be on the hill. Her favourite hiding places are there. But you must believe me, I had only the faintest sense she might...'

Holt's eyes glanced briefly upwards, as if Crown of Thorns Hill had shifted from East Thorne to Parminster. Then his eyes returned to the flickering lights on the voice machine.

'I have no memory of what time I staggered into Turks Lane. But I saw right away Biddy was back, because the rug, from Alicia's house, was lying there, discarded on my kitchen floor. Damp nightwear was on the floor, too, and fresh garments gone from the airing cupboard. Its door was open. A thousand times I've reminded her to close the airing cupboard door. She never does. Never, never does.

'Biddy was upstairs, in a deep sleep, exhausted. Attempting to wake her from exhaustion is worthless - I speak from long experience. And in truth, I could not face another moment of pain. I was beyond exhaustion. All I could think was what might happen to her, and to me, the following day.'

'And how you could prevent it?'

Holt screwed his eyes shut, to fend off the memory of one bad decision becoming two.

'Yes. Prevent it. I could see no way back for us. So any trace of where Biddy had trod, anything she'd touched, I cleaned. Cleaning, I do well. Biddy's clothes I bagged and burnt. My own, too. And the gloves Biddy wore. And of course, the rug.'

'Where?' Batten guessed the answer.

'At my compost heap. In the incinerator bins. Worthless rags, in any case. Charity shops, jumble-sales. Later, I raked the ashes into the heap. Ashes, to make things grow.'

'And Alicia Heron's clothes? You burnt them too?'

'Alicia's? No. Her bag and keys I threw in the compost heap. I have a stirring pole. I pushed them all the way to the bottom. I didn't know how else to conceal them.'

Batten swallowed at the thought of having to dig them out again.

'Her phone?'

'In our dear River Parret, Inspector. Mobile phones are a mystery to me. I was half-mad by then. I know there's some sort of bell inside. What if it rings, I thought, and keeps ringing, you know, from the grave? Better to let the river kill it, because rivers flow, don't they, and keep on flowing, till they reach the sea?' Silently, Andrew Holt stared at the flickering lights, watching his own river trickle away. 'Everything does, sooner or later, I suppose?'

He rested his head on the back of his hands, as if in prayer.

The solicitor's eyes flashed a question.

'We'll take a break,' Batten said.

Forty seven

If 'Prof' Connor thought life was back to normal, he was wrong. Half-way through his architecturally-motivated trip to Martock church, with its fine carved wooden ceiling, he was called to East Thorne, to oversee a forensic search of Andrew Holt's cottage.

Here, the plaster ceiling was mottled by sombre stains where the ancient thatch had leaked. But it was not the roof that caught Connor's eye. Biddy Holt's bedroom walls were covered in childish drawings, scratched on with pencil and pen, not a blank space between them. In a few places, someone had tried to wipe them away and given up.

More recent drawings stood out, the lines fresher, the detail bold.

The instant Connor fathomed what they meant, he was on the phone to Parminster.

Zig Batten didn't take the call. He sat opposite a rested Andrew Holt, drawn once more to the flickering lights on the voice recorder, and seeming to speak to them.

'With Biddy, one mustn't show fear or stress. She absorbs such feelings all too strongly, and displays her own version - in spades. So, next morning, I pretended all was well. Difficult, considering the clamour of police cars and the outrage in the village streets. I made breakfast, as normal, but Biddy gave me her special look, her knowing look. We signed for what felt like months. I was exhausted from the night before, and doubly so now. Our breakfast went cold on the plates.'

'Mr Holt, I should remind you DC Wilde is with Biddy now. We cross-check all statements, thoroughly.'

'In which case, I hope DC Wilde will end up less exhausted than I did. Fact and fantasy are random bedfellows, where Biddy is concerned. Only after I'd signed and signed, doing *cross-checking* of my own, was I able to reach any conclusion.'

'And you concluded what?'

'Many things. Some may not make sense to you.'

'Even so?'

Holt turned to his solicitor, who nodded.

'May I put Biddy's ramblings into some kind of shape?'

'You may.'

'"Helped, Daddy," she said. Many times. All the while looking special, proud of herself. How? I asked her, knowing and dreading the answer. On Thursday night, she said, she came downstairs and found me gone. I was out searching for Dominic. In my haste and panic I didn't switch off a single light or lock a single door.

'"Daddy was hiding," Biddy told me later, something like a smile on her face. So, she went seeking, and the lights next door drew her in. It wasn't me she found, of course. It was Alicia Heron. In Biddy's innocence, she thought I'd left 'the Jesus lady' for her, deliberately, you see, wrapped in a rug, like a present. As if I would ever do that! As if I would respond *like that* to her constant, pointless, *pointless* search for her Mummy!'

Trapped by the pain of recall, Holt swallowed a glob of tea - as greasy and brown as before. 'Afterwards, in her matter of fact way, Biddy told me, "lady's not Mummy. Too brown to be Mummy." My photographs of Elisabeth are mostly when she grew pale, so pale, as her illness deepened. But I think Biddy can be forgiven, don't you, for rejecting my 'gift' of a brown lady?'

Whatever Batten thought he knew of forgiveness, it was a whirlpool now.

'Nevertheless, Biddy didn't leave the 'lady' where she was. Did she?'

'The village would have been spared more horrors if she had. No, in Biddy's special version of Easter, the lady...became a Jesus. Kerry does his best to explain the miracle of resurrection - but Biddy's understanding, well... And Dominic would be the first to admit his old-fashioned images leave something to be desired.'

Batten remembered seeing them, in the Vestry, draped over an easel, the white symbols of Easter - and scanning them in seconds, easily absorbing their content. He remembered Biddy's slow, failed attempts at the same straightforward task.

'In Dominic's pictures, Jesus has a crown of thorns. No surprise, Inspector, if Biddy carried her 'Jesus lady' to the hill with that very name. But on Thursday night, I wouldn't - couldn't - accept she had done so. Not because she isn't strong enough, far from it. I have experienced her physical strength many a time, with bruises to prove it. She scooped up

Alicia in the rug, having done what I omitted to do - pocketed a torch - and carried her as far as the spring, on the hill. To wash her, in the pool, where the spring is dammed.'

'Why wash her? Why exactly?'

'In Kerry's Bible pictures, washing is something of a theme - perhaps you've seen them? But I fear the true culprit is me. At home, I tell her, every bedtime, no-one is allowed into Heaven unless they're clean. In the absence of a mother to do it, it's my way of persuading Biddy to wash.'

Batten needed a wash right now. Or a gallon of cider.

'And one of Kerry's most striking pictures is of Christ crucified. Perhaps you've seen it, too? Jesus, crucified, in a pure white loin-cloth?'

'Alicia's shirt?'

'Yes. Some images imprint themselves, don't they? For Biddy, this one did.'

Mind drifting, Holt sipped more brown tea from the plastic cup, ignoring the taste.

When will I tell him, Batten thought, that Alicia might have been alive, clinically at least, when Biddy Holt stripped her of her clothes, washed her naked body in cold water and transformed her into Christ? *How* will I tell him?

'Can Biddy manage knots?' asked Batten.

'Badly, Inspector, for many reasons, not least being the special gloves she must wear. A granny knot, at best. Shoelaces, no. Her shoes are specially made, with crepe soles and Velcro fastenings.'

'What size shoe does she take?'

Holt gave Batten and the solicitor a curious glance. The brief merely shrugged.

'A five. Too small really to support...her robustness. Hence the thick crepe soles.'

Too small to leave behind an eight or nine shoeprint, thought Batten, crepe soles or not. He wanted to scratch his head.

'What happened next?'

'Biddy's account was more confused at this point, Inspector. She said she grew tired. And cold, from the night and from the water in the pool. She was in pyjamas and a dressing gown. The warmest things she wore were gloves and shoes. She wanted to put the Jesus lady on the cross, for

Kerry, like the Jesus in Kerry's pictures. Quite matter-of-fact, she said she tried to help Kerry save all the sins of the world.'

'But she didn't?'

'*Couldn't*. She went to see the cross, but it was covered in plastic, tied on tight, and she had no knife to cut the string. If I have managed to instil one bit of obedience, it is to keep away from sharp objects.'

'So what *did* she do?'

'Returned to the Jesus lady.'

'At the pool?'

'Yes. And cut her nails.'

'*Why*?'

'When she told me, I would have laughed - had the circumstances not been so grim. She clipped Alicia's nails so the Jesus lady wouldn't scratch herself. The lady's nails were too long, too sharp, she said. Biddy's nails are cut very short, always – my insistence again. If *Biddy* was to scratch at herself…well, you can imagine. She has special clippers, over-sized, easy to use, with a compartment to retain the clippings. Battered old clippers, tired. Like me, perhaps.'

'And you have these clippers handy?'

'They're with Alicia's phone. In the River Parret.'

Fitting, thought Batten. Didn't Lish Heron get cautioned for skinny dipping there?

'Alicia's clothes? Did you drown those, too?'

Holt's face clouded over. He picked up his tea, saw how thick and brown it was, and put it down.

'Burnt them, Inspector. Much later. I constantly remind Biddy waste is a sin. Not because we have nothing *to* waste, but for ethical reasons. What she did, she did to help, in her fashion. I didn't know it, but she'd carried Alicia's clothes down from Crown of Thorns Hill, and re-cycled them, in a *Community Angels* bag. I have dozens, at home.'

Batten's penny dropped. 'The charity shop? The lady is with *those* angels?'

'Yes. That's what Biddy meant. 'The lady with the angels' confused me too. Worse, Biddy tied the bag closed and put it with the other filled bags. I wait until they accumulate, you see, and leave a batch by the charity shop, for the Manageress to take in. By the time I realised what Biddy meant, I'd dropped Alicia's clothes outside the door, and Evie Mellor had carried them into the storeroom.'

'So, the burglar was you? *You* broke in to *Community Angels*?'

Batten's sympathy for Holt's predicament began to falter. At what point does desperation become deceit?

'There's nothing I won't do to protect Biddy. But once a lie begins, another lie must support it. And secrets follow... I couldn't risk Alicia's clothes being found. So, yes, I broke in.'

'And sliced open a fair few collection bags?'

'Before I found the right one. I recognised the blue leather jacket Alicia was wearing. Not any old jacket. I've never handled anything so exquisite, so expensive. I remember thinking, if only Biddy could wear it. If only it would fit.'

'You made a mess of the door jamb, I'm told?'

Holt sighed. 'I didn't want to snap the lock. I only replaced it a few weeks ago. In my defence, anything I damaged, I repaired, free. And with the utmost care.'

Batten added breaking and entering to Holt's charge-sheet, and criminal damage, and theft. With Sergeant Ball in mind, he winced at 'destroying evidence'.

'So you did burn Alicia's clothes? Which you effectively stole from the shop?'

'Yes. True.'

'You missed the loin-cloth, though. Her silk shirt.'

'I knew nothing of it. Not till later. I heard rumours in the village, but it was only when Biddy told me what she'd done...and what she failed to do. If you could have seen how distraught she was, not to be able, physically, to place her lady Jesus on the cross. The knotted twine, the weight, her awkwardness, the cold - all prevented her.'

They didn't prevent *someone*, Batten thought.

'She was angry not to finish what she'd begun. Such anger, such frustration. I pray you never experience Biddy's anger. Even her signing becomes volatile. "Jesus lady on the cross, Good Friday!" she signed, elbows jagging, hands like swords. "Jesus lady rises from the tomb, Easter Sunday! Jesus lady comes down from Heaven, Easter Monday! And *all* the dead shall rise! Shall *rise!*"'

Holt's hands twitched at the memory, an echo of his special daughter's vehemence. Batten was tempted to take a break, but they'd barely begun.

'Over and over, she signed, parroting her own ridiculous Easter, parroting her Mother's *impossible* return. Perhaps Dominic should not instruct her.' Holt's fingers came to rest on the table. Thin, pale claws. 'On the other hand, what *are* we without hope?'

In the silence, Holt's face clouded over as hope for Biddy diminished, and reality replaced it. How can this stick of a man look even thinner, even dryer than before, Batten wondered? And why can't he be vicious, thuggish, and vile - to make him less gut-wrenching to arrest?

'Mr Holt. You say your daughter didn't tie the Jesus lady to the cross. Did you?'

'*Me*? *No!* How could you think it? Despair and panic I admit to. Cowardice, even, in failing to confront the truth. But desecration? I have *faith*, Inspector. So, no! And no again!'

'We'll leave that aside, for now. If Biddy couldn't tie Alicia to the cross, what did she do with her?'

'She left her, tenderly, I hope, at the pool. Washed. Clean.'

'Fingernails clipped.'

'Indeed, but with kindness. And amongst nature. Biddy loves trees, plants, orchards and everything in them. She explained it in her own way. "Kerry says all things on earth are holy. So, water is holy." She left Alicia in the holy water, "for Good Friday, when Kerry saves Mankind from the sins of the world. And *all* the dead shall *rise*."'

Without noticing, Holt drained his brown tea.

Batten was constructing the next part of the equation. Biddy didn't complete her warped work, but someone did, for savagely different motives. Was the hidden watcher on Ham Hill also watching Turks Lane? And did Biddy in her innocence drop Alicia's naked body in the watcher's lap? Easy work to slice away a plastic sheet with a sharp knife, re-use the baler-twine, and strap a ready-made Christ to a handy cross at the peak of Crown of Thorns Hill.

What an image for the sun to rise on, a crucified corpse looming from a hilltop. What an inducement it must have been, to those still living below, in Turks Lane. What a message to wake up to, on the morning of Good Friday.

'Did you bring Biddy down from the hill?'

Holt's head trembled, dropping so low to the table it almost scraped it.

'No. She came down by herself, exhausted. She managed to carry Alicia's clothes down with her. But, alas, left her own special Jesus behind, her work undone. And she came home.'

'To Turks Lane?'

'Yes, where all the lights were burning. Home, to me. But when Biddy descended from the darkness, I, in my cowardice, where was I? Not there! *I wasn't even there to greet her!*'

Face almost as white as Holt's, and before the solicitor could open his mouth, Batten said, 'interview suspended.'

Either that, or remind Andrew Holt the new reality was not being there to greet his daughter.

Forty eight

In the Parminster car park, Batten and his Sergeant breathed air not smelling and tasting of desperation.

'Jesus Christ, Ballie.'

Ball pulled a face.

'Sorry, Chris. Inappropriate. But just when you think you've heard it all...'

'I know, sir. I don't envy the CPS trying to fathom Biddy Holt.'

'And *I* don't envy whoever tells her why Daddy's in jail. Hope it's not me.'

It will be, he thought.

'Connor's waiting, sir.'

Chastened, Batten climbed behind the wheel, and in silence they drove to number 3, Turks Lane.

Where the Holts used to live.

'Prof' Connor was staring at the drawings on Biddy Holt's bedroom wall when Batten walked in.

'I wish I knew if this is evidence or not, Zig. I'm stumped.'

'Proves you're human, Prof.'

'At the risk of sounding like one of those up-themselves art historians on TV, I'd say Biddy Holt has a primitive eye, as a cartoonist. The far wall's sort of juvenilia, Zig, see? But by the bed, the lines are slicker. More detail, too. The girl's got talent.'

Batten didn't remind Connor the girl was in her thirties. Instead, he peered at the decorated walls, a visual calendar of Biddy Holt's special world, the drawings obsessive in their attention to line and shade, their human caricatures bold, lively, cross-hatched.

'She's a David Hockney in the making.'

'David who, Zig?' said Connor with a mock smile. 'Oh, you mean yon dauber from up North?'

Ignoring the jibe, Batten turned instead to a drawing which could only be Leonard Tull, a lofty figure with an exaggerated hearing-aid, frowning face and raised hand. In the next drawing, the same hand was lashing down on - Biddy Holt.

Her self-portrait, special indeed, was everywhere, the enlarged centre of each sequence, along with the achingly thin stick-figure of Andrew Holt, and a dark-robed man wearing pebble-glasses and a dog-collar. On the fringe of almost every drawing, a small female shape hovered, her clothing cross-hatched but her face never more than a white featureless shape.

'You're right, though, Prof.'

'About Hockney?'

'About whether it's evidence.'

'These bits might be,' said Connor, easing Biddy's bedside table to one side. 'I don't know if she'd deliberately hidden them, or just run out of wall. But they're a picture, eh?'

In fresh blue pen, Biddy Holt's Crown of Thorns Hill was a cut down version, its cross and thorn-tree towering over lower-slopes of shrub and upper-slopes of oak. Below them, Biddy had drawn a spring and pool, behind the dam of a fallen tree.

And the figure of a man, in a hood.

Batten's eyebrows clicked.

'And point your pupils at the next sequence, Zig. Reason I dragged you here.'

Nearer the skirting board, fresh drawings showed Biddy Holt's head peeking from a clump of shrubs. Playing hide-and-seek, alone, as usual, Batten guessed.

In the next drawing, the hooded man appeared again, higher up the hill, beyond the pool, half-hidden by trees, playing a hide-and-seek game of his own. His left arm was concealed in what looked like a hole in a tree stump. The right, drawn twice its natural size, grasped a knife sharp enough to murder a forest.

'Andy, we-'

'Already up there, Zig. If some nasty beggar's stashed a knife on Crown of Thorns Hill, we'll find it - assuming Biddy's world isn't total fantasy. There's no shortage of tree stumps to fathom, but my lot'll sniff it out.'

Crown of Thorns Hill was silhouetted against a darkening sky by the time Connor's team clambered down with their booty. Pulling on latex gloves, Batten eased open the oilskin wrapper, hidden deep inside the stump of a splintered oak.

'Bloody well-concealed, Zig,' said Connor, his smug smile now easier to tolerate. 'If I wasn't a man of science, I'd bet the little beauty in your mitt made cut-marks on your bright orange baler-twine.'

'And on Ken Leckey?'

Connor nodded, the smile gone. 'Poor bugger,' he said.

A long, vicious hunting knife was only part of the spoils. Packs of opiates made up the rest - and a bank card, belonging to one Ryan Brand.

Depositing a tray of drinks on the table, Batten realised this was the first time he'd been in The Rising Sun as a punter. At the bar, Harry Finn avoided Batten's eye, the blank face of a lost child filling the space where Flash Harry used to be.

'Cheers, sir,' said Eddie Hick, glugging a throatful of lager without spilling a drop.

'Thought you'd be elsewhere, Eddie?' said Batten. 'Don't tell me the lovely Lorna Wilde is married?'

'Can't, sir. She's not.'

'Well?'

'Soon be the weekend, sir.'

'What's happening at the weekend, Hickie?' asked Ball. 'She going to tuck your shirt in?'

Hick downed his pint with gusto. 'Not tuck it *in*, Sarge, he said. 'Not *in*.' And he strode to the bar, jarring every elbow he met on the way.

Batten's head-shake triggered a Ball chuckle – and a statement of the obvious.

'Eddie's finding himself, sir. Or someone's helping him look. All *we* have to do is find Ryan Brand.'

'We *will* get him, Ballie. But what'll we charge him with, when we do? Apart from carving up Ken Leckey.'

'Prevention of burial, sir? He planted Alicia Heron on that cross, sure as apples make cider.' Ball took a swig. 'Desecrating a religious artefact - if the law still covers such a thing? And being a vicious, drugged-up bloody arsehole?'

Despite the pub surroundings, Batten remained serious. 'But *killing* Alicia Heron? Can we prove that?'

Ball emptied his glass. 'Not up to us, sir. The evidence and the Prosecutors, they'll decide.' He went to the bar.

In the silence, Batten again asked himself, who *did* kill Alicia Heron?

He flipped a beer-mat in the air and caught it. Andrew Holt, via manslaughter?

He flipped and caught the mat again. Biddy Holt, through innocence?

The third time, the beer mat sailed high into the air and slipped through his fingers onto the floor. Ryan Brand? By stringing her unclothed body, clinically alive, to a wooden cross, for no reason at all, other than a drugged-up sense of the desires of whoever paid him?

And Batten had a fair idea who the paymaster was.

Piers Tyndale and Mal Muir might resist a further meeting, but Inspector Zig Batten's name was going in their appointment book, whether they liked it or not.

When he moved beyond the light spilling from the windows of The Rising Sun, Batten was surprised by the darkness. Thick cloud and village power-saving made for a pitch-black street.

He pressed the bleeper on his car key and the tail-lights of his Focus winked at him, from a narrow side-alley thirty yards away. He'd slowly lapped his glass of cider, to stay within the law. Ball and the others were 'staying on for a few', and sharing a taxi home, but Batten's entire body screamed for sleep.

Spring or not, the night was chilly and he regretted his thin jacket as he crossed to his car, key in one hand, the other stifling a yawn. Before his fingers even reached the door handle, before his brain had time to process the faint movement from behind, a metal cosh whipped through the darkness and slammed into the back of his head.

Without a sound, Batten dropped into the double-dark of the empty street.

The man in the brown hood poked Batten's prone frame with a heavy brown boot. Satisfied, he weighed the cosh in his hand. Barely enough light crept into the alley to glint from the metal, nor from the man's dilated pupils. He missed his scalpel-sharp hunting knife, but a cosh would do.

The nose. The groin. A knee-cap. Maybe an ear-drum. He was skilled at marking people who crossed him. Particularly if they insulted his manliness.

Enjoyed calling me Mum, did you? Enjoy what's coming next, twat. Permanent damage. That orchard twat, he was business. You, personal.

When focused on pleasurable tasks, the hooded man's habit was to grip his tongue between his teeth in concentration, and he did so now, sighting the cosh at the bone of Batten's nose.

A second later, he had bitten through the tip of his tongue and would have tasted his own blood had a two-pound-of-sausage fist not slammed into his head so squarely his lights went out like a power-cut.

Two prone bodies lay side by side in the alley now.

Beside them, in the gutter, a stubby metal cosh glinted in the white light from Sergeant Ball's phone.

Not only did Mike Brean make dinner, he opened a bottle of Malbec, and filled two glasses.

'First time I've felt like a glass of anything since...'

Magnus nodded. She felt the same. But she and Mike had begun to speak in code. Unfinished sentences, talk fizzling out. Avoiding. Pretending.

Bluntly, she said it: if the woman's *dead*, how come she's still in the room?

But she said it only to herself.

Time, Nina. Don't rush things. Time.

She raised her glass, and clinked it against Mike's - just as her phone rang.

'Nina? Do you *have* to?'

She peered at the screen. It was Sergeant Ball.

'You know I do, Mike.'

Will Mike ever accept what I do for a living? she thought, tapping the green button. Seconds later, she was on her feet.

'Sorry. I have to go. Someone's been pole-axed.'

'So? Leave it to uniform.'

'The someone's my Inspector! He's in an ambulance!'

She slammed the door.

Mike Brean poured two untouched glasses of wine back into the bottle, and replaced the cork.

Wednesday and After

Forty nine

For once, Batten did what the doctor ordered. The danger of concussion meant a mandatory stay in hospital - and much-needed sleep.

He woke on Wednesday morning, not to the glow of a pretty nurse, but to Sergeant Ball.

'Headache, sir?'

'Such insight, Ballie. What's the time?'

'Not relevant, sir. Doc says you're going nowhere till tonight.'

'Was it Brand?'

'It was.' Ball showed Batten the raw, scraped skin on his knuckles. 'Skull like a hamstone block, our Mr Brand.'

'You?'

Ball nodded. 'Left my coat in the back of your car, sir. Remembered, just as the pub door closed. Spotted the bastard.'

'I was lucky.'

'*You* were. I don't warm to violence, sir. Joined the force to prevent it. All the same, knocking Brand's lights out was a joy. He wouldn't have felt a thing, mind. Police doc said he was three times higher than the moon. Not that there *was* a moon.'

Batten remembered only darkness. He rubbed the back of his head.

'Don't suppose Brand's coughed?' he asked, trying to get up. Ball eased him down again.

'No chance, his posh lawyer's back. But Ryan Brand's going nowhere. And you, you're going nowhere but this bed.'

'I owe you, Chris.'

Ball appraised his Inspector, his friend.

'No, sir. I'd say we're even. Wouldn't you?'

Batten's return to Parminster coincided with Area Super Wallingford's return from his South African safari.

'Just in time to take over,' Batten predicted.

'And take the credit,' added Ball, with some accuracy.

'Our reward is being happy in our work, eh, Sergeant?'

The two men chinked their coffee cups in a mock toast.

'*Are* you happy in your work, sir?'

'I've still got a head, Ballie, despite a lump on the back of it. No bouncing brain for me.'

'Not what I meant.'

Batten deflected the question with one of his own. 'Brand's lawyer still here?'

'He is. But the smug smile isn't. And Ryan Brand's still contemplating the back of a cell door.'

'Then I'm happy Brand's off the streets. And off Ham Hill.'

Ball's stare kept the question hovering.

'For god's sake, Ballie. How can I be *happy* about Andrew Holt? We're putting someone in prison who's spent thirty bloody years of his life there. And god knows what we're doing to his daughter.'

'There'll be leniency, sir. There will. And you and me don't make the laws. Nor force people to break them.'

'No, Ballie. We just police the mess left behind when they do.'

'Yes, sir. While hoping something better comes along.'

Wallingford's return did at least mean Batten could take belated Easter leave, and once paperwork and briefings were done, he gritted his teeth and booked a flight to Spain.

If he *must* confront his fear of flying, he'd prefer to fly to Crete, and the easy-going villa of his friend, Lieutenant Makis Grigoris of the Greek International Cooperation Division. But Makis was not Erin Kemp, and Erin Kemp was in Spain.

And, when Batten arrived at her hotel, was still working.

'Two more days, Zig. Then we can spend the rest of the week together. In sunshine.'

'Two more? I've only got *five* days leave, full stop. I've got to fly back, Erin. In a *plane*.'

'Patience, Zig. I'm free every evening.' Erin's green eyes flashed. 'And every *night*. Or does your convalescence forbid nocturnal liaison?'

'I've missed you like mad,' Batten said, meaning every word, but without mentioning a female pathologist called Welcome. 'But I've still only got five days.'

'And for the two I'm working, I've booked you a treat. You're going on a private tour, with a driver and a guide, all expenses paid. Andalucía's a stunning part of the world. It'll take your mind off *policing*.'

Without Erin, he would have preferred to wander off on his own. But like DC Laura Wilde, Erin had an air of expertise, which reassured him.

'Fine,' he said, glancing at the hotel clock. 'But that's tomorrow. You're free now, and unless I've confused my time zones, isn't it *night*...?'

Erin Kemp was correct about Andalucía. After glorious hours exploring The Alhambra Palace in Granada, and eating tapas washed down with cold, dry sherry, next day Batten's private car rolled past fields of vines and cotton, to Cordoba.

'The Mezquita is next, and I know you will like it,' said Margarita, the pretty Spanish guide, whose English was as fluent as Sergeant Ball's - and twice as fluent as Eddie Hick's. 'It is a famous mosque, Moorish, very striking. Adapted later, of course, from the 13th Century, by Christians. A church inside a mosque, if you like.'

Batten flopped back in his seat at the word 'church.' Relax, he told himself. You're not in All Saints Church at East Thorne, and Crown of Thorns Hill is a thousand miles away.

And relax he did, as Juan, the driver, eased the Mercedes through a maze of streets, his smooth driving skills at odds with his hobby of table-tennis.

'Do not offer to play him,' advised Margarita. 'He will chop you into pieces.'

'I don't do sport,' said Batten. 'And it's too hot.'

Once they'd crossed the sun-baked square and entered The Mezquita, the cool shade was a relief. Within minutes, Batten was mesmerised - by rainbow light from coloured glass panels and by the carved geometrics of Moorish design.

Colonnades of arched pillars interlocked to his left, his right, ahead, behind, all lit by Moorish lamps dangling from an unseen roof, each colonnade flowing into the next, for what felt like miles. He stared down one row after another but from every angle the symmetry and beauty was sustained.

The building's architects and craftsmen knew their business, and even after a thousand years, still proved it. Despite the shuffle of fellow tourists, the peace of the place entered him, but with an ironic twist.

Because the name of what he felt was - serenity.

And with Serenity Developments on his mind, the long colonnades of branched arches and trunk-like columns triggered altogether different images. Against his will, memory drew him back to the threatened Turks Lane orchard, and he was no longer in The Mezquita, but staring down row after row of apple trees, their arched branches flowing and interweaving in dappled Somerset light.

An outdoor cathedral, he thought. That's what an orchard is.

Beyond the restrained Moorish columns, the later Christian part of The Mezquita imposed itself. He enjoyed it less, the ornate craftsmanship out of place, the walls over-painted in one devotional scene after another, edged by fussy ornamentation in too-shiny silver and gold. And higher up the walls, capping the altars, the inevitable crucifixes too, each hung with the dolour of a loin-clothed Christ.

Did I grit my teeth all the way to Spain, to be reminded of Crown of Thorns Hill? he thought. Staring at the clash of architectural styles, further echoes disturbed him: of one rogue developer after another, imposing new 'visions' on environments best left as they were.

His guide-book failed to sweeten the pill. The Mezquita's site had been a Roman temple, it said, then a Visigoth church. In the 8th Century the Moors moved in, erasing previous history to develop their own magnificent mosque. Not till the 16th Century did King Carlos give permission for a cathedral to be 'added' within the mosque itself.

Batten grunted when he read on.

'They have taken a wonder, unique in all the world,' the King said on viewing the results, 'and destroyed it to build something I can find in any city.'

Gazing at the clash of old and new, Batten agreed with King Carlos. Here, whether reclamation or re-development, the Christians conquered an indoor orchard of great splendour, uprooted its past and, to the glory of a rival god, killed stone-dead the restrained beauty of its arching trees, by spraying them with an ostentatious glitz of gold.

Enough was enough. To Margarita's surprise, he left the coolness of the interior and made his way back to the heat of the sunlit square, its tall cypresses framing rows of orange-trees, under whose shelter the Mercedes sat.

Heading for the car, he glanced to his left, where yet another dark reminder pierced him. Hot in their black leather boots and uniforms, a group of Spanish policemen loitered in the orange-tree shade. From their heavy belts dangled handcuffs in pouches, night-sticks, ammunition, and guns.

He climbed into the Mercedes and flopped onto his seat.

'Let's go, Juan,' he said. '*Por favor. Vamos!*'

Fifty

Spain was a distant memory as Batten's Ford rolled into the car park of Serenity Developments, for a much-delayed meeting with Piers Tyndale. Or, more significantly, with Tyndale's 'fixer'.

'I was expecting Mr Muir, sir,' said Batten, once he'd settled into a Danish leather recliner. Tyndale was the only other person in the room.

'Ah. I'm afraid Mal is no longer with us, Inspector. Business mobility. Pastures new.'

'Really, sir? And where might those pastures be?'

'Overseas, or so I am informed.'

'A little vague, sir? If you don't mind me saying?'

'Dubai was mentioned. As a jumping off point.'

Perhaps Mal Muir will jump off Dubai's famously-tall tower, thought Batten. He couldn't remember its name.

'Questioning Mr Muir may be difficult, sir. Should we have need. And since his relationship with the Council's Chief Planning Officer appears dubious - and since I'm told the Chief Planning Officer has mysteriously resigned - a need may well be forthcoming.'

Batten gave Tyndale a look, to ram home the point.

Tyndale held the stare, without flinching.

'Inspector. Should you have need, genuine need, you will not find me standing in your way. I know from experience how unforgiving the world of business can be. But I have not forgotten how business should be done. Do we understand one another?'

With a frustrated nod of confirmation, Batten climbed from his chair. Tyndale held up a manicured hand.

'Regarding Turks Lane, Inspector. I accept Mal may perhaps have been a little too...bee-in-the-bonnet where the success of our East Thorne development is concerned.'

Bee-in-the-bonnet, Zig?

'Well, the bees in his bonnet made honey, sir. If the newspaper reports are true?'

'They are. But have you a moment?'

'Try me.'

Tyndale's finger tapped a button in a trim metal widget on the glass-topped table, just as he had the first time Batten sat there. Once more, with a whirring sound, an expensive-looking wall panel opened like a yawn and, when Tyndale pressed a second button, a hydraulic shelf slid noiselessly into the room. Once more, a detailed architectural model of a vast housing development met Batten's gaze.

It was not the same model.

In this new version, the homes sat beneath the peak of a distinctive hill.

'East Thorne?'

'Full planning was granted, after we agreed the purchase of Turks Lane orchard.'

'And the Turks Lane cottages?'

'Yes. Those too.'

The access road, Batten saw, curled from the main A-road through a flattened zone at the foot of Crown of Thorns Hill. On either side of the road, thin strips of plastic trees softened dead space where the cottages and orchard once stood.

Batten didn't know what to say. He turned to go, but Tyndale held up a finger.

'I would like to point out a feature or two, if I may?'

A shrug.

'Social housing,' said Tyndale, dabbing the same finger at the doll's houses in front of him. Thirty five per cent of the entire project. More than required. *Far* more than required.'

What do you want? A bloody medal?

But Tyndale hadn't finished. His informed finger touched a building once on the village fringe. East Thorne and the new development were now conjoined.

'This, Inspector, is the existing Independent Living Centre, in East Thorne.'

The *I'll See* is what Biddy Holt called it, Batten remembered.

'How did you know about -'

'Please. Don't assume Mal was my sole adviser. I have several. Some chosen, shall we say, for their conscience? But look, here.'

The informed finger picked out a low-rise building, attached to the ILC.

'As part of the scheme, this new block will be residential apartments, and a Warden's flat. Sheltered housing, for the ILC to use as they see fit. It is a gift. From Serenity Developments.'

Clean-conscience money, thought Batten. Unless all money's tainted? He caught Tyndale's drift.

'Biddy Holt? She'll live there?'

'Is Biddy Holt the...?'

'Yes, the Special Needs girl. Woman. If you've read the papers?'

'I'm rarely hands-on, Inspector. Names whizz by. But that name is known to me. And yes, she will live there, so I understand.'

'Well,' said Batten, 'better than wondering what happened to her orchard.' He glanced at the path snaking from the ILC towards All Saints church. 'And at least she'll be close to God.'

A familiar look coloured Tyndale's face, the pained pout of a child who's bent the handlebars on his new bike.

'But it wasn't a gift you had to make,' said Batten. 'In fairness, I recognise that.'

Tyndale's smoother face returned. 'As I pointed out,' he said, 'I have not forgotten how business should be done.'

A smooth finger flicked the metal widget.

East Thorne, 300 homes to the good, slid noiselessly back into the wall.

Batten had one other visit to make. Parking his car in East Thorne proper, he walked not to The Rising Sun but to the church house of All Saints.

To say his goodbyes.

One side of the sparse kitchen/diner was full today, of cardboard boxes, stacked ready for removal. Reverend Kerry was filling the final one with dog-eared books as Batten entered, departing gift in hand.

'Too kind, Inspector, too kind,' said Kerry, opening the bottle of Speyside whisky and fetching two cleanish glasses from the drainer. 'Perhaps we should drink to each other's health? I'm pleased to see you fully recovered.'

They clinked glasses. Batten was thinking all a room really needs is a solid table and some old, comfy chairs. And maybe someone to share a bottle with, when the moment comes.

It had come for Reverend Kerry. Elbows on the scratched oak table, the old priest seemed relaxed for the first time since Batten had known him.

'My retirement may have been brought forward, but in truth, I shall be glad to go. And my extra year of peace - well, perhaps a necessity.'

Kerry glossed over his indiscretions where the Holts were concerned, and what the Church Authorities made of them. In any case, the moment he was out the door, East Thorne's rumour-mongers would get to work. He fingered a battered copy of *The Cricketer's Almanac* and flipped it at the last cardboard box, as if attempting a run-out. The book hit the rim and rebounded onto the worn carpet.

'Even a long innings must come to an end. If only I could see my scorecard. Was I leg before? Bowled? Caught in the slips?'

Batten hated cricket, but sitting at Kerry's table and sharing his whisky meant he had to say something.

'Retired out? More neutral?'

'I think *retired hurt* is closer to the truth, Inspector. But thank you for nudging me in a more comfortable direction.'

'And I'm relieved you nudged yourself in the direction of the law, Reverend, comfortable or not. Where the Holts were concerned.'

Kerry took a long pull on his whisky. 'But not without a struggle, Inspector. And not without pain. Conscience is a delicate flower. I am still unsure if my conscience won, or lost, where Andrew and Biddy are concerned.'

'And Alicia Heron?'

'Alicia too. Poor child.'

Batten could have reminded Kerry that when death is premature, nobody wins. He shrugged instead. 'When transgression is brought to book, isn't the law of the land the winner?'

'Ah. Law book, or good book, Inspector? Still a dilemma, for me. Though not perhaps for you?'

Sipping his whisky, Batten said nothing. He was better at asking questions than answering them.

'But, yes, *retired hurt* will suffice. In whatever way I leave the field, enough is enough. I trust you will reach the same state of recognition, before the umpire of the workaday world raises his finger at *you*.'

In lieu of a finger, Kerry raised his glass, chinking it against Batten's.

'Ask me again soon, Reverend, when the big four-oh rings out. Supposed to be a watershed, isn't it, your 40th?'

A rueful smile was the response. 'For me, too far in the past to remember. I suspect, regardless of age, watersheds are ever present. Lurking, invisible, waiting to be triggered - by one's actions, perhaps? Or the actions of others? Or simply by circumstance?'

Watersheds, thought Batten. He'd had a few of those. Erin Kemp had returned from Spain, only to leave days later for Germany, which seemed many a watershed away. With Erin, was he moving forward, or back?

He switched his thoughts to Somerset, and East Thorne.

'A watershed's about to hit Turks Lane,' he said.

'Ah. Yes. At least my retirement will spare me the sight of cottages being pulverised and trees uprooted.' Kerry gazed at the golden swirl of whisky in his glass. Perhaps it was bulldozers he saw in the ripples. Or chain-saws, or the dead stumps of apple-trees. 'Our last hope was poor Kenneth. And when he...'

Batten nodded. In the light of Andrew Holt's misfortune, Ken Leckey had reflected on his own traumas, and agreed to sell.

'Ken is moving to Gloucester, to hang his environmental awards on the walls of a different cottage. Though perhaps you knew?'

A nod. Batten had made sure to. He didn't much like Ken Leckey, but he liked orchards.

Glass raised high in the air, Kerry surprised him, deepening his voice into what Batten assumed was sermon-mode.

'Ah, if we but knew what we do
When we delve and hew,
Hack and rack the growing green.'

Batten remembered the poem.

'After-comers cannot guess the beauty been,' he added. 'Gerard Manley Hopkins?'

Kerry gave an admiring nod. 'Correct, Inspector. A Roman Catholic, admittedly, but poetry is an ecumenical art form, no?'

As if answering his own question, Kerry drained his whisky and - to Batten's amazement - unclipped his once-white dog-collar.

'A pleasure to have met you, Inspector,' he said. 'A genuine pleasure.'

He shook Batten's hand before slipping the dog-collar, without ceremony, into a drawer in the kitchen table.

Neither the Church officials nor East Thorne's parishioners knew the name of Kerry's replacement, nor if the Good Friday witness walk to the peak of Crown of Thorns Hill would be retained by the new man. Rumour said the new man might even be a woman.

Crown of Thorns Hill was unconcerned.

It continued to stare down, taller than every thatched cottage and stone house in the village below, taller than the apple trees in the doomed orchard, taller than the hamstone tower of All Saints Church. And it would remain taller, long after the orchard was destroyed, and the mortar joints and stone blocks crumbled to dust, and the last twig of thatch was blown away on the wind. Ancient trees had dressed its hilltop for centuries. Many had fallen, but a single thorn and a clump of old oaks persevered.

At his bedroom window, Mike Brean shifted his gaze from the fast-asleep form of Nina Magnus to a new sunrise over Crown of Thorns Hill. He was relieved to see the crime-scene tape and white police tent gone, and the one surviving thorn-tree unadorned. A carpenter by trade, wood was his life. Without doubt, the thorn-tree would succumb to canker soon enough, or to the ageing process.

But the oaks, he knew, would see him out.

To the reader:

Reviews are an author's lifeblood. If you've enjoyed this novel, please do leave a short review on Amazon.co.uk or Amazon.com.

To thank you in advance, here's a free short story about Zig Batten's early days as a keen but green Detective Constable...

Inspector Batten's New Moustache

Sergeant Ball's throat opened like a wound, and a healing pint of cider disappeared. With a single flick of his empty glass, he reeled in the barman.

Inspector Zig Batten's own golden pint was almost full. He sat easy at The Jug and Bottle's apple-wood bar, watching Ball's now familiar cider ritual. Only once had he kept pace with his off-duty Sergeant and, next day, the hangover from hell re-educated him.

'It's a sponge, zor.' Ball's Somerset twang couldn't manage 'sir'.

'What is? Your throat?'

'No. Your moustache.' Ball jabbed a sausage finger at Batten's top-lip. 'More cider there than in your glass.'

Batten ran a finger over his wet moustache.

'Shave it off, zor. It's stopping the cider going where it belongs.'

'Not bloody likely.' He gave his moustache another wipe. 'It's new, is this.'

Ball's ginger smile disagreed. 'New? Doesn't look new.'

'New shape, Ballie. Previous one was one of these.'

Batten demonstrated, index finger and thumb flicking down from lips to chin, in a Zapata shape.

'What, you had one of those Mexican moustaches? You?'

'Yorkshire-Mexican. I was young. All the rage in Leeds, back then, a long Zapata moustache. Retro.'

'All the rage with the ladies?'

'Did me no harm.'

'Bit daft you shaving the ends off, then.'

'Who says I did?'

'Well, someone must've.'

'It's a bit of a story.'

Ball's second pint arrived.

'Not going anywhere,' he said...

*

Brand-new to CID back then, lowly Detective Constable Batten was gobsmacked to be part of the big raid.

'Must be a staff shortage,' said Ged Morley, best pal and fellow DC.

Whatever the reason, in the van went Zig and Ged. Batten's toes tingled in the presence of crime, and his nervous feet tap-tap-tapped, till Inspector Farrar told him to park his shoes up his arse or he'd do it for him.

The stake-out was silent, disciplined. A warehouse, chock-full of perfume, luxury goods, designer clothing. They'd been chasing the gang of top-end thieves for weeks.

'Pint of Tetley's says I nab one of the sods before you do, Zig,' whispered Ged.

'Done', Batten whispered back. His quick frame was gangly, but could squash a crook.

When it all kicked off, Zig treated Ged to an elbow and sped from the van before his pal could recover. About to flatten what the case-notes called 'Suspect 2', he tripped on his over-keen size-nines and flattened himself instead. Where the knees of his trousers used to be, two jagged holes stared up like bloodshot eyes. Ged sailed past and laid out the fleeing crook.

'Another pint of Tetley's in the kitty, Zig,' said Ged.

'Ow!' said Batten, dabbing torn flesh.

Ragged at the knees, a young DC Batten tried hard to look suave during the post-raid grilling. No question of nipping home for a change of trousers, with five crooks to gut.

D.I. Farrar dubbed the unknown Number Six 'Mr Brain - 'because he's the only bugger from this lot who's got one.' The Mastermind proved Farrar right by being too canny to show up, or tell his crew his real name. Instead, the captive five got the hair-dryer.

'Make it easy on yourself. Just confirm what we know about your nameless boss,' Batten lied to Suspect 2. 'Sixty-odd, right? Tall, Fair. Er, clean-shaven. Sloppy dresser. That him?'

'Huh', said Suspect 2. 'Try forty, and five-foot bugger-all. Salt and pepper hair, as it happens, and long. And he dresses like a toff - a bearded toff.' Suspect 2 stared with contempt at Batten's torn knees. 'No holes in *his* trousers.'

When a squashed Batten reported this assumed pack of lies to Farrar, the Inspector's face lit up.

'Progress, Zig. That's four of 'em now, description same or similar, and no conferring. We can discount the comedian in there.'

The nearest cell door boomed as Farrar gave it a mighty kick.

'According to him, Mr Brain's real name's Winston Churchill, and he swans round in a gorilla suit and a green wig!'

The cell door boomed in response to a second kick.

'I don't care if his real name's Churchill, Stalin or Roosevelt,' Farrar told his team. 'We're looking for a short-arse with long salt and pepper hair - and a beard to match. 'So, fingers out and eyes open, all of you!'

Farrar's face screwed itself into a knot.

'Hey, Zig. What the bloody hell *is* salt and pepper hair, when it's at home?'

Post-raid celebrations began mid-evening, in a private room above The Victoria, fittingly close to the City of Leeds Law Courts. The drinking seemed never to end. Not since his student days had Batten seen so much booze downed in a single night. And the more it flowed, the more stick he took for his ripped knees.

'Air vents, are they?'

'You must be low-slung, to need a zip-fly there!'

Even the fair-minded Inspector Farrar asked to see Batten's C.I. Knee card, before sliding a pint and a whisky chaser across the table.

'Don't worry, Zig', he said, pointing his empty glass at the rest of the team. 'It's their way of saying 'welcome'. You were too quick and fell over. Forget it. Move on. Some of this lot, they can't even fall over slowly.'

By midnight, it was Batten who'd fallen over, from compensatory drink. The 'team' did the decent thing and ferried him home.

Next morning found him spread-eagled on his sitting room sofa, twin mounds of a lacy pink D-cup bra clipped across the knee-holes in the trousers he still wore. Whose bra, why pink, and how it got there he had no idea. Head like a breezeblock, he shed his broken trousers, flung the D-cups across the room, and flopped to the loo. The bathroom mirror revealed a car-wreck, with a grey face attached. Peering closer, he recognised it.

Ten tired fingers pressed and prodded his features, checking they were all still there.

They weren't!

Lop-sided, his face.

'I'm having a stroke!' he told the mirror.

No, said the mirror. *Look closer.*

He did.

'Bastards!'

To the right of his mouth, the Yorkshire-Mexican moustache bristled down towards his chin. To the left, it was sawn off at his top lip.

His fingers prodded the strip of bare flesh, dry-shaved by persons unknown while a befuddled Batten snored. It would have been baby-bottom-white, but for a long scar of razor burn - scarlet, hot - cackling at Batten from the mirror.

*

Ball's chuckles were seismic.

'Your lot stitched you up, good and proper.'

'Ta for the sympathy, Ballie. Razor burn's bloody painful.'

'Apologies, zor. But, you, a lop-sided Zapata. Can't get the image out of my head.'

'Oh, drink your cider.'

Ball needed no invitation. One long swallow and he flicked a second empty glass at the barman.

'Must've tingled all the way down to your toes, zor, when you splashed on the Old Spice?'

'Sod that. Went down the chemist shop, for some cream to rub on. I had a face like a slapped behind.'

*

'I think...let me see...this product would be best for your... predicament, sir. It's a soothing balm. A gel.'

After an age, the chemist produced a white tube of something. Batten wondered if it worked on knees.

'Soothing and healing, sir. Treats the symptoms, cures the cause.'

The chemist twirled a discreet finger at the red landing-strip scarring one side of Batten's face, then at the delicate pale-pink version on the other. All in his own good time.

A hungover Batten failed to understand how a trained chemist, whose name-badge said he was Mr Swift, could take so bloody long to lift a tube of gumph off a shelf, shove it in a paper bag and tippety-tap his fingers on a till. As stimulation, Batten semaphored with his wallet.

Mr Swift, though, was Batten's nightmare: a talker.

'Isn't life strange, sir? You're the second one this morning.'

'Second what?' asked Batten, toe-tapping the vinyl floor.

'Well. What may I call it? Second shaving incident? The previous chappie, mind, his face was Mount Etna to your little firework.'

Batten's glower said, 'hand over the gel, and *stop talking!*'

Mr Swift, inept at reading faces, babbled on.

'Razor burn *invading* his cheeks, chap before you. Never seen a worse example. Goodness, what was he thinking? His whiskers had been scythed away in record time. To match the awful haircut, I imagine. A jumping bean, the little chap.'

Batten knew how he felt. 'How much?' he said.

'How much hair?'

'No! How much for *that*?' He shook a claw at the tube of gel, still glued to the chemist's hand.

'Apologies, sir, apologies. I thought you were enquiring about his hair, the previous chap. It was short, you see. Very shor - '

'Look, can I pay for this and be on my way?'

'I do beg your pardon, sir. Of course, of course.' He reached for a paper bag, and tickled a code into the till. Talking all the while.

'We meet every type here, naturally. But when a chap comes in, razor burn aflame on his cheeks, haircut done by an untrained chimpanzee, well...'

Zig, can you arrest a chemist for Grievous Bodily Talking?

'You and I, sir, would we patronise a hairdressing salon where untrained chimpanzees wield scissors? I think not. And dare I even call it a 'salon'? 'Scene of the crime', more like, hah-hah.'

Batten's chin burnt. His hangover boomed inside his skull in frustration. But his brain sat up like a guard dog when the chemist mentioned 'crime'.

'Did you say short hair?'

'This long, sir.' He held up a finger and thumb, an inch apart. 'Snipped off by a chimpanzee. Perhaps an inverted-snobbery take on the Bohemian look? Given how expensively-dressed he was.'

'Expensive?'

'Beyond the wallets of you and I, sir. Not that it's my place to presume, of course'. He shook apologetic fingers at Batten's workaday plain-clothes.

Should've seen me an hour ago, thought Batten. Ripped trousers and a lacy D-cup bra.

'What colour was it?'

'Colour?'

Is this tosser going to repeat everything I say?

'His hair. What colour?'

'Very little hair to be seen, sir. As I said. Before.'

Mr Swift felt the jab of a Batten eyebrow.

'Oh, black and white, I suppose. Salt and pepper, isn't that what it's called?'

The hangover-throb became a tingle in Batten's toes.

'How did he pay?'

'Pay?'

A second eyebrow pierced Mr Swift. The chemist threw one back.

'It was a tube of gel, not the Crown Jewels. He paid in coins. From-his-pock-et.'

Batten couldn't decide whether to slap his own forehead, or Mr Swift's.

Blast! No numbered banknotes. No credit card trail.

Looking up at the ceiling, he asked, 'any CCTV in here?'

'Whether yea or nay, sir, we wouldn't care to advertise.'

Batten dragged out his warrant card.

'In which case, yes. We're a chemist shop. We store drugs.'

He pointed above him, at a light fitting. Batten saw only a light fitting. Hidden camera.

'Was it on, the camera? When the salt and pepper man came in?'

'It is permanently on. Except when broken. Which it isn't.'
'Tapes? You keep them, I hope?'
'Obliged to. Sir.'

Had Mr Swift not swiftly left the storeroom where the CCTV monitor lived, he might never have left at all. When Batten viewed the tape he ached for a scapegoat. The camera was set too high, its focus too narrow. All the tape showed was the tip of a nose and the top of an ugly salt-and pepper haircut. The haircut, in turn, sat above a five-foot well-dressed short-arse. No hint of a mug-shot. And expensive clothing is easy to dump.

The black and white hair might have clinched it - had the tape been in colour. But everything visible was black and white, short-arse's hair included. In court, a defence lawyer could claim its true hue was green ginger and oatmeal, and get away with it.

Batten wrote a receipt for the video-tape, his pen gouging angry deep furrows in the chit. He could do nothing more than gather up the shards of his broken demeanour, and report in.

Once he'd escaped from Mr Swift's Talk-Emporium, that is.

'I'm so sorry I could not help you, sir. But coins it was, and the camera is where it is.' The chemist tapped a finger on the useless video-tape. 'As you have seen.'

DC Batten glared.

'Of course, he did use a credit card for the other purchase.'

DC Batten froze.

'What other purchase? You never mentioned another purchase!'

'You never asked. Sir.'

The fateful gap between training and experience punched its way into Batten's memory. It would live there, a corrective note, forever. He back-pedalled, smiling as sincerely as rank hypocrisy would allow.

'Fine. So, Mr Salt-and-Pepper-Hair, he bought...what?'

Mr Swift-the-Chemist decided to work against type - by saying nothing. Instead, he pointed to a display of travel accessories against the shop's far wall. Batten stared at travel irons, continental plug adaptors, luggage scales. No surprise. Leeds and Bradford Airport was five miles down the road.

Tingling toes rattled like a drumroll now.

He followed the chemist's moving finger purely from détente, having already homed in on a rack of cabin bags, the perfect size for a plane's overhead locker. Where it would always be in sight of its owner. As he, and it, left the country.

'What colour?'

'Hair, sir? Salt and pepper. As previously mentioned.'

Batten pretended to return the smug smile.

'No. Cabin bag.'

'Black, sir. As you can see, we stock only black and mauve. Gender preference, I expect?'

Huh, offender preference, thought Batten, wondering why an absconding five-foot-short-arse, with a chimpanzee-haircut, didn't pay in anonymous cash.

'Credit card? You sure?'

Wordlessly, Swift stepped over to the till, tickled in a code, and with a conjuror's aplomb produced a carbon flimsy. The card belonged to a Jeremy Puckleton. It looked genuine - with juicy traceable numbers to kick-start a hunt. Batten mumbled humble thanks, and wrote a second receipt.

His false display of gratitude had a mixed blessing. It unlocked the chemist's tongue.

'Now I come to think of it, your salt and pepper man wanted to know where was the nearest bank. Three miles away, I told him. Our suburb is not thought significant enough to warrant a branch nearby. I mentioned this too. He seemed uninterested.'

Mr Swift gave Batten a look.

'All he did was stare at his watch. Much as you are doing now, sir. Stared, coldly, as if it was a calculator and he had sums to do. And then, presto, out comes his credit card. I surmise he carried insufficient cash to pay for the cabin bag, insufficient time to visit a bank, and had an imminent aeroplane to catch. No?'

Batten ignored Mr Swift's final flourish. Nor was he going to say, 'what a clever Detective-Chemist you are.' Instead, he checked the transaction time. Jeremy Puckleton had shaved off salt-and-pepper beard and hair in a panic, used a traceable credit card to buy a cabin bag, and headed from this very shop to the likely escape route of Leeds and Bradford Airport - less than half an hour ago.

Before Mr Swift's tongue could unleash more words, Batten was sprinting to his car-radio.

Sore knees were history.

A tube of soothing gel lay forgotten on the Chemist's counter.

*

Sergeant Ball's off-duty glass had been empty for six minutes - a record.

'You got him? Mr Brain? At the airport?'

'*I* didn't. I just got his real name and a new description. Speeded things up, though. And earned me plenty of brownie points. He was doing a runner with the laundered proceeds. Bloody cabin bag was chock-full of bearer bonds. Won them playing poker, he claimed.'

'Huh, original. What'd he get? Six years?'

'Eight. Got two extra for the crap haircut.'

Sergeant Ball's chuckles became the sound of sausage fingers tapping an empty glass.

'Right. My shout', said his Inspector.

Batten headed for the now-busy bar, but decided to keep part of the story to himself...

*

D.I. Farrar had already alerted security at relevant air and ferry ports, well before a green Detective Constable entered Mr Swift's Talk-Emporium. Checking manifests for a name like Jeremy Puckleton did make Farrar's life easier. But regardless of Batten's intervention, every forty-something five-foot male traveller would have got the once-over, whether bald, bearded, blonde, clean-shaven or dressed in a sack.

A week later, the CID team bustled into the same private room above The Victoria, for a second celebratory piss-up. So many meaty hands slapped Batten on the back he was coming out in bruises. He slid a pint and a whisky chaser across the table to D.I. Farrar, and lowered his voice.

'You told them it was me, sir. Didn't you?' Batten pointed to his colleagues, filling happy throats with beer and lager. 'You told them it was me who cracked the case? But we both know I didn't.'

Farrar flashed a knowing smile, and juggled a beer-mat.

'Integration, Zig. That's all. You're the new lad here.' The beer-mat tapped Batten on the knuckles, before pointing at the boisterous bar. 'This lot can't remember having to slog their way down Experience Street. They're so old they think they were never new. And you've got brains. You're educated. Makes 'em wary.'

'They've got brains too. They must know it wasn't all me.'

'Well, memory loss is a funny thing, Zig,' said Farrar, swallowing half a pint before dropping his voice. 'Make the best of tonight. Everyone needs a start. We've all been you, falling on our arses. You know, one leg keen, one cack-handed.'

Batten rubbed his knees. Painful reminders.

'Learn it, Zig. Learn it, store it, use it. You won't always get a freebie from Lady Luck.' Farrar drained his beer. 'She dropped in on you, last week.' With a flick, the whisky chaser disappeared. 'Bloody well put it to use, her visit.'

*

Batten placed a fresh pint in front of Ball. He was sticking to halves, not being blessed with a Ball-like mineshaft of a throat.

'There was a presentation after,' he told his cider-merry Sergeant. 'The whole CID team lined up, pints in the air, and I had to run the gauntlet from one end of the bar to the other. I was lucky. They still had a thirst on, so not much ale got wasted on me.'

Ball took a knee-jerk pull from his glass.

'When I got past the guard of honour, there was a parcel sitting on the bar, my name in felt-tip, and a big red ribbon tied up in a bow.'

'Let me guess. New trousers?'

'Close. I'd chucked the ripped ones in the re-cycling bin. Ged swore it wasn't him who fished them out, but there they were.'

'Not much of a present, pair of broken trousers.'

'This time, the buggers had sewn the lacy D-cups over both knees. Not great, the needlework, but functional. And where the cleavage goes, they'd bunged a massive fake moustache - I've still got it somewhere. Poking out the zip-fly was the world's largest tube of gel. For razor-burn. The sods pissed themselves at my expense.'

Ball joined them.

Batten made no mention of the team's second gift, carefully wrapped, nestling quietly in the pocket of his re-purposed trousers. When he tore it open, there were no hoots and jeers this time. His colleagues applauded, every one of them, meaning it.

A pair of antique salt-and-pepper shakers winked up at him.

Solid silver, hallmarked.

Exquisite.

He still used them.

*

'Ever find out whose it was?'

'Whose what?'

'The D-cup bra. Wasn't yours!'

Batten sipped and pondered.

'That's another story, Ballie. For another day.'

Ball could wait. He raised his cider.

Batten watched it disappear.

A more experienced Batten reappears in book 1, *A Killing Tree*, where he struggles with his enforced move from urban Yorkshire to not-so-sleepy Somerset. Before he can blink, hikers discover a dead body slumped against a tree on a lonely hill...
www.smarturl.it/akte

A January Killing sees Batten and his new love-interest at a traditional cider 'Wassail', in a pitch-black orchard on a winter night. Celebratory shotguns are fired into the trees, to deter 'evil spirits' and spark a fresh crop of apples. But not every shotgun fires blanks, and next day it's a dead body that has blossomed in the orchard...
www.smarturl.it/ajk

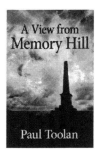
We live life forwards, but understand it backwards. In these "beautifully poignant and funny stories", minds, old and young journey through half-shaded landscapes of memory. Why not take the journey too, and see what they discover?
www.smarturl.it/avwm

And keep a lookout for book 4 in the Inspector Batten series.

The novels can be read in sequence or standalone.

Acknowledgements

A special thank-you to the many patient folk who helped during the writing and editing of An Easter Killing. You know who you are.

Extra thanks to Yvonne, Mary, Jason, Crispin and Pete. Any misunderstandings are mine, not theirs.

Printed in Poland
by Amazon Fulfillment
Poland Sp. z o.o., Wrocław